How does Nick Knight track down a murderer?

Experience.

He's been a cop for years.
But he's been a vampire for centuries.

FOREVER KNIGHT™

A STIRRING OF DUST

Nick knows one of his own kind is responsible for several brutal murders. But who is the hunter . . . and the hunted?

INTIMATIONS OF MORTALITY

A mysterious woman grants Nick his greatest wish: mortality. But Nick isn't sure what price he's willing to pay for it . . .

THESE OUR REVELS

In England of 1599, a mortal woman makes Nick question his immortality—and two new vampires threaten to reveal the vampire community to the world!

All-ne
based on the
by James D. Pa

Produced by Parago
in association w TriStar Television

FOREVER KNIGHT™

THESE OUR REVELS

ANNE HATHAWAY-NAYNE

BERKLEY BOULEVARD BOOKS, NEW YORK

FOREVER KNIGHT: THESE OUR REVELS

Based upon the television series created
by James D. Parriott and Barney Cohen.

Produced by Paragon Entertainment Corporation in
association with TriStar Television.

A Berkley Boulevard Book / published by arrangement with
Sony Signatures, Inc.

PRINTING HISTORY
Berkley Boulevard edition / April 1997

For information address: The Berkley Publishing Group,
a member of Penguin Putnam Inc.,
200 Madison Avenue, New York, New York 10016.

The Penguin Putnam Inc. World Wide Web site address is
http://www.penguinputnam.com

ISBN: 0-425-16491-8

BERKLEY BOULEVARD
Berkley Boulevard Books are published by The Berkley Publishing Group,
a member of Penguin Putnam Inc.,
200 Madison Avenue, New York, New York 10016.
BERKLEY BOULEVARD and its logo are trademarks
belonging to Berkley Publishing Corporation.

PRINTED IN THE UNITED STATES OF AMERICA

10 9 8 7 6 5 4 3 2 1

to Mr. B.B.,
the onlie begetter
of our insuing friendship

ACKNOWLEDGMENTS

For various kinds of support and assistance, thanks are gratefully offered to Mike Lifsey, Isabel Samaras, Laurie Cohen Fenster, the Wylie family, Cynthia Hoffman, Marcia Addison, Susan Garrett, Daniel Mick, Laura Waskey, Adrienne Fargas, Ginjer Buchanan, Timothy Seldes, and the reference librarians of the United States Naval Observatory, the New York Public Library (Science and Technology section), and the Folger Shakespeare Library.

AUTHOR'S NOTE

A great many facts about Shakespeare's life remain uncertain. This book assumes the following chronology, which is at least possible, and in some cases probable, based on current scholarship: early 1590s, the playwright Thomas Kyd writes the "ur-Hamlet"; it is produced and becomes an immediate flop; May 1599, the Globe Theater, standing just south of Maid Lane, opens in Southwark; June 1599, *Julius Caesar* premiers with Richard Burbage in the lead; summer–winter 1599, Shakespeare writes *Hamlet;* spring 1600, *Hamlet* has its first public performance; winter 1600–1601, the text of *Hamlet* is slightly revised by Shakespeare (for example, the "little eyases" line is added). By contrast, the February 2, 1600, private "premiere" of *Hamlet* at Lord Hunsdon's house is wholly an invention; while Hunsdon, as patron of Shakespeare's company, did host private performances of plays, there is no record that any play was given a premiere in this manner. The Hilliard family is very loosely based on the family of Henry Wriothesley, the Earl of Southampton, to whom many of Shakespeare's sonnets are addressed. The characters of Tom Saddler and Isabella are inventions, as are numerous minor characters, though the inns at which they congregate were all real places. The vampires are, of course, real vampires.

PROLOGUE

Yet can he never dye, but dying lives,
And doth himself with sorrow new sustaine,
That death and life attonce unto him gives,
And painefull pleasure turns to pleasing paine.
There dwels he ever, miserable swaine,

Now seeking darknesse, and now seeking light,
Then craving sucke, and then the sucke refusing.

—Edmund Spenser,
The Fairie Queen, Book III, verse x, 60 (1590);
Book V, verse vi, 14 (1596)

"Who goes there?"

It was a joke, of course. Only one person had the code to his loft elevator—and would use it in the daytime. The fact that the elevator had activated without a buzz from the intercom meant that Natalie Lambert, medical examiner for MetroToronto, was paying an afternoon call on Nick Knight, a homicide detective currently assigned to the city's 96th Precinct.

Nick looked up from the computer he'd set up on his dining table as Nat came in, carrying a shopping bag full of things that were guaranteed to taste terrible. Not only was Natalie Nick's colleague, confidante, TV-watching pal, and occasional companion in a night on the town, she was also, in a manner of speaking, his family doctor. For the last several years, she had been working up dietary plans, among other treatments, in an effort to reverse his particular condition.

For Nicholas Knight, in addition to being a homicide detective on Toronto's Metropolitan Police Force, was a vampire.

In 1228, he'd been a war-weary Crusader, Nicholas de Brabant, born the scion of a family of minor nobility, the lords of a small district now in Belgium. That year, he had exchanged his itinerant knight's life for that of an immortal blood-drinker, been brought across into the darkness by a vampire who had already seen a full millennium.

For a while Nicholas had reveled in his new abilities—his existence as a nearly perfect predator, the endless youth, the gifts of strength, speed, and heightened perception his vampirism gave him. He could even fly. And yet, even at the beginning, he'd felt an inward conflict over the choice he'd made. Even in the very first days of his new existence, part of him sensed that he'd embraced a terrible evil and began to want to go back. Be human again. Walk in the sun as a man.

When he met Natalie Lambert, he saw his condition only as a curse and a nightmare that he desperately wanted to undo. By the night he revived on a slab in the Toronto morgue, to which he'd been sent for her professional attention as a coroner, he'd been trying, and failing, to find a road back to his humanity for over a hundred years.

Even while still living as a vampire, he'd begun to work to redeem his soul by making up for some of what he had done. He was "dead" that night because he'd rushed in to save mortals from a pipe bomb and been caught in its explosion himself.

For Nick, the most extraordinary thing of all about that night had not been awakening to yet another extension of his endless existence. Nor had it been the fact that his bomb-shattered body had managed to restore itself in a matter of hours. Instead, it had been the way Natalie Lambert had looked at him after he'd leaped up from the dissecting table and greedily helped himself to the morgue's emergency blood supply. This doctor had been able to look at the lacerated monster in front of her and see a man who needed her help. So every time Natalie mixed up another "substitute food" with another hopeful flourish, Nick forced himself to choke it down at least once. In their years of seeking a cure together, some of Natalie's concoctions had made his system rebel with cramps and violent pain, while some of them merely nauseated him. But they all had one thing in common: none of them was a cure.

Yet.

Lately, there had been many, many days and nights when he'd wondered if there ever could be any cure, or whether he was damned for all eternity by the choice he'd made that one night so many years ago. And always in some corner of his mind, he could hear the echo of his master's voice, the seductive voice that said, *Give in: yield to what you are. Yield. It is the only way you can ever be happy.*

"Surfing the Net, eh?" Natalie joked, coming to peer over his shoulder at the computer screen. "What's new in cyberspace today?"

Nick grinned. The computer was a recent acquisition, something the Department was requiring all its employees to learn, and Natalie still regarded it with a suspicious distaste she usually reserved for toxic chemicals and really large insects.

"Well, Paul Neeson wants to do Shakespeare again," he said.

"Paul Neeson," Natalie mused, going back to the bags on the counter. "I think I read about him in *Celebrity* magazine once—the famous director whose career tanked?"

"*Celebrity* magazine?" Nick paused to look over his shoulder with a grin. His face, always boyish, took on a positively impish expression.

"At the hairdresser's," Natalie said defensively. "You just read whatever's there."

Nick's grin got wider. "Of course," he said, "and you'd never—"

"I'd never buy it," Nat said firmly.

Nick turned back to the computer, shaking his head emphatically. "No, of course not," he said, still grinning.

Nat cleared her throat firmly. "Anyway, wasn't he the guy who set *Richard III* in a sushi bar?"

"That's the one," he agreed.

"So what's your interest in him?"

"He was my student," Nick said. "In New York, about

thirty-five years ago." This got Natalie's full attention. She came and sat down at the table beside him, seeing a familiar wistfulness sweep the humor out of his blue eyes. Nick couldn't have a human life, couldn't even stay in touch with mortal friends once he'd changed lives. He had told her several times that it was best to just walk away, but the Nick Knight she knew had a sentimental streak.

"So you looked him up on the Net? Well, I guess you can't exactly go to class reunions, can you?" She rubbed his shoulder sympathetically and said, "Tell me about him."

"He was brilliant," Nick said, his mood picking up again. "It was a joy to teach him. We used to sit around coffeehouses in Washington Square and argue all night—was Shakespeare a Tudor apologist or a Catholic subversive? Was it reasonable to read the history plays as psychological narratives? Should all the women in Shakespeare be read as men since the parts were written for men to play them?"

Nat rolled her eyes. "Call me old-fashioned, but I prefer my Cleopatras without a beard. So Neeson dried out, and he's back at work? Good for him."

"Uh-huh," Nick said. "I'm thinking maybe the Foundation could help, be his backer—something." Nick had amassed an enormous fortune over the centuries; in modern times, he arranged to have it administered for charitable purposes, allowing himself the one small pleasure of giving the organization his real name: the De Brabant Foundation.

Nat grinned. "No kidding? Well, hey, if you're going to start passing out money for the thee-ay-ter, I've played Ophelia in my time."

"You?" Nick laughed. "You're the least Ophelia-like person I've ever known."

"Hah!" said Natalie, mock insulted. "That's all you know! I was a terrific Ophelia in the seventh grade." She backed away to an open area of the floor and reached back to pull the scrunchie off her ponytail, releasing the long waves of her chestnut hair.

Nick's mouth fell a little open as Natalie tossed her head back, opening her hazel eyes wide with a distracted glaze, and began to declaim, "*There's rosemary for remembrance; pray you, sir, remember . . . ,*" almost dancing around his piano, bestowing imaginary flowers on the candelabra, the ivory keys, the music stand.

It was nothing like the way he'd first heard that speech, and yet something about Natalie's ability to transform for a moment into a love-mad teenage girl with disordered wits pulled the memory forward . . .

1

. . . there is no immortality on earth can be given a man like unto plays.

—Thomas Nashe,
Pierce Penniless,
His Supplication Unto the Devil (1592)

Boar's Head Tavern, London
Midsummer Night, 1599

"HANDSOMELY PLAYED, NICK," ENTHUSED HIS FELLOW ACTOR. "'TIS madness in you to decline the player's life; you have the very pluck and soul of us."

Nicholas Chevalier, gentleman and very occasional actor, was wise enough to brush aside this amiable, but preposterous, flattery.

"Methought the chattering of my knees was less eloquent than the speech you intended," he grinned. Nicholas had been a last-minute substitute for a player laid low with a flux, cast in an act of extreme desperation for his sheer ability to memorize a part at first glance. Midsummer night meant a command performance before Queen Elizabeth herself; there could be no player haltingly reading his part from a prompt sheet by star- and torchlight.

Nicholas had managed to carry off his part with panache; a

gift that was born, though his companions could not know it, of several hundred years' practice in playing at different identities. Any vampire, he reflected, could probably serve for an actor in a pinch.

"I' faith, I misdoubted that you'd come away with your heads for playing the Shrew before a red-haired queen," he added. "It had been wiser in you to give her the boys from Syracuse."

"Nay, never say so," laughed his friend, who was also the author of the piece. "Her Majesty is the wittiest of sovereigns." Lowering his voice, he added, "And that choleric hair, you know, sprouted on some other pate than hers."

"You'll to the Tower one day, Will," Dick Burbage muttered.

"Not this night, Petruchio," retorted his friend. "And you, fair Nick: come bring your blistered spirit to table; we'll have the painted cherries off your cheeks and put real ones in your belly." He patted the bench beside him. "Faith, if you sit near enough grubby Dick, we'll have them on your smalls." Burbage paused in his eating just long enough to defend his dignity with a bearlike grunt.

"Stay, my's belly's full enough." Nick waved off the food. In fact, it wasn't, but his meal would have to be very different from theirs. Which reminded him . . .

"Knew you the man in scarlet and brown?" he asked his friends. "He stood toward the rear and left of a sudden before the final speech." And he had not been a man at all, but Nicholas could not tell his companions that, nor how he'd known.

Dick Burbage paused in gnawing at his joint of beef. "I marked him," he commented. "He hath strange eyes. But I have no name for him." He took a deep swallow of wine.

Will shook his head. "Nor I," he said and shrugged. "Who would do other than look at a queen when one is present?"

Nicholas smiled. "A most politic policy," he joked. "Perhaps you are not for the Tower yet." He frowned momentarily, wondering how the vampire had managed to insert himself in a queen's retinue, but he shook off the thought as a familiar face appeared. "Look, here's Ben."

"Well met, Nicholas," said Ben Jonson heartily, settling in at the table. "London has missed you. Well, Will, was't a triumph?" he needled. Jonson, though early in his career, fancied himself the equal of his friend Will Shakespeare, a fancy that somehow failed to diminish Shakespeare's affection for him.

"Nay, sirrah, no triumph this, only a small parade of jests," Will answered. He dropped his solemnity for a moment's satisfied smile. "But a good one."

"A travesty, but a good one," said Jonson.

"I' faith, Ben, we cannot all serve the Muse as severely as you would have us do," retorted his friend. A small, thick figure of a man whose face was familiar in every public house in town, Ben Jonson was notorious for his strict adherence to classic Roman principles of play staging, not to mention his preference for tragedy.

"And you yourself have served her a merry turn not long sin'," Nicholas added.

Jonson had the grace to smile; Will Shakespeare, the friend at whom he now jibed for not being serious enough, had indeed done him good service by taking the leading role in an exceedingly silly comedy Jonson had penned just one year ago. His principles had been forced to take a short holiday because he'd needed the money, as the others knew well.

"Nay, it was but a short sin," Jonson protested in joking surrender, "for it played not over twenty times."

"Marry, 'tis true, if one finds a merry turn, one wishes to come to it over twenty times," Burbage remarked with a bland smile, eyeing the serving girl who was refilling his glass.

Jonson laughed. "Yet one wishes it not so merry as to come to marry, look you." Dropping his voice, he added, "There's a maid we might all serve a merry turn," jerking his head toward the door.

Nicholas and William followed his gesture and found themselves looking at a spectacularly beautiful young couple, richly dressed and carrying themselves with an assured air. The other players at the table followed their glance, and some rudely appreciative noises were heard.

"She's a long sin, I'll warrant you, but no maid," Will remarked. "But he . . ."

"Also no maid, but a very long sin," Nicholas said straight-faced. The table burst out in laughter, for it was true the boy exceeded the girl in both natural beauty and gorgeousness of dress. They were nearly of a height, this pair, both nearly as slender as river reeds and almost as straight, but where her hair was glossy black, his was glowing blond; where her manner bespoke proud knowledge of her beauty, his bespoke a careless acceptance of it. For all their mutually similar adornments, there was something honest in the girl's eye that was lacking in her companion's face. It was as if she were at her pinnacle as his ornament, and happy so, whereas the boy carried himself in a manner that suggested a luxuriousness of character as well as of attire.

"Him you may call William Hilliard," said Shakespeare. "She is Isabella of no other name."

"A queen, then," said Nicholas with a smile, "for no other women are known by a single name."

"Known, I grant you; a queen, I do not," said Will, a trifle sourly. His friends exchanged a glance, sensing they were on delicate ground for some unknown reason. A patron perhaps, or a friend from the past? They dropped their joking.

"Let's greet them, then, Will," Jonson said comfortably, "and give them sugar'd wine."

The foursome rose from the table and began to work their way through the press of actors and audience who had trailed back down the river for midnight cheer at the Boar's Head.

One of the younger actors, one Thomas Saddler, wore an enormous blue hat, a tall copatain adorned with a seemingly endless ostrich feather that dipped into the faces of all who ventured near him. Just now his feather was tickling the nose of Isabella of no other name, and she seized it. Still holding the end of the feather, she struck up a conversation with the boy in the hat, complimenting his stagework, yet tweaking him for playing a female role.

"Methinks I shall breech myself, for that you have taken up my skirts so bravely," she teased.

"Why, mistress, if you breach yourself, many a man would rue the lost joy," Tom Saddler teased back. "And as for taking up your skirts, I regret me greatly that I must yield that bravery to some another." She blushed in apparent discomfort, and he softened his jibe. "Why, your tirewoman, mistress, I meant no other, sure." The blush lessened, and he realized her apparent shame had been a counterfeit.

"Nay, truly," the young player went on, "'tis pity ladies may not act their own parts upon our stage, for you would conquer it. You act yourself so well here," he finished drily, getting a saucy smile from the girl.

She was dressed to match Hilliard in deep blue velvet on which small pearls had been stitched; the darkly vivid gown set off her pale complexion, which was adorned only by two high red spots on her cheeks, as if she were feverish. She had kept her grip on the plume, and now plucked the blue hat entirely off the young actor's head and set it on her own, drawing the feather down to curl almost along the line of her chin.

"Now I am a boy and may be a girl," she laughed.

"Marry, I have seen a lady be a lady upon the stage, in Florence," said Nicholas. It was true, women could work as actors in Italy, but it was strictly illegal for them to do so in England.

"Go to, Nicholas; I think I have never seen a lady be a lady, whether I was in Florence or out of her," Ben Jonson remarked. "I marvel to hear it."

Young Hilliard drew near now. He was of only medium height, yet commanding in appearance, his features fair and finely made. His eyes shone with the look of privilege and power, yet also held a disturbing quality of corruption. His clothing bespoke both wealth and position—a rich velvet doublet slashed open to show further riches, a shirt of finest lawn, hose of silk, jeweled garter and swordhilt. Several rubies sparkled on his fingers, and pearls were scattered on the cloak that he'd thrown back over one shoulder. The cloak was lined with what looked to be sable, richly beautiful in itself, yet wrong, as that glint in his eyes was wrong.

"Faith, gentles all, 'tis a mercy England's statute spares us this jade upon our stage," Hilliard drawled. "We should all be riding to perdition with such a nag to go before us." His tone was even more insulting than his words, and now the girl blushed sincerely.

"You're for me, I think, Tom," he said to the young actor. The boy threw a sympathetic look backward at Isabella, who seemed to have been paralyzed by her companion's sudden cruelty, but allowed Hilliard to throw an arm around his shoulder and lead him away.

"There's a pretty peacock," Jonson muttered. Isabella was making a visible effort to control her misery, but her humiliation was patent.

"A cock, anyway," Burbage muttered back. "With a crow to summon the Devil, not some sweet dawn."

"Nay, no more than a coxcomb, however finely he crow," Nicholas returned, still watching Isabella. Why would Hilliard have brought her here, only to dismiss and abandon her so cruelly?

Again Shakespeare shot them a sour look, and again the others dropped their jesting and lapsed into mutually puzzled silence. What could this elegant, arrogant boy, so clearly of a class above their own, be to him? Or was it the girl, who was clearly no more than a plaything to her highborn lover?

Isabella had heard them too, and drew nearer. "Kind words, kind sir," she said to Nicholas, forcing a smile through her sadness. She looked up into his eyes and seemed pleased by what she saw. "Such nobility of nature should not go uncrowned." She took off the plumed hat and set it on Nicholas's head. "Nor, for that, should such a wealth of gold," she added, tugging at Nicholas's long blond hair with some of her earlier bold humor.

"Nicholas Chevalier, at your service," he said, kissing her hand.

"Nay, a crowned head cannot be in anyone's service," she retorted. Her eyes sparkled. "But it may kiss."

"Ho, Nicholas, so briefly a king and already a conquerer," said Will. He too kissed Isabella's hand, but with a perfunctory courtesy. "Come go with me, Ben, Dick: we are all become superfluous." But then the humor dropped away from his face as he noticed something over Nick's shoulder.

Nicholas felt the sensation that told of the presence of others of his kind, even as Burbage said, "Look you, Nick, is that not him you spoke of?"

It was. Standing just inside the tavern's entry was the vampire Nicholas had sensed among Queen Elizabeth's courtiers. The surprise had been great enough to cause him a second's delay in delivering a line, though Burbage had managed to turn his error into a good jest. One of his kind among a queen's entourage? Their life was one of shadows, of transience, of constantly changed names—how could such a one exist among a queen's court? There could be no more visible existence than that.

The man was ordinary looking, of medium size, with

medium-colored dark hair, at least what was left of it, and brown eyes. He had a notably good-humored expression on his face, and had been laughing at the play. Yet the thing that had caused Burbage, the brilliant observer of human character, to mark those eyes was a thing Nicholas recognized well. They were the eyes of a wary killer; a vampire not hunting at present and well aware that with an instant's exposure, he could become the prey.

"I know him," Will Shakespeare said quietly. "And, look you, Nick, you do not wish to. He is in Cecil's employ, and mixes with Topcliffe. Nicholas, do you mark me?" This was a serious warning: Robert Cecil was maneuvering to succeed his father, the great Lord Burghley, as the Queen's greatest and most intimate counselor, and Richard Topcliffe was the Queen's most infamous torturer.

Nicholas was not listening, however. His surprise had turned to full-fledged shock, for standing in company with the courtier vampire was the person he least wanted to see in the world. And standing next to him, all but the barest profile of her face still hidden by her hooded cloak, was the one person in the world he most dearly wished to see. Lucien LaCroix and Janette DuCharme were in the Boar's Head Inn, and a second later, it became clear they were looking for him. "It seems I must needs know him, whether I will or no," Nicholas said roughly.

He turned to Isabella distractedly. "Pray forgive me, lady, I must join my cousin," he said, but dropped her hand without further attention.

"Now I am become superfluous," she said sadly, but found her hands seized by the playwrights.

"Come, fair princess, we will form your court," said Will, darting a curious look after Nicholas.

"Aye, we will court you very fairly, so that you may fare most courteously," Ben Jonson competed. But Isabella's eyes also followed Nicholas as he joined the group at the door.

So he'd been found. He should have known it was folly to try to slip LaCroix's leash, held now loosely, now tightly, but always surely. For Lucien LaCroix, the tall, straight figure who stood still cloaked at the tavern door, was Nicholas's master, the vampire who had brought him into the night so long ago.

The woman who stood with him had also been present at the dawn of his darkness. It had been Janette DuCharme's midnight hair and moonlit skin, her thrilling voice, her shadowy blue lakes of eyes, that had drawn him forward on the night he had made his choice. He had loved her ever since, loved her across centuries, but some eighty years past she had chosen to break their bond and travel away alone.

There had been women since then: mortal women. He had even taken one to wife seventy years ago, marrying the ethereal Alyssa von Linz with the full ceremony of mortal law. On their wedding night, he had attempted to bring her across to share the night with him forever. But his effort to pass along the dark gift of immortality failed. Instead, he'd found himself with a cooling corpse on his bridal bed, with his master strolling into the bedchamber to mock his insufficiency. Miserable and embittered, he had returned to the round of attraction, love, consuming, and death that was the only love a vampire could offer mortal women. Yet always there had been the memory of Janette, like a veil through which all other women must be seen.

Nick spoke first to LaCroix, biting off his words: "I will not say well met." He had left his master behind in Italy a month ago, thinking the unfriendly climate and long northern days of England's summer would keep LaCroix from seeking him there.

"When was that ever your wont?" LaCroix said languidly, ignoring the insolence. He'd had a great deal of practice in brooking insolence from Nicholas de Brabant in the three hundred and seventy-one years since he had given the golden-haired Crusader the gift of immortal life.

"But to you . . . ," Nick began, turning to face Janette. "How shall I say that I have despised every minute without you?"

"*Exactemente comme ça*—just like that," responded Janette, smiling. "That is perfection." Nicholas raised a hand to push back her hood and get a better look at her beloved face, but LaCroix caught it.

"Save your wooing," said LaCroix. He threw back his own hood, revealing pale, severe features, hard ice-blue eyes, and the bristlingly short hair of a Roman warrior; in this gathering of casual, scruffy tavern drinkers whose hair tumbled down to their shoulders, he stood out like an eagle among larks. Yet in the next moment, the stern face softened to make way for a twisting smile with more than a hint of arch amusement to it. "Nicholas, let me make you known to Aristotle; you will mind that I have mentioned him ere now."

"Indeed," said Nicholas, allowing himself to be diverted. "You are of good fame, sir." That was an understatement. Aristotle was a legend among vampires, the amiable, never anxious companion who nevertheless had, over the centuries, established and maintained the delicate lines of communication that threaded the night-dwellers into a Community that gave no heed to mere mortal borders.

"Here I am George Dyer, in the service of the Privy Council," the other vampire said quickly, then smiled. Close up, Aristotle seemed to be no more than a slender fellow, dressed in modest taste, whose balding pate crowned a humorous face dominated by the friendly twinkle in his eye. "And Master Undersecretary Dyer is of indifferent fame at best, but he is glad to know you, Nicholas. You played well tonight."

Nicholas smiled. "'Twas a pleasant foible."

"A folly," said LaCroix coldly. "Prance and prate upon a stage. It is the act of a clown."

Nicholas ignored him. "How comes it you are of the court? It sorts oddly with . . . a need for secrecy." The general noise of the tavern around them all but ensured that he would not be overheard, but he worded his question discreetly all the same.

Aristotle smiled cheerfully. "I' truth, it sorts excellent well. Princes have greater need for secrets than any other men, and even greater need for secretive men. And I," he smiled again, showing the tiniest trace of his inner feral nature, "yea, betimes I have a mighty need for secretive men." He laughed. "So it serves me well, and sometimes well serves others who are of," he paused and twinkled again, "our sanguine humor."

"Pray heed him, Nicholas," LaCroix said silkily. "He serves us all. You travel wantonly, without paper or purse, yet you might have journeyed hence in all state with the smallest of his aid."

Nicholas grew cold again. "My methods suffice me," he returned.

"Suffice? When I am led to find you . . . a player on the

stage? In a state scarce higher than that of a baited beast?" LaCroix's voice dripped with contempt.

Nicholas opened his mouth to let fly with the scathing retort this insult deserved, but fell silent as a graceful white hand emerged from the folds of his beloved's cloak and came to rest on his arm.

"You know better than to mark our cousin's offenses, *mon amour,*" Janette chided him with a laugh. Her wide, blue eyes rose to meet his own, and her teasing smile turned fragile, as intoxicating as her touch. "He has regretted your absence and now seeks to shame you for it."

"And you, lady?" Nicholas pressed, laying his hand over hers, LaCroix and his insults forgotten. "Would you see me shamed as well?"

"Never," she promised, the intensity of her gaze closing out all the world but him. *I have returned* that gaze seemed to whisper. *Wilt thou have me again?* "It is I who should beg your pardon, *mon cher,* for not coming to you when I first heard of your sorrow—I have heard the woman called lovely . . ." Her voice trailed away into the eloquent silence of her eyes. "Can you forgive me?"

As if he could do anything other, Nicholas thought, the sound of his name on Janette's tongue the sweetest music his ears had ever heard. The image of Alyssa dissolved like a vapor in the warmth of Janette's return. A golden beauty Alyssa had been, a bright spirit draped in a mantle of bright blond curls, but Nicholas had embraced that child of light only hoping to draw her into the hollow in his heart left empty by the dark spirit now before him . . .

"This room reeks of death, Nicholas," LaCroix had taunted him, laughing at his grief for the bride who'd lost her life to his immortal kiss. But Janette could never die . . .

"A fair jest, someone, and quickly, before we all run mad with grief," LaCroix laughed now in a shockingly similar tone. "Or shall I send for a dirge-maker to sing us through the night?"

He lifted Janette's hand from Nicholas's and raised it to his own lips in mocking salute. "Your tender mercies do your soul credit, *chérie,* but in sooth, what is the point?" he continued, his icy eyes focused on the face of his vampire son. "The loss you speak of was decades since—the dead maid's grandchildren would be dying this night had she lived to a ripe old age."

"Who are you to speak of anyone's soul?" Nicholas demanded softly.

"Stay, LaCroix is right," Janette interrupted, losing patience with their posturing—how could Lucien quarrel with Nicholas's turn upon a stage, when he himself had used the world as his playhouse for long centuries? And Nicholas, forever rebuking his sire—always conflict with these two—would they never learn to bear their love in charity?

"How should we celebrate our meeting with sadness?" Janette said with a determined smile. She pointedly turned her eyes toward the mortal Isabella, now laughing at Shakespeare's every jest. "You, Nicholas, seem to have learnt comedy right well of late—and have purposed other game."

Nicholas barely spared his latest conquest a glance. "Comedy holds many charms, *chérie,* but the quarry you speak of is another man's pursuit, not mine," he replied. "I found her but tonight, and then only for a moment—and she has barely found me at all."

"Nay, Nicholas, you are too modest." LaCroix smiled, giving Janette a significant look. "You hold your chivalry and charm cheap as ever—'tis my belief you have won the young lady's heart entire."

As if on cue, Isabella let out another delighted crow of laughter, earning an anxious smile from the playwright. "Not so," Nicholas demurred, watching them. "Indeed, she hardly seems to mark me at all—my friend Will seems more her desire at the moment."

"And his attentions are caught by us," Aristotle agreed. "A pretty puzzle of affections, is it not?" It was true, Shakespeare was stealing glances out the side of his eye at Aristotle every few seconds.

"Affection has little to do with that gentleman's interest, I think," Janette answered him, slipping her hand through the curve of Nicholas's arm. "'Tis you he watches, and not in love—have you two quarreled in the past?"

"Indeed, I have yet to make his acquaintance," Aristotle said with a mischievous grin. "But perhaps my reputation precedes me."

"Yet not so far as to make an impression on the lady,"

Nicholas agreed. "And she seems determined—I'll wager she'll win him from his fear in the end."

"And will you be sorry?" Janette queried, arching an eyebrow.

"Nay, not in the slightest," Nicholas answered, smiling down on Janette. "Her heart can fly where it may—I have designs on but one such prize tonight, and its name is not Isabella."

"*Du vrai?*" Janette asked with a smile. "'Tis well spoke, sir, and your prize does thank you kindly." She bobbed a tiny, mocking curtsey, her proud bearing somehow heightening the flirtation. She tightened her grip on his arm, inclining her body ever so slightly toward his own. "But if you wish to feel its gratitude, you must value it more highly than to keep it in such squalor."

"As you wish in all things, sweet lady," Nicholas answered, returning her smile. "Come then. Let us away."

2

Death is an eternal sleep, a dissolution of the body, a terror of the rich, a desire of the poor, a thing inheritable, a pilgrimage uncertain, a thief of men, a kind of sleeping, a shadow of life, a separation of the living, a company of the dead, a resolution of all, a rest of travails, and the end of all idle desires. Finally, death is the scourge of all evil, and the chief reward of the good.

—Sir Thomas North (1535?–1601?), trans.,
Don Anthony of Guevara's *The Dial of Princes*,
Book III, ch. 48

MOST ENGLISHMEN IN THE DAYS AND NIGHTS OF GOOD QUEEN BESS found little joy in rats. Scrabbling in filthy droves through every corner of the densely populated city, the common black rat, bearer of the plague flea, was the bane and despair of every English citizen from the Virgin Queen herself to the basest Cheapside whore. And those other Englishmen, the few who lived in the dark and fed only on their fellow citizens—they had no love for rats, either, for all they had no fear of them.

But Screed was no longer an ordinary Englishman, nor had he become an ordinary vampire. Instead, he was a carouche—a vampire who fed on the blood of beasts—and rats were his greatest bliss. Just now he was tucked against the wall of one of London's poorest, narrowest alleys, whining to a largely uninterested audience of one, and punctuating his remarks with hearty slurps on his prey.

"'Tis a bloody an' ill-made night when a chap finds 'is own dear mum was sent to the cheat," he said and sighed morosely, bending to snatch another wriggling prize from the mud-slick cobblestones at his feet. "'Er neck stretched not a scanty fortnight afore we landed—now I put it to you, me unlovely Spanicky brother, ain't that the lowest o' low and cruelliest of the cruel?"

"*Sí,*" his companion agreed, though in truth he had very little notion what he was agreeing to. He ran a hand through his long black hair, pushing it out of his eyes even though the only sight to be revealed was Screed seizing the hapless rodent.

Javier Vachon, Screed's vampire maker and master, was as different from his fledgling as he thought it possible to be. Watching with unconcealed disgust as Screed sank his fangs into yet another furry little neck and sucked lustily, Vachon tried to think how to comfort him and simultaneously cursed himself for a fool for wanting to try. How he could have saddled himself with so ill-chosen a companion in the night exceeded his understanding. It was a mystery second only to his bafflement that he had failed to rid himself of the vermin-munching sailor once they'd reached port.

Unfortunately, he was incapable of expressing these thoughts in any tongue but Spanish, and the ship that was to return him to the Old World had made port in London Town. Sixty-eight years ago, when he'd left his home to find gold in the New World, England had been a dear ally and a Spanish queen had sat as consort upon the English throne. Now a Spain-hating queen ruled from that throne, and to be Spanish in London was to be a marked man.

"*Dios me castiga así.*" Vachon sighed into the foggy darkness as Screed dropped his second rat and reached for another. "God is punishing me."

"'Ere! None o' that *habla*-babble, mate," the carouche advised, shaking his still-twitching third course in the general direction of his master. "Yer sort ain't so popular in English parts, Ferdinando. There's nary man nor woman wot doesn't remember the Armada right clear-amente, so that Espaniolo-speak o' yers could land our hides in the boil, immortal or no, and I for one would lean toward not."

Vachon merely nodded, too weary to sort this out, much less argue the point. *See me home to England, and I'll never ask ye more,* this accidental fledgling had entreated, and the Spaniard couldn't bring himself to refuse. Why? he asked himself for at least the thousandth time in the weeks since the whoreson was made. Pity for his ugliness? Shame at the unmanliness of his making—Screed had suffered the ill luck to stumble literally on a sleeping vampire in the darkest reaches of his ship's hold while searching for a likely "horsey" to enter in that evening's rat race.

Roused from a torpor, having subsisted for many hidden weeks at sea on a diet of rats himself, Vachon had all but drained the sailor dry before he realized he had grabbed him. The shock had been enough to stop him before he stopped Screed's heart. He had paused to consider the possibilities—bring the sailor into the dark, risk going on deck to fling the corpse overboard, or cringe in the hold with a rotting body for the balance of the voyage—and in that moment, the Englishman did the unthinkable.

He bit the vampire back.

Even now the sheer audacity of the thing made Vachon smile on the rat-sucking seadog with genuine admiration, for all he was so inconvenient.

"So your mother is dead," Vachon said aloud, straightening up from the alley wall where he'd leaned to watch his fledgling wail and feast. "What do you do now, *amigo*?"

"Vengeance," Screed answered without hesitation, flinging another empty corpse away. "Hang an old dame as never done a crumb's morsel of harm in all the wide, wet world? That magistrate shall feel 'is crime in fires afore I'm done wiv 'im."

Vachon nodded; a life for a life, that was fair. Screed was still experimenting with his new strength, but he knew well enough how to snap a neck. "As you will," he agreed, clapping Screed briefly on the shoulder. "I wish you good fortune."

"Ye needn't think of shovin' off yet, mate," Screed retorted, a thin glimmer of fear flashing briefly in his eyes. "Layin' on for a wee squealer is but a pence worth o'evil, easily done. But a rare, juicy magistrate . . ." He clapped a bloody hand on Vachon's shoulder, physically restraining him from flying off.

An instant later, the carouche found himself slammed against the brick wall he had been leaning on, his feet dangling above the alley's cobblestones and his master snarling in his face.

"*Calm-a-tay,* matey, I meant nowt but stay a bit," Screed said submissively. The Spaniard liked to think he was being obeyed, Screed had noticed; in his years as a tar he'd had many petty officers with similar delusions. "Ye needn't cram on all sail and fly off o'er the briny, is all I say."

Vachon scowled as he worked to make sense of this. For nearly seventy years he had been a solitary vampire and happy so, wandering through unlife with the whole vast expanse of the New World for his banqueting hall. Yet even if the desire for a companion had finally overtaken him, how had he managed to bind himself to an English sailor with a mouth like one of his London's open sewers, forever spewing forth an incomprehensible flow of mottled and mixed-up language? And what demon possessed Screed, safely ashore in England, to want to stick so closely to his maker?

"I am for Spain, Screed," Vachon said finally, laboring to make sentences in this awkward, unmusical tongue. "I have tell you so many time." Screed's usual rollicking grin reappeared, and Vachon knew he'd said something wrong.

"Oi—have—TOLD—ye—so—many—TIMES," Screed said slowly, still grinning. "Never worry, it's Screedie's speedy scholar you are, Signor el Conquista; ye'll have the knack o' it in six nicks, doubt not."

"I have told," Vachon began determinedly, but his voice trailed off to nothing as his eyes flashed with a moment's green-gold fire—vampire hunger for a particularly ripe-looking doxy strolling lazily down the alleyway in their direction. Seeing she had his attention, the girl favored him with a shy-salacious smile, passing so close her wide-belled skirts brushed across him. Vachon let Screed drop to the ground and fixed his attention on the girl.

"So says yer gob, mate." Screed grinned as she turned into the avenue proper, casting a quick glance back over her shoulder to make certain her audience remained enthralled. "But them Spanish eyes seem to care right well for seeing London sights—and by the bye, mate, seeing is the best ye'll cop from that sweet bit of hard biscuit."

He followed Vachon as he followed the girl. "'Twould foster the holy cause far better if ye'd follow a more northerly compass," Screed continued bravely, giving the Spaniard's shoulder a jab and pointing him in the direction of a coach coming to a stop before a nearby tavern. "How's for that, mate?"

A plumply prosperous merchant type descended to the street, the rich dignity of his black velvet sleeves trailing in the mud at his heels.

"What of it?" Vachon muttered, barely sparing this figure a glance before returning his attention to keeping sight of the girl, still ambling slowly away.

"Why not fill gullet and purse as well, says I," Screed explained, jerking him back in the direction of the merchant again.

Catching his meaning at last, Vachon watched the mortal pay the coachman and turn purposely toward the inviting yellow light of the open tavern door, his face as round and shiny-white as the almost full moon above their heads. "I fancy him not," he told Screed, taking another step in the direction of the girl who had obligingly lingered halfway down the block.

"Hold there, Ferdinand," Screed objected, catching his arm again. "Them rooms of ours costs money, remember? Such dainties as yon less-than-maid are all very well for the appetite, but—" He stopped, his face suddenly confused. "'Ere—what in bloody 'ell . . . ?"

Vachon barely heard him, equally distracted. A sudden delicate tingle was racing through his veins. It was a sensation he'd never felt before, neither pleasant nor painful, but persistent—impossible to ignore. Looking up, he saw four cloaked figures emerge from the tavern and heard a man's imperious voice call out to the coachman to stop. "Come," he murmured vaguely to Screed as he took a step in that direction.

"Fleas, it must be; them, or crutch-cattle," Screed complained, scratching briskly beneath his hat, under his shirt, and through his much worn sailor's pantaloons. "Every time me feet steps off on the dry for more than a night's lodging— Hoy, where are you for, mate?"

Vachon barely heard him. The figures had stopped, and one of them turned toward him as he approached, the smallest of the four. "*Santa Maria*," Vachon breathed as she met his frankly hungry stare. Such eyes—had Satan himself ever gazed into eyes so blue? And the face, so delicate and yet so stern—the face of an angel, but knowing. No innocence, feigned or real, in those wide, blue eyes . . .

"Aye, I might 'ave known," Screed said with a snort of derision. "It's been a long, fair sail o'er the waters, mate, but ye've slipped off the galleon entire. That morsel o'sweeting would 'ave naught to do with the likes of you even if she weren't already engaged for the night."

"Engaged?" Vachon echoed, confused. "What is this engaged?"

"Hired on, kept an' unkempt, undone an' done for—bought an' paid for, ye ken? And 'er bottom coppered right handsome, I wager, by the look of the gents with her," Screed explained with a cheerful leer.

"*Basta!*" Vachon ordered angrily, cuffing him for his insolence. "How dare you insult a lady, a creature of such—"

"Creature right enow, but no lady," Screed retorted, taking the blow as only his due. "I know not o'the donnas of balmy Spain, but 'ere on English soil, no lady would be caught alive nor dead in such environs as this, for all she's dressed so fine. Bawd or wench, tosspot or cutpurse, gull-catcher, lightskirt, moll, meg, and stew-mutton, them's the girls 'ose parts ye'll find in these parts, mate—but never no lady."

One of the men, a golden-haired dandy, took the woman's hand and helped her into the coach as one of the others, the one whose clothing seemed richest, shot Screed and Vachon a glance of rather unfriendly amusement. "Now that's a rude 'un, ain't 'e just?" Screed muttered.

"Yes," Vachon agreed, putting a hand on his dagger.

"O, lord 'elp us, 'tis the Spanish ire rising again," Screed moaned mockingly, steering his companion away as the coach drove off. "Enough o'that, mate—it's dinner, not a duello, we're for, and a bit of palm-greasing, remember? We've not but 'alf the watch ere the sun shows 'is face, an' I don't fancy showin' 'im me own fair countenance, *oo-sted sobby*?"

Vachon sighed. One additional dram of irritation in his misery cup was the fact that Screed had but to hear a word of Spanish to remember it forever, and, what was worse, pronounce it frequently in his own unique way. "I comprehend," Vachon said wearily. "I hunt the cock, not the hen, yes? Before the dawn?"

"'At's it! That's the very trick o' the treat," Screed crowed, proud of his prowess as a teacher. "And spoke like a very Dutchman, which imports, not aright, but better than a Spaniard."

"Taste this," said Aristotle. The vampire foursome had returned to the rooms Janette and LaCroix had taken at London's best inn, pairing off to spend the daylight hours, Nick and Janette in one room, Aristotle and LaCroix in the next.

Lucien LaCroix raised a skeptical eyebrow, but obliged his old friend by sipping at the glass he'd been handed. A scant moment later, he spit the substance out, shocked.

"Turned wine and dead blood?" he said. "Have your wits melted at long last, to be drinking such swill?"

"Not in the least," Aristotle said, unoffended. "Taste again. I assure you the wine is *not* turned."

"I regret me greatly that I must decline this courtesy," LaCroix said with deadly gentleness. "Is your mind full bewildered? 'Tis mortal poison, and that's to name its charm."

Aristotle's good cheer remained undiminished. "*Some* of us are looking to the future, my friend. Have you not seen what sea travels we may take eftsoons? To the Orient, to Araby, perhaps the New World? We durst not sup on crew nor passengers through a voyage of nine weeks, so what will serve? This will." He gestured at the uncorked bottle.

"If we perish not from this venom en route," LaCroix said ironically. "How sad is the wreck of a mighty brain—or be this sly reckoning? Purpose you to kill us all?"

Aristotle twinkled. "I was ever of a solitary bent, Lucius. Perhaps I mislike my company enow for such a shift."

LaCroix smiled; there were few people on the planet who could still call him by his birth name, but Aristotle was one. "You wound me," he said playfully, "indeed you cut me to the quick"—his eyebrows arched—"but then I cannot die so."

Aristotle laughed, and LaCroix continued, only half-joking. "Yet I have counseled your love most carefully since this place was mud-walled Londinium."

Aristotle smiled broadly. "You have it still, as you well know. But as we speak of love," he nodded his head at the communicating door to Janette's room, "meseems your love is all leashed to that eaglet, and he but flaps and snaps at the jesses in requital."

LaCroix answered with a small shrug.

"What think you they do in there?" Aristotle mused. Envy crept into his voice. "Nay, what think you they do not do? I think we shall not see them rise before the moon does."

LaCroix shrugged again. "It is what I wished," he remarked.

"You would have him fly to hand unbidden, and she your lure." Aristotle construed LaCroix's intentions. "So your wish becomes his wish." He rubbed his nose. "It goes deep between those two, 'tis patent. It may serve. Yet he's a resty fledge, for that."

"Nicholas refuses to know himself," LaCroix said with a trace of a smile. *Gnothi s'auton*—"Know Thyself"—was a proverb attributed to Socrates, philosophical rival of the great Greek teacher Aristotle; the Aristotle sitting before him now had cheerfully refused for nearly fifteen hundred years to say positively whether he was the original of that name or not.

"Then you must present him," Aristotle said, eyes twinkling as he deliberately tweaked the bait. "Master Nicholas the Sullen, meet Master Nicholas the Wiser, a lad famed for how he heeds his sire. Do you not mark his happy countenance, his well-favored house? Situate you so, young Nick, leave off your sorry leavetakings."

LaCroix chuckled, but said nothing.

Aristotle dropped his humor. "Were he mine, I'd hoodwink and leash him straitly. He spoke to me of passage to the Japans, Lucius." He shook his head. "It is not proper in a son to plot so; I mind me greatly of days when it was not possible. *Lex patria potestas,* good Lucius, do you not recall?" Under the Roman law of LaCroix's mortal era, a father's dominion over a son had been absolute as long as he lived; he was entitled to the entire services and acquisitions of any child and could inflict any punishment he saw fit. Indeed, the Roman paterfamilias could even sell his children into bondage if he wished.

LaCroix's eyebrows quirked up. "Shall I vend Nicholas for a galley slave, then?"

Aristotle stroked his beard in apparent contemplation of the question, but the merriment in his eyes gave him away.

LaCroix produced a cool smile. "You look rearward too much, old friend; it is a fault in you." His eyes narrowed and his tone became steely. "The past is ash, and well so. Let it be forgot, and its habits with it. Such as we must make our own mores, or we will be buried ere we die." He stretched in his chair. "And howsomever I shall deal with Nicholas is mine own concern."

That had the unmistakable ring of the final word on the subject of Nicholas; Aristotle sketched a small bow and dropped it. He also stretched now, and settled into a comfortable position, but not without darting another sidelong glance at the bolted door. "Ah, what they may be doing," he said and sighed, folding his arms to sleep.

In fact, Aristotle would have been startled, and LaCroix no doubt most annoyed, if they could have seen just how the children had chosen to occupy themselves behind the suggestive smirk of their bolted chamber door, for Nicholas was schooling Janette in the gentle art of acting.

"All this drivel, you must learn it pat?" Janette asked doubtfully, paging through the playing script of the comedy Nicholas had performed that night at Elizabeth's court.

"Drivel? In faith, *chérie,* you are a hard critic." He knelt behind her on the bed, his doublet unlaced, and peered over her shoulder.

"Harken to this, if you list—'She is my goods, my chattels, she is my house, my household-stuff, my field, my barn, my horse, my ox, my ass, my any thing—' "

Janette tilted her face back and up to Nicholas with a decidedly martial fire kindling in her eyes, and he continued teasingly—

" 'And here she stands, touch her who ever dare.' Now say truly, beloved," he said, kissing her cheek, her ear, her neck, and finally her hair as she tipped her face away from him again. "Are those lines not well spoken?"

"*Oui, bien sûr,*" Janette replied with a secret smile. "They are spoken well indeed." She trailed her fingertips over the back of his hand, which had reached around her waist as he read. "But this copy-hand is atrocious—that you can read it at all is a marvel beyond all reckoning." She touched a series of scribbles in the margin. "What is this, pray tell?"

"Notes on performance," Nicholas explained, settling more comfortably behind her, one arm laid casually against her waist, the linen of his shirt against the thinner linen of her shift, barely separating him from her flesh. "Will is adamant I should play a duke as I should play a peasant, with action natural and speeches plain. 'Do not saw so at the air with your hands, sirrah, or you shall tear a hole in the heavens,'" he read with a grin. Janette's eyebrows went up delicately. "It is what they call the claptrap atop the stage," he explained.

"It is well that you remember his directions so clearly," Janette answered. "For you surely could not read them again." She turned her face up to his with a smile. "But perhaps you think me a fool to fault Virgil reborn as a poor scribe."

It was a dare, and Nicholas accepted it. "A prettier fool has ne'er danced on any platform," he teased, planting a kiss on the bridge of her nose. Janette in a mood to flirt: he hardly dared to trust his good fortune, having her so again. She was here and real, returned to his arms, content and playful as if she had never gone away. Their love had always been so, perfection and disaster in equal measure, with rarely a single night's duration to mark the change. Yet still he marveled at every turn, his heart leaping and falling in perfect cadence with his beloved's direction.

"Is that so?" Janette murmured, turning slightly to caress his cheek. Her golden angel, beautiful knight, blue eyes entreating her to coax him back to perfect ruin. "And how many pretty fools have counted your measure since last we met?"

His answer was to kiss her lips, pressing her close in his arms, her slender softness melting into the hard cradle of his embrace as if it were she who had been born in his love rather than he in hers. "How much do you want me?" she had murmured, lifting the hand more accustomed to a swordsman's steel than yielding flesh and leading him down into the darkness of eternal night. How many nights since then had he whispered back in his thoughts, *More than a mortal man can imagine?*

"Come away with me, Nicholas," she entreated him now, breaking the kiss to frame his face with both hands, the script sliding forgotten to the floor in an untidy heap of loose pages. "Why waste your gift in such child's play?"

His eager smile faded. "So you think me a child as LaCroix does?" he asked, getting up from the bed to retrieve his play.

Eh bien, Janette thought, *Nicholas whose moods alter faster than a cloud's.* "Why take such offense?" she retorted lightly. "Did you not just name me a fool?"

"In jest, lady," he answered heavily. "Only in jest."

"Then believe me to be jesting as well," she said, watching as he placed each page in its proper place with undisguised reverence. "Or have you no humor at all where this Shakespeare is concerned?" She laughed as she reached out to finger his golden tangle of hair. "Who is this great wit that he should be above the laughter of immortal vampires?"

"Would that I could explain it," Nicholas answered, his face alight again with interest. "You must see his plays performed to know him, *chérie*. He can take the basest of human sorrows and make one see all that is noble and good—comedy, yes, but his tragedies . . ."

He set the script he held aside on a small writing desk and took up another curling scroll. "He purposes a new tragedy, the tale of a prince, set on by his slaughter'd father's ghost to revenge. Look, here's the very speech by which the father kindles his son to rage." He unrolled the scroll and let his eyes slide lightly over the page, resisting the almost overwhelming urge to lose himself in the words scratched and blotted there. "E'en this small speech is a revelation," he said, looking up to meet his immortal lover's eyes. "A perfect poem of death and sorrow."

"Then his revelations are nothing to me," Janette retorted sharply, more sharply than she had intended. "Or to you, Nicholas. What should we who will not, cannot, die care for such a perfection of death? What is death to us?"

"Life," he answered. "From whence think you this eternal life we hold doth spring, Janette? We are violets blooming ever in the shade, not sunny roses." He saw the pain in her eyes and turned away, hiding his own as well. "I think it so . . ."

"So because lesser creatures die that we may live, we must wallow in dying like pigs in their own filth?" she demanded, getting up from the bed. "A foolish, childish notion, Nicholas—LaCroix is right—"

"Is he indeed?" He cut her off. "How so? What great wisdom has your mentor imparted that you would share with me?"

"He says that you are witless with grief, that you have lost your will to pursue any diversion but this terrible remorse which saps your strength and makes you fortune's fool," she answered, going to him.

"And whose fool are you, lady?" he retorted, catching her

wrists but unable to force himself to push her away. Her eyes flamed at him, but he continued. "Whose instrument? How long will you be a puppet for your master? How long will he command your every desire, while I—" He stopped, looking away. "While I can but entreat your presence and more often than not fail to win even that."

"Nicholas, listen to me, I beg you," she said, laying a hand on his cheek to make him face her again, visibly restraining her own temper. "I am no man's puppet, neither yours nor LaCroix's," she insisted gently. "He is my father, my master, just as he is yours. He cares for you, my precious love, as deeply as I—your pain tears at his heart—"

"LaCroix has no heart," Nicholas answered, but his will to fight her was all but lost. How could he resist her when he had ached for her so long?

"Enough," she scolded, laying a hand lightly on his shirt. "Why say such a thing when you know it is not true? Mean you to punish me, hurt me as you have been hurt?" He could not answer in words, but she could see in his eyes that this was only true in the darkest part of his soul, that the light she loved still burned strong. "Will you see me pay for leaving you?" she pressed gently.

"Nay, lady," he promised, caressing her cheek. "I would not see you hurt for all the world, far less for my own sake." His eyes fell shut as she leaned forward delicately to press her lips to his, brief and sweet as a breath of springtime air. "Stay with me, Janette," he pleaded urgently, capturing her in his arms, his lips moving feverishly against her skin. "Teach me joy again; turn my heart and mind away from death."

"Yes," she whispered, entwining him in her embrace, her very spirit melting into his passion. "Tonight we shall know only joy."

3

Then did she say, "Now I have found this proverb
true to prove
The falling out of faithful friends, renewing is of love."

—Richard Edwards (1523–1566),
"Amantium Irae Amoris Redintegratio Est," II, 7–8

LaCroix pulled back the heavy drapes as the last weak rays of English sunlight disappeared behind the spire of London's great cathedral, St. Paul's. As he gazed down on the darkening street below, he felt rather than heard his favorite daughter emerge into the room behind him, but this sensation carried no great need for response on his part. He watched the stately procession of the evening's first carriages, the flames of the torches preceding each striking his perceptions as garish and lovely in the misty dark, a welcome touch of festival in the drabness of urban twilight, a hint of the banquet to come.

At his age, LaCroix found the hunger for blood more a seductive pleasure than a compelling pain, and he savored his choice of victim as dearly as the meal itself. Who would it be tonight? A highborn female like the green-clad beauty climbing into the coach just beneath his window, her long, white throat an elegant denial of the crimson, animal life beneath her skin he could all but taste? Too close to his lodging, his lair. What of the sweet-faced clowns who pranced and preened before

Nicholas and his fellow heroes on the stage, the sweetly unnatural beasts who were painted as sacrificial virgins? Or perhaps the great poet himself?

"You should wake Nicholas," he said aloud. "Surely he is wanted—they play their comedy this night at the home of the poet's young patron."

"What of it?" she answered, the slightest edge of malice traced along the music of her tone as she moved to his side. "Such a dirty place," she mused, gazing down as well.

"No dirtier than your precious Paris," LaCroix answered, giving the word its full French pronunciation. "Methinks 'tis not London herself which offends my child."

"Nevertheless, we should never have come here," Janette insisted, turning to face him. "Let him go, LaCroix—has he not suffered enough?"

The older vampire raised his eyebrows in mock disbelief to mask his genuine annoyance. "Yes, *ma belle enfante*—indeed, he has suffered too much," he answered. "And far too long. My purpose—and yours—is to bring this suffering to an end."

"And how shall we accomplish this?" she demanded, turning away restlessly. "Is happiness a skill to be taught, joy a tonic with which Nicholas may be dosed until the memory of his lost love fades? Is grief but a scar of a disease to be cured?" She turned back to lay a hand on LaCroix's chest, her wide blue eyes beseeching. "You know but too well what it is to lose the soul's dearest hope, to have love cruelly denied," she continued gently. "Could another have set your broken heart to dance?"

LaCroix's eyes narrowed for a moment in warning. "Nicholas enjoys his grief, my dear," he chided, lifting her hand to his lips before putting her away from him. He moved away from the window toward the room's inner door, opening it to let the lamplight fall on his wayward son's still-dreaming face. "You can see this, surely."

"*Oui*," she admitted, watching them both. The sleeping chevalier, seemingly as innocent as a child, watched over with cold, knowing love from a heart like frozen fire. Her own heart's only true longings, sharers of her blood. "'Tis too true, I fear," she went on, surrendering for now to her master's will—centuries had taught her the folly of disputing him at such a moment. "And now he has found a dear companion in his misery—this damnable playwright is as drawn to death as he. They feed on each other like . . ." She let her voice trail off, the words understood quite well.

LaCroix smiled, touching her cheek lightly. "You think this Shakespeare has influence?" he said.

Janette shrugged. "So 'twould seem," she replied, turning to ring for a servant. "Bring my cloak and hat," she ordered when the girl appeared. "And have a carriage brought as well, *s'il vous-plaît.*"

"Where shall we tonight, *chérie*?" LaCroix asked lightly as the girl disappeared again. "This city you so dislike offers so little by way of amusement—I suppose 'twill be the theater again." He slipped soft, fawn leather gloves onto his smooth, white hands. "Though I must say I loathe these long days when a vampire may only enter the outdoor arenas after the third act for fear of fiery consumption," he continued. "One may patronize Her Majesty's Choir at its little indoor stage, I suppose, if one can stomach a flock of flutey boys piping at kings and soldiers." He took the cloak from the maid, who brought it to him first, before attending Mam'selle Janette. "No, I think quite not. Shall we make our introduction to the gentry, think you? Fair young Hilliard's *maman* is said to be most amusing. The relict of a minor knight, but an empress by her manner," he laughed.

"I have no stomach for any such entertainment this night," Janette answered brusquely, her perfect angel's face as blankly impassive as a statue's as she adjusted the velvet ribbons of her toque. "*Pardonnez-moi, mon cher ami,* but I had enough of young Hilliard last night. And I begin quite to weary of plays."

"Indeed?" Lacroix watched her expression for the slightest treasonous change. "Which wearies you more—comedy or tragedy?"

She tied her laces without answering, then turned to leave. "Both and neither," she said at last, her back turned to him. "I shall hunt alone tonight."

"Aye, your worships, just step, just step . . ." Every stair got its own urging, as if the Coroner to the Royal Household and Master George the Undersecretary of a Privy Councillor were balky hounds instead of Queen's men about the Queen's business.

The Silver Stirrup, the inn to which these august officials had been summoned, lay in Cheapside, only half a mile away from the great, handsome carrier inns of Gracious and Bishopsgate Streets, but for all the resemblance it bore to them, it might as well have been across the world. In this neighborhood, the houses leaned together overhead like old crones whispering, and unexpected materials were likely to be flung from their windows with no warning for those in the street.

Aristotle sighed. Ten quiet, careful years in England had accustomed him to the pleasures of the clean, orderly, and above all fragrant Court life.

Next to him, the tall, spare figure of Constantius de la Giorgi Nomus, Queen's Coroner, seemed rigid with distaste as well. Though it was hard to tell with Nomus: widely regarded as among the most learned men in Christendom, he almost never bothered to have an emotion and was often accounted a walking corpse. Of course, his companion, Master Dyer, had reason to know this was not true.

"Just step, just step . . ."

Aristotle resisted an impulse to say, *Nay, I think I'll rest me here and do you bring the room down.* The man probably just would have said, *Your worship?* in blank incomprehension, anyway.

The Stirrup's proprietor, Citizen Brewer Marcus Becker, was a man of perhaps as many as fifty years. As befitted a brewer, Becker had a florid face, red nose, and a barrel body, but none of a drinking man's jollity; instead, he had the pinched, sour features of a miser, gathered in a little bundle between his tapster's round pink cheeks.

That he was not the least bit happy to have such notable visitors to his hostelry was plain in his manner, obsequious courtesy thinly layered over desperate hostility. Still, the Queen's law provided that any death by mischance within twelve miles of the Queen's presence, wherever she might be—"within the verge"—fell automatically within the Privy Council's jurisdiction. And while the Privy Council did not always elect to exercise that jurisdiction, it was well known in the lower echelons of London society that Master Undersecretary Dyer paid a pretty penny for information of a strange death, so the news had been sent to Whitehall as soon as the unfortunate girl had been discovered.

"Just step, just step . . ." Another flight of stairs.

The variety of mortal men still amazed Aristotle. Mine host Becker, for example, had precious few hairs on his head, but that accorded with his years. However, his hair seemed not to have deserted him, but simply traveled south. Coarse wisps of it curled out from every possible opening in his clothes: at throat, wrists, below the jerkin, and where his breeches and hose met at the knees, stray strands struggled toward the light like grass sprouting through paving stones. Climbing the stairs, his visitors were afforded a particularly close view of the back of the man's neck, where heavy black curls fought their way upward from the confines of the man's rough linen shirt.

Aristotle smiled to himself, amused. Landlord Becker could never know that the sheer furriness of his fat neck protected his life, no matter how much he irritated a vampire who chanced to visit his establishment. It was just too disgusting to disentangle hair from your fangs.

"'Ere's your last step," Becker announced, to Aristotle's relief, "and 'ere be the chamber whereof she was found defuncted—" Nomus waved one bony hand to silence Becker, and entered the room.

There was a girl on the bed, lately dead—or, more to the point, lately alive. A very, very pretty girl.

Aristotle knew at once from residual scents that a vampire had been there.

Nomus brought two candles out of a pocket hidden somewhere in his drab doublet, and then a flint to kindle them. Handing one to Aristotle, he held the other over the girl's body, bringing the telltale marks at her neck to light. Her clothing was somewhat disarrayed, though not torn in any violence—so she was a ramp, or gillian-flyrte: a pretty, biddable girl with no fortune but her face, like so many others in London. The natural prey of a vampire.

"What is this wench?" demanded the Queen's Coroner.

"Light Nell, she's called," said the landlord. "Was called."

Irritation bled through his voice. So she'd paid him a bit of rent, had she? This was no bawdy house, but this landlord was of the type to demand a share of any commerce under his roof. Two pennies out of her sixpence, say, for the sort of gentleman that did not want to take his pleasure in an alley.

Aristotle sighed. With all of London at his disposal, with all of London's wonderful dark alleys and ditches and pits and open fields and a big dark river so near to hand, what kind of stupid vampire did this? A girl left gently on a stuff-mattress in a public inn, all untouched but for the small holes and the—*oh, delicious-smelling even now*—tiny dribble of blood on her throat?

"What make you of this?" said the coroner, holding the candle to light her neck.

"Plague," Aristotle said immediately.

"Nay!" said Becker from the door. "A cleanly girl, she were." Real alarm gave energy to his opinion: under the Queen's Statute of 1574, the Coroner and Secretary had it in their power to require the Stirrup to nail a white cross on its door to warn there had been plague within, and to order him and his wife to carry long white sticks whenever they went out. Such orders would ruin them.

"'Tis patent, there is neither buboes nor sores," said the coroner, feeling gently at the girl's armpit, stomach, and thighs for the typical round lumps that marked the Black Death. "I see neither botch, carbuncle, blane, vesicle, pimple nor spot apparent in her whole body, but for these at her neck." The Coroner explored under the girl's clothing with purely clinical interest. "'Tis uncommon to find life extinguished where there be but two livid tokens."

"Yet I have seen this ere now," Aristotle affirmed, truthfully enough. "One finds naught but only the little red sores such as are here, the which quickly form, and burst anon in pure blood, whereon the sufferer dies, oftimes screaming." More truth, of a sort. "You will see no yellow matter at the broken places, for this taking goes straight to the brain."

Fifty years ago, Aristotle would have spoken of a discord of humors, but the most advanced physicians these days were beginning to reject such talk. They discounted the old vegetable remedies and sought to physic the ill with compounds of minerals compounded by the new science called "chemistry."

Speak of surfaces, then: the newest talk was of what a learned doctor could see and touch. "There may be lesions that pock the skin with suchlike sanguinary sores at other points, but the throat is the chiefest."

"'Tis strange to hear," the Coroner said, shaking his head.

Aristotle found a shock of his own when he moved around

the bed. There was a bitten rat, no, two bitten rats, on the floor. "Monstrous!" he muttered.

"Eh?" said the Master Coroner.

"Look you where there are further lesions," Aristotle said smoothly, controlling his disgust. There were two, rather more ragged bite signs at the girl's wrist, which had been hanging limply over the rats. Aristotle kicked the rat bodies under the bed, beginning to be really worried. *Rats? This vampire might be worse than merely stupid.* He rubbed his eyes. "'Tis a plague, most certainly."

"'Tis an odd form of *bubonicus*, to mark so little yet destroy so quick," said the coroner. He continued to prod at the girl's all-but-perfect body with his long, dry fingers, and his voice dropped to a thoughtful murmur. "Yet how could there be what it would appear: round punctures that pierced the throat and yet let no blood?"

Nomus's devotion to accurate observation was beginning to alarm Aristotle. The vampire looked the mortal in the eye, preparing to hypnotize him.

"'Tis the fastest, maddest death ever I witnessed, this plague," he said. "Those who have it rave of yellow-eyed demons suckling at their hearts."

Nomus bridled. His mouth, always puckered with disapproval of one thing or another, shriveled to the size of a raisin. That kind of supernatural talk appalled him; he was a man of science, and was disappointed to find Master Dyer willing to repeat such rubbish. He breathed deeply.

"The disease procedeth not by demons," he said sternly. "The master physician James Quiney Thompson hath well demonstrated that pest is *esse rerum,* a physical thing. He shows that 'tis a derivative of ill air, and beginneth as a pestilential ferment insinuating itself into the blood and juices of the body, following upon which the membranes of the brain, being pricked and vellicated by the poisonous spicula, do swell. The caustick and narcotick nature of the venom causeth the victims to walk ill, as if drugged. Then appeareth mortifications caused by the extinction of natural heat upon the account of highly prevailing malignity." Nomus sniffed. "The lesions are called, by the . . . novice in physick, *tokens,* and by the learned, *exanthemata.*"

Aristotle rubbed at his beard to hide a smile; at least Nomus hadn't actually *called* him ignorant. This was the lecture, almost word for word, that Nomus gave periodically at the Royall College of Physitians. His smile widened: now *there* was an ignorant group—from the perspective of a vampire who'd already romped through the better part of two millennia.

Purely for malicious fun, Aristotle dredged up a few of the old remedies. "At that point, would you prescribe the Agua Epidemica et Pulvis Pestifugus, Mattias Plague-Water, or the Electuary of Treacle and Wood-Sorrel? And prefer you the London treacle or the Dutch?"

A tiny spasm animated the Coroner's cadaverous face. "I had liefer prescribe a dead toad."

Aristotle gave Nomus a wide-eyed stare, rocking on his feet. "Nay, so? What, consumed or hung about the neck?"

Now the gaunt doctor frowned fractionally. "You toy with me, Master Dyer."

Aristotle smiled, and bowed. "I do, Master Nomus, and do most heartily apologize. Yet you must credit me: 'tis plague we see here. I have seen this sudden-afflicted death many times before." Now the vampire was telling the truth again. "It taketh its victims most calamitously, and shows no sign but these tiny bitelike pocks."

"There appears no cause for the life to end." Nomus frowned, but he was yielding.

"And yet she is extinct." Aristotle smiled, bending a palm toward the deceased Nell.

It was working. The coroner backed away.

Aristotle turned to the landlord, who was hovering in the door. "What was the man that hired this room?"

"Two men," said Crocker. "A Dutch merchant and his lackey. There's naught to tell of them," he shrugged. "My woman saw them e'en less than I."

"Still, let us speak to her," Aristotle said. Anything to get everyone out of the room, away from Light Nell's body. "Send for the barrow to carry her out, and burn the bedding."

Becker squinted at him. This was getting off lightly. Nomus also looked askance at Aristotle.

"This small-tokened plague travels only by touch." *Another bit of the truth, in its own way*, the vampire thought. "He need not carry the rod nor mount the cross, an he touched her not."

"Me? Never!" avowed Becker.

Aristotle smiled. "Never's a long time, and that was a lie, Master Host. But not last night."

"No, your worship." Becker was humble now. Nomus nodded, satisfied, turning back to the girl's neck for one more look.

"I am like to ask a service of you somewhen," Aristotle told Becker, too quietly for Nomus to hear. "You will grant it, methinks." Becker nodded in resignation. Court gentlemen—a lot like thieves, they were.

Aristotle was wondering if he knew any vampire who was not too nice in his tastes to be willing to visit Becker's furry neck. But a landlord, that could be a useful tool to have . . .

"God's mercy, poor Nell," said the landlord, with his first trace of real feeling. "Me old woman liked her right well."

"Your good wife, who saw the men?" Aristotle said, leading Coroner Nomus toward the door.

"Nay, nay, never her. I speak o' the *first* Mistress Becker. Ah, she were a wonder and a worker, that one. Mistress Becker that is, she's a lickerish wench, begging your pardon, your worships. Just step, your worships, we'll find her i' the kitchen. Just step."

The "lickerish wench" was a thin girl, barely into her teens, dressed in a worn kirtle, bodice, and apron that hung off her limply. Her hair was tucked up under a rank kerchief rather than the neat linen caplet one might expect of an innkeeper's lady. And for all that, Aristotle reflected, she was a very lucky girl: married at thirteen or fourteen into a life of drudgery, but safe from the life that had led Light Nell to her end upstairs. Out of the grubby framing of Mistress Becker's workaday clothes shone a clean face with a smiling mouth and timid but clever eyes. She answered questions clearly and simply, and began to explain how she'd found Light Nell's body.

"So I goes to give them a basin—"

Her husband broke in. "Ay, at seven o' the clock. The *first* Mistress Becker was up betimes, and upon the market afore even the grocers or fishmongers. And she never let no man take a penny from her what he hadn't well earned, nor coal men nor pot menders nor even your thatcher. Never a-bed was she of an ague nor a humor, and her kitchen hot with cookery before the sun was ever high as the roof of St. Paul's. And she—"

"I'm sure she did," Aristotle said, cutting off the recitation of that deceased lady's virtues.

It didn't work. "Nay, *she'd* ne'er be gone three hours entire between dinner and supper—and at what, may I find? Gone with that lickerish strumpet Mistress Katherine Simons to the playhouse, so please you, to hear a comedy?"

"Indeed?" Aristotle turned to the girl. "Which one?" he asked courteously. "Did you like of it?"

She blushed at being asked for an opinion. "'Twas the midsummer dream," she said, almost too softly to be heard. "'Twas the one with fairy-folk in the forest."

"An excellent comedy," Aristotle agreed, startled to find the Coroner adding enthusiastically, "Ay, the fairy queen enamored of the weaver in a donkey's head is a rare jest."

"Bottom, he's called," said the innkeeper's wife.

"Most rightly so," the Coroner continued blandly, "for while 'tis the topmost member of *equus* that is portrayed, there's many a maid's been cozened by the other end of that beast." Aristotle choked a laugh into a cough, but the wit went right over the landlord's head. The wife might have comprehended, though, since her eyes dropped suddenly. "Now, mistress, the two Dutchmen? How did they look?"

"I was a-telling your worship, we had little sight of 'em," the husband began, but was quelled by a look from the coroner.

The wife continued in her little, squeaky voice—a voice for a mouse, Aristotle thought. "Sirs, one of them was of goodly stature, so"—she raised her hand several inches over her head—"but his fiznomy was poorly favored, and his head had no hair upon it. That was the servant, and a very rawly spoke wight he was, and rudely dress't—his breeches was blue sailor's slop-hosen stitched all from canvas, and poor slippers, but he also wore a goodly jerkin of Spanish leather."

Aristotle scratched his beard. Bald, wearing sailor's clothes? This was no vampire he could remember. "And the other one," prompted the Coroner.

She blushed. Aristotle's eyes widened. "The master," said Mistress Becker, "he was gentle enough spoke, but had little of the English tongue, being late come from the Low Countries."

"Said he this?"

"Your worship, he did not, but his servant said it upon his account."

"Now, his appearance?"

Now she blushed deeply. *So: a pretty lad,* thought Aristotle. "He lacketh a bit of your worship's height," she reported faithfully. "His hair is black, all undressed and uncut, and falls free at his face and shoulders. His beard is trimmed indifferent short, that's black also. He spoke me little, saving only," she darted her eyes at her husband, "'Good e'en, mistress' and 'Good morrow, mistress,' yet he had a mild, courteous eye—a very gentlemanlike eye, very brown and soft like a hound's eye."

A pretty lad who knows how to use it on women, Aristotle thought, remembering the dead girl upstairs. "And his condition seemed good," Mistress Becker went on, "his doublet and hose of taffeta, his boots well enough, his cloak lined well."

The landlord had had enough. He broke in roughly: "He had great black brows, black eyes, and a black heart. He was a Spaniard, or I'm an ass."

A Dutchman for certain, then, thought Aristotle. A glance at the Coroner told him Master Nomus was thinking the same thing.

"The *first* Mistress Becker spent no sighs on foreign devils," Becker continued. "She looked no further than her own door until the day she died." His tone became piteous. "Oh, I remember the day well . . ."

"Happiest day of her life, I doubt me not," Aristotle murmured, and drew a small, flashing smile from the wife.

"No more do I," she whispered back in her little mouse's voice, then said aloud, "Will your worships be wanting a tankard, then?"

"My hairs!" Tom Saddler somehow injected an anguished screech into his whisper. "God's lingering death, *where are my hairs!*" The tall boy tossed frantically amid the gowns and props for Rosalind's wig.

The company had acted an entirely different play that afternoon and were able to prepare to come across the river for the evening's private performance only after the last of the groundlings had been ushered out of the Globe. While Lady Hilliard, who had commissioned this performance at her big riverside house, was giving her noble guests six or eight courses of dinner, the Lord Chamberlain's Men were hastily unpacking their trunks, swiping makeup onto their faces, and praying not to mix up their speeches when these well-bred, well-fed notabilities sat down to be entertained. It was not unheard of for an actor who had conned a Merry Wife of Windsor for the afternoon to accidentally let slip a few of her lines into a speech of Titania, Queen of the Fairies.

In the great hall of a private house, such as the one in which they played tonight, the Lord Chamberlain's Men were often lucky to have so much as a curtain draped over a rope to separate their backstage dressing area; the tidy order of their backstage management gave way to a chaos in which only the location of the promptbook was known for sure. Tonight, though, playing in the seemingly endless long gallery of Hilliard House, they had more than ample backstage space. Not only was there room for a tiring place, a well-lit area for the bookholder to stand and prompt missed lines, but there was even space for an impromptu "green room," where players could lounge a bit between cues.

"Every night the same thing," groaned Will Sly, teasingly. "Where's me 'airs, where's me 'airs? Where's the chopine shoes?"

"Oh God, the chopines!" whimpered Tom, his head bobbing up from the trunk he was pawing through. His face was chalked white for a maidenly complexion, rubbed at the cheekbones with brick dust to give him an enchanting, blushful quality. Sheer anxiety was giving his eyes a moist, dewy look.

Sly had an ear tuned to the performance; he knew Saddler's cues as well as he knew his own. When only a minute still remained before Tom would have to make a disastrously wigless entrance, Sly laughed, said, "Tom?" and pointed in the direction of the company's resident poet.

Will Shakespeare, who was in only the first and last acts, had settled down to chat with young Hilliard and Isabella, both of whom apparently already knew what was going to befall the young lovers in the play. Isabella had spotted a small scroll tucked into Will's doublet and teased him to bring it out for her. It turned out to be a freshly written scene.

"Will?" said Tom Saddler uncertainly, looking back at the grinning Sly. "Hast seen my hairs?" His voice was nearly inaudible. A young actor did not like to have to pester one of the company's shareholders for his wig.

Shakespeare didn't answer. He was attending to a different performance.

"One woe doth tread upon another's heel, so fast do they follow," pretty Isabella intoned. She was reading the foolscap aloud by the light of a bright double flame set in a sconce high on the wall, the rich scarlet of her velvet gown changing hues with every movement as she strolled, tilting her script to catch the light of the flambeaux behind her.

Two feet above Isabella's head on the stone wall, another torch holder stood empty—but for a wig.

"Villain!" hissed Saddler, making a heroic leap to pull the wig down from its perch. Sly shrugged.

Isabella's dark head turned from the blotted parchment as young Thomas, fully gowned and painted, flew into the air next to her, landed heavily, clapped the wig on his head, and pressed a kiss for luck to her half-covered bosom before sprinting for the stage and his cue.

Watching him go, Isabella raised a hand to brush back her hair. "We're doomed in sooth if they follow as fast as that," she laughed. Moments later, they heard Tom delivering his line in the half-distance, his breathlessness turned to account as maidenly reserve.

Isabella turned back to her text. "'Your sister's drowned, Laertes'—Drowned? Good heavens, Will," she laughed, incredulous. "I thought as all who died in your tragedies were stabbed or bludgeoned—now will one be drowned? And a lady yet."

"How else shall one kill a cat?" Hilliard teased, catching idly at the bell of her skirt as she passed, but making no great effort to pull her closer.

"More kit than cat in this case, Adonis," the player-poet answered. Willy had become quite bold, bringing his lowborn mistress all but under his proud mama's highborn nose. He was keeping her hid behind the actors' arras, 'twas true, but 'twas a brave stroke, nonetheless. "The girl who's drowned is a virgin."

"A tragic tragedy indeed," Isabella said, pulling a solemn face at her patron. "So the lady is drowned—Who sings here of her death, then, sirrah?"

"Her lover's mother." Mischief glinted in the playwright's eyes.

"O ho, then 'tis a happy speech!" she crowed, stepping aside to allow a pair of lesser boys to admire themselves in the wavering brass mirror. "Think you not so, my sweet?"

"No doubt, my demon." Hilliard returned her smile.

"So I am to think myself the mother of the lover of a virgin," Isabella mused, one hand falling to her seated lover's curls, twirling them idly round her slender fingers in waggish imitation of the lady they could all have seen by leaning around a curtain.

"The Queen of Denmark," Shakespeare elaborated, suppressing mirth. No doubt Hilliard would be less than charmed were he to perceive his mother so cleverly aped.

"A great lady indeed," she answered, fluting her voice ever so slightly through her nose. "Aye me, 'tis much to ask, O Great Greatness, i'faith too much."

"Then let it lie," Hilliard suggested, tugging her roughly into his lap as Tom Saddler and the other leading "lady" came back in. They saw Saddler launch a kick at Will Sly, who avoided it easily, a good thing since the stage directions called for him to bound onstage, not hobble. Saddler came to lean against the wall at a spot where he could watch Isabella.

"I'll none," Isabella retorted, kissing her lover briefly but firmly on the lips—*Take that, young Tom,* Shakespeare thought with an inward sigh. "The Ancient William has besought my help; shall I refuse him?" She took up the parchment again, studying it from her perch in Hilliard's arms, ignoring the shadow that flickered across Will's face at the word "ancient."

"Drowned, drowned, drowned . . . ah, 'tis here . . . 'There is a willow grows askant the brook, that shows his hoar leaves in the glassy stream . . . therewith fantastic garlands she did make of crowflowers, nettles, daisies, and long purples, that liberal shepherds give a grosser name, but our cold maids do dead men's fingers call them.'" She stopped, her brow wrinkling slightly in a frown. "Would a queen make such a vulgar jape as this, sweet William?"

"She would if I should play her," Tom laughed.

"No doubt." Isabella pulled a face at him.

"'Tis hardly carved in stone," Shakespeare answered, losing patience with the jests and eager to hear her continue, a woman's wind through the flute of his play. "Go on, 'twill be better by and by."

"By and by is easily said," Hilliard grumbled as the girl got up.

"'There on the pendant boughs her crownet weeds clambering to hang, an envious sliver broke,'" she continued, her eyes widening in horror at the tale, her voice rising to match. "'When down her weedy trophies and herself fell in the weeping brook. Her clothes spread wide—'"

"Now come we to the argument," Thomas murmured to Hilliard. "A virgin with clothes spread wide—"

"'And mermaidlike awhile they bore her up,'" Isabella read on, entirely oblivious to all but the words in her hand. "'Which time she chanted snatches of old lauds, as one incapable of her own distress, or like a creature native and endued unto that element'—Will, why . . . ?"

"She is mad for love and grief," he explained. "Go on, go on . . ."

She nodded, barely glancing up. "'But long it could not be till that her garments, heavy with their drink, pulled the poor wretch from her melodious lay to muddy death,'" she finished, letting the parchment fall. "'Sblood, Will . . ."

"Fair verse by fair lips told," a new voice spoke from the shadows. The Frenchman LaCroix, late arrived, had apparently taken a wrong turn and found himself amongst the rabble. "A new play, sir?"

"A piece of one," Shakespeare answered, rising reluctantly to meet him. Nicholas might call this man friend, but he himself found little to love in either his manner or his person—a proud man, and perhaps a cruel one. There was something strangely lawless about the way he kept his hair, close-cropped as only a warrior or an invalid would have. And this man was patently no invalid . . . "The lady does me service to read it so well."

"And now she shall do me service to leave you," Hilliard said, barely sparing LaCroix a glance as he got up—What care should he have for the French patron of a drunken actor who could not be troubled to leave his bed before sundown? "Come, Isabella."

"Nay, my lord, I beg you," she answered, handing Shakespeare his page as she watched this LaCroix. Something in those eyes—ice and fire told in blue . . . "Shall we not wait for the play to be done?"

"We shall not," Hilliard said, annoyed, taking hold of her arm with no great show of gentleness. "Come, lady, I would have you come away."

LaCroix watched with barely suppressed amusement as the girl's eyes flashed dark fire of their own. "And I would stay where I am," she said defiantly, jerking free. "Go wait upon thy lady mother and leave me to my own obliging."

"Isabella, I release you from your promise," the playwright began, obviously hoping to keep peace. "Go as our Adonis bids you—"

"Nay," Hilliard interrupted, the blood rising in angry splotches on his pretty white cheeks. "The Queen of Denmark shall do as she will." Making a bow to LaCroix so slight as to barely escape offense, the young man took his leave.

"We needs must pardon him, my lord," Isabella sighed, offering LaCroix her hand for his kiss. "He broaches no courtesy beyond sight of his *chére maman*."

"A worrisome fault," LaCroix agreed, obliging her.

"Nay, not when taken all with the whole great barrel of him, by my troth," she laughed, glancing around at the other players, all of whom seemed comically anxious to find themselves someplace else. "I wonder that such a sour moon hath drawn all the tide of merriment out behind him."

"Perhaps it is not your lord's absence but my present discourtesy puts them out of humor," the vampire said, casting a significant look in Shakespeare's direction. "No doubt they think me forward and ill-bred to so present myself in closeness unbidden."

"Then 'tis the dawn of a prim new age," she answered. "Shall players now stand on the ceremony of their betters? A wonder indeed . . ." She moved aside to clear a path to the promptbook for another anxious actor. "Nay, sir, a true stranger would scarce be marked," she continued, pressing nearer to LaCroix in the process of making way. "But you . . . I hear it whispered about that your face has been seen amongst these men ere this," she confided with a charming grin.

LaCroix smiled, thinking of his one appearance on an English stage . . . four devils for the wage of three—a pretty bargain if ever he'd seen one. "Can such pretty ears be privy to blasphemy?" he demurred.

"Yea, and often," she shot back with a laugh. "And you are

e'en the patron of the handsome Chevalier, *n'est-ce pas?* Know you where he bides tonight?"

"You think him handsome?" he parried.

"Have I no eyes?" she retorted. "I think your lordship thinks him handsome too, for he has no love for his acting."

"Verily, lady, I am no patron," LaCroix said.

The girl looked momentarily confused. "I'faith?" she said. "Then you must pardon me, sir, for I have mistaken your face—"

"No patron but father," he interrupted.

She stopped, her eyes widened in a pantomime of shock to impress the farthest reaches of the gallery. "Nay, it cannot be," she cried. "Chevalier is a pretty youth, 'tis true, but he carries more age than your years have strength to bear."

"You flatter me," LaCroix replied with a cryptic smile.

"Yea, verily," she retorted with a laugh. "But in this matter I speak but truth—you have not the age to be that man's sire, unless you got him in the cradle."

"Monsieur LaCroix means to tease you into error, lady," Shakespeare said, putting on a mask of good humor. "He is a gentleman of infinite jest." He looked up as Nicholas himself appeared in the doorway, his clothes and hair as rumpled as if he'd flown the five miles from his lodging. "Is't not so, my errant actor, most tardy lord?"

"Pardon me, Will, I pray you most humbly," Nicholas said, shooting LaCroix a murderous glance. "My rest was so deep I took more than my fair hour climbing back to labor, and none were so kind in my house as to wake me."

"'Tis no great matter," Will answered, his mood growing lighter in truth as well as presentation. "Condell's flux has run its rapid course and left him hungry for applause. 'Tis two shillings' fine to miss rehearsal; we'll assess you so." The thought of fining the well-born amateur brought a smile to his face; two shillings was a serious penalty for a working actor, but less than nothing to a man like Chevalier, whose doublet alone must have cost fifty pounds.

"So little?" Isabella said playfully. "For myself, I have missed the golden monsieur—such an ornament as this must be prized, superfluous or not. And what is the value of gold at his weight?" She tweaked his hair.

"Fair e'en, lady," Nicholas said, absently kissing her hand, his eyes still fixed on LaCroix.

"Why blame me for your lateness, Nicholas, when 'twas your cousin who gave you such repose?" LaCroix said. "Have you no thought for her?"

"Naught else but so," Nicholas replied, dropping the mortal girl's hand.

"A fair compliment," Isabella laughed. "Heard you, Will, how neatly courtesy may be set by for true affection?"

"Aye," Shakespeare agreed. "Methinks good Nicholas has remembered his hour but quite forgotten his heart—or, more like, lost it."

"Many years past," Nicholas admitted.

"Then alas for such poor creatures as I who shall sup alone tonight." Isabella sighed.

"Not so, *ma belle,*" LaCroix protested. "Your beauties make you as necessary an ornament as Nicholas—and as you can see, the first lady of our play has not appeared. You shall dine with us."

Nick opened his mouth to protest—some excuse to spare her pride as he sought to spare her life—but the girl laughed before he could speak. "So shall I play the understudy to thy cousin's part?" she asked him. "What think you, Will? Shall I taste French entertainment?"

"Ask me not, Isabella," the playwright replied, using her Christian name but refusing to meet her eyes. "The Queen shall do as she will."

She colored slightly at this, crimson at her throat to match the roses in her cheeks. "Just so," she murmured, her eyes clouding at some memory.

"Last night a princess, tonight a queen," Nicholas said gallantly, looking from the girl to his master's smirk and back again. "Think you, LaCroix, that our company may tempt such a regal lady?"

"Tempt me, yea, and much," she said, coming back to herself with a smile. "But not so much as to damn me as yet." She bent to press an impudent kiss to Shakespeare's balding brow. "I must away to my lord." She made pretty curtsies all around, lingering before LaCroix. "So sirrahs, I bid ye good night."

"A pretty creature," LaCroix remarked when she was gone.

"And scarce a whiff of the gutter left about her—my compliments, Shakespeare. Or was her tutor young Hilliard?"

"Neither," the playwright said, his head bowed over his pages in a scant attempt to disguise his dislike. "Isabella is a prodigy, a product of her own fair design." He gave Nicholas a grin. "So, laggard, wilt thou join us despite thy sloth, or art thou otherwise engaged?"

"I fear I must compel his company," LaCroix injected smoothly before his errant pupil could reply. "We have been so long parted—"

"Nay, sir, save your noble breath." Nicholas cut him off. "Think you I fear your damnation so profoundly as the pretty chit who left us? I am no juggler to be compelled to dance and prattle for my dinner."

"I'faith, I think never so," LaCroix replied, after a moment's pause. He arched one eyebrow. "I but believed you courteous and fond."

"Then mayhap you know me less than you believe," Nicholas said coolly, meeting his eyes. "I shall do my own will this night."

4

This pleasant lily white
This taint of roseate red,
This Cynthia's silver light,
This sweet fair Dea spread
These sunbeams in mine eye,
These beauties, make me die.

—Edward DeVere, 17th Earl of Oxford (1550–1604),
"What shepherd can express," v. 7

VACHON TOOK A SEAT ON THE TAVERN'S CREAKING COMMUNAL BENCH A short, safe distance from his latest and unloved prey, watching with disgust as the rich, young fop quaffed down yet another goblet of wine.

"*Maldito, porcino . . .*" The vampire swore under his breath as the boy snatched a greasy leg from the goose carcass before him and tore into it with gusto. Only the thought of returning to Screed empty-handed kept him still for such a display—he knew the rat-drinker would never leave off howling if he sought more thrilling if less profitable pleasures now. Particularly since Vachon himself had insisted on mounting the evening's enterprise alone.

"A bit o'friendly succor ne'er hurts, mate," Screed had warned him, the cockamamie voice of reason. "Wot if ye must needs chat the capon afore ye stuff it?"

"I manage," Vachon had answered, hellbent to have his way in some small part of this foolishness. *Worse than a bad marriage, this partnership of blood.* So now here he lurked like some barmaid's ghost at the heels of a drunken lamb barely old enough to bleat, sworn irrevocably to a quest that had liked him little in the first place. He had smelt gold on the boy as soon as he saw him skulking out of a Deptford bawdy house and had stalked him all night, his patience wearing thinner by the moment. He must leave the light soon enough, Vachon soothed himself, a small smile flirting with his mouth as his quarry took another long draught of wine. And death would be waiting in the shadows.

Suddenly, the same queer tingle he had felt the night before swept over him like the fog-soaked draft from the gaping tavern door. The vampire turned sharply in his seat, his quarry momentarily forgotten in his eagerness to make himself certain . . .

At first he could discern nothing more captivating than the usual lowlife press. Then he found her—the beauty he had seen the night before, his porcelain angel of the night-sky eyes. *Beautiful* . . . Tonight she was alone, moving with a shadow's silent grace through the vulgar mass of men, making his heart leap with fascinated joy. A bawd, Screed had called her. Gull-catcher, stew-mutton—how could such words have any commerce with such a dove, no matter where she might choose to light? How could mere gold purchase the favors of a queen? Such paradise must surely be priceless.

Janette felt eyes on her—vampire eyes. Turning warily, half-expecting LaCroix, she found quite a different breed of wolf, a mere cub by comparison. Surely he must be young; no revenant of any age could have gaped at her so openly, with no attempt to hide the admiration in his ebony eyes. A love-struck hound. *Who are you, garçon?* she thought, amused and rather charmed in spite of herself. *Whose pretty, young demon are you?*

"More wine!" a mortal boy at her new swain's table suddenly crowed, all but banging his cup on the board in his eagerness to make himself more stupid. The vampire watching her glanced back at him with a look of such contempt Janette nearly laughed aloud to see it—emotion danced on this young one's face like moonlight on a pond. So, this wastrel was his purpose, his prey for the night—a canny choice. *C'est bien.* They should both have a bit of sport.

"Patience, *chérie.*" The blue-eyed beauty scolded the mortal sweetly, taking a pitcher from a passing wench and filling his glass herself. Vachon's eyes widened, and she smiled at him with kittenish charm before turning away to settle herself on the bench beside his prey. "Let me help you," she continued, wiping goose grease from the drunkard's chin with her lacy handkerchief.

"Good e'en to thee, fair mistress," the mortal said boldly, sweeping his hat from his head in a mocking salute. *He thinks her a trollop as well,* Vachon thought, seething with a fair new purpose to his murderous intent. *Have no care, angelita oscura . . . He shall suffer rare torments for his insolence.*

"Fair night to you, milord," Janette said, giving the silly bit of youth her most salacious smile. "Shall we be merry, think you?"

The boy at least had the presence of mind to be dazzled to stammering by this. "Yea," he managed, his watery eyes struggling to focus on her face, powerless to resist the whisper of her unspoken command. *Come to me, little pig boy . . . I hunger, and you shall oblige.* "Give me but a moment, and I shall entertain thee right merrily," finished the prey.

Janette resisted the urge to glance over her shoulder to see the horrified look she could already feel burning from the vampire at her back. Why risk losing quarry for trivialities? "Why beg my patience, monsieur?" she inquired aloud, lightly touching her dinner's slobbering mouth.

"Necessity, lady," he answered, blushing. "Mistress Nature hath spoke for me first."

The lovely vampire laughed, her mood improving by steady degrees. *Nicholas should be here to share such delightful game.* "Mayhap Nature and I may share you by turns," she said, rising to join him as he fumbled to his feet. "Forsooth, we share a shopfront."

"So, Nicholas, where will you now?" Shakespeare asked as the rest of the company threw off their imagined figures and became plain weary men again. "The comedy is done."

"Think you so?" Nick asked, canting his head to indicate Saddler, his face and eyes still gaudy with maid's paint, tearing out of his wig and chopines and flinging them to the winds as if he would never need them more.

"The scripted one, in any case," the Lord Chamberlain's Man chuckled. "But I am earnest—will you while the evening with us or mend your quarrel with your cousin?"

Nick snorted. "My quarrel with LaCroix may not be mended in a single night." He frowned, thinking of the vampire household whose members were in such disarray this night. "In earnest, good Will, would I stay here—or rather, go with you. I would see the Globe," he explained.

"Then go you shall," Will answered, pleased. He tried not to puff it, but the playwright clearly loved his new theater heartily. "And welcome—" He stopped, his expression clouding, and Nick turned to see William Hilliard making his way back into the makeshift tiring room.

"I thought him departed," Nick remarked as casually as he could manage.

"As did I," the playwright replied, matching his tone. And yet, what had Hilliard done to offend Nicholas? His young patron had settled himself on a chair in the midst of the chaos and was pretending to make himself content examining the jeweled hilt of his dagger. Will met Nick's eyes and rolled his own expressively heavenward. "I would see the last of this merry carnage stowed before I leave in any case," he said. "Go you on ahead with the others—I'll meet you presently at the Swan."

"I'll attend you," Nick promised. Making a brief bow to Hilliard, he left.

Shakespeare waited until most of the rest of the company had gone before addressing himself to his young patron. "I thought you would be with your lady," he remarked, rolling up the promptbook and securing it with a ribbon.

"Mean you my mother or Isabella?" Hilliard answered with a cheery insouciance all the more winning for its meanness. "In either case, the word is most sadly abused."

"Isabella hath gone to attend your coming."

"And well she might. But she hath accustomed herself to waiting."

"'Tis true, and 'tis pity 'tis true." Shakespeare stared down at his play; his smile was not one of enjoyment. "Come you then with me; the Chamberlain's Men have missed your wit of late."

"Thank you, no," Hilliard got to his feet with the insolent grace of a sleepy cat. "I've no great love of drinking with Frenchmen."

"Then mayhap I'll see thee later, to mend thy faults privily." The boy answered him only with a sullen glance, but the player's tone softened nonetheless. "I'll seek thee in thy lady's house." Turning away, he wondered if he'd just done Isabella a favor, or a harm.

This is not possible, Vachon thought, watching his heart's desire steal his long-stalked prize with little more than a well-batted eyelash. This beauty, this angel could have no such designs . . . yet there she went, all but leading the fool into the street. He followed them at a discreet distance, watching as she lay a small, white hand on the sleeve of the boy's velvet doublet and tugged him from the main thoroughfare into an alley. The guiles of a strumpet, no question—*Come, sweeting, I know a fair place* . . . He had heard such a siren's song often enough himself.

"No," he said aloud, shaking his head for emphasis though no one stood by to mark him. Why should a common strumpet so fire his immortal blood that he should feel her very presence, no matter how lovely she might be? Loveliness was no rarity, even in such a godforsaken sty as this London. Even now, as he thought of it, the tingle overtook him, freezing fire just beneath his skin.

"What ails ye, me a-may-go?" Screed demanded, sliding out of the shadows like one of his own precious rats. "A fair banquet set before ye, and yer gaping in the street."

"What do you here?" Vachon demanded through teeth clenched and aching to be fangs.

The carouche had the good sense to feign sheepishness even if he didn't feel it. "I thought as 'ow ye might need a bit o'lookout," he confessed. "An' now sees I ye do."

"You are with me all night?" Vachon asked grimly.

"No insult, mate, nowt i' the world," Screed assured him. He looked anxiously in the direction of the alley. "They're fair to away already," he pleaded, pointing.

"Wait here," Vachon ordered sternly, no hint of friendship or even familial obligation in his tone. "No follow me, Screed. I warn you."

"Righty-o, senoro," Screed promised, discreetly resisting the urge to correct his master's English just this once.

Vachon moved a short distance into the winding alleyway, then leapt easily to the tavern's roof, his heavy boots coming down on the thatch above the rooftree as softly as a wolf's pads. Crouching and all but silent, he moved swiftly down to the roof's edge, stopping just above his prey, his angel-seeming whore now locked in his sometime-quarry's arms.

Janette held the mortal's smelly weight from her with a well-placed hand on his chest as she crooned to him with hypnosis as tender as a mother's lullaby. "Such a sweet little pig," she lilted, smiling to see him smile back, oblivious to his doom. "Too bad you've spoiled your blood so with wine . . . but no matter, *chérie*. No matter at all."

Suddenly she felt her audience of one catch up, and her smiled widened, her blue eyes going gold. Sparing a moment's glance upward to meet the other vampire's eyes, she sank her fangs into her victim's throat.

Up on the roof, her audience's eyes had opened to their widest, and his jaw dropped in astonishment. Vachon could scarcely credit his sight—blue eyes turned to gold: an angel indeed—an angel as he had thought only he could know her. He smiled with near-childish delight as this delicate beauty took down the prey he'd meant to have for himself, holding the barely struggling youth helpless between her slender hands as if she had no notion that he was twice her size. *A blood-drinker . . . Santa Regina . . .* He stepped down from the tavern roof like a man in a trance, landing at her side just as she let the empty corpse slump to the ground at her feet. Janette snarled for a moment, but Vachon backed away instantly, raising his hands in smiling, delighted surrender.

"*Mon Dieu,* my aching head," Janette murmured wearily as the cheap wine wriggled through her consciousness. English tastes in wine were terrible to begin with, but why must the fools add sugar to it?

"It passes," Vachon assured her with a cocky grin.

She shot him a sidelong look. "*Oui, je sais,*" she answered wryly. "I know that." She swiped her mouth with her fingertips, and started to lick the blood from her skin, then waggish inspiration struck. Turning to the wolfling with her sweetest smile, she offered her hand to him instead.

Vachon's eyes widened again—was she serious? But who should question an angel? He caught her by the wrist and lowered his mouth to the crimson stain, her gasp as sweet to his ears as the blood was to his tongue.

"Stop it," Janette ordered as his teeth scraped teasingly along her wrist, the weakness in her knees at his rough caress quite spoilt by indignation. "*Arrêttes-toi, garçon, à l'instant!*"

"*Sí, mi linda,*" Vachon replied as his fangs grew sharp, saying yes to this beauty, neither knowing nor caring what she meant to tell him.

"I said stop!" Janette roared, flinging him away with sufficient force to send him crashing into the brick and plaster wall on the other side of the alley.

Vachon recovered his balance before actually slumping to the ground, but only just barely. "*Santa Maria,*" he swore, wiping his throbbing mouth. And yet his delighted smile returned the moment he looked back at her: this great beauty, a hunter in the night as he was.

"*Pas de tout,*" Janette retorted. "Just the opposite, I assure you." The vampire glow faded from her vision, leaving a clear picture of the look on his pretty and so dirty face, and she could barely suppress a smile. "What think you, garçon, that I am the cheap doxy in truth?" she demanded sternly.

"No, lady, I swear it," Vachon hastened to assure her. "You are . . ." He struggled to find words in his pitiable store of English sufficient to express his wonder—such a vision was a creature like himself? He barely had the Spanish to speak of such a miracle. "*Un angel,*" he blurted out in a fevered rush. "*La noche te ha echado una de sus tigres a causa d' una invidia la mas pura que debe sentir . . . tu no debes pertinecer al sol, pero solamente a la luna—*" He broke off, embarrassed but dazzled by her sudden, lovely smile.

"*Merci beaucoup,*" Janette said lightly. "Thank you, I think." She frowned. "But speak you no civilized tongue? I would know how I am flattered. Speak French to me, *garçon.*"

"You forgive me, I cannot," Vachon confessed, falling to his knees before her. "But I swear you I am to learn." He reached for her hand again, and she gave it, smiling again as he kissed it as prettily as any royal courtier for all he was obviously starving.

"*Très bien, monsieur,*" she said, raising him to his feet. "Very good." She looked him up and down, shaking her head. "But, *vraiment,* you do our kind no credit looking as you do. Fear you water, Monsieur Espagne, that you avoid it so? Think you a vampire is a cat to be washed but with his tongue?"

"Vampire?" Vachon's eyebrows quirked up. His features lit up with a predator's flashing grin. "That is how we are called in this English? Vampire . . ." His eyes glittered with pleasure.

This one is so young, Janette thought, enjoying his naïveté. *He knows nothing yet.* She turned and retrieved the dead man's purse from his pocket. "Is that why you sought this, *mon petit*?" she teased. "To buy yourself a bath?"

"*Sí,*" Vachon replied tersely, his pride beginning to taunt his chivalry for a coward. He frowned, his heavy eyebrows drawing together in a black chevron above his dark eyes. Angel or no, she had deprived him of his quest—must she insult him as well?

"Then here," Janette said, tossing him the purse. "Now have we both our desire." She could feel the tingling presence of another youngling, and she gazed up at the rooftops with bemusement. If this were the general, what must his lieutenant be like? "Farewell, *monsieur,*" she said aloud, then glanced pointedly at the corpse. "I shall depend upon your discretion."

"*¿Cómo?*" Vachon asked, genuinely puzzled. He had barely kissed her hand, and besides, what care should a vampire have for her reputation?

"The boy, yes?" Janette explained, struggling to be patient as the game began to wear thin. Suddenly she wanted no more than to lie herself beside Nicholas and sleep and sleep and sleep . . . "He must be disposed of, hidden from view." She eyed the young vampire doubtfully. "You will do this for the gold, think you?"

"I will do this for you," Vachon promised.

She smiled. "A fair answer, *chérie,*" she said. "*Au revoir.*"

Nick let Burbage and the rest of the players think he was staying behind with Shakespeare.

Waking late, he'd rushed to Hilliard House without feeding,

breaking his careful rule about sating his dangerous hunger before daring a lengthy period among mortal friends. Now, walking alone toward the riverbank, he felt the desire to feed like a claw tearing at his guts, and his vision kept fading to patterns of glowing light and dead darkness as his vampire's body sought out the heat of living blood and reduced all else to nothing.

The Golden Swan's doors were flung open, the light from inside pouring out into the street, along with the songs and jests and general drunken happiness of men he could almost call friends. But he was not one of them—for all that he was the most apt player of them all . . .

"Failed of your cue, sirrah." A feminine voice spoke just at his elbow, startling him badly.

Looking up, he saw the girl as a sketch in blood, a pattern of glowing light, and he struggled to regain some semblance of humanity. "Pardon, mistress?"

"You have forgotten your hour again, and your fellows play the drinking scene without you," she explained slowly. "Though from your manner, I would say you have well begun without them in some other house. Or perhaps you seek your bed . . . ?" Her voice became uncertain.

"Nay, mistress." Nick demurred with a smile. He focused his mortal sight and remembered the face before him—one of the chits who were wont to hang about the players in their haunts, doing bits of sewing and other womanly tasks for those among the Lord Chamberlain's Men with neither wife nor mistress. His senses quickened with her scent, and the hunt began in earnest. "Good e'en to you . . ."

"Lisa," she supplied with another bold grin, reassured. "Lisa Burstiner."

"Milady Lisa," he agreed, returning her smile with his own, a wide, happy, boyish smile. Another friendly, foolish drunkard, naught to fear in the world. The vampire in him smiled inside, differently.

"I am one Nicholas Chevalier, yours to command," he said lightly. The girl's face showed surprised pleasure. Nick essayed a bow, and found himself wishing in his heart that this were no mockery, that they two were somewhere in the mortal world being courteously introduced. That wish was Alyssa's voice in him, but now the voice of LaCroix rose from within as well, mocking his foolishness. *Look well around you, Nicholas, and be what you are: a vampire in a dark street who has not fed for many long hours.*

His next words could never have been said by that imagined mortal man to that gently bred imagined mortal maid: "How is't you have not yet found your bed, Mistress Lisa? The chimes have long since struck."

"Mayhap my bed has not yet found me," she parried. No, these were not the words of a delicately schooled girl. "And you, sir knight Chevalier, what is your quest this hour? Do you seek the Grail? Or is a unicorn thy pursuit?"

"I'll bring you both in time, milady," he retorted, offering her his arm. "But first I shall take myself to supper."

"So late and yet still hungry?" she asked, playing a game she thought she knew well, allowing him to draw her down the dark street toward the river. "Forsooth, you must be famished."

"Just so," he answered. "Wilt accompany me?"

The girl's eyebrows quirked. "You'll not sup at the Swan?"

"Nay, other fare likes me better," Nick said gruffly, both loving and hating the scene he played. "Come up the bankside with me a bit." The water stairs were not far, but likely to be crowded with boatmen; better to walk her toward the unimproved bank, toward the better houses upriver. A quarter mile farther on, the little road ended near Essex House—a perfect place, since the Earl himself was off bungling a war in Ireland, and much of his household was gone with him.

And the house had a quay all its own.

"Do we sup with nobility?" The girl recognized her surroundings.

"Let us tarry here a moment," said Nick, leading her onto the private dock. At its far end, he took her into his arms, leaning her back against the railing. To anyone passing by on the river, they would be but another set of less-than-noble lovers, probably servants in the famous house, taking a profligate's ease beneath the moon.

She rested easily in his arms, thinking she knew well what was to come. Instead, the knight kissed her lightly, the smallest, most respectful salute she'd known since the very first peck she'd had as a very young girl, the offering of a baker's boy who'd adored her chestnut locks and laughing eyes, who had given her the kiss, then blushed fiercely and run away.

She laughed at Nick a little, but the laugh altered as she pulled back to look at his face. Her knight, she thought, looked the part, though he could never bring a unicorn.

The moon was near full and low in the west; its rays gleamed off the small river waves at a slant, played in the man's fair hair as if it were the topmost grasses of a hayloft, and shone almost directly into the man's eyes so that she saw them as if by daylight. His eyes were blue, with the tint of a shallow stream running across a meadow, and they did not look like dull, drunken eyes at all. Instead they were very much like a true lover's eyes, lit from within somehow. Even as she allowed herself this fanciful thought, the man bent his face to hers again, offering another gentle lover's kiss—this was not the hasty pawing she'd expected, and she yielded not only her body but part of her heart to the knightly pantomime.

Nick kissed her cheeks, her face, her throat. Her kiss tasted like sugar'd wine, and the soft skin beneath her jawline smelled vaguely of the powder on a player's face. He brushed his face against her cheek, and heard her heart quickening, his world beginning to shrink to the small area in her throat where the great vein ran so close to the surface—he could see it pulsing under her skin, an invitation, a command—mayhap she'd been abandoned once already tonight . . . Nick pushed the thought away—all thought—and sank fangs into her flesh, the vampire emerging to have what it must.

She cried out once, and he felt both her pleasure and her pain as she yielded to his final kiss, but his hunger was such that he drained her to weakness within seconds, making much struggle impossible. Her fingers grasped his cloak as her heartbeat slowed, then fell away as all was silence.

Nick's silence was the rapture of utter possession; no crevice of her life was closed to him now. She had liked his kisses, the unexpected chivalry . . . She'd been thinking, *Kiss me more* . . . and the thought came to him unbidden, *Yes, if you wish it.* But it was impossible now. He bent his head against hers again as if he would drop another gentle kiss on her soft skin, and felt his rapture dissolve into bitterness.

Still holding her around the waist, he swept the cloak from around his own shoulders and wrapped it around her, head and all, avoiding looking into her face. He looked around with vampire vision but could perceive no one in sight, no one to witness as he tumbled the convenient girl over the rail.

He watched the wool billow slightly, then sink beneath the surface, his desire to hide his deed for once more than the mere duty of discretion. How was it that he should accomplish such a feat, wipe a human soul from the face of the earth, with never a trace to mark her? He thought again of Alyssa: a bridal bower, a coffin decked with flowers—

He turned away, shivering as the wind coming over the water seemed to slice him to the bone, and headed back toward the Golden Swan.

Vachon watched with the guileless grin of a child as his idol disappeared into the night. "*Que bonita,*" he murmured, turning away with a sigh. So that tingle meant a vampire was near . . . and a vampire could look like an angel: look . . . smell . . . taste?

"The fair sail bein' we got the gold, eh, mate?" Screed said, dropping down beside him and shattering his reverie to bits. "Though I'll avow as 'at was a nice bit o' toast—an' a fanglette in the bargain—"

"*Shut . . . up,*" Vachon ordered, his eyes glowing, his lips drawn back in a snarl.

Screed's own beady eyes widened as much as anatomy would allow. "Nowt o'that, senor-ay—'tis well, 'tis well," he promised hurriedly. The glow left his master's eyes, and he breathed a sigh of relief. "No need to take on . . ."

"Screed," Vachon warned, making the carouche fall silent with a single pointed look. "I am hungry," he announced, tossing the heavy purse to his companion. "I go to feed . . ." He glanced impatiently at the corpse. "You get rid of him," he ordered.

"Right-y-o, mate," Screed grumbled as Vachon took flight, knuckling his forehead in salute as he'd done thousands of times as a sailor. "No insubordinin' 'ere; no fear o'that." He grabbed the dead boy's shoulders and hauled him upright. "Wot say ye, mate?" he quipped, peeling off the velvet doublet. "They makes a pretty pair, yer dos amigos . . . An 'ere, you, stand at attention!" Screed stood the corpse as straight as could be managed.

A rat scurried over the corpse's boot, and the carouche let

him fall. "Hungry, 'e says, like as 'twere a private condition," he muttered, snatching up his tiny prey and draining it dry in an instant, his task immediately forgotten.

"A nice li'l sip," he said and sighed, tossing the carcass aside. "But no meal fer a man . . ." He noticed the dead man's boots jutting up alongside his own tattered sailor's shoes and grinned. "A bit more booty," he decided, grabbing for them. "Two boots to boot oh it's bootiful booty indeed . . . ," he sang, deciding he wanted the man's shirt as well. "Two boots, two boots, then off to the hunt fer young Screed . . ."

Will Shakespeare was just going into the Golden Swan with the promptbook tucked safely under his arm when Nick returned. "Did you lose yourself?" he joked.

"Long ago," Nick joked back, his vampire's satiation still warring with mortal pity for his prey. He shook his head, pushing his thoughts away. "Come let us go in, and make up the lost time." They passed Ben Jonson and Phillip Henslowe, who owned the Rose, another Southwark playhouse, coming outward, clapping each other on the shoulders and laughing. The sight of the two men walking off together caused Shakespeare to turn his head and look after them. When Nick looked a question at him, he waved a hand and said, "'Tis naught," but then he turned his head and looked again.

It turned out that much of the Lord Chamberlain's company was still inside.

"Why, Will, well met!" said Burbage tipsily. "'Tis thirsty work, walking home, is it not?" Will and Nick sat down at a long board where Burbage, Sly, Heminges, Saddler, Pope, Phillips, and the apprentice Jack Wilson were already carousing. Traces of flour and ink remained on imperfectly rinsed faces, though their red cheeks came from ale, not makeup.

"So then, 'tis true you own the Globe?" Nick pursued as they sat down.

Will chuckled. "Do I look like the king of Spain? I make no such silly claims, even whilst I too possess a Pope to support them." Tom Pope, one of the younger players, was used to this joke. He grinned and made an elaborate sign of the cross over Tom Saddler, who was drifting off to sleep.

"Nay," said Shakespeare expansively, "'tis the Burbages who own the world."

"Not I," said Dick, with a cheerful, crooked smile. "I do not own the Globe nor even a poor dog-christened turve of grass till Her Majesty's courts do affirm it." He grinned. "Or until I do beat the same from out Master Giles Allen's ears."

"That's pretty talk," said Nick, startled.

"Why, Nick, we are a villainous rabble," joked Tom Pope. He ran a hand over his ruddy face. "'Tis true our company has no one to rival Ben Jonson, who hath fought a duel and killed his man. Yet here's Dick Burbage, the famous puller of noses, and late triumphant in the War of the Broomsticks. Masters Heminges and Sly, they too are very mischancy men, though 'tis true they endanger mostly ladies, as doth our William the Conquerer."

Young Tom Saddler frowned, counting on thick fingers. "*Henry Four, Henry Five, Henry Six . . . Richard Second, Richard Third . . . William*? I do not think we play a play of that name." His eyes shut, and his head slumped down to the table.

"Ah, now that's a tale I can tell," said Nick, grinning. It had happened on his previous visit to England, seven years before, when he'd literally stumbled into the players' world. "Marlowe told it: it is that you," he pointed at Burbage, "playing King Richard, did plot to meet a lady privily, but when you came to her chamber, were met only with the message that William the Conquerer had gone before Richard II." Nick's grin got wider. "So, I am to credit this scandal?"

"It was because of what he said to me," Will said. His face showed nothing but his customary mild good humor.

"Never say," said Dick, taken by surprise. "What said I, said what?"

"Quoth you," Shakespeare said emphatically, "'Never do that to me again.'" Burbage looked blank for a moment, then began to laugh. "Whereupon, as a gentleman and your loving friend, I resolved to give you just cause for those words, so that you should not face the final reckoning with such an injustice to your most loving friend scriven 'pon your slate."

Dick was roaring with laughter now, but no one else understood the joke.

Will sniffed exaggeratedly. He sat up very primly on the bench, wrinkling his nose like a fop who'd smelled skunk, and explained: "It was upon a performance of that most excellent history, *The History of Richard Second,* the which was writ, gentles all," Shakespeare sniffed again, "by me, that this Dick"—he stretched his arm out to its full length and pointed a finger almost into Burbage's eye—"this pustulous murdering whoreson Philistine hairy-shanked paint-spattered ale-soaked cup-shotten louse-scratching beshitted sack of a baseborn braying jigger—in sum, gentles all, this very witless Dick before you, did presume to mislike a speech he was given to say." Will gave himself a dramatic pause. "A most excellent speech, sirs. Writ . . . most excellently . . . by me."

"No, Will, no!" roared Burbage. "Never a jigger, God save me! Never call me that!"

"What, Dick? Thou'lt not dance a morris for us now?" Will Sly chimed in, raising his tankard. "I think we'll have one—holla, landlord, bells! Bells and ribbons fit for our Dick!"

"Crows pick out thy eyes, Sly!" laughed Burbage. "There is no riband in England long enough to compass me! And you, Master Poet, I put to you again—retract your insult, sirrah, for if you call me jigger, I call you out! And I have my steel to hand!" Burbage reached for his stage sword, lost his balance, and slid off his stool. The noise woke Tom Saddler abruptly.

"Jiggerer, then," amended Shakespeare. "Jiggerer and pokerer." He leaned over the edge of the table and looked down into Burbage's face. "Now say, gentle Dick, wilt thou have a duel with Will at dawn or no?"

"A-mercy for thy kindness," laughed Dick, still on the floor. "Keep thy blood, gentle Will, and my goodwill with it. 'Twas only that to be bad Will Kempe is a fate I could not bear." Kempe, the great actor-clown who'd left the company only months before, was not remembered fondly by these men.

"'Tis crime enough you've been Dick Burbage," Shakespeare agreed. His face grew solemn. "Nicholas, you look upon the only man in England who hath ever stol'n a building entire."

Nick gave Shakespeare a look that suggested the poet had had a bit too much ale. "'Sooth," Will affirmed, "he took it down in Shoreditch and raised it up in Bankside, which act is even now complained of to the Queen as a great and felonious and forcible enterprise. He owned the building but not the land—though the owner of the land does presently dispute the law appertaining." He grinned. "I doubt but you'll visit Dick in Marshalsea Prison any day now."

"Let's have the bill of particulars again, Dick," said Tom Pope.

"Aye, let us hear it!" seconded Heminges. "'Tis better than most songs."

"And all jigs," finished Burbage, climbing back on his stool. "You'll have it? Here, your worships, is the tale of the Globe Theater, *domum novum edificata,* that is, a house newly built in the Liberty of the Clink, as well as that of the theft of the old Theater, a house that late stood in Shoreditch, et cetera. The events we are to relate took place upon the night of St. Innocent's Day, a time most befitting the high crime and misdemeanor you shall hear related. And all must join with me upon the choruses."

He belched, shook his body to settle it comfortably on his stool, and commenced:

"The complaint at law to the Queen's Majesty of one Giles Allen, citizen. Viz., *The said Cuthbert Burbage—*"

"That's Dick's brother," Tom Saddler muttered to Nick.

Burbage decided to orate standing up and rose, though keeping his balance proved to be a challenge. He affected the prissy, clerkish voice of a well-known barrister who specialized in pleading the greedy causes of the rich in the Queen's courts:

"*—unlawfully combining and confederating himself with the said Richard Burbage and one Peter Street, chief carpenter, William Smith, and divers other persons to the number of twelve, to your subject unknown, did about the eight and twentieth day of December, in the one and fortieth year of Your Highness's reign—*"

"Wednesday, three days after Christmas last," Tom Saddler continued. "Or nights, rather—for they all went down in the hour after midnight with axes." Burbage paused in his oration to glare down at Tom, who clapped a hand over his mouth.

"*—and sithence Your Highness last and general pardon by the confederacy aforesaid—*"

Now Burbage interrupted himself. "My children, stout parishioners, and worshipful guests, we come now to the chorus of this holy hymn, whereat we must jointly and severally sing our song of praise—all together—" Burbage lifted his hands, and the actors all said:

"riotous—"

Burbage belched, and resumed: "*—riotously assembled themselves together, and then and there armed themselved with divers and many unlawful and offensive weapons, as namely swords, daggers, bills, axes, and such like, and then and there armed as aforesaid, in very—*" He gestured.

"Riotous!" shouted the players, and Nick with them.

"*—riotous, outrageous, and forceable manner, and contrary to the laws of Your Highness's realm, attempted to pull down the said Theater. Whereupon, divers of your subjects, servants and farmers, then going about in peaceable manner to procure them to desist from that unlawful enterprise, they, the said—*" He lifted his hands.

"Riotous!" Drinkers at other tables were also joining in, enjoying the free show.

Burbage changed his voice and posture, affecting the stoop-shouldered stance and peeringly benign smile of a country parson, to whom he gave a lisping Welsh accent: "*—bpersons aforethaid, notwith-thtanding bprocured t'hen t'herein with kreat fiolence, not only t'hen and t'here forthibly and—*"

"Riotous!"

And now Burbage straightened, threw his shoulders back, and became Julius Caesar, the role with which he'd opened the Globe, stretching his hand forward as if to address the Roman Senate, his words pealing out like the tolling of a majestic bell: "*—ly resisting your subjects, servants and farmers, but also then and there pulling, breaking, and throwing down the said Theater in very outrageous, violent, and—*" He cued his chorus.

"Riotous!"

A drunkard now—no great feat of acting in his present condition: "*—sort, did then also in most forcible and—*"

"Riotous!"

"*—manner take and carry away from thence all the wood and timber thereof unto the Bankside, in the Parish of St. Mary Overyes, and there erected a new playhouse with the said timber and wood.*"

Burbage then pinched his nose shut and whined, "Further than the which Your Majesty's humble humbilissimus deponent sayeth naught."

"Amen!" roared the players.

Whereon Burbage bowed deeply, lost his balance, and crashed to the floor again. A round of applause rewarded the performance.

"Come, Nick," said Will, "that's all the merriment we'll have from him tonight. And I'll forget this," he waved the prompt-book, "if I drink any deeper. And you wanted to see the Globe."

"Certes, yes," Nick said.

"Aye, you puling poet, push off!" agreed Dick from the floor, spraying the knees of everyone around him with his p's. "Go pen your proper prating play of . . . what was it?"

Nick stopped and turned back at the door, taking in the cozy scene as if he would paint it, drunkards and bawds and all. The memory of his late victim's face rose before him, and he pushed the image aside, opening the door to go out into the night.

Shakespeare shrugged. "A father, a son. A kingdom, a murder. Nothing."

5

If you can, either for love or money, provide yourself a lodging by the water side; for, above the convenience it brings to shun shoulder-clapping and to ship away your cockatrice betimes in the morning, it adds a kind of state unto you to be carried from thence to the stairs of your play-house.

—Thomas Dekker (1570?–1641),
The Gull's Hornbook, "How a Gallant Should Behave Himself in a Playhouse"

ISABELLA'S EYES FLEW OPEN, HER HEART POUNDING FROM A DREAM THAT evaporated at the first touch of real firelight bouncing off the plaster walls of her cozy bedroom. "'Sblood," she murmured, reaching out for the pillow so lately abandoned by her lover, pulling it close to bury her face in his comforting scent.

"Hast sunk so low as to blaspheme in thy sleep?" Hilliard remarked, watching her from across the room. He knew she would have thought him gone, had even considered letting her sink back into dreams unaware, but something about the way her bare, pink leg curled itself around an embroidered pillow made him want to make his presence known.

For her part, Isabella couldn't have been more pleased, the last vestiges of the nightmare swept away by the knowledge he had stayed.

"Yea," she answered, favoring him with a disheveled grin.

His wont had always been to make his escape as soon as she dozed or even loosed her hold on him, even in the greenest days of their now-grudging romance. "Will you bide the night here, then?" she asked.

"Not likely," he muttered. "I should have gone long since were thine ancient William obedient to his hour."

"Ah," she replied, disappointed but hardly surprised. There was explanation enough—he was waiting for Will, not for her. The lodging Hilliard gave her had long been the favorite meeting place for these two, even when she had herself become superfluous. But now, it seemed, it was Hilliard's turn to be superfluous. "Mine ancient Will? And thine, still ancienter, methinks," she taunted to cover her hurt. "'Tis passing strange he has not come ere this."

"Yea," Hilliard retorted sarcastically. "Passing strange indeed . . . but then you say Chevalier had lately arrived when you left him."

Aye, and little would suit thee better justice than to be scorned for Chevalier, she thought but dared not say. 'Twas true that of late Shakespeare had seemed to grow more fond of this Frenchman at the expense of his Hilliard-crony, and few who knew both men could blame him. But Isabella knew the truth of it. She knew the depth of the player's feeling for this sullen angel now sprawled in an opulent chair by her fireside, scowling and half-naked. She knew because she felt the same herself.

But unlike the player poet, she had neither healed herself of the malady of loving Hilliard, nor found herself another disease to replace him. Looking at how the light played on his golden hair and fair skin, she instead found herself suffering fresh hurt. And feeling love, she softened her approach.

"'Tis more like thy lady mother keeps him late amusing the guests you yourself abandoned," she said, reaching for the linen blouse he'd left hanging on the bedpost. "If he did swear to meet you, surely—"

"He swore me nothing," he said, cutting her off, still glaring balefully into the fire. He was beautiful, yes—but the dancing shadows sliced his handsome face into an evil mask as he tipped back the bottle in his fist, making her shudder, the memory of her dream threatening to surface. She pulled the blouse over her head, pushing the thought away.

"And yet he should come," Hilliard finished, looking up. "Modesty, lady? 'Tis late in the game for that."

"Chills, more like," she confessed.

He took her onto his lap with little more protest than an impatient sigh, still holding his bottle.

"Feel you not the cold?"

"Nay, I find no chill in midsummer, sweeting," he answered, letting her nestle close. His brows flickered with surprise as she curled into him. "But you are burning up."

"'Tis nothing," she promised, taking the bottle and drinking from it as she tucked her feet between his well-turned legs to warm them. "My feet were wetted picking through good William's bog—no doubt the wine will warm me."

"Aye," Hilliard growled, wrapping his arms more tightly around her waist. He bent to kiss her throat, and caught sight of a small gray head emerging from beneath the bedclothes across the room, its eyes glittering in the firelight. "Hold still," he ordered his lover, bending down to pick up his heavy boot. "You need new lodgings—since when do you have rats?"

Isabella turned to look and screamed. "No!" she cried, catching his arm as he threw, making the boot fall short with a thud. The tiny head disappeared, but the air was suddenly full of angry mewling. "'Twas no rat," she explained, going down on her knees by the bed and reaching underneath. "Ouch! Little wretch . . . come here then, since you've learnt the way out of the basket."

"God's death," Hilliard groaned as she pulled a tiny kitten into the open. "Worse far than a rat! Why did you stop me? Here, open a window—I'll warrant I can make the river from here."

"Bite your tongue," Isabella scolded, bringing the kitten back with her. "How durst you speak such knavery before Queen Catherine?" She held the ball of fluff up to her face and smiled. "Isn't she a beauty?"

"'Tis but a rat with hair on its tail, and the sooner killed the better," he said scowling. "Cursed, devilish creatures—they taint the ear with their witchy wailing. How many plague you, lady?"

"Why none," she joked, but Hilliard was in no mood for wordplay. "Cheer you, Will, there be not so many, and not a one of them cursed," she said. She kissed the little creature's nose and put it into his hands.

"'Swounds, girl, and for mercy," he protested, holding the squirming thing away from him as if it were a scorpion.

"Hold her close, and she'll not be frightened," his mistress ordered as she dragged a basket from beneath the bed. "Come and meet the royal family—it will put you in a better humor."

"Only if I may put them to the knife," he snarled, though he did draw Queen Catherine closer to his body, allowing her to curl herself among the golden hairs on his stomach as he stroked behind her ears.

"This is Queen Jane," Isabella went on, lifting out and kissing a white kitten with startling blue eyes, setting her aside, and taking out a tabby with a perfect white boot on each foot. "This was supposed to be Anne Boleyn, but that seemed unlucky," she explained, kissing this one too, before setting her down with her sister. "So I call her Felicity instead."

"Very wise," Hilliard said sardonically. "A veritable infestation of queens. When may I begin the executions?"

"These queens shall outlive their master, thank you kindly," she retorted, lifting the mother cat from the basket and cradling her in her arms. "And here is their dame whom you've met before, remember? This is La Celestina."

"Still working the docks, I see," he retorted. "Squashed by a carriage was my guess."

"We mustn't hear him, Celestina," Isabella said soothingly, kissing the velvet head tucked so trusting beneath her chin. "We'll 'scape drowning and squashing and all, for all we are both harlots."

"And I am to sleep in a cat's house to keep you company?" he asked, suddenly losing patience. "I think not—put them outside."

"As you will, of course, my love," she said appeasingly, dropping the mother cat gently into the basket and gathering up the kittens. "Will you send fair Catherine to the Tower as well or keep her in your favor?"

"Wring its tiny neck for all I care," he snapped, snatching up the sleeping kitten and flinging her away.

"Will, no!" Isabella cried in horror as the kitten crashed to the floor. She picked the tiny creature up and cradled her against her breast, relieved to hear her begin to mew in protest.

"You could have killed her—dashed out her little brain or broken her neck," she scolded, stroking her fur and rocking her back and forth. "They're very fragile—"

"Not fragile enough, else I had rid the world of that one," he snarled, getting up. "If you do love these vermin so well, I shall leave you to them—mayhap they can settle your debts."

"Nay, Will, wait," she pleaded, dropping the kitten into the basket and running to him before he could get out the door.

"Go to," he grumbled as she twined her arms around his neck.

"I'll none, but to go to you," she retorted, planting kisses all over his face. "Stay with me and be easy for once—'twill be your secret, I'll never discover it to a soul."

He tried to turn his head away, but she would not be put off, and in truth, his heart wasn't in it. "My head aches," he complained, still as a statue in her embrace.

"Then shall I soothe it," she promised, leading him toward the bed. "Do but let me put the kittens outside, and I'll be all your posset and balm."

Will and Nick had themselves ferried across the river rather than try to pick their way through the mucky street of London Bridge by the light of Will's weak lamp. Will stumbled a bit and near fell into the boat, flailing his arms out to keep the promptbook dry even if he should tumble into the Thames.

The waterman chuckled. "Made a bit too merry this e'en?" he asked, offering his hand to Nick. "Well, 'tis late for gentlemen to be abroad . . . bound home, I am, but one more fare shan't kill me . . . Daniel Mickel places himself at your service, sirs, and undertakes to get ye home dry."

Nick didn't answer, not trusting his voice or wishing to invite further conversation. The wind was northerly, bringing a waft of blood on the air, or so it seemed to him. Whatever the reason, the oarsman and the playwright had both resolved into hot red images in his mind.

He tossed the man a coin and settled heavily into a seat, a mortal drunkard for all the world—the glorious vampire-player in his greatest role to date.

The boat landed them at the Paris Garden stairs, near the bear-baiting ring; now they were walking past it on Bear Alley, headed for Maid Lane. Even at night, there was a racket from the caged animals. Worse, the scent of blood on the air proved to be real, not just a fancy of a vampire's guilty mind, rising not only from the ring wherein dogs were pitted daily against bulls, bears, and apes, but also from the riverside, where the newly dead animals were flung. It was not human, but it was fresh blood in the open air . . . It quickened Nick's hunger despite his recent feeding.

He'd brooked his master's anger, and the scorn that was sure to follow it, to spend his time with the players. Their good fellowship almost made him forget that he was not human. But only almost.

He could swallow a little wine, at need, but nothing like a night's worth with these hard-drinking players. Some wine could be "accidentally" spilled; sometimes half a glass or so could be poured under the table for dogs to lick up. Some wine could be tipped down a dark sleeve. But it was a risk, always a risk; something could happen—a scent of fresh blood, a provocation . . . Nick's ready acceptance of Will's wish to leave the inn came not just from his eagerness to see the theater. It also made him safer, meant he no longer had to keep up the dangerous charade—particularly among men who, as actors, knew very well how to spot fakery.

Nick shook his head, disliking these thoughts. He needed to distract himself.

Will himself had seemed distracted as they were rowed across the Thames, and had remained silent as they walked. Now Nick broke his reverie: "Penny for your thoughts?"

"Nary a farthing's worth," scoffed Will. "Only that it seems Ben hath repaired his quarrel with Master Henslowe."

"What quarrel was that?"

"You never heard?"

Nick shook his head.

"Why, that Ben depriv'd Henslowe of one of his good players just at the close of last summer's season." Will's voice invited further questioning.

Nick obliged, adopting the light voice of a player who must set up the jest so that the other player could reap the crowd's applause. "And how contrived he to do that deed, worshipful Master Shakespeare?"

Will rang a change on him and answered with perfect seriousness. "That was the duel, Nicholas. The man he killed in

Hog's Den Field was one Gabriel Spencer, player of the Admirals' Men—Henslowe's men."

"Ben slaying a man—'tis hard to believe." Nick shook his head.

"'Twas an unfair contest, to boot, but th' advantage was with the other man." Shakespeare continued soberly. "He was younger, higher of stature, and his blade a full ten inches longer than Ben's—Ben took a bad stab in the arm to get within reach. 'Twas providence he prevailed. Gabriel was a man of rich jest, witty parts, and mayhap the foulest temper I have ever known."

"And yet, a player to be a killer . . . ," Nick murmured. "'Tis strange to me."

Will snorted. "Nay, Nicholas. We are men, like all others."

"Just so," Nick retorted. "Few men are killers."

"Gabriel Spencer was one. Himself had killed a boy called Feake the year before. 'Twas some stupid brawl in a barber's shop. The boy made to brain Gabriel with a candlestick, Gabriel drew steel and stabbed into his eye. The boy laid abed three days before he died." He spread his hands. "Eleven months later, Spencer thinks to kill Ben. He fails. *Explicit* the history of a bad man." Nick shook his head in disbelief.

"We are a very sanguinary mystery, we guild of players," Shakespeare chuckled, and his voice grew humorous. "Aye, and play-poets too: one killed another this very year. What, have you never murdered a man, M'sieur Chevalier?"

The question was like a knife in Nick's heart. It was a bitter reminder that there weren't two men walking down Maid Lane, exchanging gossip. There was a man, and there was a vampire. *Few men are killers . . .* but all vampires were.

After a moment's pause, Nick answered with the truth, delivered as mockery. "Murdered a man?" he asked, remembering Lisa's kiss. "Why, not tonight, Master Shakespeare. But what of you?"

Will laughed. "No, not tonight, sweet Nick."

Neither man spoke again for some minutes.

Nick didn't know what thoughts were occupying Will, but he himself was raging inwardly at his nature. There was no M'sieur Chevalier, occasional visitor to London, occasional player, cultivating a friendship with the English poet for whom he had done a chance favor a few days since. Or rather, there was—but he was a cloak, a mask, a counterfeit to be thrown aside in twenty years' time, or before, if he ceased to serve. And under that?

Under that, a hunger that endured forever. A hunger that burned on its own satiation. He knew so well what it was to be a vampire, had gloried for centuries in his difference—yet even from the beginning, a small voice inside said, You were not meant to be a killer.

These past seventy years, the voice of humanity that beckoned him had grown ever stronger. It sounded like the simple trusting love of Alyssa von Linz, who had gone to her grave as Alyssa de Brabant. Alyssa, whom he'd seen only by night, though for him she shone with a sweet golden light like the lost sun—her hair, spun gold in candlelight, her skin a soft dawn with its tinges of rose. And her nature had been simply to love. To love him. There had been no questions, no suspicions, no servants bribed to inquire into the true nature of Nicholas de Brabant, who could court her only by night, who must have a marriage at night. "Trust me," Nicholas would say, and she always did. Nor had there been coquetry, the arch, demanding, witty, tantalizing expression of female strength. "I love you so much my heart cannot contain it," she said, long before he'd offered her much more than ordinary courtesy. Not from simplemindedness, but from simplicity itself. For Alyssa, love had been much too important to clutter with masks or denials.

He'd thought he could marry her and keep her light with him forever. He'd placed a golden ring engraved with the de Brabant arms upon her finger—the arms of a lineage now centuries extinct, as she could have learned if she had sent a letter to Brabant to inquire. But that was not Alyssa's nature. She simply loved. He was what he was. How had Alyssa loved him? She had. Somehow, somehow, the girl who had been all that was sweetest in the mortal world had loved him.

Alyssa: the sweet bride he had offered to his hunger, and delivered to her grave. He shook his head, trying to send these thoughts away. Yet what would she have been if he had succeeded? How would Alyssa have endured the sudden hunger the mere scent of animal blood could awaken in their kind? What would Alyssa have looked like when she killed?

And yet . . .

"Think you any man may come to kill?" Nick ventured. "Not in soldiering, but in the ordinary way?"

Shakespeare looked at him curiously. Nicholas Chevalier struck him as an odd man altogether. His English was perfect, an odd fit with his claim to come to England so rarely. His gift of reading a playscript once, and that speedily, and having the lines was a player's godsend—but if he were a gentleman, why was he a player at all? And his quirk of never rising before late afternoon, never coming forth before evening—well, the quality did as they willed, since they could pay for the privilege. Altogether, one might take him for a silly fellow of the better class, idle wealth looking for ways to amuse itself. And yet—his companions, particularly the "father," were not of that mold, a much sterner pair, though clearly as full of wealth as Nicholas himself. And this question . . . it was not the question of a silly man.

"'Tis the very matter my prince argues against himself in this new piece," Will answered thoughtfully. "He hath the greatest urging to a murder any man ever could—a father murdered by his brother, a king usurp'd, a queen adulterously wed. Yet his hand stays itself."

"So your prince is a man who can never murder?"

Will smiled. "Come to the Globe in the spring, and see."

Nick laughed, and they walked on in silence again.

"'Ere's the poor devil," the constable said, leading his small group of followers into a lightless alley. "The Watch tripped on him. Watch told the warden, warden told me—and I determined to send to Your Worship . . ."

The man's voice trailed off. If he, Constable John Smallberries, had dragged a Court gentleman out into the night on a false alarm, things could go hard with him. He shifted nervously, torn between the pleasure of being the one to bear important news and the terror of being so close to a man of great power: George Dyer, Secretary to a Privy Councillor, a man rumored to be one of the Queen's *privadoes,* a man who had Her Majesty's liking—and her ear. Still, they did say about town that this particular gentleman had a specially lively interest in strange deaths. And he'd come as quick as was humanly possible, with no fewer than three lampbearers and a body barrow in train. And he had thrown Smallberries a piece of gold.

A corner of the constable's soul yearned to throw the coin

back at him, but gold . . . and besides, for all he was a mild-faced man, there was something mischancy about this gent. He was peering through the darkness at the still figure on the ground, and smaller, equally still figures around it, like as they were Holy Writ instead of the grisly and all-too-common sights they were.

"You did right to summon me," murmured the Court gentleman, himself almost invisible in his dark cloak.

"Even so," said the constable, freshly emboldened. "What but plaguey madness could cause the wight to shed doublet, blouse, boots, and hosen? Nay, 'tis the heat seized his brain, and fluxion of vap'rous blood—'tis the very mark of the last takings."

Takings, Aristotle agreed mentally, beckoning the lampbearers closer. They lowered the lanterns almost to the ground, permitting him to see quite clearly what he already knew: there were two small holes in the pale corpse's neck, each weeping a tiny dribble of blood.

Since he'd first arrived in England, he'd arranged that tales of plague deaths were to be brought to Master Secretary Dyer's ear in order to protect his own small Community—which had nothing to fear from the harmless bubonic plague—from an entirely separate set of dangers. He rubbed a hand over his beard, and sighed, shifting his attention to the litter of curled rat bodies that surrounded the dead man. Though human senses could not know it, the rats were as drained of blood as the dead youth.

"Happen the rats bit him and died of it alike," the constable hazarded. "They do say 'Near rat and cat do fever breed,'" recited Smallberries. He puffed out his cheeks. "'Do dog and gypsy fever speed.'" He peered at the corpse. "'A don't look like a moon-man, happen."

Aristotle recruited his patience. "He is no Gypsy, but a gentleman of breeding unlikely to belong to this parish." So much changed from generation to generation of mortal men, but their love of superstition and their fear of foreigners appeared to be as immortal as he was himself. "You do great ill to sully good men's ear with such brute report," he added. Whatever method might be needed to deal with this problem, mob slaughter of all the Gypsies in London would not help.

Smallberries marked the insult, and grunted. "But it be the Pest?"

Aristotle stroked his beard again. "Aye, 'tis plague." Not so foul a lie, he reflected. A careless blood-drinker was plague enough for him. And one with an appetite for rats? Could a vampire's wits addle? What else might explain this?

The lampbearers backed away, muttering curses. To be in Dyer's service was to do strange things, but this was too much. Only six years had passed since the Black Death last ravaged London; having escaped it then, they had no wish to fall prey to it now.

Smallberries nodded importantly, standing his ground. "Ay, she's a corruption i' the air. Be it summer, the time for her. I myselfen," he bounced on his toes, "do eat every morning a little London treacle, or the kernel of a walnut, with five leaves of rue and a grayne of salt beaten together and roasted in a fig. Happen I never stir out fasting, neither."

"And 'tis effectual?" This was the anxious voice of a lampbearer, a few feet behind him.

"I bain't taken o' the Pest, clodhead." The constable was nettled. "She'm effectual, what you will."

"I thought the receipt was half an ounce of nutmegs cooked o'er the fire, add three pen'worth of treacle, and a quart o' angelica-water," the clodhead retorted.

"Me grandmother sweareth by her pomander," said the youngest lampbearer, a red-haired boy whose voice was still breaking. "'Tis herbs of rue, wormwood, zedoary-ginger, myrrh, and others, also some roots."

"Wear a meadow at your neck?" The third lampman scoffed. "Nay, get you but one good toad, dry and flat, and 'twill draw the ill o' the air by swelling."

"Toad's good," nodded the clodhead. "Seen it myself, I have. Or I once heard ninety-eight walnuts stuffed with mercury and mussels would ward you."

"Anyone tastin' that will care nothing for plague," chuckled the old one. "Swallow quicksilver?"

"Gran burnt feathers and old harness in the house to keep the ill air out," the boy said. "And kept caged birds, for the flutter of wings do keep air from pooling and going to rot within doors."

"Rot?" echoed Smallberries contemptuously. "How may air rot?"

"How did you?"

Smallberries whirled, but was unable to tell which man had made this remark. Insulting the law was a popular sport, for all it was illegal.

While the mortals bickered, Aristotle had been wracking his brains. In the better part of two millennia, he'd simply never heard of a vampire that left rats hard by its kills. London was a gossipy town; if this kept up, it had best be talked of as plague. Especially with such a wonderfully authoritative civil authority as Constable Jack to spread the talk.

"Air may rot," he announced, raising a hand for their attention. "'Tis a matter of influences, aspects, conjunctions and opposition of ill planets, the eclipse of the sun and moon. Through the immoderate heat of the air, where the temperature of the air is turned from its natural state to excessive heat and moisture, which is the worst temperature of the air; which time vapours being drawn up do rot, putrify, and corrupt."

He made his voice even more portentous. "The which corruption brews a venomous miasmata that takes men ill and drives them mad." He gestured at the dead boy, lying on the grimy street with nearly all his clothes gone.

Clothes gone? *A rat-drinking thieving vampire*? Aristotle allowed himself to fancy that he was getting a headache and rubbed his eyes.

The lampbearers were backing even farther away, and now Smallberries slid a few steps backward as well.

Darkness and solitude, a vampire's eternal allies. Aristotle knelt next to the victim, on pretense of looking closer at the neck. His head dipped close to the wounds, his fingers slipped across them . . . The others were reflexively stepping even farther back from such foolhardy exposure, and would not see what he was going to do. Darkness and solitude, just enough—Aristotle called his vampire senses forward.

Scent of his kind, a subtle tinge in the air, and far different from the sickly sweet odor that even the mortals were able to detect on plague victims. Aristotle swept the blood onto a finger, and bent his head . . . not long dead, still some impression to be had . . . Beautiful dark woman? *Janette? Janette would walk i' the sun ere she'd taste a rat.*

• • •

Eventually they left Maid Lane to cross a field, and then a little bridge. Nick couldn't help but notice that almost all the land here on the Thames's south bank was soggy. As their boots squelched into the soft earth, he wondered at the wisdom of putting a playhouse in a swamp, though he knew the Globe, the Rose, the Swan, and the Bear Garden were all set within a few hundred yards of one another here in Bankside.

As if reading his mind, Will remarked, "'Twas difficult to foot the theater in this muck, but we contrived, upon pilings near strong enough to raise London Bridge—sail ho, there she is." The small upper house of the Globe was in view, and as they came out from behind some trees, Nick saw the whole theater.

It stood three stories high, black timbered and white plastered, a little jagged circle of a building with a steeply pitched roof thatched with river reeds. Its sign hung over the door: a painting of a man holding up the world—the Sign of the Globe—beneath which was the Latin motto "*Totus mundus agit histrionem.*"

"All the world goes playing," Nick translated softly.

Will smiled. "I'd render it, 'All the world's a stage.' No truer words are writ down anywhere, if it be not blasphemy to say so."

They walked through the entry passage, a purposely narrow tunnel that allowed the Globe's doorkeeper to collect pennies from even the most determined gate-crasher. They walked through easily, even though the hall was unlit, Shakespeare knowing his way from habit and Nick able to see in the dark. They came out in the theater's open yard, where the groundlings stood for a penny a play, and walked round to where a stage jutted into the courtyard.

"Who goes there?" A candle appeared, and with it a hand and a rather severe face, from one of the doors at the back of the stage.

"Will Shakespeare, and a friend," Will called back.

"Well, then," said the voice. Its owner showed himself, a thin man with a sweep of gray hair pulled back from bright gray eyes, who lifted his candle and took a good hard look at Nick. "The wagons all been back an hour," he said. "What want ye here?"

Nick looked at Will, a smile brimming in his eyes. Was the man to be barred from his own theater? What sort of creature would even try the trick? Will patted the promptbook tucked under his arm. "I bring tidings of mismarriage in Verona. Do we pass?"

"Happen," said the watchman, and produced a grin that was only half teeth.

"Nicholas Chevalier, be known to honest Tim Seldes," said Will, "who, having circled the world with Drake, the Burbage brothers thought most meet to watch over our little globe."

"'Tis a right fair choice," Nick agreed.

"Ay, and he's fought at Agincourt and carried a spear in Caesar's legions too, though Plymouth-born in the reign of Harry Eight," Will joked. "Yet I've a bone to pick with him," he added, "for he swears poets should get thruppence ha'penny for their plays, and not a groat over."

"And the reason of this is . . . ?" Nick raised his eyebrows humorously. Will looked at Tim, who lifted his chin and set himself in a square stance.

"Well, sorr, here's the matter of it," the watchman began firmly. "A waterman getteth but a penny to bring a man, or a lady, sorr, across yon Fluvius Thamesis, which is to you, the river, sorr, which labor costeth an honest man twenty minute of time, happen thirty if tide's against, whereas a play taketh up ninety minute of an afternoon, which is three times more. And 'twould be more than that, if ye allow the jig and interludes, but since he," Tim nodded at Will, "writeth them not, I pay him naught for them."

"Ha'penny?" Nick raised his eyebrows again.

"Ha'penny o'er for the tip," Seldes said. "Which a waterman may have if he comports him all courteous and do not spit at the swans, et cetera."

"There's a reckoning," Nick laughed. "Tragedy, comedy, what have you, by the minute."

"'Tis but a free man's opinion, sorr, but it is that," said Seldes with dignity. "Good e'en t' ye, then."

"And to you," murmured Nick, but the man had already walked away. "A character fit for a play," Nick marveled, turning to Will. "A king in his own country."

"Just so," Will chuckled. "But there's a good round truth in't: my weaver who drowses with an ass's head within the forest, my goodwives who foil old Sir John Falstaff, or the usurped king I purpose now—all are one to the passing hours. And when those hours are gone, all still one, all still."

"A father, a son; a murder, a kingdom," Nick said, more to himself than otherwise, but Will heard.

"A dead father with a quick son," Will said, walking to the edge of the stage and looking out. "'Tis a history in Saxo-Grammaticus, and Kyd botched it on the boards once. A father who cries vengeance, that blood must be answered in blood. Yet there is that in the son which is not ready to the task, and so his troubles enlarge themselves upon all his house."

Will paused, and swept an arm toward the galleries. "This house. And that father, his angry thirst unslak'd, who comes again and yet again?" He smiled, patting his chest. "I shall be that father; 'tis Dick I will vex. I shall come from Hell," he pointed to a trapdoor, "for this father hath not merited a higher seat." He looked up to the Globe's heavens, bright with a gaily painted moon, stars, and a zodiac.

"A father who comes from Hell," Nick said. It suddenly seemed quite real to him; where else had LaCroix sprung from to haunt his life forever? "A father who never lets go his son, but comes from Hell to rule him." His mood turned bleak in an instant. An eternity of submitting to LaCroix, or rebelling and being whipped back into place—now that would be a story for a poet to tell. Will was watching him curiously, marking his abruptly clouded humor.

"What comes from the heavens, then?" Nick said heavily.

"Why, God's grace, if He's a will to it," his friend answered. "Or so we may all pray." He peered through the darkness at his companion and added a joke: "Betimes a spillage of unlooked-for rain, if the tireman drops his pail." Will smiled broadly, a cat full of cream, and folded his arms across his doublet. "The fine for which is three shillings, which we never assess upon a god."

Nicholas tried to laugh, but the small stage was affecting him more than he dared say.

There was something friendly and sweet about the new made theater; the reeds of the roof's thatch were still releasing a bit of their scent, and the new wood and limed plaster that had been added to the timbers the players had brought across the river were also still fresh. It was almost intoxicating to stand on the stage of wide oak boards. Nicholas had seen stages in Italy set upon marble palaces with gilded props, and yet this homely outdoor circle touched him more grandly than any scene in Venice or Florence had ever done. It was indeed easy to look up at the planking of the tireroom above and imagine a surprising drip of spilled ale falling through the crack to baptise the players below.

Burbage would know just what joke to make for such a mishap too, Nick thought. Or Phillips, or Will Sly, or even phlegmatic John Heminges. And yet any one of them could in the same space of time counterfeit a god descending and make a thousand people in a rough building believe it.

"Mere oaken boards." He scuffed one boot at the stage.

"Planking for a deck that sails the wide world," Will returned easily. "What is this melancholic humor that bites at you? Here's a place for jigs." The middle-aged playwright threw his arms askew momentarily and essayed a mild hop, nothing like the wild antics of the clowns who jigged at the close of each play, but far from his usual sober motions.

Again Nick laughed, but again it died away quickly. "'Tis true, I have seen it: here's a castle's flagged floor, strewn with pretty lovers come to a doleful death, or your Roman forum with its Caesar bleeding like a stuck hog—yet five minutes hence, four fond actors are jigging upon that grave." He was remembering a performance of *Romeo and Juliet:* its tragic priest's speech followed on the instant by Will Kempe's clowning dance, a-leaping like a frog with flux, as had been justly said of him.

Nicholas kept his gaze on the stage, sweeping his feet over it, pushing the rushes about. "How like the world that is, a wide grave where those who go above do dance in ignorance of all the death about them."

"Avoid!" exclaimed Will, pantomiming an old woman's superstitious gesture. "What fiend is this in you?"

"A fiend," Nicholas agreed bitterly. "I know it better with each passing season: a fiend." He drew a long breath of the night air, and looked past the ragged fringe of thatching to the starry sky.

Not for him the happy sight of a new play of Will's being premiered on one of the Globe's sunny afternoons. Never for him.

A few, precious times he'd seen a whole play of Will's in its natural setting, simply standing in the audience and laughing at the jokes like anyone else. Seven years ago that had been, back when the Lord Chamberlain's Men performed in the courtyard of the Cross Keys Inn in midwinter, starting at four in the afternoon instead of two because the innkeeper insisted his yard be free for the arrival of travelers most of the day. Days when the sun went down just after half past three . . .

Nick had stumbled into his first stint as an amateur player then, happening along as a well-looking man who could remember his lines at first glance and did not sound entirely like a talking tree when he delivered them. That was how he'd first met Will Shakespeare . . .

But he would never get to play this small sweet stage, open to the true heavens. He might know the flag went up at one o' the clock to signal a performance at two; he could know the admission would double to tuppence when a fresh new marvel was to be acted; he might con the lines from the promptbook and have them, in his vampire's memory, readier to his tongue than any player ever could, for the rest of eternity—but experience the thing itself, the theater swelled with groundlings and lords on the cushioned seats, the cries of men selling fruit and nuts, the actual sound of Dick Burbage making the man real for the first time, bringing out the first act when this prince's life was full of choices? Never.

He, Nicholas de Brabant, had chosen. He had been offered life and strength forever under the cover of the night sky, and he had taken it. He stared into the stars, cursing them momentarily for their familiar travel in the heavens. *Change!* he thought, *Be only once changed, and I with you!*

"'Tis only the fifth act that's familiar," he murmured to himself.

"What is't you say?" With his accustomed courtesy, Will had simply waited out Nicholas's strange, silent taking.

"That I know endings best of all," Nicholas answered, pulling himself to the surface. "And so I know that never to end, which once I thought the happiest state, can be a great curse."

Will's brows knitted together, but again he answered with humor. "Certes, never to end is never to send the players to bed—which of itself may be well enough," he grinned, "but yet it is also never to send the audience away, and thus never to have them back and collect more of their copper and silver the next day."

Nick laughed. Will's hair was askew, tugged a little by the light evening breeze, and his wide forehead was a bit decorated with loose strands, and his pouched eyes, always a bit owlish, now seemed positively night-round. What could be more human? What more transient?

"You make an excellent show of being pennywise." Nick smiled, letting his spirits be raised. "Yet I know you for a toppler of the throne of Egypt, and tupper of innocent maids."

Will laughed. "Sooth, and would do again for half the pay," he said cheerfully. "But you must not tell anyone I have said so."

"Your secret's close in my breast," Nick said lightly. His humor fell away again for a second. "And I am a most excellent keeper of secrets."

"Which minds me," said Will, "I must lay this," he patted the promptbook, "to rest." Will led him backstage through the door Seldes had used, and back to a little counting room, lighting a candle to show the way.

There was a small humpbacked chest sitting unlocked on the floor. Will swung the lid open and knelt to deposit the sealed and beribboned promptbook of *The Taming of the Shrew.* A stack of similar books could be seen in the box.

"All your plays?" Nick said, gesturing at them.

"Mine own and other men's," said Will. He patted the chest's rounded lid, swelling with the Lord Chamberlain's repertory. "Here's love's labor won, in very sooth," he said affectionately.

A note of eagerness came into Nick's voice. "Might I stay to read them?"

Will looked over his shoulder. "Come see them, rather."

Nick shook his head. "I may not. My days belong to my cousin. 'Tis only nights such as this, in a private house, when I may hear them."

Shakespeare's expression flickered. The cousin was the explanation? Did Nicholas know this "cousin" claimed to be his father? Whoever he might be, Will misliked him. It wasn't hard to believe that the tall, severe LaCroix was able to compel a grown man's attendance, even when that man was clearly a gentleman who should have been able to do his own bidding.

Yet to leave Nicholas alone with the chest of playscripts was much to be asked. Plays were a player company's greatest asset. And the Lord Chamberlain's Men did not generally allow their plays into print, though a few had been pirated by greedy publishers—and maybe once by jigging Will Kempe, though they had never proved it. Henslowe routinely sent spies to take shorthand notes during performances, but what might he pay a man like Nicholas, who remembered everything at first sight? It was more than he should take upon himself to permit.

He shook his head. "I may not allow it, except with Dick's consent—he and Cuthbert hold half the shares. Come another night, and 'twill be possible."

Nick's disappointment was evident. Nor was there any trace of thwarted greed in his expression, so Will thought of something else. "Here's other matter for your eyes, if you'll have of it." He closed the chest and shot the lock on its hasp. There was a small box upon the desk, shelved sideways next to the account book. "Take these, and bring them to me when you have done."

From the box, Will drew a roll of paper, not a scroll like a player's script, but loose leaves rolled and tied. "They are little poems I had writ some years past."

"Your sonnets?" Nick asked happily. "I have heard of them. I have heard them called most excellent mellifluous."

"Then you've had speech with the spirit of Euphues," Will laughed, "for since that poor man died, no one else hath abused the language so. But see if you like of them." He handed them to Nick. "And now it's time to be off, and let Tim bolt the door and sleep."

He led Nick out of the Globe, shouting loudly to the unseen Seldes, "All a-gone."

6

Whenas in silks my Julia goes,
Then, then, methinks, how sweetly flows
That liquefaction of her clothes.

Next, when I cast mine eyes and see
That brave vibration each way free;
O, how that glittering taketh me!

—Robert Herrick (1591–1674),
"Upon Julia's Clothes"

THERE WAS A DELICIOUS MURMURING OF VOICES SOMEWHERE JUST beyond the edge of his dream—women's voices—

"*Bon Dieu,* how you tarry! No, no, 'twas but a jest. Well, give me the smock—"

"*Oui, ma'mselle,*" said a compliant voice. Somewhere in a corner of the dreamer's mind, the voice was identified as Dianne, Janette's tirewoman.

Since she and LaCroix had come from France with almost no preparation, Aristotle had undertaken to supply them with servants who he warranted would be discreet. He had also, wizardlike, produced several trunkloads of appropriately elegant clothing and bespoken one Master Clutterbook, tax collector and draper in Gracious Street, to attend immediately upon any alterations that might be required.

Janette had fretted a little at having strange mortals near her, but LaCroix had laughed: servants supplied by a spymaster? What could be better? The women who had come to serve Janette proved to be a trio of sisters—Mary, Marcia, and Dianne Wickes—who were clever with both their hands and their minds. Janette was beginning to wax content.

There was a rustling, and somewhere in his dream Nick felt his shoulder being touched—"*Dormez-vouz?* Nicholas, it is time to get up. Nicholas? *Eh bien, cinq minutes au plus.*" The rustling went away, but the murmuring started up again. In his sleep, Nick smiled and rolled onto his back, stretching and snorting softly.

"Bring the damask quilt bodice with whalebone, *oui,* that one. Bah, the lacing is broken, it will not serve—the green silk, then. *Ah, oui, ça va bien.* Then the petticoat of wrought crimson velvet, *bon,* and the underdress? *Un petit moment, Dianne—*"

The rustling again, a more complicated sound. Now the delicate touch came at the side of his face. "*Nicholas, levez-toi, hiên*?" And then a tiny laugh, as the question answered itself. "*Non.*" The rustling gone.

"He sleeps like one drugged today. Silk hose, *je pense.* No, not slippers, give me the leather shoes, for we may walk. Give me the smock again; he must be roused."

The rustle approached again. Nicholas heard the outer door close heavily; the thump jarred his dream to fragments. He roused and rolled over with a groan, burying his face in Janette's abandoned pillow. "Wake yourself, my love," she chided him gently, smiling. Such a sweet, vulgar oaf, her *cher chevalier*. "The sun has long since set."

"What of it?" he grumbled, reaching for her blindly, last night's wine still throbbing just beneath his skull.

"No," she protested with a laugh. "Nicholas, get up!"

He dragged her into the bed, mindless of her heavy smock and the complicated garments that it protected. "Janette, come down," he growled, climbing over her.

He kissed her hard and deeply, the muffled voices of LaCroix and his ancient friend drifting from two rooms away through the half-open door of their antechamber, only to be lost in lovers' fevered breathing. Nick's fangs descended and he kissed Janette's neck, pressing their tips to the point where the vein stood so close to the surface.

"Ah, Nicholas, please," she pleaded. "I am so hungry." Nick paused.

"So am I," he admitted, raising his head away from hers to flash her a bleary-eyed grin. Janette slid out of his arms, giving him a fiery smile that promised much for later.

She went back to her tirewoman but left the communicating door open now as she resumed the management of the gowning process. Nicholas sat up slightly in bed, watching with pleasure.

"The French hood, *oui,* and the small border of rubies." The great ritual was in its last stages, hairdressing followed by the application of the magnificent outer gown, velvet embroidered with pearls, and the long, delicate process of lacing together the points of the gown, sleeves, farthingale . . . "What has become of the buske point?"

Last of all came the delicate matched ruff and cuffs, the linen stiff and snowy, carefully arranged upon its wire supporter until it seemed to float by art, not artifice, around Janette's exquisite neck.

"I will return in a few minutes. Set the gloves here for me, and you may go." The rustling again, muted now and accompanied with the smallest tapping of shoeheels on the floor—

Janette sailed into the room like a galleon under full sail. Nick caught his breath. Janette was never less than beautiful, but dressed like this—

"You are a queen," he said, catching her hands to kiss each one of her jeweled fingers.

"Then I command that you rouse yourself, sir knight!" she ordered with a smile, giving him a most unmajestical sharp poke in the ribs that sent him rolling, groaning, laughing away . . .

"Your wayward son contents himself, then?" Aristotle asked dryly as he cast a pointed glance at the door.

"Of course," LaCroix replied. Pride would hardly allow him to share his concerns at Nicholas's insolence of the night before, even with his oldest equal. The remedy would be his alone; so should be the problem. "Did I not predict as much?"

"Indeed," Aristotle agreed slowly. "He shows no more signs of melancholy, then? No hint of madness in his habits?"

"Madness?" LaCroix echoed, incredulous.

Janette came through the door then, pushing an errant curl into place. "Monsieur Aristotle," she said, coming to greet them. "*Bon soir*. I am most obliged to you for Mistress Dianne, she is *très amiable*." She swept forward in full magnificence, her hand raised to be kissed.

The ancient vampire seized it, but rather than presenting his lips, he lifted her wrist to his nose. "Aha," he said, his tone more sad than triumphant.

"What is this?" LaCroix demanded. "Some new form of English courtesy?"

Aristotle's only response was to tear open the flesh of Janette's wrist with his teeth, making her cry out in pain.

"Have you gone mad?" LaCroix protested angrily. "Let her go at once!"

"In a moment, my friend," Aristotle said. He tasted Janette's blood with great delicacy, a mere droplet on his lips, then let her wrist fall. "Where is he?" he demanded, addressing himself to her. "And who?"

"I have no notion of what you mean," she snarled, holding her wrist, where the small punctures were already healing themselves. "*Vraiment,* I cannot believe—"

"You must answer me for this," LaCroix said coldly, watching his fledgling's face. She *was* hiding something.

"Of course," Aristotle's tone was perfectly mild, "I shall answer you, Lucien, then this one shall answer me—and perhaps others." Both Janette and LaCroix stiffened slightly.

He offered Janette his handkerchief, which she took with no good grace. "London has of late been littered with corpses even more so than usual," he began. "A strange new plague has arisen among us, striking most commonly in Eastcheap and Deptford."

Janette made a dismissive sound. "I do not even know this name, Deptford."

"All who die are found drained of all blood, with no sign of their malady but for a pair of bloodless wounds. The author of these heedless kills signs his work with rats. He is working his way upward in the world, having risen from trollops to a boy of some degree, whose person I have myself seen—who bears two small wounds . . . just here." He demonstrated on Janette's throat, making no move to stop her when she jerked away. "The blood of the last of these can be tasted in Mam'selle

DuCharme," he finished. "So I ask you, lady. Have you done these deeds yourself, or have you a reckless new lover?"

"I will not speak to such lies!" she cried, glowering at her master as if to demand his protection.

"Mortals tell me of a young foreigner, Spanish or Dutch, with black hair and eyes," Aristotle continued, watching with bemusement as golden Nicholas staggered groggily through the room and out the other side. "Speak me truly, pretty one . . . I hold you no ill will. But see you not the peril of such a course? Unexplained plagues that can be traced to creatures who drink living blood? And what of the vermin that garnish these kills?"

"A disaster in the making," LaCroix agreed slowly, still watching her face.

"*Oui, sans doute,*" she retorted. "But not mine."

"Have you no remembrance of the boy in green velvet breeches?" Aristotle resumed. Observing his old friend, LaCroix believed that there was no shred of doubt anywhere in Aristotle's mind that she did. "I pray you think, milady: he was found this night dead in an alleyway after leaving last night with a wench."

"And you think his wench was me?" Janette demanded hotly.

Aristotle's manner was always humorous and twinkling, and it was easy to forget what power lay behind it—power in both mortal and immortal circles. He smiled now as if it were no great matter, saying lightly, "'Tis said blood will tell, lady. I think it has told."

"I think this inquisition has continued long enough," LaCroix said gently. He moved between them, taking his daughter's wounded hand and drawing her gently to his side.

His face expressionless, LaCroix turned his eyes to Aristotle. "*Mon ancien ami,* if Janette avows that she knows of no such plague, we needs . . . must . . . take her at her word."

Aristotle met his friend's eyes for a long moment. That drifting, soft diction was Lucius's way of marking a battleground. Was now the time? So far, the mortals had all believed the plague story. "Of course," he said, sketching a small bow. "My mistake, my lady. Pray forgive me." He watched Nicholas stagger in again and collapse into a wide, cushioned chair, holding his head as if it hurt him. "So I shall take my leave."

"*Merde!*" Janette swore as soon as he was gone, to LaCroix's amused astonishment. Whatever lie Janette was protecting, it must vex her greatly to move her to such vulgar gutter speech. "*Imbécile! Bête!* Stupid Spanish dog!"

"I thought he was actually Greek," Nick mumbled.

"What of this plague, *chérie*?" LaCroix asked, shooting his young crusader an amused glance. His children could really be so diverting.

"A plague on him!" she retorted. "And on you, *mon cher* LaCroix, for allowing me to be so used."

"I do crave pardon, my love," LaCroix soothed. "But you must admit—"

"I must admit nothing," she said flatly, storming from the room to call for her cloak.

"What happened?" Nicholas asked, watching her go.

"Nothing of consequence," LaCroix assured him. Which was his actual judgment of the situation: Aristotle had been stalled, if not entirely mollified; Janette was enraged but in no real danger, despite her lie; and there was a new player on the board, but unlikely to be anyone of consequence.

LaCroix smiled, thinking of the scene just enacted. *Ay, no one of consequence, but quite possibly a source of entertainment for the future.* While a rat-sucking vampire was an abomination never to be embraced, it was rather interesting to see Aristotle's feathers ruffled . . . how long had it been? That affair of Berta Broadfoot and Pepin the Short, perhaps? Through them, Aristotle had fancied manipulating France—only to have them whelp Charlemagne, a mortal prince who'd brook no rule from anyone, let alone a night-dwelling heathen. Or perhaps it was the time he'd propped up the puppet Pope at Avignon?—well, one had to admire the conceit, a vampire seeking to co-opt the entire Christian church. Yes, let Janette keep her lie . . . for now.

Seeing no immediate threat to his family, LaCroix was prepared to let the situation play itself out, and to be amused.

He gave his son a jaunty smile. "Come, Nicholas—we will taste of your fair London's best delights."

Nicholas should have known Janette would have been less than impressed by the Mermaid Tavern—his fastidious beloved had already declared the English "*les cochons des cochons,*" pigs of pigs, for their dress, their speech, their table manners. "The greatest minds of the century, and they eat with their hands?" she sniffed, poking at the greasy joint of beef the serving girl had deposited on their table as soon as they came in, without bothering to ask if it was wanted. "Where are the forks?"

"Forks are not an English use, *ma chére,*" LaCroix explained with a thin smile. "Over-dangerous by half. Picture you this menagerie managing to sup a banquet entire without bloodshed were they so armed?"

Nicholas shot his master an impatient look, and LaCroix raised his eyebrows, daring Nicholas to contradict his facts. When Nicholas held his peace, LaCroix added, "In faith, I have heard it bruited that their upper classes trust each other with blunt knives over beef."

Nicholas looked away in disgust. "Pray take this away, mistress," he ordered, catching a passing girl by the elbow and indicating the dead chunk of cattle with a grimace.

"Oh, sir, was you wantin' o' the stew?" the serving girl said earnestly.

"Wine," said Nicholas. "Nothing more." He was tempted to order three steaming bowls of the Mermaid's fish stew just to watch LaCroix's reaction as it was delivered, but forbore.

"The social graces of the English do leave much wanting," Nicholas resumed. "Yet cannot you feel the brilliance in this room, the life?" He looked around at the teeming mass of drunken mortality with undisguised delight, making his companions share an indulgent smile.

"These men may eat as peasants, but they dream as gods—this language of theirs which you value so little has laid the human heart open and bare on the stage like the sections of an orange, inviting us to take it up and eat it with our fingers. Shakespeare and Jonson and—"

"And pretty Kit Marlowe, who was stabbed to death in a pig lot very like this one," Janette finished for him. "How am I to marvel at a city that kills its finest wit?"

"—whilst he himself conspired against his shriveled little monkey of a queen," LaCroix picked up the thread. "And not, look you, with a fork." LaCroix was enjoying himself now. "Or plotted he *for* her? Their animal manners be clear, but the politics of this ragged little isle are altogether too subtle to be understood. Was Marlowe the Queen's toy, or the Pope's? Put to it, the man himself may not have known."

"Lucien, now you exaggerate," Janette said, laying a hand on Nicholas's arm. "As usual." She looked around with an airy sigh. "*Oui,* Nicholas, there is life here, beauty in this squalor. But is it enough?"

Nicholas watched the old sadness creep back into her eyes, the same delicate fire that had first drawn him into her darkness—into the darkness they shared. Had her restlessness come again so quickly? He laid his hand over hers and restrained himself from squeezing too tight.

"In ancient times, they smeared their faces blue and beat upon their shields to affright their foes," LaCroix added, undaunted in his scorn. "In sooth, that was a less fearsome sight than a score of them at table tonight."

His ice-blue eyes widened slightly, and the corners of his mouth curved upward in amusement. "Stay, Nicholas, here's a spectacle would make a Pict proud. Is't not your little friend with the large hat who goes there?"

Hilliard was a vision as usual in ruby-colored velvet slashed in doublet and breeches to reveal cloth of gold so bright it shimmered even in the dim, smoky light of the alehouse. But for once, his little mistress quite outshone him. "*Mon Dieu,*" Janette breathed, amused and appalled at once. "He has her dressed as a boy."

Isabella's doublet had obviously been patterned after her lover's, its shortened lines over a white linen blouse clinging to her sharply corseted form to accentuate rather than disguise her shape. But far more shocking were her breeches—gold brocade and barely ballooned, in the style favored by the more outrageously fashionable of Venetian youth, a waggishly obscene compromise between a gentleman's attire and the golden bloomers of an Oriental courtesan. Her abundant black curls had been gathered and tucked into an approximation of a page boy's bob beneath a modest ruby velvet toque, and her pretty round calves were barely concealed beneath tight, clocked stockings with the garters crossed. In short, she was a caricature of the most ridiculous extremes of masculine vanity—the folly of mortal youth displayed on his prettiest toy, revolting and irresistible.

"Beauty has been breeched at last," spoke a voice over Nicholas's shoulder. Turning, he found Will Shakespeare in the crowd at the long table, watching the girl's performance as they did. She stopped before one of Hilliard's wealthy acquaintances and made a deep, theatrical bow a few scant feet before them.

"What think you, Nicholas?"

"At last?" Jonson spoke up morosely, down the row from his colleague. "The breach in that particular fresco has been opened by half the wits in London, and her friend seems prepared to see it broken more."

Isabella looked up with a feverish light in her eyes, but her smile was bright. "And how shall such a breach be mended, sirrahs?" she demanded, releasing her hold on her lover's arm. "Surely not by neglect." She grinned at Nicholas and winked. "Pray you, love, advise me," she called, going after Hilliard. "Wise Will and his good friends think me cracked—shall I send to the City for a plasterer?"

Nicholas laughed with the rest, but his mirth died when he saw his own lady love's face. "*La pauvre petite,*" Janette said, turning to him sadly. "They think her drunk . . ." She wrinkled her delicate nose in disgust, speaking very softly. "She is full of pox—can you not smell it, Nicholas? The disease is far advanced in her."

"Faith, mistress, we've a bricklayer to hand," laughed one of the wits, indicating Jonson, who had been licensed in that trade before his playwriting days and hated to be reminded of it. "Shall we have him set his hand to you?"

"Hath he never done so before now?" another added from across the room. "Behindhand thou art, then, Ben."

Isabella raised a hand to her face in an obviously false imitation of maidenly shock, but Jonson seemed genuinely incensed, reaching for his sword.

"Nay, sir," Shakespeare interjected, putting a hand on his friend's arm. "Behind is never where the hand goes in, nor in amatory nor military nor yet in builder's parts." Jonson subsided into his seat. "And we have no brick to hand," Will added, glaring down the table at the wits, "unless blockheads do suffice."

A general laugh diffused the tension, and even Jonson was seen to smile wanly. "Once more unto the breach, dear Ben!" shouted a voice hidden in the throng.

"You see, Will, they will mock you out of humor as well," Isabella laughed. "I do but turn jennies into men, but they'll turn your Henries into Bens." Now she got a general laugh too, all the more hearty for her neat appropriation of Hilliard's horsey insult to her from the night before.

"And Hilliard, the loathsome angel—see how he allows me to be used?" She turned and caressed her lover's cheek. "Yet I have won him at last, have I not?"

Hilliard pressed the girl's hand briefly to his lips before pressing a goblet into her palm. "Some cracks are meant to be kept open to admit light into our darknesses," he answered, turning to Thomas Saddler, the young actor whose hat Isabella had pilfered some nights before. "What think you, Tom—shall we have the little monkey sealed?"

"Forgive me, my lord," Thomas stammered, blushing scarlet. "I know not what I should think."

"Aye me," Isabella sighed in exaggerated regret. "But then, you're so young yet, dearling—no doubt the thought shall come to you in time, if coming is the thought." She turned again toward Shakespeare and the vampires. "But what of Willie's Frenchmen?" she laughed, moving toward them with the slightest of staggers. "They know what to think, I'll wager."

She stopped before Janette and pressed a hand to her heart as if struck by her beauty. "But then, they needs must be courteous in the presence of such a lady," she concluded, lifting the vampire's hand to her lips in perfect imitation of her lover's gallantry. "Or am I deceived again—is this an angel come to save their damned French souls?"

Janette caught the girl's hand between her own, her intense blue eyes alight with sympathy. "Leave this place, *chérie,*" she urged in her low, thrilling vampire's voice. "This man—he means you only harm."

"Say not so," Isabella protested, her mask of merriment fading with shocking speed under the effects of the hypnosis. "My lord cares for me—I am his love—"

"You are his plaything, less valuable than the boots he wears and more easily replaced," Janette insisted, cruelty shaded for kindness. Her eyes met Nicholas's ever so briefly, as if in pleading, as LaCroix looked away, shaking his head in disgust. "You are ill, *chérie*—"

"What mean you, lady-lad, with these uncourteous attentions?" Hilliard interrupted, coming to lay a possessive hand on Isabella's shoulder. "These gentlemen are out of your class, and the lady." He smiled, the blessing of an angel with the eyes of a snake. "You must forgive her, mademoiselle," he said to Janette, taking Isabella's hand from hers. "Having exhausted all the men in London, *ma* Belle has apparently decided to take on fair ladies instead."

"Yea, my lord, 'tis true," Isabella replied, an angry lucidity lighting her eyes as she turned to look at young Thomas for a beat. "'Tis pity, lady, and I beg your pardon. My patron has himself found such delight in Roman tricks, I thought to try them myself." She turned her glare on Shakespeare, still standing behind their table. "Like our sweet William, I have made his exotic rose my noble pattern."

Hilliard raised his hand and struck the girl to the floor in a single fluid motion, the effect of his blow quite distracting the crowd from the effect of her words. "Strumpet," he spat, flushed scarlet with rage. "Whore! You should die so, in the filth that bore you." The girl looked up at him, her bleeding mouth opening to reply, and he struck her again, the back of his hand sending her sprawling.

Nicholas half-rose in his chair, but LaCroix laid a hand on his arm. "Be still," he ordered quietly. "What will you do in such a rage?"

He was right, Nicholas realized through his fury—he could feel the red glow coming into his eyes even before he moved. One cross exchange, and the vampire would feast before all. He turned to look at Shakespeare, expecting to see a mortal's outrage, mortal shame—surely an artist of such sensitivity could not watch such a performance in silence. But the playwright seemed barely aware of his own living self, so engrossed was he in the brutal pantomime before them.

"Tomorrow is Saint Valentine's day, all in the morning betime," Isabella half-laughed, half-sang, crawling slowly to her feet. Thin tendrils of her hair, knocked loose by her lover's blow, floated around her head in wild strands.

"And I a maid at your window to be your valentine." She dragged the mannish toque from her head and shook the rest of her long hair free, her gaze unfocused and wandering as if she had suddenly found herself alone and lost.

"Then up he rose and donn'd his clothes, and dupp'd the chamber door," she sang on, her voice seeming to find strength in the song, rising above the whispers of the crowd and moving them to silence. "Let in a maid that out a maid never departed more."

"What means this mad chanting?" whispered an actor. "The lady's wits are gone altogether."

"The chuck sings her own tragedy," Jonson muttered under his breath.

Isabella turned to him and laughed as if delighted he had noticed. "By Gis and by Saint Charity, alack and fie for shame!" she sang, turning so quickly toward her still-furious lover she nearly tumbled over again. "Young men will do't, if they come to't, by cock they are to blame." She stopped before young Thomas Saddler, her spinning changing to perfect stillness in an instant.

"'Tis true, is it not, sweeting?" she said with a smile full of innocent light. "By cock, we are to blame . . ."

"Nicholas, for mercy, do something," Janette whispered urgently, her nails digging into his wrist. "Save her, kill him, burn this pigsty to the ground—only put a stop to this madness before I run mad myself."

But young Tom, to his credit, was quicker. "Come, then, Mistress Izzy," he soothed, putting an arm around her shoulders. "We'll go have a sleep until your fever passes, and you'll be quite your lady self." He led her toward the door, the crowd parting slowly before them, then stopped just before the door.

"Noble or not, you're a whoreson dog, William," he said without turning around, the girl breaking into sobs against his shoulder. Hilliard, lounging negligently against the wall with his rapier slung before him, did not so much as bat an eyelash at the insult.

After a moment, allowing Hilliard a decent amount of time to challenge him as honor should have demanded, Tom began to move again. "White-livered coward, to boot," he said contemptuously, and even now Hilliard did not respond. Tom bent his attention wholly to Isabella. "Hush now, little chick," he mumbled against her fallen curls. "And you, Will—both you Wills . . ." He broke off, blushing. "A pox upon you each." Gathering his charge closer still, he pushed into the street.

"A more appropriate curse I can scarce conceive," LaCroix muttered, turning away. "Indeed, Nicholas . . . they dream as gods."

• • •

"A fair word and a nod and we've clear sky and smooth seas, all aboard and safe away, but never say so, not for Señor el Grandiosissimo Windy-Jowls . . ."

"Shut up, Screed," said Vachon. A big knife cut was healing itself on his face as they walked along Deptford Strand.

"*La barba de tu madre,*" Screed imitated, ignoring his master's instruction. "Thinks ye a-pickin of his purse, and him on the dubbing cheat 'imself—'tis 'is honor, and all you has to do is say him nay, it's not a crossbite, thievin' of a thief, but no, el vam-peero magnificent-ioso has to go and shoot off 'is Spanish mouth." Screed's voice took on a shade of approval. "Still—'yer mum's beard,'—right wicked one that is." The carouche's voice resumed its disapproving tone. "But here's the prick of me point: then there's nothing for it but slip 'im the fang right where there's torchlight and us could be prigged—"

"*Basta,* Screed," Vachon said, but there was no heat in his words.

He agreed with Screed that he had been stupid to let the pickpocket make him angry, and stupider yet to curse the man in Spanish, but he was damned if he would say so. And once the man had sliced his face open with a knife, the vampire in him retaliated unthinkingly. Besides, he thought, he was paying enough of a penalty already: the Englishman had been drinking cheap beer which some enterprising tapster had cut with lime powder to make it shine like a better class of ale, and now the vampire's head ached of it.

"There it is, again, that Espan-yolo babble." Screed threw his arms wide in the air, but Vachon gave him no reaction.

Screed caught up with him and resumed his griping. "'Ere's me cudgeling me briny brain day and night, and what d'ye do wi' th' English I give ye but pick a fight straight so's some peevy lubber cudgels me brain for me. And me—what devil's in me to take up for you—well, it's the onliest and lastest of times, by my fay, or I'll find me 'ead wi' yours on a pole at Temple Bar, and the mean o' mean time, I've gotten splinters itching me skin all in my face—"

It was true—Screed had jumped down and taken a blow in the face from the pickpocket's accomplice, a blow that had been meant for Vachon. That man had gotten off lightly, left alive but somewhat dazed, Screed testing his new gift of hypnosis with delight while his master feasted on their attacker. If that other man had gotten a chance to strike with the old spar . . . Vachon stopped and looked at his creation and largely unwanted boon companion.

"Thank you, Screed," he said in carefully correct English. "It was well done of you, and I shall remember it."

The shock of this stoppered Screed's mouth for a minute; the two paced the Strand in silence, listening to slurp of the waters, while Vachon's face continued to heal to a point where he was willing to show himself at their inn. "See her silhouette, there?" Screed said. "She's the *Golden Hind,* what Drake sailed right round the 'ole world. Queen Elizabeth rode down and knighted the man 'imself right there on 'er decks. Ain't she a lovely 'un, though?"

Vachon shook his head, though he looked where Screed pointed. One ship was the same as another to him, though even in the New World he had heard his countrymen speak of the terrible Drake, the English dragon-pirate who sailed the seven seas, plundering Spain's treasure ships. They said blood rose in the wake of his ships, and that he had cast splinters upon the Channel waters, only to have them rise up as fireships against the Armada. *That little thing?* he thought, looking at the wooden hull, permanently retired in Deptford. *That, to terrify a whole empire?*

On a whim he took to the air and flew to the hulk. She was listing a bit, but sound, though a bit the worse for wear where the curious had chipped splinters off her mainmast and her decks.

"Ah, that's the motion," Screed said softly from beside him. The rising tide of the Thames had set the ship to rocking slightly, and while Vachon took a wider stance for balance, Screed simply adjusted with the habits of a lifetime.

In the next instant he was gone, and Vachon felt more than saw him up in the ship's rigging. Screed beguiled the next few minutes darting between the maintop, the foretop, the bowsprit, and the poop like a restless bird, then landed next to his master again. "King Neptune's mama's beard—if I could show the lads that." Screed shook his bald head in amusement, producing a broad grin. "Set sails in a blinky-wink, flitter to the maintop in a freshenin' breeze or the teeth of a nor'east gale if ye fancy . . . flitter right off above the maintop . . . who'd reck it?"

The grin faded, and Screed sucked at his lips. He darted a glance at Vachon. "Us was five on a rat in the mess betimes . . ." He rolled his eyes, and his lips pulled back over his teeth, but not in a grin. "Kegs o' stinkin' beef, weevils wot drank ale, barnacles . . . scurvy . . . apple-scrapples once in a year, lucky-duckies, them none cleaner than uslike, knacker yer knicks in one shake and ask sixpence . . . then 'twas back belowdecks an' snuggle wi' squealers." Still swaying easily with the motion of the ship, Screed willed his fangs down and reached strong, callused sailor's fingers up to touch them. "Ah, me sweet squealers, Screedy 'ardly knew ye, did 'e then?" He stretched his jaw open wide, baring the fangs as if to bite.

Screed darted a sidelong look at Vachon, who was understanding about one word in ten. "Are we the Devil's work like they say?"

Vachon laughed shortly, but shook his head. Screed take a blow for him? Screed ask a serious question? This *was* a strange night. Vachon looked over at his fledgling, and his eyes warmed with a smile. "You were *un hijo del diablo* before ever you meet me."

Screed flashed his toothy grin, reveling in this first gleam of appreciation. "*Met,* ye mean," he said. "Met me."

"*Sí,*" Vachon said with another smile. "And me," he added with a quick grin, "the ladies call me devil's seed before I am fifteen." Screed rolled his eyes at the boast and let the Spanish go. Vachon swiped a hand over his cheek, feeling the wound. "It closes," he said.

Screed peered at him, still unused to this aspect of vampire life. "God's death," he marveled, "'tis shut tight as a nun's knees."

"So let us to house," Vachon continued.

"To home," Screed said, but Vachon had flown to the riverbank, where he dipped a hand in the water and washed the last of the blood off his face. He'd simply thrown away his bloodied shirt and jerkin, and taken the pickpocket's clothes—a linen blouse of finer lawn than Vachon had had before, its collar edged a bit with lace, and a sober woolen doublet whose intricate fastenings annoyed its new owner.

• • •

The host of the Anchor and Hope was still awake in his dooryard when Vachon and Screed came through the entrance, but disappeared at once into the stables. "A fine welcome," Screed scoffed, but an instant later, the innkeeper's wife poked her head out of her own kitchen window and looked around.

"Oh, Master Bowsheet," Goodwife Crocker called, trying somehow to screech softly. "Master Bowsheet" was the closest she could come to pronouncing de Bosschaert, the name Screed had picked for his "Dutch merchant" master when they rented their room. It took Vachon a moment, and a helpful jab from Screed's elbow, to remember that this was himself.

"Javier, madam," he said, walking over to the window and essaying a small bow. The lady had opened the mullioned window and was leaning on its sill. She'd taken off her kirtle for the night, so only her thin shift was left for a gown. Screed leered at her openly, and she leaned forward, plumping her charms on the windowsill and deliberately improving his view.

Vachon smiled, his dark eyes luminous with the pleasure of her attention. He brushed his hair back and reached for her hand to kiss it.

The young woman made a face at his gallantry, but also tried to tuck away a wisp of blond hair that had escaped its moorings. Her head bobbed as she dropped a tiny curtsy, and her tone became flirtatious.

"Well, Master Javier, there was a Court gentleman sought ye here not an hour since," she said. "Asked for you particular, though he allegated as he was looking for a Spaniard." She frowned. "Though how a body's to be Spanish being Dutch . . . allroads, my Robin's sure to have gone a-horseback to the constable this minute, for Secretary Dyer, which was his name, did command him to." She cast her eyes upward and recited by rote, " 'Send to me directly upon the hour when the Spaniard do return.' " She sniffed. "Though what I say is tish-tosh and fiddle-faddle. As if I would not know a wicked spying Papist from an honest Dutch merchant!"

Her speech was a bit beyond Vachon, who was thinking about her eyes. How many years had it been since he'd seen anything but eyes as dark brown as his own, or even darker? So many of these English maids had blue eyes, and there were so many different shades of blue—one would have eyes like the last sky before darkness, the next like rivers in sunlight that he remembered from his mortal life. And their golden hair . . . that cast him back even further. There had been a girl, when he was a young man in Spain, with golden hair and a bold heart . . .

Vachon reached out to tug the stray strand of the girl's hair back out from under its net, but Screed forestalled him. Unlike his master, Screed was quick to grasp what the girl was telling them. He plucked at Vachon's sleeve, trying not to betray his agitation, yet nearly dancing with it.

"Give you good thanks for this intelligence," Screed improvised, "for they did say at Court they'd be a-wanting of our spices, did they not, Mynheer de Bosschaert?" He pulled at Vachon's sleeve again.

"*Sí,*" said Vachon unthinkingly. The vampire in him had fixated a bit too intensely on Mistress Crocker's lovely neck, down which that golden tendril curled so alluringly, and he'd had to close his eyes momentarily to regain control.

Screed's agony doubled as the Spanish syllable came out, and the young wife rumpled her brows. "Be that a Dutch word, 'see'?" Mistress Crocker queried.

"Ay, 'tis very Dutch, 'tis in Dutch for 'say,' which is to say, 'Say you that in sooth?' " Screed gabbled, leaning toward their room. Vachon reopened his eyes, grasping that aught was amiss, but not precisely what. " 'Tis not the Spanick tongue, no never, 'tis but the Dutch manner of saying, 'so and in sooth,' and . . . and . . ." But Screed's powers of invention deserted him in that moment and he simply grabbed his master's arm and pulled him away.

"God give you good health, lady," Vachon called back to her as he was dragged off.

"God give *you* English manners and Dutch wits, you whoreson Spanish marplot," Screed snarled at him, perfect fear driving out love. "D'ye not fathom, 'tis the law as seeks us? 'See is the very Dutch for say,' " he mimicked himself in a high, nasal voice. "Pox on't! Sea is where they'll toss our moldy bones if you say '*sí*' but one more time!"

Vachon pulled away from him as they reached their room, and shrugged carelessly. "You mistaken," he said. "They cannot hurt us, but with fire or wood in the heart."

"I mistaken?" Screed's voice ran up an entire octave in one

word. "You *are* mistaken, bully, and *I am not* mistaken, and we both shall be taken if we harbor here one more minuto, you *sobby*? D'ye ken the constable comes for us e'en now, if not someone worse? El prison-o, you know that one? Or the Tower? Topcliffe's toy-house, they calls it, where 'e pulls out the guts of the living and drapes 'em round their necks? Not for old Screed, *gracias* very much, I'm absento starting this very tick o' the tock. You with me?"

Vachon's face was a picture of unconcern. "I tell you, you are mistook altogether," he said. "No Topcliffe is no danger to us, comes he not with fire or wood. But I will go with you, say to where."

"Me say?" Screed paused with a sudden grin, biting back the correction he'd been about to make. This was an unexpected bit of fortune. He paused from frantically stuffing the clothes he'd stolen over the last week into his sack and rubbed his bald head in thought. "What port shall we steer for, eh?"

Inspiration came to him: he had a favorite hunting ground which, now that he bethought him of it, was perfect for them both. "Tell 'ee what, Southwark be our compass, Vachonendez. 'Tis crammed with the squealers we both loves best—rats and lasses, mate, cheer alike for thee and me." With luck, they could even take a room in a brothel, Screed thought—that ought to keep the Spaniard out of mischief, if he could be persuaded to feed away from home.

"There's a lady called Doña Hollandia Britannica 'oo's acquaintance ye're wishin' to make. She'll Dutch yer scuppers proper—but mark me," Screed shook a finger at his master, "never mark 'er." Vachon returned him a solemnly innocent look. Screed went on planning. "We'll make you a Frenchie this time—and godspeed Mynheer de Bosschaert, may he rest in peace."

"Amen," grinned Vachon, with unexpected comprehension.

Nicholas caught the chamber door a scant moment before it slammed shut in his face. "Janette, my love, I beseech you," he said soothingly, going to his lover and placing his hands on her shoulders. "Calm yourself . . . Why should you be so upset?"

"*Ah, oui, bien sûr,*" she retorted, tearing free of him to pace the room like a tigress. "What is there to upset me? What in the world? Only a woman turning to rot for hatred and indifference before my very eyes—what great tragedy is that? Hardly worthy of a dumb show in one of your precious plays—surely no cause for alarm."

"Indeed," LaCroix said dryly, coming in after them.

"The girl's situation is pitiable, certainly," Nicholas interjected, shooting their "father" an angry glance. "To be so ill-used by one for whom she obviously bears great love—"

"Yes, and what will you say in his defense?" Janette cried, turning on him in a fury.

"Nothing, lady, by my troth," he protested.

"Why not so?" she demanded. "You were as quick as any wit in London to make her the pith of your jests some two nights since. Indeed, sir, you did pay her mocking court right well, as I recall."

That was before I knew you had a care for her, beloved, Nick thought but would not say. "I had little thought of her illness," he said instead. "Nor knew I how dearly Hilliard did abuse her."

"And dearly doth she cherish him for it," LaCroix said impatiently, as if the entire subject bored him beyond all bearing. "Really, Janette, why waste your tears on a whore half-dead already?"

Janette's eyes flashed blue fire at this. "Why indeed, LaCroix?" she asked acidly, the pain he could hear behind her fury making Nick flinch and turn away, heartsore and furious on her account. "Of what use is a whore, dead or alive?" LaCroix moved to turn away, but she wouldn't allow it, catching him hard by the sleeve. "Tell me, *mon père,* since you are so wise tonight. Why was I so much more deserving of pity when I danced in that girl's shoes? Why offered you me so much more kindness?"

"You know full well my reasons," LaCroix chided her gently, his voice almost tender as he lifted her clutching fist to his lips. "But your case is well driven, *ma petite* . . ." He let her go with a speculative look. "If fair Isabella is to become our project, why not take her on entire?"

Nicholas's bowed head snapped up at this. "What mean you, LaCroix?"

LaCroix raised an eyebrow. "That if our Janette would see this chit escape her cruelest fate, we should oblige her," the older vampire said. He opened his hands languidly. "Why not bring the girl across?"

The question hung in the air between them for a moment, palpable as the London mist. Janette started to speak first—

"No," Nick said flatly, cutting her off.

"Why not?" she demanded, curious and annoyed in equal measure. How dare he so dismiss her—and why did he so dare?

"Yes, Nicholas," LaCroix said, watching his errant son's face. Would the crux of his malady fester out of this trifle? "Why refuse Isabella the help she so desperately craves?"

"I have no objection to helping Mistress Isabella," Nick said. "But that I will not do—I will not make her a vampire." He turned away from his vampire family, turning in his mind to Alyssa's cold, dead corpse. He had sought to save her from death and brought it down on her instead, cut down in the flower of her youth, innocent affection turned to carrion beneath his kiss. Not again, not even for Janette . . . "Never that."

"She seems a bit uncultured, I admit," LaCroix laughed, though his eyes showed no mirth. "But surely in time we might teach her to behave."

"Nicholas, what is it?" Janette asked, going to him as he had tried to comfort her. "Where are you, my sweet love?" she whispered, curling close to his back.

"Here," Nick promised, turning to her with an attempt at a smile. "With you, *ma chére,* as ever."

She searched his eyes. Was this sudden mask but the melancholia LaCroix decreed they must cure, this wild ache she could almost touch but another symptom of his grief? Or was there something more? She demurred, touching his cheek. "I think not so."

He drew her into his arms, and she allowed it, let him crush her close. "Promise me, Janette," he begged, but his eyes were focused on LaCroix, and their light was anything but pleading. "Promise you will not make this girl as we are."

"If you wish it not, then no," Janette promised softly. "I have no talent for such arts in any case . . . You know I have never yet been able to share this gift."

"Nor I," said Nick simply.

"Ah, *la mortelle* . . . Alyssa," Janette realized. Her head bent: she had attempted to share her immortality once or twice, but it was not in her nature to draw back from the ecstasy of feeding before it was complete—and too late for the mortal. Yet none of her efforts had touched her heart, whereas Nicholas had chosen to attempt this for the very first time with a mortal girl he had loved enough to marry.

And had destroyed her in the attempt. It was Nicholas whom Janette pitied in this story, appalled when she learned of it decades later. One little mortal? It was as LaCroix had said; even her grandchildren would be withered crones by now. Nicholas was the sufferer. For Nicholas was the vampire, the one who would live—the one who had to live. Still, she knew Nicholas believed that the girl Alyssa had been the sad figure in this pathetic little accident.

Nick shook his head, though neither of them knew exactly what he was denying. "Let the mortals take care of their own," he said roughly.

"*Oui, mon coeur,*" Janette said, thinking, *Yes, let them, and you come back out of their world of death.* She drew back and framed his face with her hands, making him face her. "Fear me not, beloved," she said to the ghost haunting his eyes. "We will but stay we three, and care for each other."

"Forever," Nicholas said, still in the strange, rough voice, in the instant before his teeth found her throat.

7

. . . those puppets, I mean, that speak from our mouths, those antics garnished with our colors . . .

Yes, trust them not; for there is an upstart crow, beautified with our feathers . . . with his tiger's heart wrapt in a player's hide . . . and being an absolute Johannes fac totum, is in his own conceit the only Shake-scene in a country.

—Robert Greene,
A Groat's Worth of Wit, Bought With a Million of Repentance (1592)

VACHON COULDN'T CHOOSE BUT SMILE, WATCHING HIS UGLY FLEDGLING muscle his way through the riverfront throng like a bantam rooster pushing through his hens. After a few nights' careful research in all Screed's old familiar haunts, the carouche and his Spanish master had at last pinned down the identity of the "cruelly villain" who had sentenced Dame Screed to the gallows, run him to ground in an alehouse, and trailed him to his domicile across the street from where Vachon now stood. All that was left was the vengeful deed itself—once that was done, Vachon was done with London. "Harbor o'er till I 'ave me justice, and I'll ne'er ask ye more," Screed had said.

The Spaniard settled himself more comfortably against the weathered wooden piling, closing his eyes to let the thick tide of English voices swell and eddy around him. If he stayed so for any time at all, they would not know he was there at all—a vampire trick he had honed to near perfection in the untamed forests of the New World. Five minutes of stillness, and the prey would forget to see him—until a few scant seconds too late. His vampire's ears were catching sounds from inside the house that suggested Screed was in no hurry to end the agonies of the magistrate who'd set his mum "a-dancin' on the air."

"A doctor?" a woman's voice laughed, slipping by Vachon's perceptions like a single silver trout in a pond full of dull brown mud. He sniffed the tang of fever sweat as she passed, a dusting of lavender. He opened his eyes just in time to see a slight figure in white linen and black brocade fade into the press along the quay. Trailing in her wake was a boy in robin's egg blue—a peacock enamored of a wren. The vampire barely glanced in the direction his sworn companion had gone—the opposite direction—before heading off in stealthy pursuit.

"Think you to cure me of love, fairest Tommy?" the girl was laughing on.

"Nay, Izzy; that cause be lost," the boy in blue replied as he shifted the bundle in his arms to a more comfortable position. "But th' effect might well be trod out, particularly now . . ." A blush rose in his maiden-milky cheek as he let the suggestion die in the chill night air.

The girl stopped and turned to face him, showing her predator bright blue eyes and a pert little chin beneath the swaddling of her white linen kerchief. "Now that the worm's begetter hath moved on to fairer blooms," she finished for him, making him blush the brighter. "Nay, Thomas," she sighed, moving on. "Such cancers know no such physic—absence is no cure for me."

The boy reached and caught her arm, stopping her and turning her back to face him. "Izzy—Isabella," he stammered, "I beg of you—" but then choked on his own words.

The girl shook her head again. "Give over, sweet Tom, there's nothing for't."

"There is," he said fervently, startling both the girl and the watching vampire by dropping to his knees on the street's greasy cobbles. "Be my wife, Isabella. Be my care, my keeper and kept one, my heart, my dove . . ."

Isabella laughed out loud before she could stop herself. The boy swayed as if struck, but then straightened his back again, proud and honest on his knees.

"Oh, Thomas," Isabella said sadly. "What a beautiful scene thou play'st me, but truly thou must needs play the maid, not the man. There's so little dove in me as God alone could find, if even He. And thou," she reached down and caressed his barely stubbled boy's cheek, "thou must have a true maid, a girl who will bring a true dove-white heart to thy altar."

"I am of age," the boy said stubbornly, and it was true: at fifteen, the law of England regarded him as a man grown and legally able to wed.

"Then I am of too great age," Isabella responded. "I beg you, Tom, be my true friend, and seek not to be husband of a false wife. You know me well; what else should I be?" Still unnoticed by both mortals, Vachon was beginning to grasp the gist of this strange conversation, and now his eyebrows rose. What else indeed? London was proving to be stuffed with interesting girls.

"You would not so use me," the boy said steadily. "I know it, lady, e'en if you do not. You would love me all honestly."

Isabella found the image of herself that was shining out of his eyes all but unbearable. "Get up, Tom," she said, almost harshly. "The curtain's rising on a different scene." Then her voice grew sweet again: "Gentle Tom, forbear your arts. Be Izzy's friend again. Rise, sir Tom, and walk with me a bit further." She turned and moved up the street again, walking slowly.

The boy's bravado lasted only a moment longer; he jumped up, slapping at the ruined knees of his hose, crusted over now with all the street refuse he'd kneeled in. He made a face, snatched up his bundle, and ran after Isabella.

Vachon followed as they turned off the main thoroughfare, trailing at a discreet but convenient distance through the darkly shadowed lanes until they stopped at a narrow doorway lit by a single flickering torch. The boy made bold to go inside, but his lady wouldn't hear of it, relieving him of his burden and sending him on his way.

Vachon crept closer to peer in through the shop's dusty window, the girl and her goods reduced to circles of fish-eyed glass but still caught in his watchful gaze. A stooped figure was opening her bundle, riffling through the contents—silks and satins, jewels and laces, even cunning little gold-encrusted slippers. Vachon could feel the pawnbroker's excitement even through the glass, so lively was his greedy little heart, but his expression was solemn as an empty grave. He said something to the girl, his eyes bright with expectation, spoiling for battle.

But the girl simply nodded, turning away.

The pawnbroker seemed shocked, and perhaps even disappointed, but only for a moment—he recovered himself with admirable speed, sweeping the entire lot up in his crooked arms and spiriting it out of sight through a curtain at his back. He returned in a moment with a tattered leather purse which he held out to the girl. She glanced inside, then turned and left without another word.

She didn't see Vachon as she came out, didn't even glance his way. He watched, fascinated, as she moved drunkenly down the street, weaving along the gutter's stony edge as if all her strength and reason had been pawned with her jewels. He could even smell her sickness more clearly now, fever boiling her blood, making her all the more tempting a morsel to the vampire closing in behind her. A beauty with a freshly filled purse . . .

Suddenly she stopped, lurching toward a nearby post with a muffled shriek, clinging to it as if for dear life. She pressed a hand to her stomach where the bodice of her gown made a deep V into her skirt, her breath coming in painful gasps. "Nay," Vachon heard her snarl in fury. "Not here—I will not die alone—"

"Not alone," said Vachon.

She whirled around, nearly losing her balance, catching the post just in time to keep from landing on her knees at his feet. "Where did you come from?" she demanded angrily. "I heard no one—"

"No," he interrupted, taking a silent step closer. "You do not hear me."

She stopped, rage seeming to melt into fascination on her palely pretty face, her sick-bright eyes losing focus. "No," she repeated, almost smiling. Her expression made Vachon wonder if his English had gone astray again. "I would not have heard you."

He reached for her kerchief, and she made no move to protest or shy away. "*Que bonita,*" he murmured, tugging it from her head to release a cascade of curls as black as his vampire angel's—a little mortal sister to his idol.

"What are you, I should have said," Isabella said, gazing up at those ebony eyes, her pain all but forgotten. "Nay, tell me not . . . I ought by all rights to have known you."

"Why think you so?" Vachon asked, genuinely curious. Were all English women mad?

"You mean to set me free, do you not?" she asked, the rightness of the vision making her feel something like joy. "Good Queen Bess would have us know the Devil for a Spaniard—perhaps her crown hath given her sight beyond our earth."

"You think I am the Devil?" Vachon's voice crackled with amusement, but his face belied his innocent tone with a vampire's green fire eyes.

She gasped, but happily—a child's delight wrapped in a madwoman's smile. "My devil, *señor*," she told him, going to him. "One of wild Kit's demons has come for me at last." She closed her eyes and opened her arms, the pliable mistress of this welcome Death.

But Death found himself not so willing. "No," Vachon said, taking a step back, hunger cursing him for a fool. Why not take what she offered? What honor should he lose to oblige her?

Isabella opened her eyes and stared at him, aghast. "No?" she repeated, incredulous.

The Spaniard looked away, suddenly unwilling to meet those eyes, mortal or not. "I cannot," he explained with a shrug.

Where was the glow she had seen before, the emerald fire in his eyes? Had she only imagined it? Now he looked as young and silly as Thomas. "Surely you jest," she protested.

"No, I do not," he assured her, the accent that had seemed so enticing a moment before now setting her teeth on edge. "You forgive me, lady—"

"For not killing me in the street?" she retorted, the pain taking charge of her again, lessened perhaps, but hardly banished. So much for the devil's magic. "Yea, sirrah, I shall certainly try," she said, turning away.

"Wait!" Vachon ordered, cutting her off with vampire speed, making her gasp again. "Where is your home, *mi linda*?" he asked, giving her back her white kerchief. "To whom do you belong?"

Isabella laughed—was this not her most dear-loved query? "*A nadie, señor,*" she answered him, in his own language, walking off into the darkness. "Nobody at all."

Vachon watched until the scrap of white in her hand disappeared from his vampire sight. "*Las damas,*" he murmured. He shook his head slightly and turned back the way he'd come. "Women."

He reached the house just as Screed was stumbling back across the street, wiping his mouth, tongue and all. His clothing was liberally decorated with blood. Vachon smiled at the sight; only on Screed could gore seem comical. "There ye are," his fledgling grumbled. "I'll tell ye true, Har-vee-toe, Oi dunno how it is ye stomach the taste of yer two-feeted rats. Give me a squeaker all betimes, an' I'll live an 'appy sod."

"Happy," Vachon echoed, grasping that much of Screed's speech. "Then all's well," he replied, clapping Screed briefly on the shoulder. "Now, come—I am for Spain."

"What holds him?" Janette grated. She'd been tempersome since their arrival at this misbegotten alehouse.

"He brings the passports presently," LaCroix said. "Patience."

He knew Janette's restlessness had less to do with Aristotle's tardiness than with the fact that the landlord had winked at him, one man to another, when he'd commanded a private room. LaCroix had merely smiled at the wink, but Janette had drawn herself up in her most imperious great-lady posture and glared. Mine host had blanched and scuttled away, but Janette was still angry. LaCroix smiled. *Well, we know where my lady Janette sups tonight; where shall I?*

Besides, they were leaving for Paris on the next tide if all went well. Aristotle's providence would give them Court papers for travel, which would ensure a wonderful servility as they traveled. With a Queen's patent backing their voyage, they would find any whim of theirs served without question—a handy accommodation for vampires.

So Janette was also fretful because they could not set sail soon enough for her. She would have, as it were, one last taste of England and then on to Paris, her beautiful, soothing Paris.

LaCroix liked Paris, but he also liked Rome, Vienna, Avignon, Wittenberg, Constantinople . . . He'd even begun to like London, and was considering accepting Aristotle's invitation of taking a trip up to the university towns of Oxford and Cambridge and imbibing the scholarship there.

Through the thin walls of their private room, Janette and LaCroix heard a group of voices they recognized, coming in and settling at a table.

"Nicholas's players, are they not?" Janette said, with little actual interest. "I thought he was with them tonight, no?"

"No," said LaCroix. "Only with his Will, the one he most favors. No doubt they two are somewhere bidding each other a tearful farewell."

"*Très bien,* let him weep, so long as 'fare thee well' is said," snapped Janette. "And right speedily—when does the tide rise?"

LaCroix smiled: for his Janette, the world was Paris and Everywhere Else.

They both sensed a vampire's approach; a moment later Aristotle bustled into the room, frowning and rushed.

"Where's Nicholas?" he said first.

"Give you good evening," LaCroix said. He saw no reason to inform Aristotle of his son's whereabouts. "How do you fare?" The use of commonplace courtesies would communicate that quite adequately.

"No more than middling fair," said Aristotle. "I cry pardon for holding you in wait here so long. An undersheriff came—"

"An undersheriff," said Janette in her best bored voice. "*Quel horreur.*" It was useful that Aristotle mixed in mortal affairs, but did they have to hear about it? An undersheriff—what was that? And in truth, who cared?

"Perhaps you may aid with the undersheriff's cause, lady," Aristotle said through gritted teeth. "He led us to the chilly corpse of a magistrate, who lay dead and bloodless in his house with only a pair of likewise bloodless rats to serve for his clerks. There was no discretion in this kill, madam: the man's blood was on his walls, his chairs, his linens, his floor, in sum, madam, everywhere. The time has come for you to yield up your Spanish swain, Mistress Janette; he threats us all."

Janette bridled; every tendon in her throat stood out as she drew breath to blast Aristotle.

LaCroix spoke first. "I thought that question settled," he said gently. He raised a finger to scratch momentarily behind his ear, the picture of mild disinterest.

"'Tis not." Aristotle almost never used few words when many would do. LaCroix ceased his scratching and raised his eyebrows minutely, questioning his daughter.

"Bah!" broke out of Janette. First the pig landlord, and now this. "I will see you at the ship," she said coldly to LaCroix and left the room.

Aristotle looked after her, weighing the merits of picking a fight with LaCroix over one of his fledglings. Well, they were leaving London; maybe she would take the stupid vampire with her. "Here, Lucius, are passports for the three of you. You have also letters of passage under the names we agreed, with a Privy Council seal upon them; if anyone thinks anything, 'twill be only that you are spies."

LaCroix smiled. "Only that."

The courtier vampire slid his fingers lightly over the wax of one of his forged seals. "The hand that made this," he tapped the seal gently with one finger, "helped take off the head of an anointed queen not so long ago." LaCroix tilted his head. "She of Scots, do you recall? The letter that sealed her fate was forged, her words false—and her seal remade by this knave."

"Artist, rather," LaCroix corrected him with delicate humor. "Such gifts as killing queens must be fairly honored."

Aristotle leaned back in his chair with his hands linked behind his head, and sighed lustily. "These *are* good years, Lucius, are they not? We may travel abroad in their carriages, go voyaging in their ships, and make them thank us for it." He tilted his chair back against the wall and grinned.

A companionable silence fell. Janette had left the door open as she left; now the players' conversation drifted through.

"There is talk of a lost city built of gold bricks, that lies on an island in a lake at the top of a mountain," Tom Pope was saying. "Theodor de Bry pictures the emperor thereof being powdered with gold dust each morning."

"There is talk of another pitcher of wine, which is a deal more to the purpose," muttered Burbage.

"'Twas called 'El Dorado,' by the Spaniards," said Condell. He was older by a decade than many of the players, a solid citizen among flighty young men. Most players lodged in Southwark, near the theaters where they worked, and also near the stews, bear baiting, and inns where they took their leisure. Condell, though, lived comfortably with his wife and ever-increasing brood in the highly respectable parish of St. Mary Aldermanbury. He kept the company's books, was kind and moderate of temper, and was loved by them all. Since he rarely took time away from his family to join them in a tavern, they harkened to him.

"Methinks the city of gold was never more than a Spanish lie," Condell opined.

"Which minds me, Lucius," Aristotle said quietly. "This reckless vampire I seek is perhaps a sailor, and likely Spanish. He is described to me as black in hair and eye." He smiled wickedly. "And heart, though I'm not like to hold that against him. This, I think, is the one that met with Mistress Janette."

LaCroix gave Aristotle a cold look. Aristotle wrinkled his brow but did not retreat. "They did meet, Lucius," he said, softening the blow with an almost apologetic tone. "You may like ill of it, but 'tis so."

He was struck by a thought. "Can it be there are two? That this Spaniard sailed to the Indies and the ratting one is some pet he gathered and brought from the New World? There have been few carouche in Europe for many, many years." Carouches were usually accidents; the vampires of the Old World had learned from many fiery lessons that their stupider, animal-feeding brethren were dangerous to harbor or create. "Yet there is talk of an uncouth servant . . ." His voice trailed off.

LaCroix shrugged fractionally. "The Iberians were always messy killers. As for the rats," he remarked, "perhaps it is two mad Spaniards; I doubt mingling with the savages of the New World hath rendered them nicer in their tastes."

Aristotle made no answer, but sat scratching his beard and thinking.

Out in the main room, Condell was wrapping up the conversation about El Dorado. He had a way of speaking ponderously, as if he expected his thoughts to be the last word on any subject. "In sooth, methinks the tale of this golden city was a scurvy trick o' theirs to get our honest sailors to wreck their ships where their Armada was not able. For look you, Raleigh hath broken both his spirit and fortune in pursuit of it." Condell sighed. "A poor expense of either, by a very great captain."

"Well, he lodged on the Queen's generosity long enow," Sly said caustically. "Though I hear the rents on yon Tower are nearly so bad as goldsmith Langely charges in Southwark."

"Perhaps he did turn the Tower's iron bars to gold to pay," said Saddler, "for I have heard the School of Night went to visit." Raleigh was famous for his interest in the science of chemistry, conducted with friends at night in his private rooms. The little group called itself the School of Night and sought, among other things, the lost knowledge of transmuting base metals to gold. Even in prison, Raleigh had pursued his experiments.

"'Tis meet his rent was dearer than yours," said Ben Jonson, smiling. "Her Majesty's lodgings are better, as housing a selecter breed of rat."

"Ay, and his wife was allowed to him," said Sly.

"Ah, but for that, they must lower the rent," Ben laughed. "It merits a pretty premium to keep a wife at bay."

"Raleigh should not have sailed so far across Indies waters," Condell said. "'Twas unpolitic. Better he had sailed waters closer to home and taken Spanish prizes."

"Piracy? Nay, 'tis the Queen should have sailed her Water close to home," said Jonson, invoking the Queen's pet name for Sir Walter, "and used the water consequent to that voyage to get us what we would most dearly prize, which is one little boy only."

"Why, Ben," Pope said blandly, "are you of Kit Marlowe's stripe after all? 'Tis a chary cat you are."

"Sublime Walter's water to get a boy upon a virgin queen? There's an alchemy the School of Night could master," Sly said wickedly.

Jonson squirmed a little. "You know what I mean. May she live forever, but since she will not, could she not lower herself but once, to but one man, and give us a lusty bawling boy? And now she will not stoop to give us a grown man."

Pope had touched one finger to the side of his nose. "*Soît sage, mon ami,*" he muttered. "Be quiet, lest you be quieted." The Queen had ears everywhere.

Jonson would not be halted. "Name the King of Scots for heir, is all I mean," he growled. "God's death, Your Holiness, they say she takes a spear from the guards and pokes into the arras of her bedchamber."

"'Tis true," murmured Aristotle. "The Queen's mind weakens. A great and dread sovereign she hath been, but e'en she must fail."

"You like her," LaCroix said.

"I like good princes; order serves us well."

"You like her," LaCroix said more positively. "Will you—"

"Nay, never." Aristotle sighed. "She must rule kingdoms; we must be secrets. 'Twould be a rare disaster to introduce Eliza to our night."

At the table, Condell wanted the conversation to change course. "That lady knows well how to feign sick to bring a commonweal to health. She hath cozened the Spanish king with counterfeit illness many times before now."

"She is not feigning barren," argued Ben.

"Soft, Ben," said Pope, laying a hand on his arm. "Anyone may listen."

"And anyone may hear!" Jonson shook the hand off. "Burleigh's dead, Essex is a self-loving fool, Cecil's another, and we are like to become another famous island sunk under the waters with legends told over our graves."

Condell tried turning the conversation again. "They say there is such a wealth as that under the waters closer to home, where old Atlantis stood." This was a shrewd tactic: Ben Jonson could not be chaffed out of a temper, but almost any mention of something Greek or Roman would distract him.

"Oh, Atlantis," agreed Burbage, raising his cup to the name. He knew Will Shakespeare bore Ben great affection, but Burbage found him very irritating. "Me old auntie's from there. And me uncle's from Hy-Brasil."

"There's a tale in Italy of a town in Roman times that was burnt all to ash by a flaming mountain, and drowned under rivers of fire," Jonson said. Condell's strategem had worked. "They say 'twas founded by Heracles in ancient days."

"Your walls of gold standeth not well up to your rivers of fire," Burbage remarked. "'Tis quite a runny mess they become, like your crack'd eggs—or crack'd brains, of which we have several examples at this very board."

The players laughed. "Are you not curious, Dick?" Jonson was nettled. "Does Antiquity hold no philter for your love? Or are you incurious as one of your painted planks?" Burbage had been trained as a joiner as well as a player, was still happy to turn his hand occasionally to assembling and painting stage properties, and was no worshipper of books. Jonson, toiling through his bricklayer's apprenticeship, had been famous for the books, preferably in Latin or Greek, that were always poking out of the pockets of his jackets. Young as he was, and without a university degree, scholars were beginning to acknowledge Jonson's learning. "What of Seneca, Plautus, Horace, Ovid, Tully?"

Burbage belched, simply to annoy Jonson. "Why, are they good, obliging wenches?" He rubbed a hand over his face. "Sooth, Ben, the fancies you describe are good tales to hear, but naught to us here in England. Raleigh's golden city might as well be in Cloud Cuckoo Land, and, on my honor, honest Ben, a commodious wench is river of fire enough for this Dick."

There was a groaning laugh. "Philistines, each and every," Jonson muttered.

"You were born too late, Ben," said the easygoing Condell. "The audience for your classical trigs has lain underwater on Atlantis since the world was young."

"Aye, under water, as that one must needs have water upon the brain to reck of it," said Burbage, finishing his cup of wine. "Look you," he said seriously, "player and householder at the Globe, I've little enough care for your antique unities in a play. 'Tis present pennies that allure me. And another pot of *wine, please you, mistress*!" Raised, his voice carried through every wall in the building.

"I've business elsewhere," Jonson snapped. He threw a couple silver coins on the board and stalked out of the tavern.

"Why, Ben," said Burbage sweetly to the closing door, "was it aught I said?"

"O never rare enough Ben Jonson," agreed Sly.

"Drowned in a river of fire," LaCroix echoed softly. The vampires had been silent as they eavesdropped, LaCroix occupying himself with picking the odd bit of fluff off his elegant black doublet. "'Twas mine ancient abode, and now it is babble for drunken jugglers."

Aristotle looked at him curiously. Of all the vampires he had ever known, Lucius was best able, or so he thought, to adapt to each successive era of mortal society. "You pronounce it like a man who misses his own country," he said.

"I?" LaCroix pursed his lips. "No, my friend, that failing I bequeath to thee. If there is a time or place I yearn for, it is what has not yet been, and where I am yet to travel. What a quest it is; their puny voyages across oceans are nothing to the journey you and I are on." He shook his head minutely. "They think they sail the world, but we sail time. 'Tis folly for us to look anywhere but forward."

Aristotle scratched one side of his nose. "A plausible speech, yet you have not spoke your mind entire, Lucius," he said quietly. "'Tis in your eyes that some splinter of the past yet festers in you."

LaCroix looked askance at this uninvited perception, but won no retraction from his old friend. He leaned back against the wall and folded his arms, letting his eyes wander the little room's unadorned walls. Aristotle waited.

"I do remember a house," he conceded. "One I owned, though I slept most nights at . . . elsewhere." Aristotle raised his eyebrows, but was denied. "That house I owned was set high in the fields, among vineyards—a pretty place, with a cooling breeze even in the worst of summer. What I recall most of it is one painted chamber wall, a scene of gods sporting."

He stared across the table, not really seeing his friend anymore. "Returned from war, bloodied with the gore of some Gallic rabble, I did lie oft on my couch, drink new wine, and look at those unaging gods." His eyes roamed the walls. "But not with envy. Even then, methought my life greater than theirs; I despised their bootless frolic. And yet I remember the afternoons of lying on that couch, looking at that painted wall . . ." He smiled again, and met Aristotle's eyes. "Perhaps it mindeth me that even the least hour of my life now is greater than the greatest hour of that old life."

"A pleasant conceit," his friend agreed.

"And you?" Lucius prompted. "'Tis only just that you requite my remembrance with one of your own. What images harbor in your memory hoard, Aristotle? Can you tell me of the gold and crystal towers of Atlantis? Of Ilium? Were they the same city?"

Aristotle laughed. "Marry, I must needs find a scholar to tell you someday," he said cheerfully. There was to be no new fact for Lucius's slender trove of information this night. Then he repented. "In my time I heard men say there was once an island called Thera," he said. "They did say it exploded itself from off the sea." LaCroix was skeptical.

Aristotle laughed again; his humorous way of dealing with things meant that even his serious answers were doomed to go doubted. "Sooth, I swear you, Lucius, I am not as old as Ilium. Even in my youth, 'twas said the place is but legend."

"And now pretty Pompeii is a tale in the mouths of drunken Angles," LaCroix finished. "Perhaps any buried thing is destined to become a rumor."

"Just so," Aristotle agreed. His humor bubbled up again. "Think you that we shall live to see these men, once buried," he waved at the outer room, where the players were falling asleep over their wine, "be talked of as doubtful legends?"

LaCroix's eyes flicked to the open door. His mouth twitched. "Unlikely."

"Still, I do yet hope to meet a Trojan vampire." Aristotle's face took on a thoughtful cast. "I would hear of this Helen whose face launched a thousand ships. What might her body have launched, I ask you?" He waggled his eyebrows in lascivious suggestion.

LaCroix snorted. "You are worser far than they."

Aristotle smiled ferally. "Aye, far, far worse," he agreed in sudden, perfect seriousness. His warm brown eyes flushed to a hungry yellow. "I shall miss you dearly, Lucius. Before the tide turns, shall we have a hunt?"

Nick left his last errand until late, careful to sate his hunger first. It would not do to have this meeting made difficult by the pressures of hunger as well as those of sadness.

Evenings after a play, it was easy to find Will Shakespeare. It was a safe bet he would be at one of the three taverns on Southwark High Street, sitting at a table just to the side of the hanging wagon wheel that was a tavern's usual chandelier. Will would find himself a bit more than one man's space at a common table, and settle in with a tankard of small beer, a pot of ink, an individual candle, a penknife, and a few quills—all clustered a few inches from his right hand. He was a neat man, and even the sheets of paper he covered with his crabbed, spidery hand contrived to be set into a single tidy stack.

This night he was in the taproom of the White Hart, scribbling away, sitting alone at his work, though Nicholas sighted Ben Jonson with Philip Henslowe again, in company with Ned Alleyn, Henslowe's partner and son-in-law, and the greatest actor in the company at the Rose. Henslowe was considered a bit of an odd fish in the players' world, forever invoking Jesus yet invariably conducting his business in a tavern, if not a brothel. Still, few words were heard against him, since the religious side of him was greatly prompted to such acts of holy charity as paying the bail for drunken or bankrupt actors who happened to find themselves involuntary guests of Her Majesty. The three men looked to be finishing up both their business and their beer.

Nick walked over to where Shakespeare sat and looked over his shoulder at the foolscap he was filling with the new play.

"'Tis true you never repent a line, then?" Nick said, craning his head at the pages of evenly written dialogue that had already been completed, and finding no scratch-outs. Shakespeare was famous for never blotting a word as he wrote; his actors said his first drafts could serve for fair copies.

"Good e'en, Nicholas," smiled Will, looking up. "'Tis not the lines—a sheet of paper's dearer than a bread loaf. I'd repent me the shillings." His smile widened. "Or if I did not, my fellow shareholders would repent them for me."

"So that's true too? You own the Globe?" Nick sat down across from him.

Shakespeare chuckled. "An eighth of it, howbeit. Cathay to O-tahiti, let us say. Or the empire of Muscovy."

"There's times I've wished you in Cathay," Henslowe said, walking up and clapping a hand on Will's shoulder, Alleyn and Jonson in his wake. He peered at the written pages. "What damage to my purse do you purpose tonight?" He looked at Nicholas and winked. "Every word this fellow pens is tuppence I never see, and when he indites a Romeo or a Caesar, 'tis shillings and golden angels."

"A rose by any other name would sell as sweet," Will said calmly.

The others laughed out loud. "'Tis true, the Rose is no great loser of pennies," Henslowe admitted.

He looked over at Nicholas again. "Know you the origin of Master William's little joke?" Nick shook his head. Henslowe smiled. "'Twas our drain he meant. Of a steamy August afternoon the Rose's little ditch can be quite fragrancy—and here's Will serving up his maiden Juliet cooing to the moon how sweet a rose must always be."

Now Nick laughed too. To a vampire's acute senses all of London was pungent, but it was true that the Bankside district had a special reek all its own.

"I doubt not the laugh was heard across the river." Henslowe's voice took on a sour note. He shook a finger at Shakespeare. "Do not bankrupt me, Will; it would leave you all a-lonesome. What's this one to be, eh?"

Shakespeare knew he was being baited; Henslowe was notorious for getting the competition's scripts. He smiled thinly. "A play."

Jonson broke the tension, roaring as if shocked. "God's help, a play!"

"Why, what manner of play, sweet Will?" Henslowe said in a loud, stagy voice. The other patrons turned around on their benches and stools to watch, recognizing the actors and writers. "A comedy? Tragedy? History? A historo-tragical, like your sad Caesar? Comico-tragical-Senecal-Ovidian, as Ben oft charges that you write?"

Shakespeare went along with it, stroking his beard and pursing his lips as if pondering deeply. "It is a play," he affirmed, then twinkled. "It hath in it a father who has a son."

"A father who hath a son!" bellowed Jonson to the whole room. "The heavens do ope'!" The tavern patrons, recognizing their cue, cheered lustily.

Now it was Will's turn to grin. "And a ghost," he added.

"A ghost?" said Jonson. "O ghost who walks!" he howled, evoking gasps and screams of fake fear from the rollicking audience.

Shakespeare rolled his own eyes in mock terror and sprang to his feet, shouting: "Yea, 'tis the madding shade of one Benjamin Hieronymo-son, who doth tramp the stews and bawdy houses, crying, 'Bring me the hollow pampered jades of Asia!' "

Alleyn jumped in, capping Shakespeare's pun with one of his own: "Outside the which William the Conquerer most piteously begs, 'A jade! A jade! My kingdom for a jade!' "

"Oh, take me!" cried one of the serving girls, getting into the spirit of the thing by laying herself down on the table. "I'll be thy jade!"

"Nay, me!" cried another.

Ned Alleyn, the great master of entrances and exits, floated out of the White Hart on the tide of laughter that greeted these sallies. Jonson and Henslowe paused a moment to say good night, and followed.

Nick also rose, pulling out the sheaf of sonnets, meaning to hand them back and say farewell.

Will forestalled him. "Come sit, I'll not drive you off."

"If you're writing . . . ," Nick said.

Will smiled, tapping at his high forehead. "'Twill not disappear from this old globe if I pause a bit." His smile turned sly. "Nor even if Master Henslowe jokes me for hours. It will out."

Nick sat down, suddenly feeling a great constraint. There was so much he wished he could say, if only it were possible to speak directly to the man in the poems. His apparent companion, the always good-humored and friendly Will, was not that man. This Will was a surface—like his own surface, the golden-haired knight who changed names and countries so easily. His eyes dropped to the sheaf of manuscripts he held in his hands.

The candle sputtered and hissed. Nick sat silently, trying to find the words for what he felt.

"Ned Alleyn did regard you odd," Will ventured.

"I was there at Dulwich," Nick answered, relieved to have a topic of conversation. He knew his friend would understand the reference.

Will laughed. "The night of the devils? 'Sblood, 'tis rich."

Nick grinned. "I was a hired devil, mind you, earning my shilling. But perhaps Alleyn's fancy remembers me as the uninvited one."

"Did'st see the extra fiend?"

There was genuine curiosity in Will's voice. Shakespeare's even temperament did not lend itself to the enthusiastic interest in alchemy, apothecary-mixing, or even arcane speech that many of his players shared, although he was as willing as the next writer to give audiences ghosts, devils, fairies, necromancers, and witches for their pleasurable affrighting. Such stuff was grist for his writer's mill, and he soaked up knowledge of it as he did of the law, of medicine, country courtship, superstition, sea lore, and anything else that crossed his path. Writing plays, he used it all—but believed none of it.

Ned Alleyn, on the other hand, was a credulous man, like many among the player companies. Players, so dependent on the mysteriously unpredictable whims of audiences, were great believers in luck, both good and ill, drawn to signs and portents and ever willing to credit things unseen, or seen only by the baneful light of a bad moon. And Kit Marlowe—even seven years after his death, Christopher Marlowe remained a figure of whispered rumors: atheism, alchemy, buggery, counterfeit coining, treason. Since its premiere, there had been tales that extra devils could sometimes be counted onstage during Marlowe's *Dr. Faustus.*

Nick had once been present when the story came true.

He nodded, his face lighting up with mirth, for reasons he could not share—not entirely, anyway—with Will. "Not I, though certes I saw his effect. 'Twas all one murk of yellow smoke and sulfur stink downstage, the which made mine eyes weep with stinging," Nick recalled, "so I saw naught." In fact, he'd actually been turning his back, wiping away the incriminating red tears before someone could see, at the moment when LaCroix appeared, fanged, demon-eyed, and hissing, swirling out of the stage smoke just inches upstage from poor Ned Alleyn, all tricked out in inked-on wrinkles and white horsehair beard as the wicked Faust.

"All of an instant," he smiled, "Alleyn went white under his flour, the groundlings shouted, and then," Nick waved a hand in the air jauntily, "*Exeunt omnes.*"

Nick's smile became a wide, boyish grin. The simple stage direction, "Everyone exits," wildly understated the rioting run for the Guildhall door when the audience had set up its screech of "Fiend! Fiend!"

"Mind you," Nick added, "Ned Alleyn swore to't later, and I did believe him to be in earnest."

Of course, by the time Nick caught up with the horrified actor in a tavern, he knew, much better than Alleyn ever would, what devil had haunted that night's performance of Marlowe's scandalous play. For, minutes after the panicked race for the doors, when Nick was left in sole possession of the stage, LaCroix had shown himself again, looking considerably more like a cheerful cat than a fiend. "A most excellent diversion, this playacting, Nicholas," his master had commented. "Indeed I do perceive the charm it hath for you. I must take a role more often."

It was blackmail, of course, and, also of course, it worked. The thought of LaCroix terrifying audiences all over England with unscheduled visitations by fiends in such gory current plays as *Tamburlaine, Titus Andronicus,* and *The Spanish Tragedy* had been enough to get the elder vampire what he really wanted, which was Nick's leaving England in his company. At the time, it had made him angry, but now, seven years later and on the boards again himself, Nick found it amusing.

"More than swore," Will chuckled. "Alleyn wears a cross now whenever he assays the blasphemous doctor and has pledged to found a college with his sinful playerish gains." Will chuckled again; the sinfulness of the theater was a favorite sermon of the rising Puritan preachers, who blamed plays and players for everything from rain to plague. "Ned says he will call it God's Gift College, i' thanks for his life."

"Do you believe in devils, Will?" The thought of LaCroix gnawed a bit at Nicholas.

"Certes," Will said promptly. "I believe they prance about the stage and bring me many pennies." He sighed. "More largely, I could believe 'twas a devil that brought me a wife."

"But you do not fear for your soul?" Nick joked.

"Not upon the boards, Master Nicholas," Will said easily. "Elsewhere, I cannot avouch, but needs must hope God's grace will shift for me later," his eyes twinkled, "whilst I shift me a shift or two now."

"Ah!—wherein the matter cometh to the Dark Lady in these poems," Nicholas said, mock formally. "Come, Will, say who she is." But in the next second he raised his hand, saying, "Stay. That is not what I wish to talk of." Again Nick fell silent, searching for a way to express what he felt—how powerfully he'd been affected by what he'd read.

"These poems will carry your name into eternity," Nick said, cursing himself for the inadequacy of his words.

Will smiled courteously. "You say too much. Into next week, mayhap," he said.

"Nay, don't turn me aside with a jest," Nicholas insisted. "There is great matter in these songs. There is a man's soul."

Will met his eyes patiently. "These loves hurt you," Nick said simply. "When I heard these poems called 'sugar'd sonnets,' I expected quite other than this."

Will's eyebrows flickered, but his expression was neutral. "What words I knew for what I felt, I used."

"'Th' expense of spirit in a waste of shame,'" Nick quoted.

"Seed spilled upon the ground, Master Nicholas," Will said softly.

Nick leaned forward across the table. All trace of boyishness was gone from his face. His hands opened, almost imploringly.

"I know this lust," he said. "I know the fire i' the blood, and how it is quenched and then burns upon its very quenching. I *know* the bitter disgust of it."

Will swallowed, folded his hands together, and dropped his eyes, seeming to study his fingers.

Nick knew he was forcing confidences on a man who kept his own counsel—and yet—the voice in the sonnets, the man who suffered that pain, *that* man had to be able to understand. That mind, that heart, could encompass the hunger that owned Nick's soul, the hunger that sent him into the darkest streets every night; the hunger that even in its feeding seemed to starve him, to give him equal measure of joy and torment but most of all to give him an ever-renewed need. Even LaCroix and Janette seemed not to comprehend, but the man with the mild face sitting across from him had burned it onto the written page.

"Don't deny me, Will," Nick said from pure need. "Let me tell you this. I have felt those things. I know these words are not ornaments or foibles but plain speech."

Will sat silently for a long moment. When at last he spoke, his voice was even, yet charged with intensity. "You mention eternity, Nicholas? I would scant it for twoscore years of a boy's time. My eternity is in the ground."

"Your son," Nicholas said simply. Alone of the Lord Chamberlain's Men, Will Shakespeare did not keep his family with him in London. Instead, they had always continued to live in his native town of Stratford: Anne, the wife who was his elder by eight years, two daughters, and one son. And then the son, Hamnet, had died.

Will nodded. "Near three years since. Buried the eleventh day of August—St. Sulpicius's day, *anno* 1596, and I away playing somewhere in Kent, unfound by a letter." His eyes wandered to the candle flame. "My father knew the boy best. One could pity him the loss almost more sharply than mine own."

"'Tis no easy thing to be a father," Nicholas said. He was barely able to attend to the conversation, though; his mind had ripped loose and gone back to a stone manor in Brabant, to cold rooms, to a mortal father he scarce remembered. Four hundred years ago, he had been a boy like any other, making noise and trouble, stealing fresh hot bread from the cooks, getting his tunic dirty—defying his father. Who could have told that boy that he would never die—but also never live to have a son of his own? He had last visited that place with the immortal father he could not acknowledge—the father he could never lose.

Will smiled a little. "'No, nor no easy thing to be a son."

"Sooth!" It came out more sharply than Nick intended.

Will's smiled widened. "I hear a tale behind that oath," he ventured. "Shall we have it?" He stretched and eased his posture, palpably putting the thought of his lost son away. "And shall we have more ale with it?"

Nicholas returned the smile. This small, balding man who was so apt with listening silences, who could sit at table between hotheaded Burbage and quarrelsome Ben and keep both mild in his presence—such listening was a gift. And beneath that listening, somewhere, had to be the heart that had written those tortured poems. The temptation to meet the excellence of his listening with the plainest of trust was almost overwhelming. But then what?

"You have seen my father," Nick said carefully. "He came among us at the Boar's Head some time gone."

Will's eyebrows rose. "Your father? I had not known him for such." His lips pursed. "You have little look of each other."

Nick laughed. "Fairly said. Indeed, we have no look of each other, but who would make sport upon it?"

"Not I," Will agreed.

Nick grinned, reading his mind. "No, not baseborn." His friend had the grace to look a bit embarrassed. "My parents died, and he nurtured me—he is all that I have of a father." This was an easy, practiced explanation; how many times across the centuries had Nick explained LaCroix that way? LaCroix, of course, never bothered to offer an explanation to mere mortals, and mortals who chose to challenge LaCroix's word on any subject were unlikely to survive the night.

Will rubbed his face. "He hath a quelling eye." In fact, Will thought both of Nick's "cousins" had some frighteningly hard and cheerless quality shining out of their eyes, but that was far too much to say to any man about his kin. "Or compelling, I might say," he amended.

Nick smiled. Shakespeare was responding to the vampire in LaCroix's nature, certainly, and Nick had a very good notion of what was going unsaid. For all Will's courtesy and easy manner, the poet's aversion to the elder vampire had not escaped his notice.

Nor did that reaction fail to satisfy Nick. There were aspects of his existence that Nick still enjoyed very much, and the natural tendency of mortals to perceive vampires as their betters was one of them. Their natural disdain for mortal limitations gave vampires an air of aloof superiority that allowed them to pass unquestioned in many situations; it translated into the unthinking air of mortal aristocracy. The other side of the coin was that the mortal aversion to that chilly superiority kept the best among them, such as Will, that much safer.

All this ran through Nick's mind in an instant as Will watched to see if he'd taken offense.

"He compels me presently to Paris," Nick said easily. "I came to bid you farewell."

This took Will by surprise. "But you meant to stay . . ."

Nick cocked his head. "We spoke of difficult fathers, did we not? Yet there is some duty left in me."

This wasn't quite true, and Will noticed it, thinking, *So 'tis the lady who compels him, then.* He did not press it, though. Instead, he nodded and responded with a small personal revelation of his own. "Aye, and in me. My father hath not always known justice, and I find that I seek it for him upon occasion."

Nick smiled. "The arms," he guessed. It was notorious in player circles that Shakespeare had revived his father's old claim to the one great hallmark of a gentleman, a coat of arms approved by Her Majesty's Herald of Arms.

Shakespeare smiled. "Not without mustard," he joked: it was the mocking mistranslation of the family motto, *"Non sans droit."* It was a mark of his liking for Nick that he would offer the joke himself.

Nick laughed. "Well then, I shall have a pot of the stuff for you, come you ever to Paris."

"Nay, come you back to us, gentle Nick," said Will. "Methinks London likes of you, and you of her. And I will have this play."

"The play," Nick agreed, abruptly somber. This was a play after all, was it not? Yet he could not say as much to Will. Nor say the truth: *I go to Paris to live as a vampire again.* "Ay, the play's the thing—a play of a son with a crack'd heart."

"And a compelling father, albeit dead," said Will, declining to be somber. "Safe journey, Nicholas. And send to me with the name of your lodging."

8

*Kno'well. My son is not married, I hope! **Brain-worm**. Faith, sir, they are both as sure as love, a priest and three thousand pound–which is her portion—can make 'em: and by this time are ready to bespeak their wedding-supper at the Windmill, except some friend here prevent 'em, and invite 'em home.*

—Ben Jonson,
Every Man in His Humour,
Act V, sc. i (1598)

December 31, 1599
Paris

FEW CREATURES COULD CELEBRATE THE TURNING OF A CENTURY AS happily as a vampire. Standing beneath a freshly painted springtime sky, LaCroix felt himself the center of a perfect world of his own creation—his favorite place to be. Over the past six months, he had transformed this ancient château on the outskirts of the city into a contemporary paradise. *La Maison des Enfants LaCroix* was just that, a house where his children could be happy, their every whim indulged, where he could enjoy their happiness. Now that this dream was complete, he had chosen tonight, the start of a new mortal century, to share the outward trappings with the city that would feed them in every possible sense. Standing at the center of his new grand hall, he was surrounded by the cream of Parisian society, mortal and immortal alike, all gathered to pay homage to his vision. What could possibly have been more appropriate?

One of his guests managed to catch his eye as she passed, a mortal whose gilded mask presented the face of a lioness. A smile curved beneath her glittering whiskers as she touched the jeweled brooch pinned over her heart, a pretty bauble in the shape of an Egyptian ankh. *The symbol of life,* the vampire mused, returning her smile but turning away untempted. Sapphires and a come-hither smile—a worthy pursuit for some new fledgling, but hardly a prize for the master of the hunt.

His game of the ankh was simple but deadly, an amusement worthy of those of his guests from a far more ancient peerage. Each coveted invitation to *Les Enfants* sent to a mortal had included a gift, some jeweled brooch or comb or pendant fashioned into this same shape. "Why the ankh?" Janette had asked him, admiring a ruby pin before it went on its way to a duchess. But this was one jest LaCroix was unwilling to share even with her.

The value of the jewels adorning each token indicated the point value of the kill, a number based on such variables as beauty, wealth, social prominence, purity of spirit—mostly the calculations of LaCroix's wicked whim. The merely lovely wore pearls, the rich and handsome emeralds, the righteous and admired rubies, and so on. Most would likely live to wear these riches into the dawning light of this new age, never guessing how closely death had passed them by. But many would lose both prize and blood in the dark.

Janette stood beneath a potted pear tree gilded with real gold, surrounded by admirers, each more besotted than his neighbor and with good reason. Or so Nick thought, watching her from a distance. His immortal beloved had bloomed in Paris, the ennui she had shown in London falling away like dead leaves to reveal a gorgeous new flower that opened most freely to him alone. Tonight her happiness glowed outward to take in the entire gathering, the finishing touch on the pure nature and priceless art of her beauty. She had worn her hair to suit her lover's pleasure rather than fashion, the ebony waves released from their usual sleek rolls to fall around her shoulders, ornamented and restrained with only a delicate arch of woven silver wire. But if her coiffure defied *la mode,* her costume made up the quarrel. Her overgown was a rich purple, almost black, drawn back with silver cords to reveal a pale green shift—the colors of deadly nightshade in softest silk and heaviest satin brocade. Rather than the more common vermilion favored by mortal ladies, her lips were painted crimson, a pigment that would have poisoned mortal lips but which complemented the unearthly pallor of vampire skin and the dark light burning in eyes that were hers alone.

Feeling his gaze upon her, Janette gave up her pose to join Nick at the center of the hall. "*C'est forte amusante, d'accord?*" she said, taking in the entire scene with a single sweep of her hand. "LaCroix's little game—do you like it?"

"Most diverting," Nick agreed, barely noticing the crowd at all. "You look beautiful."

"A most artful compliment," she retorted, but her eyes sparkled. "I hope you can devise a prettier speech for your prey, or we shall never take the prize."

"You are still so determined to win, then?"

"*Bien sûr.* If we do not win, why bother to play at all?"

"My thought exactly," he said, leaning closer to speak for her ears alone. "Can you not imagine more choice entertainments?" he asked, moving to kiss her lips.

"*Ah, oui,*" she said and smiled, stopping his kiss with her fingers. "But only after the prize be ours."

Nick made his most menacing frown, but her smile never wavered. "*Eh, bien,*" he said, relenting, and kissing her palm instead. "You have a plan, I trust?"

"*Mon cher,* you know I do," she laughed. "I have found the most rare of LaCroix's little treasures, his lives of diamond." She moved behind him and turned him toward the thick of the crowd. "Mark you the young one looking so tragic, there, standing by the fire?" she said, her lips brushing his ear.

Nick looked as bidden toward the fireplace, broad and tall enough to have sheltered a small brigade of guardsmen with their brothers on their shoulders, except for the roaring flames. A youngster dressed in murky black leaned his curly head against the mantel. "The one who seems to practice for perdition?" he asked sardonically.

"Just so," Janette chuckled. "And he burns inside as well—

poor Abelard—yes, Nicholas, that is really his name—is in love."

"And his lady hath refused his suit?" Nick guessed.

"Nay, not a whit," she answered with arch pleasure. "His Heloise doth burn as hot as he and sigh as loudly." Janette gave him an example of a young girl's deep sigh, and Nick all but laughed aloud. "But their fathers, once as dear to one another's ease as food and water, have fallen of late into a most grievous quarrel. Now their children, sworn since infancy to marriage, have been most cruelly parted, and many fear 'twill mean their deaths."

"My love weaves a fair and touching tale," Nick teased. "'Tis pity she so disdains the stage."

"They have fallen into despair, *tu sais,*" she sighed tragically. "*Les pauvres chers* . . . I'faith, 'twas but a few nights past that *le beau* Abelard swore he would fall upon his sword if he may not straightaway be joined to his soul's completion." Janette crossed her hands over herself in a parody of corpse's repose. "All have but little doubt Marie-Alise would do the same." She circled around to face him again. "Only think," she said and smiled, her eyes glittering with anticipation, "a pact of self-slaughter from a pair of pretty virgins—hath LaCroix not chosen well?"

Nick could barely find breath, much less voice, looking full into the face of this unearthly flower who thrived in darkness and fed on blood. His Janette . . . how could he resist her? What imp of perversity could ever move him to even try? He longed to take her into his arms, but he knew she would not allow it, not now—she had a more immediate purpose, and when her will was set, his own would count for naught. "Yea, a fair conceit," he allowed slowly. "All in all a fine first act. But will you teach me now my part?"

"Yea, and straightaway," she answered, taking his arm and cleaving to his side, his reward for such perfect compliance. "Thy study must be brief, or we shall be too late—they wear their tokens prominently. I have already taken the girl away to wait, but you must go to Abelard."

She caught her breath for a moment, thinking, two fingers touching her chin, her deep blue eyes searching the ceiling for inspiration. "Yes," she said, mostly to herself. She swung her gaze to Nicholas, and touched one gloved finger to his cheek. "Go to the boy. Say you are my love and I have sent you."

"No great art in that, for it be but simple truth," Nick said, kissing her hand.

"Say that I have heard of his plight and do much pity both him and his lady," she continued, her musical voice dropping to a thrilling murmur. "Tell him 'tis my wish that he speak to his love, that I have arranged for them to meet in secret in our private chapel—to speak, mind, not to touch." She smiled. "My own piety forbids I should give him leave to dishonor so fair a maid."

"The chapel?" Nick asked, feigning shock. "You do astonish me, lady—does your wickedness know no bounds?"

"Bah!—not a one, as you should know," she scoffed elegantly, her smile widening with pleasure in her plan. "Put the ram in the east confessional and bid him await his lady's voice. I shall move the ewe to the closet on the west and await you in the center." She touched his cheek, fingertips in velvet on his skin. "So tell me, my heroic player—will you accept your part?"

"The tragic villain?" he teased. "For surely 'tis tragedy indeed when two such innocents must die for love. And most excellently wrought as well—yea, love, I should be honored to be your actor."

Young Abelard was pathetically easy to convince, dissolving into happy tears at the very mention of Nick's purpose. "*Vraiment, monsieur,* your lady is an angel, *une sainte!*" he enthused, following the vampire through the dimly lit corridors. "To speak to my love—only think!"

"*Une ange véritable,*" Nick agreed. "But mind you keep her terms, *garçon,* and give the maid your words alone."

"May I live everlasting in hell if I should fail her," the boy swore dramatically.

Nick stopped, pausing at the archway into the chapel so abruptly his companion nearly crashed into his back. A chill deeper than death seemed to race through his empty veins, drowning out even the warmth of his hunger. "What spoke you, *monsieur*?" he asked, turning to look back at Abelard's face, flushed with eager love. *To live everlasting in hell . . . never to die, but to live . . .*

"I say I shall do all as she hath bidden," Abelard answered, his expression clouding, a ghost of suspicion in his eyes.

Nick smiled. "*Bon,*" he said, clapping the boy on the shoulder and drawing him into the chapel. "Then all must needs be well."

LaCroix's chapel was his favorite room in the house, the gaudiest jewel in the crown of his new château. A team of artisans and painters had worked for months to create the murals for the ceiling, and vampire carpenters had repaired or replaced all the medieval woodwork with ornate new carvings in the Italian style to match. "More cherubim per square foot than any other room on the continent," LaCroix had laughed when it was done.

All that was missing was the cross.

Nick led Abelard to his appointed confessional, then hurried deeper into the chapel, the tingle of his lover's presence goading him on. "Were you successful in your quest, sir knight?" she queried, meeting him at the altar.

"Could I so fail my mistress and yet still live?" he queried back, drawing her into his arms. He bent to kiss her, and this time she allowed it, opening her mouth to his. "So what next?" he said softly, his lips sliding over her cheek.

"But little and that too sweet," she breathed. "Tell me, *mon coeur précieux* . . . can you still play the besotted swain so well as you play the villain?"

"No villain I," he protested. His words echoed inside his heart with a resonance deeper than his intent, but the echo was lost in love for her he held. "I do no evil but for love . . ." He kissed her again, pressing her close.

"Love or hunger, *mon cher*?" Janette laughed softly as she broke the kiss. "*Quelle félicite* that for us they are one and the same!" She stepped back and clasped his hands. "She is there," she said, nodding in the direction of the opposite confessional. "Feast you well, then do call for me again."

Nick slipped into the confessional, the warm perfume of sweet, young blood closing in around him in a cloud. "My love?" a tremulous voice spoke from the other side of the screen.

"Yea," he answered, sinking down on the prie-dieu.

A tender gasp, a sob denied. "*Mon Dieu,* Abelard," the girl wept, so close by the lattice she must surely be pressed to the rail. "What can we do?"

"Hush yourself, sweet love," Nick said soothingly, using the barest touch of his model's inflection to color his voice. "All will be well—"

"How?" she demanded, his deception achieved. "I want to trust you, *ah non,* I *do* trust you, *de tout mon coeur,* but I cannot but think . . . when I heard you had said that you would die—Abelard, you must swear me now to do no such sin."

This was not at all what Nick had expected to hear. "Sin?" he echoed, catching up.

"If you have no care for your own immortality, think you then of mine," she pressed on. "You know if you plunge into darkness, I needs must follow you . . ." She broke off, her breathing ragged, obviously fighting tears. "I do love you so," she almost whispered.

"And I you," Nick responded, his frozen heart melting in spite of his hunger. This was no courtier's plaything, no society coquette. No wonder LaCroix valued her death so highly . . . He paused, one hand laid against the screen as if to touch a lover's cheek.

"You speak of immortality," he began. "Think you I hold your soul more cheaply than your person? And for that I would give my life—to touch you now—"

"Nay," she cut him off. "You must say no such thing."

"Why not, when 'tis but truth?" he protested, finding his theme at last. "How long must I keep silent?"

"Until we are joined by God," she replied at once, quick enough for catechism.

"Hath God not joined us long ere this?" Nick pressed. "From whence comes this sweet pain if not from God?"

"From the Devil," she insisted. "Satan causes us to burn to tempt us into sin—"

"Can you truly believe this to be so?" he said urgently. "In faith, *chérie,* can such love as ours lead to damnation?"

"I know not what I should believe," she admitted with a hysterical laugh. "In my heart, I know my love to be pure, but I am so afraid . . ."

"Of what, *mon ange*?" Nick asked, suddenly unsure if the words he spoke came from Abelard's role in this deadly farce.

"Think, Abelard, only think," she said urgently. "Can we be

sure? If we break faith with Madame DuCharme this night, if we allow our souls to fall, they might ne'er rise up again."

Suddenly the priest's nest in which Nick perched seemed too small and close to hold him, the mortal girl's words a dissonant music twanging in his brain. Why should this child's pious prattle so unnerve him? "Are you certain 'tis thy soul for which thou fear'st?" he demanded, grasping control of his wavering emotions. "Or have you perhaps found another swain whose attentions suit you better?"

"You know well 'tis no such matter," she replied without the slightest trace of the righteous indignation he'd expected. "I want you now as you want me, my desire pricks as cruelly. But I would have you mine forever, in heaven as on earth." She paused, her breath coming short, a hand coming up to touch the screen, her warm flesh pressed to his cold palm with only the thin slats of wood between them. "Am I wrong to worry so?" she asked, a musing sigh. "Will you tell me I am wrong?"

"No," Nick replied, the word catching in his throat. Had any creature ever worried so for him? The night Janette invited him into eternity, his soul had not been her concern. This immortal soul for which little Marie-Alise wept and ached and burned—was it worthy of such attention? Was its loss such a cause for grief?

"But yes," the girl said suddenly. "I *am* wrong, Abelard; I must be. God is love, *n'est-ce pas*? Does every priest not say the same?" He heard her take a long, deep breath. "Come," she whispered. "Before this coward can change her mind."

No! protested some perverse good imp in Nick's secret heart even as he climbed to his feet. *You can't; you shan't; you mustn't—* But he was a vampire, not some fond and foolish husband, certainly not a priest—all trappings to the contrary, this was the house of LaCroix, not God. No doubt this sweet fool carried her salvation even here and would find her mate in heaven—'twas certain Nick would never seek her there.

He opened the confessional's other door and found her waiting, a beautiful young woman with serious green-brown eyes. The diamond pendant hung around her neck, sparkling just about the pulse, marking her as his prize. "What is this?" she whispered, breathless with shock.

"What you asked for," he answered in his hypnotic vampire's voice. "Was it not you who bid me come?"

"No," she said weakly, falling back as he moved closer. "I know thee not."

"But you do, Marie-Alise," he insisted, cradling her cheek in his palm. "I have sworn my love." She opened her mouth to protest, her will to love her mortal boy fighting even his vampire power, and he kissed her . . . warm lips, soft body held taut then yielding, melting into his embrace—another lesser creature conquered. He deepened the kiss, an actor's parody of love, and she sighed, her hands clasping him closer, never pushing him away. He lifted his head to look down into her eyes . . . eyes of a fawn, trusting, brimming with a desire to be prey. He let the vampire come, her face dissolving into a pattern of lurid light, her maiden's blush a crimson stain across her burning shape—food, no thought; a creature nothing like himself. His fangs grew sharp, his lips drawing back in a snarl, the leer of the ravening wolf, and even then she made no effort to be free, only hid her burning face against his shoulder. He slid behind her, one arm curved around her slender waist, catching her tight against him, making her cry out—was it fear or desire he heard? *Perhaps they are both the same,* Janette's voice murmured in his brain, an echo woven through the thunder of this mortal woman's heart.

He laid a hand on her burning brow, pulling her head back to his shoulder, exposing her tender throat. With the glowing vision of his hunger, his eyes could trace the flow of blood beneath her skin, an adornment far more precious than her diamonds. He let his head fall back, gathering force for the bite to come . . .

"Forgive me," the girl said softly, weeping. "Forgive me, my only heart . . ."

Nick froze in mid-strike. He caught her by the shoulders, leaning, reeling as if from some heavy blow that had split his heart in two. "No," he said numbly, flinging her away, a perfect vessel filled with poison. "I cannot . . ."

The girl tumbled forward, falling to her knees on the cold, stone floor, her senses returning with the shock. "*Mon Dieu,*" she gasped, scrambling to her feet, scarcely able to tell where she was or how she had come to be there. Turning, she saw a monster in the shape of a man, a golden-haired angel with the teeth of a beast and the mad, glowing eyes of a demon. "No!"

she screamed. "Help! *Aidez-moi, a moi, a moi!* Someone, please—Abelard!"

Janette tore open the chapel door, the blood of her own prey smeared across her pretty mouth. "Enough!" she snarled, catching the girl by the hair and snapping her slender neck in a single efficient motion, cutting off her life in mid-scream. She let the body slump to look at Nick, standing there with his vampire nature exposed but with the expression of a horrified priest. "What is this?" she demanded. "Are you out of your senses?"

Nick looked from Janette to the dead girl at her feet, her face frozen in terror forever. Terror of a monster, a monster who was himself . . . "Yes," he admitted, speaking in a dream.

"How did this happen?" Janette cried, too furious even to hear him. How dare he stand there mumbling when he had nearly ruined them all? "Was the girl a resister? Why did you not take her at once?"

"No!" Nick snarled, confusion giving way to an inexplicable rage. The world seemed split in two with a river of fire between, an unbridgeable rift between himself and this woman, this vampire he loved more than his own life. "Have I failed thee, mistress?" he roared, his monster's voice rattling the flimsy walls. "Shall I lose thy favor?"

He reached down and snatched the diamond pendant from around the dead girl's throat. His voice thickened and grew cold with contempt. "May I buy it of thee with this?" he demanded, stepping over the corpse to shove the trinket under Janette's nose. "What is thy price tonight?" *Your lady is a saint,* the voice of a dead boy said mockingly in his memory, the words casting him back to the image of Jeanne d'Anjou, so small a girl, her hair cut around a bowl like a boy's, who had preferred to die in a fire kindled by greedy bishops than to live forever in the darkness offered by a vampire. Joan of Arc, they called her now, Saint Joan to whom God Himself had been willing to speak, her soul was so great . . .

"How?" Nick had asked her. How could she make that choice? "Faith," she had said, almost baffled by the question, its answer so obvious to her, so painfully difficult for Nicholas de Brabant to hear, "pure simple faith."

"What price tonight, my sainted lady?" Nick's words came out like lashes of a whip, scourging himself as well as her.

"How dear shall your holy favors be bought at the brink of a century? What penance will you have of me for failing to kill one innocent child?" Janette gasped in horror—she herself must have run mad—he couldn't have said such a thing. LaCroix, yes, in his rage he might be so cruel, but Nicholas? It wasn't possible.

"You *are* mad," she breathed, backing away, out of the tiny closet.

"Not mad, lady," he answered, following her, still holding up the diamonds. "A monster. *Et tu—tu etes une salope immortelle.* Here," he said with brittle contempt, "consider yourself paid." Dropping the pendant at her feet, he turned and fled the chapel.

LaCroix bid the lady vampire lately arrived from the Japans a polite *adieu*—what elegance they had, these women of ancient Heian-kyo. Artists, musicians—truly he must visit the place someday.

His thoughts thus pleasantly occupied, he began making his way toward the hall's eastern entrance. Both Nicholas and Janette had passed this way some hours past in the company of the most valuable prey at the gathering, but neither had as yet returned. Now the city chimes were ringing midnight, and still neither was in sight. While he saw no great cause for fatherly concern, he was nevertheless intrigued.

He found Janette on an upper terrace, gazing out over the battlements like some lost princess of yore. She turned at his approach and moved to meet him, this in itself something of a wonder. "Have you tired of Paris games already?" he scolded her playfully, holding out his hands. "Or do you and Nicholas prefer hide-and-seek?" He stopped, shocked, as he caught a fleeting glimpse of scarlet tears on her cheeks as she flung herself into his arms.

"*Il est derange,*" she wept, clinging to her master like a frightened child—most out of character for his usually fearless Janette. Even on the night she was made, she had repelled such an embrace.

"Who?" LaCroix demanded, covering his sudden unease with impatience as was his wont. He caught her chin and snapped her face up to his. "Who is mad?"

"Nicholas," she retorted, jerking free of him. "We were

about to win your little game when he lost his mind. He showed himself to a victim—a silly girl, a sheep, the sort of chit he should have devoured in an instant." She shivered. "But he would not take her life. He showed his true nature, then simply stood there and let her scream."

"Impossible," LaCroix insisted.

"No," she answered. "Though truly, *mon amour,* if I had not seen it I would have said the same."

LaCroix studied her closely, but she seemed sincere. Besides, what cause could she have to lie? "Where is this unfortunate creature now?" he asked aloud. "Still screaming?"

"Dead, *bien sûr,*" she snapped. "I killed her myself—quickly, not neatly. Such a wreckage—" Her face shaped itself into a remembered mask of horror. "LaCroix, I swear to you on our lives Nicholas has lost his wits—there can be no other explanation. *Never* have I seen him thus, not even on his first night with us." She looked up. "Not even when his sister still lived—"

"Enough!" LaCroix cut her off. "Where is our witless madman now, think you? Weeping over his corpse?"

"*Non,*" she answered evenly, though her eyes narrowed in fury. "I know not where he may have gone; I could not think . . . He called me a whore and himself a monster, then fled from me altogether."

"Can this be?" LaCroix mused softly, more to himself than to her. "*Non . . . c'est impossible.*" That Nicholas could be so stupid as to call himself *un bête* was no great shock to his master. Indeed, LaCroix had seen the first bright sparks of self-damnation in his eyes on the night of mortal Alyssa's all-too-timely demise. But for him to turn this revulsion outward, not on the master he hated as well as he loved, but on his precious Janette, his soul's one worthy desire . . .

"Nevertheless, it is true," Janette said as if to finish his thought. A tear glistened on her otherwise placid cheeks; she was a statue with a broken marble heart.

"Rare jewels indeed," LaCroix said, capturing a droplet of new-wept blood on the tip of his finger, his heart touched in spite of himself. "You must not squander them on trifles, *ma fille.*"

"When have you seen me do so?" she retorted bitterly, but there was an unmistakable plea in her eyes.

"*Ne commences pas maintenant,*" he ordered, licking the blood away with a single, efficient flicker. "Dry your tears, *ma daimone* Janette." In his mouth, the appellation of demon was a loving compliment. LaCroix's eyes grew icy. "I shall fetch back your little lost lamb."

Nick stumbled along the bank of the Seine, the real world of the Paris night lost to him in a screaming whirlwind of memories. Looking down at the sluggish crawl of green-black water, all he could see was faces, drowned and staring, wide-eyed and gape-mouthed beneath the surface, the horror of innocence lost in a moment frozen forever, like fish in a winter's pond. He reeled out on a wide stone bridge and leaned heavily against the balustrade. He swiped his palm across the jagged stone, tearing a deep gash from whence oozed sluggish blood . . . Whose? he thought as he watched the skin knit itself whole in the moonlight. Whose blood had provided the physic to work such a miracle? Where was the blood that might heal the gaping wound now torn deep in his soul? What magic could make him forget he had no soul at all, now that he'd remembered it was so?

He felt the approach of a mortal, felt the thief's presence as soon as his boots touched the bridge, his vampire senses still painfully acute after his thwarted kill. But where little Marie-Alise's heart had drummed and fluttered like a bird caught in a snare even before she knew him for a monster, this man's heartbeat was measured and calm—he was another predator like Nick himself, stealing food in the night, his hunger as mindlessly cruel as Nick's own. The vampire closed his eyes, feeling the fangs fall, curved sharp against the inside of his mouth.

"Is this what you seek?" he snarled, turning just as the man reached him, eyes glowing gold as the moon rising over the water. He grabbed the wrist of the hand that held the knife, snatching the man close enough to smell stale beer and rancid onions on his breath. "Have you come here looking for Death?" The sound of muscle torn from bone was music more pleasing than madrigals as he tore the arm from its socket. "You have found me."

"Mercy!" the killer shrieked, his eyes as silver-white as his knife with pain and terror.

"Of course," Nick responded, striking raggedly at the throat, blood gushing forth to bathe his face, his throat, the patterned silks his beautiful mistress had chosen for him to wear in her play. He drank deeply until the fountain in his grasp began to turn to carrion, the flesh under his fingers hardening, the blood oozing cold against his lips, and he felt his own nerves shiver as if in sympathy.

"How charming," LaCroix said dryly, coming to rest before him, a fashionable seraph fallen from the sky. He looked Nick and his prey over with the dispassionate expression of a jaded patron presented with a tedious objet d'art. "For this you abandoned the game?"

"Get away from me," Nick snarled, letting the dead man drop. "Go back to that nest of vipers."

"And leave you alone in such a state?" his master retorted. "I think not." He took note of the blood left untouched on his son's face, the wild grief glowing in his eyes. "'Tis ill, Nicholas," he scolded warily. "*Très mal, et très dégoûtant*—why quench your thirst from so disgusting a bog when you might have drunk from the sweetest pool in Paris?"

"Get you hence," Nick cursed him, but his strength was beginning to fail, the burning rage giving way to a chill despair. "Go back to your silly devil's game if it amuses you—me it delights not at all."

"Indeed?" LaCroix became arch. "*C'est bien*—for i'faith, Janette was little amused by your forfeit." He caught a glimpse of more lucid pain in his son's eyes at this and pressed on. "Sooth, she is overwrought."

"You lie, LaCroix," Nick said, but his face reflected doubt. "When have I held power to give Janette such pain?" The memory of Janette abandoning him in Florence lent bitterness to his words.

"Are tears not proof of sorrow?" LaCroix was gratified to see Nick start. "Yea, Nicholas, Janette has cried this night for your madness," he went on. "As for your cruelty—i'faith, I knew you not so hard."

Janette weep? Had he ever seen such a thing? He thought back to the chapel, his love's angry face, bloody diamonds, a roar and then a hiss that he recognized as his own voice. "Ah, Janette," he breathed, his heart twisting at the memory. *Salope:* there was no crueler word he could have hurled at her. And he—of all people living in the world, he knew best how terribly that one insult could hurt her, could strip away centuries of elegant self-possession in an instant. Yet she had not allowed him to see it—or was it that he had not stayed even the single instant that would have allowed him to see?

"You would tell me such things just to tighten your hold," Nick said roughly. Yet his eyes rose to meet LaCroix's with a question.

"Perhaps." LaCroix drew out his syllables for emphasis. "But not tonight." A trace of satisfaction came into his voice, seeing Nick's horror. "Now, Nicholas: will you let her sleep so uneasy?"

By the time Nick reached the château, the ball was over. All the surviving mortals were gone home to their safe, warm beds, never dreaming what revelations of death the new day and new year would bring. The vampires were secure as well, tucked into various rooms throughout the château behind heavy shutters to wait out the fast-approaching dawn. Nick ran through the deserted corridors at vampire speed toward his lover's private rooms, desperate to reach her and beg her forgiveness.

"Janette!" he called, pounding on the heavily bolted door that led to her private suite. "Janette, let me in! I beg you—"

He heard a bolt sliding within and took a step back, searching madly for words that might win her pardon. But when the door opened, it was not Janette he saw but her maid.

"The Lady Janette demands that you go from here at once," she said, taking in the blood on his clothes and face with a single, horrified glance before focusing her eyes on the wall behind his head.

"I must see her," Nick insisted, struggling to remain calm. Forcing his way into her bedroom was hardly the best way to regain Janette's favor after such an offense as his.

"She will not see you, *m'sieur,*" the girl replied, quaking at having to defy so frightening a figure. "She says that if you wish to spend the day in this house, she suggests you do so in the chapel and pray forgiveness there." She looked at the blood again, and was barely able to squeeze out her next words. "She says you have . . . a mess . . . to clean up."

• • •

"I take it she hath banished you from the temple of delights," LaCroix quipped as Nicholas came into the chapel, though the stricken look on the younger vampire's face was grievous enough to give even him pause.

"Aye," Nick replied woodenly. "She sent word I should come here and clean up my 'mess.'" He looked around, his blue eyes empty glass. "Where is it?"

"The children are gone, Nicholas," LaCroix said with a frown. "They will be discovered in the morning in the girl's bedchamber—all will think the boy strangled her, then poisoned himself." He held out a small, glittering object—a diamond ankh. "So you see, Nicholas—you have won the game after all."

The glassy blue eyes clouded with a burning rage, a perfectly acceptable sign of life so far as LaCroix was concerned. "Go to hell, LaCroix," he snarled, turning away.

"I am loath to deny you any wish," LaCroix purred, "yet I must decline to gratify that one." One eyebrow rose contemplatively. "I cannot but wonder, *mon ami*—how will you win her back?"

Nick stopped, despair washing over him again. "I know not," he admitted plainly. "I'faith, LaCroix, I know not even how to begin."

"Then let me school you," LaCroix said, softening his tone. "Look at yourself, Nicholas, for mercy." Nick looked down at the blood drying to a crust on his clothing, smelled the dead thief's stench rising from himself in a noxious cloud. "Knowing our fair companion as you do, think you she can be charmed by such a suitor?" LaCroix pressed.

"Nay," Nick admitted. Suddenly he was tired, his newfound doubts like an ache in his bones. "What ails me, LaCroix?" he heard himself ask without ever truly meaning to speak.

"But little," his mentor assured him with an inward sigh of relief. "Come, Nicholas—I shall give you the physic you require."

By the next sundown, Janette had regained her outward composure if not her inward calm. Her parlor was filled with all the favorites of her vampire acquaintance—all, that is, but one. And all who were present were making every charming effort not to notice the conspicuous absence of that one, talking to her and one another about a thousand empty topics and saying nothing whatever about the subject that so obviously preyed on their venial little minds. But when Nicholas did appear in the doorway, the illusion was shattered, and all conversation ceased.

"What do you here, monsieur?" Janette said haughtily, her voice ringing strong through stony silence.

"Janette, please," Nick began, taking a step inside.

"Have you come to show your friends the evil of their ways, *mon frère?*" she went on mercilessly. "Or mean you to condemn only me?"

"Never," he swore, coming to her.

"Nay, not so," she laughed. "*A vrai dire,* 'tis scarce a night's passing since you did so last. Most convincingly," she added, after a pause.

"And verily would I take that night back again were it possible to do so," he said urgently, speaking to the pain he could see so clearly in her eyes, the fascinated witnesses forgotten. "I beg you," he continued, falling to his knees, sending a ripple of shock through the room. A vampire on his knees? "I know not what madness seized on me last night. Th'effect of the chapel or . . ." His voice trailed off in hopes she would respond, but she kept silent, one delicate brow raised in question, but her jaw strongly set in denial. "'Twas but a passing fever—you must believe me."

"Must I?" she asked coldly.

"Yes," he swore, clasping her hand. "Can it have been but so? Think you, love—could I ever be aught but your slave if not in madness? You are my life, my eternity—banish me from you, and you banish me to the sun." Another shocked gasp swept over the crowd, while LaCroix turned away with a private smile. Nicholas had become a rare player indeed, a most apt actor. Or perhaps he believed with all his foolish heart the lines he'd been taught.

"Say no such thing, you fool," Janette ordered, shocked herself.

"A fool," he agreed. "And only your fool, love. I speak but plainest truth." He pressed her hand to his beatless heart, making her lean down from her chair to meet his eyes.

"Forgive me, beloved," he pleaded. "Give me mercy this night, and I swear I shall ne'er deserve your hatred so again."

"A pretty speech," she said, but he could see a smile melting through the marble mask. "'Sooth, you do play the lover better every night." She stood, allowing him to keep hold of her hand. "But I cannot let you burn to prove your faith." She sighed. "So take my pardon, love, and mend."

"Well done!" one of the other vampire ladies cried, expressing the general sentiment. When Nick rose and took his lady in his arms, he kissed her to a round of applause.

"A pretty accord if ever such were seen," LaCroix agreed as Janette led her prodigal to his chair. "But what is this?"

A servant had appeared carrying a packet on a silver tray. She rushed forward and presented it to Nick. "This just arrived, monsieur," she explained, quaking under LaCroix's impatient glare. "You said if anything should come for you from England—"

"*Merci,* Sophie," Nick interrupted, taking the letter. "You may go."

"What is it?" Janette asked, annoyed, as he tore it open.

"Forgive me, *chérie,*" he said absently, scanning the page. Shakespeare had written him once or twice over the past six months, sharing ordinary news of London and asking the same of Paris, and yet, almost as an afterthought, including in each note a line or two mentioning the new play that, even in these sketchy accountings, seemed to burn upon the page. Now at last the play was finished. *You did speak once of reading a man's soul in a hotchpotch of sonnets,* Nick read. *That soul hath writ this play. And, my friend, it is to debut at night, Thursday month.*

"I must go to London," he said, looking up. "Janette, come with me—"

"More madness?" she demanded, appalled. "Of course I will not, nor shall you—"

"I must," he insisted. "Not forever, I swear it. But a month, a week—one night would be enough."

Janette opened her mouth to repeat her refusal in even less uncertain terms, but LaCroix cut her off. "One night?" he asked, intrigued. "What urgent quest may be fulfilled in a single night?"

"Shakespeare has finished a new play," Nick explained,

struggling to keep his voice neutral. He was somewhat embarrassed to raise this question so soon after regaining Janette's favor, and even more so still to be playing for a salon of fascinated vampires. Still, he was determined to have his way. Janette might stay behind if she wished, but nothing would prevent his going to London, however briefly—"It is to be played at night."

And yet it would tear his heart in two to leave Janette at this moment, when, more than ever before in their long history, he owed her the unmixed devotion that would be needed to heal the wound he had made. He took Janette's hand, willing her to comprehend what it meant to him. "He is my friend, lady," Nick said softly. "Accompany me, I beg you."

"Hath he ne'er writ a play before, that this one should be such an event?" Janette said sarcastically. "Verily, no—"

"Nay, be not so crossed," LaCroix interrupted with a smile. "I think we shall all see this play." Both his children looked at him with surprise: LaCroix was counseling Nicholas to indulge his taste for mortal company?

LaCroix enjoyed their incredulity. He smiled upon them paternally. "*Sic volo, sic jubeo,*" he said softly: Thus I wish, thus I command. They were words he had spoken to entire armies in his mortal days, but speaking them then—and finding himself unconditionally obeyed then, even unto death—had never given him a tenth the pleasure that seeing his children smile at each other and accede to his wishes was giving him now.

9

Our players are not as the players beyond sea, a sort of squirting baudy comedians, that have whores and common courtezans to play women's parts and forbear no immodest speech or unchaste action that may procure laughter . . .

—Thomas Nashe,
Pierce Penniless, His Supplication to the Devil (1592)

London
February 2, 1600

Each of the Lord Chamberlain's Men, from the meanest spear carrier to great (or loud, at any rate) Burbage himself, was as well accustomed to the role of mover as to that of priest or king. During the long, dark months of the English winter, their collective livelihood depended greatly on their ability to transport their stock and trade to private homes, crossing the river to play comedy, tragedy, or whate'er else might be required for the pleasure of any nobleman with the wealth to pay them and the wit to call them forth.

But their task on this uncharacteristically bright morning held special promise and peril, the unlooked-for sunshine discovering them each one harried and happy by turns as they loaded wagons with scenery, costumes, paints and fabrics and fairy dust—all the ingredients required for their mechanical world of illusion. For tonight, they would play for Lord Hunsdon, the Lord Chamberlain himself, their own rare patron, at his house in Blackfriars, off Water Street. And the play they would present had ne'er been seen before.

"What fair new lad is that, Thomas?" joked one of the carpenters, himself slated to play a ghost-affrighted guardsman, as he passed young Saddler and a friend standing by one of the wagons in the icy muck, the two boys dressed as similarly as peas in the proverbial pod.

Then he caught clearer sight of the second boy's face and blanched. "Ne'er mind me," he muttered, giving Thomas a long, stern look before turning pointedly away. "I ne'er saw half a thing."

"Look I so ill as that?" the second boy joked, pulling his hat more firmly downward toward his brow. He was a pretty youth, no question, prettier e'en than Saddler himself, but the haunted, hollow look in his blue eyes mocked his beauty and his sunny smile as cruelly as the frosted mud below their feet mocked the fair blue sky above.

"Climb on," Thomas replied, ignoring the question to give his companion a boost over the side of the wagon. "Mind your hat," he ordered, pulling the tarpaulin back to reveal a tiny hollow among the gilded thrones of Denmark just large enough for one small human, assuming he kept his knees close by his ears.

Isabella took a deep, rattling breath of fresh air before wriggling into this seat, trying not to think of the long, stifling ride across the river.

Or the drama waiting to be told on the other side.

"Snug, are you?" Thomas teased, his tone softening in spite of his anxiety. She looked so sweet in his clothes—no wonder Hilliard had so fancied her this way. But she looked so fragile too, the skin on her pretty face worn thin to near-translucent over the delicately sculpted bone. "Promise me, Izzy, for your own dear sake," he pleaded, resisting the urge to touch her, mindful of who might see. "Promise me you'll stay well out of sight, most carefully from any who might . . ." He let the plea die unfinished, loath to hear her reply, whatever it might be.

She smiled again, her feverish blue eyes twinkling. "Speak

thy speeches well, sweet maid," she scolded, reaching for the tarpaulin. "I shall hark to thee right close."

Janette came down the broad and brightly lit steps, her displeasure patent on her lovely face despite her gorgeous costume. "Remind me, Nicholas," she said acidly as she allowed him to hand her into the coach. "Why is't again that we needs must fly the pleasant society of friends in Paris to return once more to this fogbank?"

"A fogbank with rare accommodations, as't turns out," LaCroix quipped, climbing in and signaling the coachman to drive on. Given a fortnight to prepare for their arrival, Aristotle had proven his gifts admirably, arranging for the vampire "cousins" to be housed in a residence of the Queen herself. Elizabeth was not currently at home at Whitehall, 'twas true, but the idea of living like royalty suited LaCroix rather well nonetheless.

"Explain to me again, *s'il vous-plaît,*" Janette persisted, ignoring their mentor's good humor with catlike disdain. "What mortal quest hath so straitly compelled your attention?"

Nick suppressed his own sigh of impatience, unwilling to rejoin a battle long since won and lost. "Forgive me, *ma plus cher amour,*" he begged, reaching again for her leather-gloved hand.

"Were you so unhappy in Paris?" she demanded. "Has the company of your own kind become so offensive that you must seek the comfort of mortals or run mad?"

Nick could see LaCroix's fine-drawn lip curling in amusement, for all he pretended to watch the London scenery go by. "You know not so," he chided his immortal beloved, leaning close in a futile attempt to speak for her ears alone. "Paris is as dear to me as ever, and your company ever more so—why else would I risk your displeasure to bid you accompany me here? But I came at a friend's bidding, as you know."

"To punish me for my devotion, or so I begin to think," she retorted fretfully, being purposely perverse. "LaCroix, please—close that window, *à l'instant,* or I shall faint." The thought of Janette fainting made Nicholas smile: she had indeed recovered her spirits if she would threaten something so absurd. She covered her face with her free hand and coughed theatrically. "A pigsty, this London—and we must return to wallow in it for the sake of a silly play?"

"Not *a* silly play, but the *only* silly play, *chérie,*" LaCroix said, his voice dripping with merry irony as he ignored her request to close the window. He rather enjoyed the smell of the night, even when the darkness hid a sewer. "Good Shakespeare's very soul upon the boards—was that not how he expressed it, Nicholas?"

Indeed it was, though it pained Nick deeply to hear LaCroix say it so mockingly. He had shown Will's letter only to Janette, but apparently she had thought it necessary to share its thrust with their mentor. "One night, my love," Nick said to Janette, ignoring LaCroix as well as he was able. "One night, and I shall return with you to Paris or the very moon if you so desire it."

"In faith, a pretty promise," LaCroix judged playfully. "Come, Janette, be not so unkind to our dear Nicholas. He has so few vices; surely you can allow him this one. 'Tis only a play, after all."

"I allow?" she demanded as the coach pulled to a stop before a modest town house. "What is it to do with me? When have I a word to say that can call or send either of you?"

At this, both of her companions laughed aloud, and Nick and LaCroix looked at each other with the affectionate harmony that had ruled their threesome since LaCroix had chosen to make a paternal command of Nicholas's much-wished return to London. "When indeed?" LaCroix said. "When has a word been required?"

"I shan't be long," Nick said, kissing Janette's hand and opening the door. He had hoped to find Shakespeare at home, diverting their coach all the way across London Bridge on this fruitless errand. They could have no private words with the other vampires present, it was true, but he was eager to at least see his face.

"Why so peevish, *chérie*?" LaCroix asked his daughter. "Sure this speaks of more than the fog or stench of poor slandered London."

"I cannot believe you still choose to indulge him in this," she said urgently, now they were out of Nick's hearing. "After what happened in Paris—I cannot believe you do not see where this indulgence will lead him. He had just determined to be happy again, now you allow him to come back to this disagreeable island with its disagreeable plays and poets. You had done as you promised, made him wish to be one of us again—"

"No, Janette, you saw it: he had just determined to be utterly miserable. And within the hour of his repenting that wish, he received Shakespeare's summons," he finished. "I have commanded what I could not escape, and you would be wise to do the like."

"And how is that possible?" she demanded. "How is it that a mortal man should command the heart of a vampire? How should he so much as know the name of our house and be made privy to the comings and goings of a vampire?"

"Madness, I quite agree," LaCroix said. "Though I know not how to prevent it, except I end the playwright's life . . ."

"For which Nicholas would ne'er forgive us," Janette finished, the possibility having obviously occurred to her before. "I still cannot believe this urgency has all to do with a single play. There is something more; there must be."

"Perhaps," LaCroix allowed. "Though knowing what I do of Monsieur Shakespeare and of Nicholas, I can well believe a play might so demand their mutual attention. And if it is something more, best we should know of it and quickly." Nicholas was emerging from the house again, alone. "Would you have thought it meeter we allow him to come here alone?" he asked.

"No," she said quickly, looking up, alarm flaring blue in her eyes. "No, Lucien, far better that we should be with him. But far, far better still that he should never have come here at all."

"He's already gone," Nick said, fighting disappointment as he climbed back into the coach. "I ought to have known—no doubt he's been with the players since dawn."

"No matter," LaCroix said as they drove off again. "We shall all see him soon enough."

Screed hated being alone. As a mortal, he'd never had the opportunity to discover this particular nugget of truth regarding his character, as he'd gone from being midways in a passel of brats to being well crushed in a family of sea dogs, with nary a pause for breath in between. But this vampire jaunt was an education in more ways than one, and a long, lonesome sail around the Horn for those as had no mate in murderosity.

He'd spent the first month or so after the black-eyed Pride of Espagne had left him feeling naught but sorry for his plight, snatching up rats and bits of talk with equal uncaring. But time and experience had since taught him to pick out his own among the rabbling crowd, at least so much of his own as could be picked in a stray tingle among the dying press. Still, very few of the other night creatures he'd sniffed cared to spare more than a mo' and a sneer on the likes of a vermin-sucker birthed from the lower-class womb. The closest kin to mates he'd been able to muster was a pack of boyish-looking clowny sorts who made a game of loitering about the districts theatrical, preying on such mortal dims as yearned for the sugared kisses of youth. These fair and silly lads tended to find his dirty linen and sailor's ways more lark than disgrace and had even gotten him a bit laid on to tragedies with their talk. The playhouses all standing right along o' the haunts of the Bear Garden rats, Screed had taken to sleeping under the tireroom floors at the Rose and Globe, where, of a sunny afternoon, he heard the drama both onstage and back. Over time, he'd found much to like in the current state of English theater. But 'twas not a candle's spark to real company, and many and long were the nights he wondered how Vachon was faring in his quest for his *tierra madre.*

Still, there was a bit of a thaw on, and with it enough game to satisfy the hungriest of rat hunters, particularly if a chap knew where to look. He stopped along the riverside to peruse a new broadside—the Bear Garden had finally reopened and was going *to play five dogs at the single bear, and also to weary a bull dead at the stake; and for your better content shall have pleasant sport with the horse and ape and whipping of the blind bear . . .* Screed closed his eyes and ran his tongue around his lips just thinking of it: the blood of rats that had fed on the blood of bears—nectar of the gods, to him. "Now 'at's a fair bit of news if e'er the like was writ," he said aloud, paying the odd looks of the odd mortal no mind in the least.

Vachon leaped lightly from the barge to the shore, his eyes focused on his fledgling with something like real fondness. It had taken him a month of halfhearted searching through the dark corners of this London to find Screed again, a month wherein his English had improved but his spirits had fallen steadily, continuing the decline that had begun almost as soon as he reached Spain. Even after nearly six months, he wasn't sure he entirely understood it. He had been so eager to see his mortal home again—the thought of it had haunted him constantly from the moment it first occurred in the depths of the South American jungle. But once he was there . . .

He had expected things to be different in his home village of Sarriá—any fool would, after more than sixty years. He knew his mother and father would be in their graves, that his friends, if alive, would be stooped. Even so, the experience had defeated his imaginings. He had walked through the churchyard on his very first night, gazing down on the graves of many he had known before and feeling almost nothing. He was a vampire; what had these dead bones to do with him?

Like every other village in Spain, Sarriá had an inn where old men gathered. They'd heard of the fate of the tanner's boy; gone to Barcelona, to sea, and then dead in the dirt of the New World somewhere. Not one of them had peered into his face and asked, *Was that your father? your grandfather?* Even with the same face, he was too different for mortal recognition. Paying for the old men's ale, he'd heard the words go by on their lips—Javier Dionysios Vachon y Gaytan-Feria—and realized that name was no longer really his. It was just something for him to use while he passed among them, or, in this one little village in this one little district, something for him to avoid using. The first thing, the name his mother had given him for reasons she would never explain—yes, perhaps he was still Javier. The rest was purely arbitrary: a pagan saint on whose day he'd been born, a stepfather, a mother's father, a carefully retained record of the taint of bastardy tagged onto his mother's name. It was a catalogue of things that meant nothing to him now, a tool of their world, as an ax or a bucket might be.

He was other. He was a vampire.

Then, on the second night, he had learned how much he remained the same. He'd seen a girl, barely more than a child, and her face had been completely familiar, a face he had carried with him in the warmest part of his memory all through the decades. She had seen him watching her as she walked down the twilight street, and she'd smiled at him, almost as if she knew him too. His heart had leaped—*he* was still young, still hungry—could it be? He'd followed her, keeping a predator's distance, seen her go into the same tiny house he remembered. But when he'd drawn close enough to peer through the unshuttered window, he had seen the truth—an ancient crone huddled by the fire, whining to this beautiful child in the curdled echo of his former lover's voice.

In that moment, he had known Spain was no longer for him—or not yet for him.

He left Spain and wandered, but all of Europe was just as dead. In this new life, he was a creature of the New World.

He expected Screed to look up as soon as he got within clear sight of him—surely he could feel the same tingle Vachon felt himself. But the carouche didn't look up until he was almost upon him, and then he barely seemed to credit his senses. "Faith 'n' chancery," he swore, his crabby tone spoiled entirely by the grin on his face. "Th' Armada's gone an' landed on the Thames."

"A happy thought, but no," Vachon shot back, grinning as well. "Only one soldier, and that one weary of the fight."

"Then stay an' welcome," Screed said. "Though I thought as how ye'd pushed off these shores for good an' all to hunker on Spanish soil."

So did I, Vachon thought but didn't say aloud. How to explain to this Englishman barely as old as his boots the pain of seeing a world grown out of one's reach? "I am for the sea, Screed," he answered instead.

"Get out," Screed answered. "How do you propose to manage that miracle, me lovely lunkhead? A sailor earns his tack in the sunlit rigging—"

"I am for sailing to the New World," Vachon explained slowly, his English still hard-won. "I do not belong here anymore, Screed. I am going home."

"Home? A wilderness squealing wi' savages?" Screed demanded.

"So you have no wish to come with me?" Vachon asked, disappointed and angry to be so. What did he care whether or not the carouche came with him? Since when did he require companionship, particularly such companionship as this? Had he not felt relief to be done with Screed these few months past when he left him behind in London?

"Hold, I never said that," Screed hastened to assure him. "But a bloke's got a right obligation o'reason to know the destination afore he hops beneath the sail."

Vachon was spared the effort of answering this by the sudden tingle of other vampires closing in on them. Looking up, he saw a carriage pass by, its windows thrown open on either side in spite of the evening chill. "*Santa Maria,*" he breathed, the blasphemy falling from his lips in reverent tones. "It is her."

Janette had barely noticed the frisson, but she saw the young Spaniard plainly enough, standing in the street and gaping at her as if she were a queen in royal progress passing strictly for his peasant entertainment. "*Mon Dieu,*" she breathed, turning away from those ebony eyes.

"What is it?" Nick turned his head to look behind them, seeing nothing particularly amiss.

"Not what, but whom, Nicholas," LaCroix said playfully. "Did you not see the boy standing there in the gutter staring at our *cousine précieuse?* Who was that, Janette?"

"Nobody, I assure you," she said testily. Nick looked back again as the carriage rounded a corner.

"Aristotle suspected you had taken a lover of somewhat coarse refinements," LaCroix teased, enjoying her obvious discomfiture far more than he expected to enjoy the blasted play to which they rode. "But I never imagined you had sunk so low as that."

"So low as what?" Nick demanded, turning back to his beloved.

"Ignore him, Nicholas," Janette insisted, glaring murder at her vampire father. "I meant nothing, only a sigh, but he thinks to torment you with it."

"Indeed, I should think it was you who would torment Nicholas, keeping company with such a ruffian," LaCroix said, softening his tone nevertheless. "But perhaps I mistake me after all."

Lord Hunsdon's main hall, always grand, had been transformed to a place of dream for the first performance of Shakespeare's newest and, rumor had it, best tragedy. Tall candelabra stood all along both sides of the room, their flickering tongues of firelight reflected a thousand times in the tiny diamonds of mullioned glass in the windows that lined one long wall. More single candles, as yet unlit, lined the stage at the room's far end, pasted into shallow plates with their own wax and left to await the play, ready to illuminate another world for the pleasure of the rulers of this one.

The Queen had sent word just that afternoon that she herself was too immured in affairs of state—puzzling over Essex's latest disobedience, most like—to attend the performance, but most of her faithful peerage had come just the same, filling the Lord Chamberlain's hall to overflowing. Many of the seats in the bleachered galleries had already been filled by the ladies, their velvets spread around them like jewel-encrusted petals, with more streaming in through the huge double doors, their maids trailing in their wake. No less splendid were the gentlemen, an ever-changing kaleidoscope of multicolored peacocks that milled back and forth before the galleries and around the chairs set up before them for Hunsdon's own household and honored guests. All in all, a scene rich and varied enough to satisfy even Janette's thirst for beauty and splendor as she entered through the doors between her cousins. "Very pretty," she said, one hand laid lightly on Nicholas's arm. "One might even imagine oneself in civilization."

Nick was himself unimpressed by the gorgeousness of the hall, concerned only with his friend. He scanned the crowd with a vampire's expert eyes but could find no sign of Shakespeare. "Most like he is behind the scene, fretting the last detail," he said aloud, barely aware that his words did not match his beloved's. "Prithee pardon—I shall return anon."

"Nay," Janette said, catching his arm more tightly. "Stay with us."

Nick lifted her hand to his lips before handing it to LaCroix. "I'll be back long ere the play begins," he promised.

The scene behind the curtain was far less grand but no less crowded, the small space filled to overflowing with the Lord Chamberlain's Men. The company seemed to rush as a whole in every direction, trailing false hair and laces and weaponry behind them, putting the entire household in perpetual danger of immediate immolation from the candles stuck everywhere, on every available bare space among the chaos of costumes, props, and general rubbish. Young Thomas Saddler had apparently commandeered a roasted capon from His Lordship's kitchens and was now hosting an impromptu dinner party for the minor players in the direct center of the room as everyone rushed to dress. He snatched a leg from the carcass and used it to gesture at one of his fellow "actresses" as the other boy was fitted with a gold-foil crown. "Have a care his wig ne'er covers his eyes, dearie," he cried in a mincing falsetto that would have earned him a rain of orange rinds had he adopted it on the platform at the Globe. "Her Majesty needs must see the lines she hath privily penned on her wrist."

"Dog!" the other boy cried, breaking free of his dresser to pelt Thomas with stray bits of his queenly costume.

A roll of horsehair missed Burbage's head by inches as it flew by, shaking him from his own private ritual of preparation. "Someone take these pups away and drown them," he rumbled, bringing the laughing fray to an immediate and total halt. High spirits were all very well, but he who dared to annoy Burbage just before a performance would find not only his job but his life threatened. With a final friendly exchange of grimaces, the boys went back to their respective preparations, and some semblance of peace returned. Satisfied, Burbage picked up the paint pot and began to coat his own visage with the glamor of youth these boys had by grace of Nature.

Suddenly he caught sight of another face reflected in the glass. A golden-haired man stood in the middle distance, no player but a gentleman, hunting for something, his looks familiar, but— A shiver raced down the actor's spine. Then he recognized Nick Chevalier.

"But here, 'tis the very face I require," Burbage said, covering his foolish fear of a moment before with false good humor. "'Sooth, Nick, you come most happily on your hour—sit by me that I may have a fair model for my prince."

"Nay, not so," Nick said with a smile. "'Tis sure this Hamlet must resemble no man but thyself."

"Then why have you risked your unblemished soul to consort with sinners so soon after reformation?" Burbage asked. "Would you rather take a lady's part? Forsooth, I would you would change frocks with Saddler—look at him, I pray you." Thomas gave Nick a resigned grin. "I put it to you straight: is that a blushing virgin?" Burbage went on. "Tall as a guardsman's spear with beard as thick as mine own, yet I must woo him for a maid."

"Or else die of old age so I may take thy part," Thomas shot back saucily, yanking on his wig.

"'Sblood, a rat!" Burbage thundered, rising from his chair with his sword drawn, sending the boy laughing away. "Yea, go to and stay gone," the actor finished, sitting down again.

"Where's Will?" Nick asked.

"Purgatory," said the actor. "The Ghost cometh thence."

Nick gave this joke its smile and silently repeated his question.

Burbage shook his head, his face turning serious. "Best not ask," he advised grimly, returning to his painting.

"I would have a private word with him before the play is

set," Nick explained, surprised to see Burbage look so solemn even if he were about to play such a melancholy part.

"Think you I would not?" the actor countered, an edge of rancor creeping into his tone. He stopped and shook his head. "But you must pardon me, Nicholas—my nerves are drawn tight as Cupid's bow this night and will stay so until the play is done. As for the Conqueror, we needs must both be disappointed. He who hath his ear just now will suffer no other hearers." He glanced up and saw Saddler watching them in the mirror. "Poor boy," he muttered, tossing away his paint rag and reaching for the inks.

"Mean you Saddler there?" Nick asked, confused. Burbage fixed him with a pointed look, and the truth of the matter came clear. "Or do you mean young William Hilliard?"

"Poor in purse or poor in spirit," Burbage replied with a twisted smile. "'Tis for a philosopher or parson to split that hair, not a poor player." He turned in his seat to look the vampire in the face, his sharp eyes seeming to pierce Nick's skin in search of his very heart. "Will doth love thee well," Burbage said slowly, interrupting Nick's thoughts. "No doubt he will tell thee all now thou hast returned." He turned back to his own reflection. "For myself, I will say but this," he finished. "You spoke of Hilliard? Find him, and you've found Shakespeare."

Janette watched Nicholas disappear behind the curtains with what looked to her vampire father like genuine fear. "What think you he will encounter while yet still so close?" he chided her gently. "A dragon?"

She forced a smile. "Much more deadly game: a poet."

"Soft you," LaCroix soothed. "Here, let us find you some diversion—ah, just the thing. Not dragon, but gorgon." He smiled as a lady in deep purple velvet pushed her way through the doors with a queenly air, a small army of servants all but clinging to her skirts. "See you that creature there?" he said, indicating her with a nod.

Janette was in no mood for LaCroix's perverse humor, but he left her little choice. "Which one?" she sighed.

"In the purple," he said. "'Tis your favorite Englishman's precious dam."

"Shakespeare's mother?" Janette asked, confused. "I thought him more common—"

"Not Shakespeare," LaCroix corrected. "William Hilliard."

Janette's eyes narrowed slightly before she took a closer look. "*Ah oui,* I see a resemblance," she murmured as the lady gave one of her footmen a brief cuff to the face with her glove. Madam was elegant, no question, in the fashion of a lady who knows she is past her bloom and seeks to compensate her loss with riches. "Her son has her golden locks."

"And her gentle temper," LaCroix agreed silkily. "Come, I will make you known to her."

Janette reluctantly allowed herself to be led to the front of the room, where Lady Hilliard lingered, clearly expecting to be met. "My lady," LaCroix said, making a deep bow.

"Monsieur LaCroix," the mortal woman answered, her languid tone belied by a light in her eyes that Janette found rather interesting—so, she was a conquest as well as a diversion. "Come, sit here by me."

"Many thanks," LaCroix answered, shooting Janette an amused glance. "May I present my cousin, Janette DuCharme?"

"But of course," Lady Hilliard answered graciously. "What a pretty creature—in truth, LaCroix, you are much blessed in beauty."

"I thank you, your ladyship," Janette replied, making a slight curtsey, her head bowed to hide her smile.

Lady Hilliard turned to look around the room again with a barely suppressed sigh of annoyance. "I must tell you, Monsieur LaCroix, I begin to despair," she said. "My son— But you have charge of a young cousin who consorts with players; you understand my plight."

LaCroix suppressed a mocking laugh and made a sympathetic face instead. "Indeed, dear lady," he agreed. "And sooth, he is my heart's sore plague. Is he not so, Janette?"

"Just look you, pray," Lady Hilliard went on, indicating the room full of nobles with a heavily ringed hand and giving the other female no time to respond. "The greatest men in England gathered together in high good humor, and where is William? Mining some value from his wretched association with this pack of gypsies by diverting their betters? Nay, he cannot be bothered—he is too much occupied in wallowing in the gutter." She looked Janette up and down again, a thought seeming to occur. "Tell me, mam'selle—have you met my son?"

"Yea," Janette answered, covering her contempt with a catlike smile.

"Brilliance breeds perversity, madam," LaCroix said soothingly, giving his daughter's hand a warning squeeze. "Particularly in youth's full bloom."

"Full bloom indeed," Lady Hilliard replied bitterly. "'Tis all very well for your Nicholas; he is near to blown entire and may hold his own state among them. But my son is still in his first man's fledging, too fresh for such frivolity as this—'twill leave him bent."

"He is a tree, or a flower?" Janette puzzled with apparent innocence. "Nicholas," she smiled, "*mais, il est un bête.*" LaCroix's shoulders shook slightly.

"Bird, beast, fair or foul—'tis time he gave up such amusements and made his place in the world." Lady Hilliard was nettled.

Janette drew breath to reveal just exactly what she thought Hilliard's place ought to be, but just at that moment spotted Nicholas coming toward them. She let go of LaCroix's arm and went to join him.

"Nicholas, thank heavens," she said, taking his arm and leading him back toward LaCroix. "*Le grand chat* has scented a mouse, *je pense.*"

"So 'twould seem," Nick said with a grin. "How think you he means to bait her?"

"With himself, *sans doute,*" Janette replied. "She seems quite taken with him."

"So she does," Nick agreed. "We must hope she can escape being taken by him as well."

"Why must we?" Janette countered, a challenge in her eyes. "If we are away tomorrow, what matter will it be what LaCroix does tonight?"

What matter indeed? Nick thought, the answer coming not from his vampire head but a new spark burning in his mortal man's heart. Why should LaCroix not take whatever pleasure this noble harridan could give him; indeed, why should they all not do as much?

"Perhaps her son would mourn her passing too grievously for my conscience," he said sarcastically, pushing these rebellious thoughts aside. "Look you, beloved, where he comes."

In truth, young Hilliard made a far less pretty picture now than he had some six months before. His clothes were as rich, his jewels as bright, but he seemed far less pleased with his place in Fortune's parts for all his wealth, his curls not so crisp, his eyes glazed over with a sheen beyond mere tedium. He was making his way from the curtained arras before which this new *Hamlet* would be played, to his mother's platform, like a warrior on the field of battle, sparing no notice to the right or left.

Janette's pretty mouth curled in a lethal smile. "And LaCroix insists there is no justice in Nature," she quipped. "The pox he set upon his lover has returned to devour his heart."

"So 'twould seem," Nick agreed, far more interested in his lover's satisfaction than in wee Willy Hilliard's appearance. She looked positively gleeful . . . Was this boy so deserving of death in her eyes? He thought of little Isabella, likely dead these six months past, sprawled in the dirty rushes of a tavern at Hilliard's feet and Janette's sore grief at the sight of her. "*Oui,* beloved," he said, lifting her hand to his lips. "I should call that justice myself."

Shakespeare emerged abruptly from behind the corner curtains, his fine brow, painted to ghost-white, drawn with pre-performance fretting, though he still wore his own linen shirt. He spared the assembly the barest glance before going after Hilliard, touching the young man's arm as he overtook him, but Willy was having none of it. He flung the older man's hand away with the hauteur of an Oriental prince. Though even Nick's vampire hearing could not pick up what he said, Shakespeare's sudden flush was unmistakable. "Your scribbler has not always been so fortunate in his passions as he is with you, Nicholas," Janette said as the two men came closer. "Yet he seems to be as fond as ever even so. 'Tis odd . . . Why does he yet have a care to that whelp?"

"Perhaps he is as devoted to his friends as I—or you," Nick said evenly. Janette looked at him sidelong, wondering how many layers of meaning Nick really intended with that barb, but Nick's eyes were fixed on his mortal friend.

"Your servant, my lady," Shakespeare said, making a bow to Lady Hilliard as his peevish patron stopped at his mother's other side. "And look you, gentles all, you have arrived at last."

"Did you doubt us?" LaCroix asked him archly.

"Nay, sir, never for a moment," Shakespeare answered amiably, refusing the bait. "Monsieur LaCroix . . . Mam'selle DuCharme." His brown eyes twinkled as he glanced pointedly at the way Janette held Nick's sleeve. "For shame, Nicholas—your gracious cousin doth fear you fickle, that you may fly off with the players again."

"I'faith, Will, if your tragedy be as you styled it, I shall be sorely tempted," Nick answered.

"A hope to make all merry," the playwright replied with a grin that looked very strange on the dead-white, black-eyed ghost face. "For in truth, we have missed you as sorely, good Nick—though as I am an Englishman, I can yet well discern the beauty of France, particularly to a lover's eyes." He made a bow to Janette. "'Sooth, it fair dazzles even mine."

"Your friend is well versed in flattery, Nicholas." Janette's smile held little warmth. "Shall his players speak his rhymes so well as he spins them himself?"

"Far better, lady, I assure you," Shakespeare said with a smile. "But shall we speak apart, Nicholas? If the *belle* Janette be so offended by my crude courtesy, I quake to imagine her pain at my plainer speech."

"You must forgive Janette, good sir," LaCroix explained with an enigmatic smile. "She hath felt ill humors since the hour we embarked."

"Nay, not so," Nicholas demurred, pressing his lover's hand. "Yet, Will, I would walk with you—"

"Nay, do not," Janette interrupted, holding him fast. "Think you not the play shall begin in a moment? I fear *mon anglaise* will not suffice to follow it without you."

"Then stay, Nick, by all in heaven," Shakespeare laughed with the dead King's face. "I would have my verses understood before my affections sated." He glanced over at LaCroix. "And indeed, you must all give me true reports of the play's effect," he continued. "It speaks much of fond sons and their fathers, false and true."

"And much other matter more diverting, I assure you," Hilliard injected dryly.

"A banquet of a tragedy," Nick said. "I cannot wait to devour my fill."

"Then let us wait no longer," Shakespeare said, conducting them to seats of honor near the place of the Lord Chamberlain himself. "As for you, Nicholas, we shall speak when the scenes are done."

"I'll not fail thee," Nick promised, receiving a smile in return as the playwright took his leave.

"Yes, do let us get on with it," Lady Hilliard grumbled as she seated herself. "Though I faint with the heat—Addison!"

A pretty wench in a serving maid's gown appeared as if by magic from the corner. "Go fetch me my pomade, the one for heat," Lady Hilliard ordered. "And wine. And be quick—"

"She cannot be quick enough," Hilliard snapped. "Come not back in until a break in the scene."

"Aye, milord," the girl agreed quickly, dropping a curtsey. "My lady." She scampered for the doors at the back as Hunsdon's servants began to light the stage candles, preparing for the play to begin.

Lady Hilliard's long-suffering chambermaid slipped around the outside edge of the grand hall, her faculties sore pressed to pay proper respect to the noble guests without treading on their noble toes—an exercise she would no doubt repeat a dozen times over before the night's entertainment was done. Her ladyship found little diversion in the antics of players, but she never tired of watching her tirewoman scamper to and fro.

"I boil, Addison; fetch my pomander," the girl muttered, aping her employer's pinched-nose tone to comic perfection. "I faint, Addison; fetch my physic . . . I thirst, Addison; fetch me wine." She rounded the corner into the servant's hall. "I tire, your ladyship; kiss my bum."

"Talking to yourself, sweet Marcia?" Osric, the steward, teased as he handed her his own brimming mug. The two had met many times before at such functions, and the Lord Chamberlain's servant rather fancied the girl, sharp tongue and ample bum alike.

"What of it?" the maid retorted before taking a soothing swig. "I ought to've run stark lunatic long since, the trials I bear with that woman." Her sharp eyes caught an unfamiliar face in the crowd of grooms and footmen loitering between the fire and the courtyard door. A face to give a healthy lass a fever—big black eyes and an angel's own mouth, and long, black locks to make wee Willy turn more orange than was his wont with envy. "Catch me, Oz," she said, feigning shock. "I'faith, I swoon . . ."

"Waste not your vapors on that one, lass," Osric retorted

dryly. "A Frenchman, and not much for the parlay-voo. His shadow's a bit more natural, but ne'er smells o'er-sweet to my nose. They've bided here an hour past, and nary a sip of ale nor friendly glance between them."

"Mayhap he don't thirst," Marcia said with a grin. "A Frenchman, say you? No doubt he serves them three which my lady hooked."

"Aye, I have seen them." His mouth turned downward. "Mark me, lass, all of them unnatural, gentry and servant alike."

"'Swounds, Osric, you've the sweetness of a bulldog and half the looks," she laughed. "The nobles are strange, no question, but this lad seems naught but shy to me. His older lord and the lady are the Devil's own proud—perhaps he fears his place if he speak too free with us."

"An' you mean to set his foreign fretting soft, no doubt," Osric said sarcastically, taking his mug back. "Saint Marcia Addison, patron of the wretched, so long as ever they be handsome."

"So long as that," she agreed, laughing. "But I must go back to my mistress—guard him for me, good Oz. Mayhap I can return at more leisure—the thing's tragical, and she's bound to nod off by and by."

"Shall I be a Frenchman's panderer?" he shot back. "Go to, wench, go to."

"You first, old goat, and quickly," she laughed, patting his cheek. "Now fetch me a bottle of wine while I see to the matter myself."

Vachon watched the girl approach with a lightening heart—green eyes could serve as well as blue when a vampire began to feel hungry. Following the fancy vampires to this estate had given him no great trouble, once Screed's disappointment at missing the Bear Garden had been appeased with the promise of stable rats to come. But while his English and his clothes were far better than they once had been, Vachon still knew better than to attempt any foray into the polite society of the main hall—the society of the dark lady he sought. So he and Screed had been biding here among the servants, waiting for the lady to emerge.

Still, lady or no, he could see no good reason to let such an opportunity as this girl pass him by unnoticed—the fondest lover still had to eat.

"So tell me, sirrah, since none else braves the asking," she said, pulling a stern face as she looked him up and down. "What manner of man art thou who stands so at the fire and gives no man his voice? Will you give it to no woman, neither?"

"Mayhap I will give it to a girl, if she be so fair as you," Vachon responded with his most endearing smile. "I am Javier, mistress, so please you. I serve a lady within."

"The Lady Janette, yes, I know," she answered, smiling back, all pretense of reserve abandoned. "The Frenchwoman with the ebony locks."

"Janette, yes," he agreed, mentally recording the name. The vampire lady was Janette . . .

"She is a rare beauty, your lady," the girl teased, half-turning away as she strolled toward the deserted hallway. "I wonder that she keeps such a ruffian as you in her service."

"You wound me, mistress, to the quick," he answered, following.

"Marcia, sweeting," she responded. "I think I am no man's mistress."

"No?" he asked, glancing back to where Screed sat by the fire giving him an evil look before leaning in closer to his prey. "I'faith, sweet Marcia, that seems past all believing. 'Tis a terrible waste of a flower not to be plucked."

"Your wine, Mistress Addison," the steward intoned, coming around the corner with a dusty bottle in his hand and a disapproving expression on his face. "No doubt your ladyship has long ago expired from thirst."

"My ladyship is far too hateful to be killed by so natural a means," the girl shot back, ducking under Vachon's arm to take the bottle. "But she may well be plotting some such fate for me." She turned back and smiled at the vampire again. "Mayhap your mistress will give you liberty enough to see me later," she said.

"If you wish it, I shall certainly try," he answered.

"Oh, I wish it, monsieur," she said, pronouncing the word well enough, considering. No doubt she found it easier than his name. "I wish it very much indeed."

10

ISABELLA. *So that you say this herb will purge the eye*
And this, the head?
Ah, but none of them will purge the heart.
No, there's no medicine left for my disease,
Nor any physic to recure the dead. (She runs lunatic.)

—Thomas Kyd,
The Spanish Tragedy,
Act IV, sc. i, 1-5 (c. 1587)

"BURBAGE HAS CONNED HIS PRINCE'S PARTS RIGHT WELL, THINK YOU not?" Nick whispered to Janette as the Danish prince Shakespeare had spent the long months perfecting flung his boy/girl ladylove from him with a curse. "To a nunnery, go and quickly, too!" he shouted with all the thunder his considerable lungs could muster. "And young Saddler makes a sweet lady, for all he has grown so tall."

"I tremble to hear you say so," Janette retorted, stifling a yawn. "In truth, I expect the boy to bash in the man's brains at any moment for these insults—no noblewoman would bear such discourtesy, even from a prince."

"Go to, I'll no more on't; it hath made me mad," Burbage continued, his fine eyes bright with feigned outrage as he towered over Thomas's half-prone form. "I say we will have no more marriage. Those that are married already—all but one—

shall live. The rest shall keep as they are." He grabbed the boy's arm and made as if to snatch him to his feet, trusting the agile ingenue's own strength to complete the motion. "To a nunnery, go!"

Thomas made as if to prevent his Hamlet's leaving, reaching out with his hands as his mind reached for some great sadness that might call up a few dewy tears for his own fair speech to come. A noise from the back of the hall made him turn, and there he found a portrait of woe sufficient to weep an ocean, for himself and the other as well. "'Swounds and bleeding heart," he murmured in a voice quite wrong for fair Ophelia, making the crowd gasp as one. "Isabella . . ."

At first, Nick could not tell what he meant. Peering into the darkness at the back of the hall, he could see only the usual crowd of favored servants, standing to watch the play. Then he saw one of the page boys moving closer, making his way through the crowd, coming abreast of the gallery and closer still, his eyes focused on the brightly lit stage—

"*Mon Dieu,*" Janette whispered as she reached for Nick's hand, recognizing the girl at once. "She lives."

Only then did Nick really see Isabella.

Isabella, and yet not. The witty, dancing girl of the tavern party was near a wraith now, the illness having chewed her body down to its essence so that her skin seemed a bare transparency. Her face, its eyes huge and fever-bright against her pallor, shone almost as black-and-white as Will Shakespeare's painted ghostly King had done in the first act. She moved like a wraith as well, gliding over the floor and seeming barely to touch it.

She reached up and caught hold of the boyish hat she wore much as she had that night in the tavern, dragging it from her head and shaking her long, wild locks free around her shoulders, making a frame of darkness and glimmering candlelight for a face pale as moonglow. She caught hold of one of the white cloths covering the tables set just behind the honored guests' chairs and dragged it around her waist, knotting it loosely over her boyish doublet. *Now I am a boy and may be a girl*, her voice whispered in Nicholas's memory as she reached the platform and turned, her eyes focused solely on the young mortal man sitting nearby.

"O, what a noble mind is here o'erthrown!" she said as if

speaking only to Hilliard, a sibilant whisper which reached the farther corners of the hall.

"What player's trick is this?" Lady Hilliard demanded, shifting as if to rise from her chair. "Silence this person—"

"Nay, lady," LaCroix interjected, cutting her off with a vampire's persuasive touch as he watched his fledglings' faces. "Let her speak."

Nick turned and saw Shakespeare standing on the makeshift stage balcony, still wearing the dead King's face and armor, his sword drawn and half-lifted as if in royal salute. "Will knew naught," he whispered to Janette. "Look you how his wits are driven out." Janette paid the playwright a scant glance before looking back to the central performance.

"The courtier's, soldier's, scholar's, eye, tongue, sword," Isabella continued, her voice gathering force, the dullness leaving her eyes, burning up in fevered fire. "Th'expectancy and rose of the fair state—The glass of fashion and the mold of form . . ." She took a step toward her lover, raising a slender hand as if she longed to touch his fevered cheek. "Th'observed of all observers," she said more gently, the sad smile on her lips contradicting her madness. "Quite, quite down."

"Enough of this!" thundered Hamlet. Burbage moved from the stage as if to lay hold of her, but Tom Saddler lay hold of him, Ophelia bending her prince to her own will at last by force.

"Leave her be!" the boy ordered through tears that had naught to do with acting as the girl looked over her shoulder at him, including him in her smile.

"*Mon Dieu*, Nicholas," Janette breathed, clutching his wrist in a death grip, "look at young Hilliard's face."

For once, there was no art in the young nobleman's expression, no weariness or calculation. He had risen from his seat, and tears welled in the bright blue eyes that had so inspired the poet's verse, a flush deeper than fever coloring his perfect cheek.

"And I, of ladies most deject and wretched," Isabella cried, falling to her knees. "That sucked the honey of his music vows—O woe is me, t'have seen what I have seen, see what I see!"

"What does this creature here?" Lady Hilliard shrilled,

turning to her son. "Tell me what you know of this woman—"

"Indeed, milady, 'tis a most diverting tale," LaCroix said, putting a hand on her shoulder and pushing her gently back into her chair. "But hardly fit for such a company as this."

Hilliard seemed not to have heard his mother nor indeed to know aught but the sight of his abandoned mistress, now kneeling before him, his tear-streaked face bent over hers. It was his mother he answered, though the words were spoken into Isabella's stricken face.

"'Sooth, madam, the Frenchman speaks aright," he said, an acid tone brushed rough with weeping. "Not fit in any fashion." He looked away from the girl toward the doors, his gaze flicking over the balcony where Shakespeare no longer stood. "Hath the Lord Chamberlain no servants, no guards?" he demanded. "Shall we bear the sight of this monster forever?"

"Bastard!" Thomas roared, lunging for Hilliard. Burbage caught hold of the boy by Ophelia's skirts as servants streamed and clattered up the aisles, ordering him to remember his place, his honor, their lives.

"No!" Nick shouted, as Isabella slumped to the floor in a dead faint at the center of the pandemonium. "Leave her—let her go!" He leaped to his feet, but Janette held him fast. "They will hurt her," he protested, turning to Janette.

"*Vraiment,* they will not," she promised, rising to meet his eyes. "How can they hurt her now? Come, Nicholas, come away from this place—"

"No," he insisted. "I cannot. I must not—"

"Nicholas, she has what she wanted," LaCroix urged, joining them as Lady Hilliard rose to rebuke her son. "She has her revenge—let her die now in peace."

"In peace or in prison?" Nick craned to see as two of the servants lifted the girl's seemingly lifeless body. Holding her between them like a sack of offal, they headed for the nearest doorway. "Hilliard has condemned her—what peace do you think she will find?"

"Content you, Nicholas, your friend Shakespeare will see her safe," Janette insisted. "Look where he goes after her even now." It was true, the ghost King had come back to earth and was trying to reach Isabella through the confusion.

"A poor player whose present safety is far from assured," Nick shot back. "Indeed, lady, a fair savior he will make—

mayhap they can share a cell." He moved to extricate himself from her grasp, and she let him go at once, turning away. "Forgive me," he said, glancing at LaCroix for a long moment before turning and going after the guards.

"So what think you of the play, *mon père*?" Janette asked, faux bright, her eyes focused on empty space. "Is it all that you expected?"

LaCroix watched her, thinking of how best to comfort her, but the effort seemed far beyond the goal. "A masterpiece," he pronounced, turning away.

By the time Nicholas escaped the sudden chaos of the hall, Isabella and Shakespeare had both vanished. He made his way against the tide into the backstage area and found most of the players still gathered there, sullen and fearful and drowning all in Hunsdon's beer, like soldiers who'd found themselves abandoned by their commander in the very thick of the fray. Thomas Saddler was half-reclined in a far corner, still wearing his now torn and bloodied gown, attended by one of Hunsdon's serving maids. The girl obviously saw neither blood nor the gown as a detriment to romance—she was clucking over him as diligently as any pretty hen.

"Well met, husband," Thomas honked, referring to their late turn in the *Shrew*. "Lovely evening, think ye not? Dick went to grovel to Hunsdon, singing for all our suppers."

"Hang Dick; where are they, Tom?" Nick asked, looking away as the girl flung the bloody handkerchief she'd been holding at the actor's still-streaming nose past his own and replaced it with a clean one. Blood—why must every mortal crisis be soaked with blood? "Isabella and Will—"

"Izzy's to be arrested." Tom sat up and pushed his nurse gently aside, taking the handkerchief from her and wadding it more efficiently—this gentle maid had apparently brawled before. "Will went to stop them, but . . ." His shrug did little to conceal his misery. "If you can help . . ." He searched Nick's face, and smiled. "Then come, Lucentio, if thou wilt—let thy Bianca conduct thee to them."

Standing just outside the courtyard doorway pleading his case with all the wit he could muster, Shakespeare felt he was doing well. Perhaps the ghoulish mess on his face enhanced the drama of the story he told, for he could feel the sergeant's cynical heart melting under his words. Indeed, who would not feel sympathy for Isabella, in this ghost-king's tale an innocent maid driven to madness by fortune, unjustly accused, wronged by all and sundry, and now held shoulder and foot by two clodpole constables? It would make a turnip weep, and this sergeant was very turniplike.

Unfortunately for her otherworldly champion, Isabella chose the very pinnacle of his argument to open her eyes and utter her maiden lines.

"Whoreson poxy dog!" she screamed, sinking her teeth into her first captor's beefy wrist as she kicked at the other, struggling to plant her feet back on the ground. "Go to, I say! Let me go!"

One of Hunsdon's own guards raised his cudgel to give the girl's wits another rattle. "Nay, sirrah, have a care," Will warned, taking a step forward and wishing for King Hamlet's sword.

"Stay, man, the poet speaks aright," added another voice of reason—Nicholas Chevalier, just coming out the door, trailed by young Thomas. "Hilliard may take offense at the poor maid's madness, but by my troth, the Lord Chamberlain will think less well of the sight of her brains on his doorsill." He reached into his purse and withdrew a fistful of coins. "Of what crime is the lady charged?" he asked the sergeant as his underlings still fought to control her.

"Lady, what lady?" the sergeant retorted. "I'm thinking to clink her for dogbite—'tis Bedlam for this one, and no mistaking."

"God's blood, a blessing indeed!" Isabella cried, pausing briefly in her struggles. "Hear you what he says, Will? I shall be a penny player at last!"

"Izzy, for mercy, shut up!" Saddler pleaded as Will and Nick shared a worried look. It was true; if she were placed in Bedlam, Isabella would indeed be on a stage of sorts—the madhouse was a favorite entertainment for the same crowds as frequented the Globe's pit, for much the same price. One of the deputies mistook her momentary stillness for yielding, tried to scoop her up again, and received a bite on the chin deep enough to draw blood for his trouble.

"This honest sergeant is but intent upon his duty," Will said solemnly, wincing at the deputy's yelp. "He warrants for a warrant—you must put away your purse, my friend." Turning as if to leave, he winked at Nick.

"No need to be hasty, milord," the sergeant protested. "As the player says, she's a delicate creetur, no question." The delicate creetur's fist made crackling contact with the second deputy's bearded jaw.

"Isabella, stop," Nick said, catching the girl's flailing arm and her attention. "Calm yourself," he ordered, using his vampire will to speak directly to the demon in her mind. Suddenly the tussle ceased as quickly as it had begun, every ounce of strength and will seeming to bleed from her as she stared into the vampire's eyes.

"This gentleman seems right able to bring the chit to heel," the sergeant said, taking the gold. "Release her to him and welcome."

The deputies both let go, and Nicholas caught her in his arms as she fell forward. "Soft now, Isabella," he murmured, eliciting a muffled sob against his chest. "All will be well."

"Liar," she wept, clinging to the front of his doublet as the carriage in which Nick had come pulled up before them. "Sweet, sweet liar—"

"Where has she been, Thomas?" Will asked, turning to the boy player with a voiceless sigh of breath.

"I'll take you," Thomas said, climbing into the coach.

Nicholas hadn't realized how powerfully accustomed he had become to luxury until he saw the mean quarters to which Thomas Saddler led them, a ramshackle inn in Cheapside that from the outside looked a more appropriate habitation for ghosts and goblins than for any solid creature, mortal or otherwise. "'Swounds, Thomas," Will said as they got out of the coach, the momentarily quiet Isabella still carried in Nicholas's arms. "Why let the girl bide in such squalor?"

"Might you have changed her plight?" the boy shot back with unaccustomed insolence—ordinarily he was the very soul of filial loyalty and respect to the player-poet. "Would you replace the lord that furnished her previous comforts?" He watched with unmistakably jealous eyes the vampire and his burden as they went inside. His voice softened. "Nay, Will, she wouldn't ne'er allow me to tell you—and more, I knew not where to find her myself until a fortnight past."

"They bore him barefaced on the bier," Isabella began to sing as they crossed the freezing cavern full of broken benches which apparently served as common room, her head falling back limp as that of any corpse. "Be those not the words, my dearest master player?"

"Yea, chuck," Shakespeare replied, trailing with Thomas behind them, very like mourners in procession.

"Hey non nonny, nonny, hey nonny," she sang on as Nick carried her up the stairs, her voice a raven's croak playing at lark song. "And in his grave rained many a tear . . ."

"She did bid me straitly to hold my tongue," Tom went on as Nick laid her on the bed. "I doubt not but what she would have put me out of her seeing as well, had I not had the maid Ophelia's verses to bait her."

"And daily sight of her lover," Nick added as he felt the girl's brow, red-hot beneath his palm.

"'Tis true, she did ask after Hilliard most carefully," Thomas admitted.

"'Tis Tom should sing, for I am dead," Isabella insisted. "And you, Willie, you may dance, and Chevalier may take the chorus." She sat up, her fever-wild eyes locked to Nick's. "Sing thus, pretty—'A-down, a-down, a-down . . .'"

"Peace, Queen Isabella," Nick said, to soothe her. "Thomas will wait upon you whilst Will and I see you fixed."

"And what manner of mechanical shall accomplish that?" she laughed.

"Enough, Izzy," Tom said, pushing Nick aside to sit by her on the bed. "Enough of this madness," he insisted, pushing her down again. "You are not so far gone as this."

"Am I not?" she asked lightly, allowing him to cover her with the blanket. "How fortunate for me, to be not so nearly dead."

Will followed Nick back out into the hallway. "This is well done of you, Nicholas," he said. "The girl would ne'er have borne Bedlam."

"Nor Bedlam the girl," Nick agreed, going downstairs. An old woman dozed by the dying fire in the otherwise deserted common room, and he moved to her with more purpose than these environs had likely ever seen. "Wake up, mistress," he ordered, giving her a shake.

"Go to," she muttered, then opened her eyes and caught sight of her tormentor. "Pardon, sir, I pray you," she amended hastily, struggling to her feet.

"I require food and drink," Nick told her. "Fresh bread and thick broth—send to a better house if you have not the makings here." He tossed her a generous handful of coins as carelessly as a rajah, making his friend raise a quizzical brow. "And a clean tub of hot water brought upstairs—quickly."

"A basin mean you, milord?" the woman asked, his tone obviously as frightening to her as the richness of his garb.

"Nay, a tub," he answered. "Big enough to hold me, at least—bigger if you have it."

"This gentleman is French, mistress," Shakespeare explained calmly. "Indulge him."

"Aye, sir," she agreed, scuttling away with Nick's gold clutched tight in her claw.

"You mean to give our Bella the cure, then?" the playwright asked. A hot bath to steep out all poisonous humors was the most popular remedy for pox.

"It can do her no harm, think you not?" Nick asked wryly. "And in truth, a bath may do much toward regaining her former charms."

"Will you leave Saddler your purse then, that this good physic you prescribe may continue?" Will asked sardonically as the old woman's fellow innkeepers began to stumble seemingly from the woodwork to assist her in performing Nick's bidding.

"I will stay with her myself," Nick answered.

The player's face was eloquent of surprise. "Have you neither fear nor obligation? I speak not of Hilliard—he is but a painted soldier to you, I know—but what of Lady Janette and your other good cousin whose name I'd durst not hear in such a house? Will they suffer your absence kindly?" Was Chevalier going to brook his "compelling" father's anger to wait at Izzy's sickbed? Will had seen for himself that this father grudged his son even a few hours' unasked absence.

Nick didn't answer, even after a long silence. But the dark desperation clouding his bright blue eyes, plain evidence of the same melancholy that had so infused the poet's own Danish prince, spoke more than any words could have done. "Why, Nicholas?" he pressed, touching the young man's arm. "What's Isabella to you that you would risk such trouble for her sake?"

"What is she to you?" Nick countered, an obvious but effective evasion. "You risked your liberty to plead for hers. Why soft the rage that did consume your soul's first play?"

"Yea, and would again," Will answered. He went over to the unwatched keg and drew himself a mug. "She would be heard, Nicholas, and I . . . 'Tis years since, but I did burn for her. And was cindered, and now Hilliard doth the like to her. But you—you scarce have met—you owe her no such favor, unless I mistake me greatly."

"She is dying, Will," Nick answered. *And I cannot,* his mind silently added. "Why shall I not use the means I have through no labor of my own to bring her such ease as I may?"

"Would that Hilliard reasoned so," Will sighed. He frowned: Chevalier seemed always to be speaking the truth, but never quite all of it. "There, sir, your tub begins its journey up by the stairs. Let's to Saddler before he loses his own wits for love."

Will's jest was truer than he could have known. "Izzy?" the young actor ventured, touching a wisp of the girl's hair. When the poet and her savior had gone out, they had apparently taken the last spark of Isabella's spirit with them. Now she lay curled on her side as still as death, staring in fixed fascination at the candle by the bed, refusing to answer him or even acknowledge she'd heard.

"Well-a-day, sweeting," he muttered, turning away.

He glanced down and noticed he still wore Ophelia's gown, now ripped down the front from Burbage's attempts to keep him out of jail and bloodied from his own still-aching nose. "Christ's holy bones," he grumbled, grabbing the skirt and yanking the garment and its petticoats over his head. A pretty picture indeed—no wonder the girl wouldn't talk to him.

"Isabella, listen to me," he pleaded, turning and falling to his knees by the bed, stripped to breeches and bare skin. "You needn't stay here so any longer—Hilliard is lost."

"And I am dead," she chirped, looking at him at last, but with eyes too cold for bearing.

"Nay, not so!" he protested angrily. "You live; you breathe; you even yet love, though why is a devil's own puzzle. You might be happy if you would but abandon this last." He clasped her thin, cold hand between both of his own, all that was sweet and young and kind in his soul shining in his face. "Or but give it another," he urged. "Marry me, Izzy—love me as you've fought so long to love Willy—let me love you and keep you safe."

"Marry, I'll not," she repeated, her eyes still dead with shock. "Nay . . ." A cruel smile twisted her face. "Are you mad?" she cackled, sitting up. "The form of man is lost, so I must wed with his shivering manikin?"

"Nay, lady, be not curst," he pleaded, still holding her hand.

"Why should I not, who am curst of the gods?" she demanded. "Who are you to say me nay in aught, little maid?" She jerked free and stood, looking down on him like the perfect picture of disdain. "Husband? What practice hast thou known of such a part as this? Better thou shouldst beg me take thee to wife."

"Isabella, please," he said softly, tears sparkling in his long, dark lashes.

"Go to, boy, go to," she answered scornfully, catching hold of the back of a chair for support as Will and Nicholas came back in. "Your pretty maid is tired, Willy," she managed, her nails digging into the wood. "Take him home with you to bed."

"Monster," Thomas said, more sorrow than malice in his tone. "I do love thee well, for none's benefit but thine." He tossed the ruined gown to Shakespeare and shot Nick a look of purest hatred as he walked out of the room.

"You have learnt your lines all well, Isabella," Shakespeare said mildly, watching her thin shoulders begin to shake. "Hilliard has taught you well."

"Follow him, Will," Nicholas urged as the servants rolled in the tub he'd ordered, and let it settle with a thump before the fireplace. "Give him this before he freezes." He threw his heavy cloak to Will, who with a bemused smile tucked it under his arm alongside Ophelia's dress. "The Fates alone may tell to what his desperation may drive him thus."

The poet gave his friend a long, searching look, but Nick's mask was well intact. Still, he could remember a night not so very long past—*"Th' expense of spirit in a waste of lust,"* he had said, quoting Shakespeare's own lines. *I know this lust . . . fire i'the blood and how it is quenched and then burns upon its very quenching.* Was this sympathy a symptom of this same remembered pain, to be salved by the very woman for whom the lines were once indicted? Could he mean to debauch her? A rich man of handsome parts, good humor, a quick and mobile wit: what could he want with this fevered, skeletal, and, most of all, doomed, girl? "You'll not be dissuaded?" Will said aloud.

"Go," Nick repeated, meeting the mortal man's eyes but unwilling or unable to show him more.

As soon as Will was gone, Isabella let go of her chair and slumped to the floor behind it, weeping as if her heart were truly cleft in two. "Forgive me," she whimpered to the dirty rushes. "Pray you God forgive me."

"There's naught to be forgiven," Nick promised, bending beside her as the old woman brought in the tray of food.

"So lost . . . His poor child dead," she wept on. "I would have soothed him well, would haply hath waited on him e'er." She looked up into the vampire's face, but her eyes saw another man. "Had he thine eyes, this sweet Hamnet?" she asked, touching Nick's face but seeing another, speaking the name of Will Shakespeare's dead son. "Yea, it must be so—sweet brown and mild . . . What shame to weep before me, for all I am a whore? I was not always thus, and I do love thee well—doth my heart count for naught in this?" Her expression cleared, her eyes seeming to focus on Nick's face at last. "But 'tis no matter now," she murmured, turning away.

"Leave us," Nick told the woman. He went to the room's only window and fastened the shutters, warped but thick as ship's decking. The seal was fair as well—any cracks could be closed easily enough. Picking up Thomas's discarded petticoat, he tucked it all around the shutters, sealing out any sign of dawning light. Then he turned back to the girl, still sprawled among the rushes, though her remorseful tears had stopped. She let him lift her to her feet and lead her to the chair, then chewed and swallowed every morsel of food he put before her without a word of protest or question of his intentions, either utterly trusting or utterly beyond caring.

"Have you had enough?" Nick asked when she had set the last empty bowl aside. "Shall I send for more bread? Some fruit?"

"No need," she said dully, leaning her head on her hands as

if too weary to hold it up, as a knock came on the door. "Unless it be the Queen, I am not here," she joked as Nick went to answer.

"Sadly, the Queen is otherwise engaged this morning," Nick replied, letting in two men bearing buckets of steaming water.

"I'faith, I regret her not a whit," Isabella replied. She sounded far more like the witty girl she'd been when Nick first saw her than he'd ever hoped to hear again—but tired and impossibly sad.

"Tell me, Isabella," he said as the servants filled the tub, "why did you so this night, take on Ophelia's part? You could not fail to be arrested."

"I thought not so far beyond the speech," she admitted, looking up. "I'faith, pretty Nick, I thought to die as soon as my love refused me."

"Then you knew Hilliard would be angry?" This elicited a laugh.

"Yea, sir, I knew it well," she said with a bitter grin. "But in his secret heart . . . 'tis where I dwell most freely, I promise you." She shrugged. "I can give him naught so fine as Will's verses, but I would give him something even so . . ." She smiled. "He'll need rare will to forget me now, think you not so?"

"Yea, lady, too rare for such as he to boast for all his riches," Nick agreed. "But why think of giving this evil boy aught but scourges when he hast ta'en so much already—your honor, your comfort—" He stopped himself.

"My life?" she said wryly.

Nick took a deep breath. "Particularly when you knew right well how dearly he should despise you for it?"

"'Tis a mystery stranger than angels, is't not?" she laughed, a shadow of her former charm more sweet for its very weakness. "Tax not thy wits, fair Nicholas—a creature such as you are could ne'er credit such reasons as mine."

"A creature such as I?" Nick echoed, a sudden thrill of apprehension in his stomach.

"A man, sweeting," she laughed. "Are you not a man?"

And how might the vampire answer this? "Come," he said, bolting the door behind one last servant. "A bath, fairy, and you'll feel more yourself for all."

"I think not so," she said warily, climbing to her feet.

"Verily, Bella, 'twill do you good," Nick promised. He reached for her and received a surprisingly powerful cuff for his trouble—no wonder those deputies had been so quick to let her go. "None of that," he ordered, ducking behind her and laying hold of both her arms.

"No!" she screamed, struggling mightily as he dragged her toward the tub. "Go to, you bastard—damned French pig!"

"Flattery will serve you nothing," he grunted, lifting her off her feet and braving sharp kicks to both his shins instead of one. "'Twill do you no harm unless you move me to drown you."

"Please," she pled tearfully, trying another tack. "I die, 'tis true, but I would had not freeze beforetime."

"The water is hot, I swear it," Nick promised, dumping her in, clothes and all.

"Yea, verily," she retorted furiously, laying hold of his doublet with both hands. "Come, rogue, feel for thyself." Before he could regain his balance, she'd dragged him in after her, his weight pushing both their heads beneath the surface, the girl screaming all the way.

"'Tis well, sweeting," Nick said, sputtering and laughing as he emerged, yanking her upright before him.

She stared purest murder in response, her dark hair plastered and streaming over her face. Then she burst out laughing as well.

"Aye me," she sighed as Nick climbed out. "Forsooth, Nicholas, you are a devil, but I forgive you." She leaned back in the tub, letting the water rise to her chin. "Why not die of one thing as another?"

Nick flung his soaked doublet aside and turned to say with perfect sarcasm how pleased he was to hear her so yielding. But then he saw her, and the words died in his throat—a sleek, warm, living creature with a heart and blood that burned, gazing up at him with a challenge in her eyes. He took a step toward the tub, all but tasting her on the air, her lips, her throat . . .

He stopped. "Wash yourself," he ordered, turning away to hide the bright fire he could feel burning in his eyes, the fangs against his lip.

Isabella watched his back for a long moment. This beautiful, inexplicable Frenchman—what did he want of her? Why was he here—what favor did he hope to win? "As you will," she said aloud, wriggling out of her gown and tossing it out of the tub to land just before his feet. "Have you soap?"

"By the tub," Nick replied, struggling to keep his voice even, not to shout above the sound of her heartbeat in his ears. He took another few steps away as he heard the water slosh and splash around the form he wished he could not see so clearly in his mind.

The girl scrubbed herself quickly and well—for all her fearful protests, this was far from the first time she'd had a bath, and the luxury of it was something she'd missed of late, even if it would put an end to her. "I'm cold," she announced as she rinsed the last of the soap from her hair.

"Have you a clean shift?" Nick asked, moving to the trunk at the foot of the bed, his back still safely turned.

"Yea, 'tis there," she replied. "But I faint—I cannot get out by myself."

"I will call the mistress of the house to help you," he said.

"No." She would know his game now, before the fever she could feel returning took her over again entire and she lost all strength to fight him. "You cast me in, pretty. You may come and fish me out."

Why not take her? Nick's brain insisted in a voice very like LaCroix's as he turned and saw her, even more tempting now, her skin scrubbed pink as no vampire's could ever have been. Listening to the irregular throb of her heart, he was more certain than ever that Death was upon her—his fatal kiss could be deemed sweet blessing—she would likely think it so herself.

He went and took her hands, raising her up, and she stepped from the tub and into his arms. *Yes,* the mindvoice murmured as he kissed her lips. *Just so, Nicholas; she is yours.* He crushed her closer, savoring the mad rhythm of her heart against his empty breast, only the thin, wet linen of his shirt between them, only her tender skin separating his hunger from her hot, sweet blood . . .

"No," he snarled, pushing her away as gently as he could manage. His fangs pressed like tiny daggers against the still-burning flesh of his mouth as he turned his back again on a prize he should have claimed without a thought. "Do not touch me," he rasped, feeling her fingers stroke at his back, his neck.

"As you will," Isabella repeated sadly, reaching for her shift instead. Her head ached so, 'twas likely just as well. "Verily, Nicholas, I blame you not at all—any fool can see the truth of my madness, th'effect." She snatched the simple gown over her head with her last burst of energy and sank down on the bed with ragged breath. "You've better wit than to lie with pox, even for pity."

"Nay, lady," Nick protested, love of a sudden making him face her when hunger could not. "The cancer is not yours, dearest girl," he promised, lifting both her hands to his lips. "'Tis mine, I swear it."

"Such a sweet nature as this must be cherished," she answered with a weary smile. "No wonder your lady doth hold you so dear."

"Think not on her," Nick urged, drawing the blankets up warm around her. "Think on naught now but your sweet rest."

11

"Yes, come," quoth he,
"my thirst is not quenched; for the first draught
gave me but a taste of sweetness . . ."
And therewith another cup of the same blood
was given him to drink.

—Thomas Deloney,
The Gentle Craft, ch. iii (1597)

VACHON AND SCREED HAD EMERGED INTO THE COURTYARD FROM THE servants' hall at the first loud shriek of commotion and had drawn ever nearer as the violent farce proceeded. "I know her, Screed," Vachon explained, remembering as he watched this hellcat tear at her human bindings, the lost and pretty girl who had asked him to help her die. She seemed eager enough to fight for life this night, he mused. Perhaps he could better help her now . . .

Then he'd felt the presence of another vampire and seen Janette's golden dandy emerge with his magic purse.

"Yon lordling seems to 'ave all well in 'and, wot say ye?" Screed said sarcastically as the girl collapsed in the blond man's arms. "A bit o' the vampy mutters, an' 'e's one lovely loony more blessed."

"I fear you've the truth of it, Screed," Vachon answered sadly, barely conscious of how easily he could now find meaning in his companion's babble. "The girl is his now."

• • •

The chaos in the main hall had spilled outward in every direction as soon as *la petite derangeé* had been carried out, with Janette's lover following like a dog. Now the vampire was pushing her own way through the press of nobles who apparently thought Isabella's sickness would infect them if they stayed calm at Hunsdon's house another moment. For herself, she only wished her reasons for fleeing the scene were so simple.

Not mad . . . a monster. The memory of Nicholas's furious, grief-stricken face in the false confessional haunted her like a ghost, refusing to be banished. Now the image was born anew, reflected almost perfectly in his anguish as this pitiable Isabella had fallen. Ridiculous . . . What could this English tart have in common with a rich French virgin? Nothing but death.

She summoned one of the footmen standing and looking overwhelmed in the teeming courtyard, calling him to her with a single, imperious gesture. The man, who had been gaping at the chaos, seemed relieved to be commanded, galloping to Janette's side as if she represented the last shred of order in the universe.

"I am Madame DuCharme," Janette informed him, using small words so as to be understood as quickly as possible. "I know not where my own footman may be. I care not where my own footman may be. Bring me my coach *à l'instant.*"

"A thousand pardons, milady," the footman stammered, recognizing her accent if not her face. It was more chaos, after all—did this lady not know? "I cannot—"

"Why not?" she demanded. "Shall I describe it to you? Are you so stupid—"

"Nay, milady, 'tis not that. I know it well enough," he hastened to assure her, absorbing the insult as only his due. He continued, his voice miserable with failure: "I'faith, I did see it not a quarter hour past—driving away with your lordship, them two players, and that crazy lass in it."

"*Incroyable!*" she hissed, her creamy complexion going whiter with rage. So the wench would have her carriage this night as well as her Nicholas?

"A thousand, thousand pardons, milady," the wise footman muttered as he beat a most hasty retreat.

• • •

Vachon, meanwhile, still stood where he'd watched the wealthy vampire drive away with his acquisition.

"A fine thing," Screed said with a sigh, echoing Vachon's thoughts. "She made 'erself a fair ruckus afore they bagged 'er, though—a body'll give 'er that much. Hoy, but weren't that a lovely sight," he grinned appreciatively, "see a mad mort sink 'er teeth into one or two official 'ands." He looked around the bustling courtyard with a cheerful grin. "All of a jig they are, each 'n' ev'ry. Make a fanger of 'er, I says," he said approvingly.

Vachon was barely listening to his fledgling, but this last remark registered. He gave Screed a sidelong glance. "She wants death."

"She never—the more fool 'er," Screed snorted, rolling his eyes. "Worms and green grass when it could be a jolly nightride and pricky-nicks in the neck?"

Vachon shrugged. Would the golden vampire give her the death she so craved? Or would he bring her into the night?

A moment later, Vachon forgot these thoughts entirely.

"Screed, *mira*—look," he said, correcting himself and pointing. Standing just outside the great house's main door was a far more worthy object of interest, looking fair for murder and most fair indeed. "'Tis the lady."

"Lady? Wot, yer little fanged night-dove? Ain't we Fortune's fav'rits," Screed said sarcastically. "'Er weather eye ain't told 'er yet the golden wind blew off with the squall," he grinned, enjoying the sight of an aristocrat's discomfiture.

Vachon was already walking away, his eyes fixed on Janette. Behind him, Screed rolled his lips, making a rude noise. "'Tis a stormy compass ye've steered," he said to Vachon's back, leaning against a wall to watch his master try his luck.

Scarcely daring to believe his luck, Vachon approached her and swept his hat off in a graceful salute. "Milady, we meet once more," he said gently.

Distracted by irritation over her coach, Janette barely spared the other vampire a glance. Some lackey of Aristotle's, probably. Then she remembered him, and looked back: this was the fledgling who had brought her that unpleasant visit from Aristotle.

"You are exactly the same," said Vachon, almost reverently.

"You look much better," Janette said. His foolish gaping of earlier notwithstanding, the unkempt vampire of the back alley was now a handsomely dressed young man, with his beard neatly trimmed à la Cadiz and his hair clean and combed, if still rather long. Dressed as a citizen rather than a lord, but certainly presentable. She held out one gloved hand.

"Thank you, milady," Vachon returned, taking her hand and bowing over it. "I am Javier Vachon, at your service. I speak a goodly English now, as you bade me."

Janette's eyes began to register boredom. What was the point of learning to speak if one uttered only platitudes? "I believe I asked you to address me in a civilized tongue," she said. "English, while a language, is not a civilized tongue—though I grant your performance of its intricacies has improved greatly since last we met, for which I felicitate you."

"I learned this tongue most of all to converse with you, milady," Vachon said softly. At that moment, it was the truth.

Janette shrugged slightly. "Even a gray parrot may be taught to say *prithee* or *bon Dieu,* but it doesn't make him a knight. Nor do I recall that I offered you aught for it. Certainly not my hand," she added tartly, pulling it away from him.

"I see that you have no carriage," Vachon pursued. "Come with me, then. The world is open to any pleasure we may want to prove on it. Come to the New World with me."

Boredom flushed to incredulity. "You jest, *garçon,*" Janette said flatly. "Or are you mad?"

"You don't understand," the fledgling said. "We are different."

"*Mais oui,* extremely different." Her voice was cold. "From courtesy, I will mention only that you do not wear skirts, whilst I . . ." Her hand brushed lightly at her velvets, the damasked farthingale pulled back to reveal an underdress of delicately figured silk.

"Ah, milady, no," said Vachon urgently. "That is not my import. I mean, such as we both are—we, who are not of their world at all." Now it was Vachon who gestured, the sweep of his hand taking in the household from stables to kitchen to great chambers—the whole panoply of the mortal world. "We are . . . special and apart," he said earnestly. "We must always be so. It is our great glory, this liberty."

Janette laughed shortly, amused despite herself. What a pity that it was this uncouth Spaniard and not Nicholas who wished to celebrate the pleasures of his existence in the night, who was imagining he could pass them along to her.

"Ah, *mon brave,* I think it is you who do not understand," she said, more kindly than she'd intended. "You are still a very new one, are you not? I know the pleasures of our existence well—very well." A smile of feral pleasure crossed her lips, her eyes flashed briefly, and she said once more, "*J'ai une bonne connaissance des lesquelles, on t'assure.*" Her attention returned to Vachon. "*A vrai dire,* I am much older than you, young one." She shrugged her shoulders in mock despair. "Ah, but a woman should never say such a thing to *un gallant,* no?"

Genteel wordplay, particularly when liberally salted with words from a language he did not speak, was beyond Vachon's immediate experience. What social conversation he had indulged in with ladies in recent years had not involved the small delicacies of upper-class flirtation. But the flash of Janette's proud blue eyes, in the moment when she smiled as a huntress, struck him like lightning—a beauty, and one of his own kind.

"But you must understand me," he said intensely. "None of the old errors rule in the New World. It is all fresh morning there." He smiled slightly, acknowledging the incongruity of his image, but continued. "It can be our morning." His brown eyes were huge with desire, his soft lips were slightly parted, and the black locks that framed them tumbled incontinently around his shoulders. "Come and find it with me."

Janette laughed at him. "The New World? *Mon Dieu,* young one, I have no wish to live with savages in jungles. *Bien sûr,* I do not even wish to drink at the fountain of such creatures. It is the merest accident that you even find me in this England with its rude manners and ugly houses. Me, I belong in Paris."

Stung by her mockery, Vachon stepped back. The pleading quality left his voice and his face, and something of the predator in him looked out at her. "Then you truly do not understand, milady. This world," he nodded backward at the house, "is one colossal death. It shines only with its own slick decay. It is not for such as we, who will never be so touched. Let them have it, the mortal ones who pick at its bones. Let them drown in its swill."

Vachon looked at her steadily. "The New World may be

rough, milady, but it is as we are." He shook his head slightly, and his voice dropped even lower. "It is of our very nature."

Janette favored him with a small smile, finding Vachon more appealing as a predator than a suitor. "That is one truth, *garçon,* but not the only one." She continued, exaggerating his phrase a little. "Yes, it is important for 'such as we' to learn that we must make our own world, but there are other lessons awaiting you. Perhaps some day you will come to Paris, to *la vielle cité*—the old city—and learn another truth."

"Paris." Now Vachon shrugged. "Is that where he'll take that girl?"

Janette spoke softly. "Go away now, *garçon.* I thought you held some promise when you could not speak, but now you have expressed yourself and I see that I erred. You are a peasant pig. *Va't-on,* Vachon. You have exhausted my interest in you entirely."

Aristotle had not so much as left his seat during the uproar over Isabella's sudden performance as Ophelia. How rare to see Old Punctilioso, Lord Hunsdon, bearded by a chit in his own den; how interesting to see a base young female devise a way to give her highborn lover, Hilliard, a bit of his own back again. And there was something between the girl and the players too; the part seemed to have been struck off her. A mad girl playing a princess drawn from a mad girl? Yes, a rare show.

Well, time to go home, the cream of the jest had been savored. The candles set along the edge of the stage were still less than halfway consumed; no one had thought to extinguish them in the collapse of the performance. Aristotle strolled to the window wall, mildly curious about the noise in the yard.

What he saw destroyed his good cheer in an instant: there in the courtyard stood Janette. In itself, that was nothing to alter his humor, but Janette was making a gesture of dismissal at a young man with dark eyes, black brows, and long black hair. And the young man went.

The Spaniard served her? All this time, this untidy marplot had been at her bidding? Was he on his way to make yet another ridiculously public mistake—mayhap he would sup on some wench there in the courtyard?

Aristotle hurried for the stairs.

• • •

The crowd in the back courtyard, having lost the spectacle of Hilliard's mad lightskirt being dragged off to Bedlam, had begun to break up, the nobles either climbing into carriages or drifting back inside to hone their bits of testimony to razor-sharp gossip for the morrow at court, their servants resolving into a loose circle around those of the Lord Chamberlain's Men who'd drifted out with the rest. Vachon and Screed moved through this pattern in halfhearted opposition to both groups, and Screed was singing:

Was not good Kyng Salamon
Ravished in sondry wise
with every livelie Paragon
That glistered before his eyes?

He paused, waiting for Vachon to tell him to keep his peace. But his vampire master was obviously not listening—indeed, he had such murder in his expression Screed thought it best not to look at him at all.

If this be true as trewe it was
Lady lady
why should not I serve you alas?
My deare lady.

This earned him a pointed glance, but little more. "Alas, lay-day, why should I not serve *you*!" Screed finished, throwing in a little hopping dance for good measure as Vachon pushed through the open door into the servants' hall and disappeared. Finding himself suddenly the only vampire in the crowded courtyard, Screed scurried to catch up.

"'Ang on there, a-may-go," he pleaded, overtaking the Spaniard as he passed out of the hall into the house proper, through the arch at the other side. "Just where is't yer thinkin' o' landin' yerself, if I may be so bold to ask?"

Vachon didn't answer, pausing at a stairway that curved both upward and down, lifting his chin as if to sniff the air. "Go away, Screed," he ordered, half-consciously quoting this proud Janette who'd held his favor so cheap.

"I'll none," the sailor retorted indignantly, though his courage threatened to fail. He had seen Vachon kill before—indeed, he'd felt the fangs barely hidden behind that wenchy pout stuck sharp in his own skinny neck. But he'd never feared him, at least not after that first moment. Not, that is, until now.

He cast a despairing glance back at the relative safety of the outdoors before following Vachon up the stairs. "So what if yer lines ran a-foul o' Lady Not-So-Fair?" he persisted. "Told yer to shove off—what o'that? Hoy, that's what ladies does. No need to take a taking from it—find another and be done."

Vachon stopped to look at him, his eyes as black and empty as the night. "I am," he answered mildly, but the threat was unmistakable. "Now go."

Screed met the Spaniard's glare face-on for as long as he was able, but he could stare down death only so far. This wasn't hunger, and Screed knew it. His master was headed for a leeward shore with all sail crammed on—he'd come to hold his own brand of squealer a powerful grudge and naught would dissuade him from vengeance. A little boy's trick of temper, no question, but best to let him howl it out alone. "Lay on, me lovely infant," Screed grumbled, turning away. "But ne'er say I didn't warn ye."

Vachon watched until his companion made the turn in the stairs, defiantly repeating his song. Then he turned and went back to the hunt.

In the jungle, he'd learned to hunt a single prey for the sheer sport of it, sometimes stalking a lone mortal hunter for three nights together before finally taking him down. But he'd never had so much trouble isolating a single scent as he had finding Mistress Addison again. The upper floors of the house were a chaos of perceptions, a cacophony of unintelligible voices behind thick stone walls. The vampire slipped through the shadows like a panther in the night, sometimes passing unseen within inches of one of the servants dashing to and fro to put the highborn cattle in their proper stalls for the night. Every time a door opened, he listened for his prey, until at last he picked her voice out of the din. Slipping into an alcove behind one of the heavy tapestries, he waited for her to emerge.

Marcia had been hard-pressed to draw breath, so occupied was she in keeping her mistress from losing her mind entirely. For herself, she hadn't a clue who the doxy who'd embarrassed young William might have been, but she was more than a bit conflicted in her hopes for the woman's future. On the one hand, she had no great objection to seeing Willy squirm. But the consequence for herself was none so pleasant—Her Ladyship was indeed fit to be tied. And gagged.

Promising once more to send for William straightaway, she backed out of the door and shut it as quick as she could. "Most like he hath gone to take his vengeance," she muttered, turning to head down the hall.

Suddenly a strong, strange hand shot out from behind the tapestry and yanked her into the dark. Opening her mouth to scream, she found herself kissed instead.

"Go to!" she hissed, giving her captor a sharp cuff to the side of the head. Pulling back, she found herself nose to nose with the handsome Frenchman she'd met a scant hour before. "Are you mad?" she demanded softly, mindful of her mistress just across the hall. "Let me go."

"Yes," he answered with a wolfish grin, bending to kiss her again, brief and soft on the lips. "And no." She opened her mouth to protest, and the vampire kissed her more deeply, pressing her tightly to him as he backed her against the wall. "You bid me meet you, did you not?" he murmured, brushing his mouth across the curve of her tender cheek.

"Yea, but not here," she protested, a muffled giggle escaping her as his breath tickled her ear. "Go to, I say—my mistress will miss me."

"Horribly," he agreed as he kissed her once more, holding her mouth captive until she grew willing in his embrace, her heartbeat calling him on. He nuzzled her throat, savoring her sigh as sweet as her scent, the warmth of her blood just beneath the pale pink, tender skin. Her arms slid up tighter around his back, and he smiled. "What think you, mistress?" he whispered, kissing the nape of her neck.

"I know not," she admitted with a gasp. "If I were wise, I should have screamed long since."

"And now 'tis too late," he agreed, putting a gentle but implacable hand over her mouth as he sank his fangs into her throat. He felt panic, fear like a spice in her blood, cinnamon in honeyed wine, then a resignation that was sweeter still, an inclining of her will like the yielding of her body, surrender to his murderous embrace, to the soft, contented rumbling in his throat as he fed from her. He lifted his hand from her face, letting her sigh escape as he drew the last sweet drop from her heart, a whisper of deathly rapture.

He lowered her to the cold stone floor, mesmerized by the play of fractured moonlight falling through the mullioned window onto her peaceful face, glittering in her empty eyes. "*Adios, cariña,*" he murmured, kissing her cooling cheek. He tugged the concealing white cap from her head, revealing a halo of reddish-blond hair, fine as silk between his fingers. Lovely . . . but wrong. Kissing her lips once more, he left her to her moonlit niche.

By the time he reached the servants' hall again, a veritable carnival was in full swing, with drunkards holding court inside and clownish players making merry just without. "Well met, you popish bastard!" one of the drunkards hailed the vampire as he came back through the arch. "Comment tally voo—back to have a bit more stand about and stare, are ye?" Vachon turned to snarl at him and got a bottle pressed into his hand instead. "Good Rhenish tastes as well here as in France," the drunkard laughed in sodden good humor. "Drink ye something, for Christ's sweet blood."

Vachon uncorked the bottle with his teeth. *Why not?* he mused as he tipped the bottle back to general applause. The wine burned his throat, the taste making him gag. Rotten fruit, essence of this corpse of a continent . . . He took another long swallow, feeling the alcohol rise to his already-buzzing brain.

By the time he stopped drinking to look around, the man who'd forced the bottle on him had already disappeared into the mass of mortal celebration, one of the maggots feasting on the corpse of Hunsdon's party, themselves a collection of overripe grapes waiting to be tasted, for vampire teeth to free their juice. Their faces seemed to dance in a morris ring on every side—not an unfamiliar sensation, now that Vachon thought of it. This England was not so different from Spain, much as he had tried to prove otherwise. Many was the night he'd spent in such a stupor, blending into the throng, waiting for some pretty baggage or another to find him, give him a warm, soft haven in which to rest between bottles, a cushion on which to finally collapse.

He thought of his latest conquest, her blood still warm beneath his skin, bits and pieces of her memory swirling through the dizziness of wine. Her happiest moment remembered at the moment of her surrender, a walk in Whitehall gardens with a boy she liked on a spring afternoon, all the bushes coming into their green and flowers blooming in the raised beds, feeling a flower herself—simple sweetness, his for this moment, fading as he thought of it. Had this Janette ever carried such sweetness in her blood? Not likely, and never for him . . . *Vat'on, Vachon.*

He lurched back to his feet and out the door, a slight stumble as he brought his false mortal drunkenness under vampire control. The loose circle from before had become a proper audience, the players' clowns finding a way to recover some profit by performing various tricks and gambols for whatever pennies these peasants might throw. What had Fortune meant him to be, peasant or clown? Well, he had cheated Fortune, as he would now remind her. *Vampire, is that how we are called?* he remembered, losing himself in the crowd, seeking new prey as eagerly as if he starved. And on the edge of the throng, he found it.

She was tall, almost as tall as Vachon himself, but delicate, with the long, white limbs of a nunnery madonna. Even better was her hair, a tangle of heavy black curls pulled back from her high, white brow with a simple band and allowed to tumble all the way down her back. But best of all were her eyes—the deep, rich blue of the midnight sky and the shape of perfect almonds, tilted upward at the corners to lend an air of catlike intelligence to an otherwise innocent face. He watched her try to push her way to a better vantage point, but she met with no success, and drew back with an impossibly lovely pout. "*Santa Maria,*" he murmured, moving purposefully to her side. "Thy pardon, mistress? We have met ere this."

"Think you so?" she laughed, turning to him at once, the mocking, flirtatious twist of her mouth folding his time in on itself, transforming this sweet poison to another, though this one wore a peasant's apron and cap. "I warrant you I should remember," she said, fearlessly returning his gaze.

"Do you not?" he asked, mock-serious, as he lifted her hand to his lips.

"'Sooth," she murmured, making wide eyes at him. "I am tempted to say you yea, for all it be a lie." The crowd let out a collective shout of approval, diverting her attention for a moment—she put her hands on his shoulders and pressed forward to see what was going on, unconsciously offering him her throat as she craned for a better look. "A pox on't all," she swore, falling back again, unable to see past her taller, quicker companions.

"What ails thee, my pretty one?" he asked, closing his eyes lest he frighten her away while he regained his composure.

"'Twas the Devil's own task convincing my papa to let me come out so late to see the players," she pouted. "Now I cannot come near enough them to see."

"Your papa thought it best you stay at home?" he asked, pretending an interest he did not feel for the pleasure of hearing her speak.

"He thinks little good of players," she answered. A thought seemed to occur to her, and she grinned mischievously. "Of course, Papa would have me beat near dead if he knew where I dallied now—and having converse with a stranger, e'en so."

"As well he might," Vachon scolded, grinning back.

"Go to," she cried, giving his shoulder a playful swat. "As if I cannot keep me well alone without his care."

Vachon touched her cheek. "Just as if," he murmured, capturing her completely with his eyes.

"'Sooth," she repeated, the intensity of her tone somehow endowing this simple, girlish oath with the depth and emotion of a sonnet.

"Come with me," he urged with a smile, taking her hand and leading her away from the crowd, toward the privacy of the stables.

She came to his arms with the eagerness of an experienced courtesan, wrapping herself around him almost before they were out of sight of the crowd. "What think you your papa might say now?" Vachon teased, freeing her hair from its band as he led her to a horseless stall. He backed her against the rough wood of the stall and loosed her lacings, sliding one hand inside her blouse to touch the warm, soft skin, while the other traced the lines of her lips, caressed at her brow, her ear, her jaw.

"Naught but ill," she admitted with a giggle, shaking her head to fling the stray curls from her eyes. "But what is't the old wives say? What he doesn't know can't hurt him?"

Another proverb proved false, Vachon thought, biting

through her tender skin so gently she would barely feel a sting. She sighed and curled closer into his embrace as he lowered them both to the straw, her delicious warmth like a summer wind captured in his arms. But as he drew the life from her throat, he felt her arousal melt into an icy terror in the midst of her heat. "Papa!" she screamed as he captured her mouth and her cry with his, kissing her deeply one last time before snapping her delicate flower-stem neck.

He lifted himself from her and sat back, gazing for a moment on her beauty, perfected for this single moment, her blue eyes wide with shock, her lips parted for his kiss. Best to leave her now before the illusion was shattered. Turning away, he strode back out into the night.

Screed, watching the clowns, had felt Vachon emerge from the house and had turned in time to see him peel a pretty off the skin of the crowd and lead her to the stables. But he'd felt no burning desire to see him make the kill. "Fair sail an' I wish ye joy," he'd muttered, a sailor's marriage blessing, as he turned back to the show.

But now as he thought him of it further, it seemed meet he should have at least a peek. He slipped through the wooden stable door, hardly surprised to feel a telltale tingle in the air, then dove for a shadowed hayrick as a vampire he didn't recognize ran past him into the night.

"In livery yet," Screed muttered, shaking his rattled bones back into place as he got back to his feet. "A fair gentleman's gentleman and a fanger to boot." A fat and sassy barn rat darted over his foot, and he took another dive into the hay. "A lil' nip to settle me nerves," he said, coming up with the squirming body between both hands.

The first rat drained, he crawled forward and laid hold of another—the hay was fairly crawling with them. Two . . . three . . . four . . . Ahhh," he gargled, lifting red teeth from the last of them, "there's pearly-precious; nectar for ol' Screedy is wot." He reached out once more, feeling a bit of the glutton, and his fingers made contact with something softer and infinitely less lively. "Blast me to Hades and kiss the Devil's bum," he muttered, sitting back on his heels to look down into a dead, blue-eyed stare.

• • •

Janette stripped out of her gloves and flung them on the low table by the window, her fingers fairly itching to wrap themselves around the nearest handy throat. "*Merci,*" she said tersely to the servant who had shown her and her own Dianne to this chamber, turning away before the creature could complete her curtsey. "Dianne, go with her and fetch Monsieur LaCroix at once."

She turned away from the window restlessly, pacing the room like an angry cat. Could this night be any worse? First Nicholas had behaved like an utter fool, leaving LaCroix and herself stranded in this house full of mortals—windows in her bedchamber; how was she to manage that?—to chase after some lunatic on the brink of death. Then that Spanish brat had appeared as if by magic—*quelle dommage!* As if she could possibly be persuaded to go tramping through some savage jungle . . . Verily, things could not get any worse.

"Have you lost your wits entirely?" Aristotle demanded as he came through the door unannounced. "Where have you sent him?"

"Who?" she retorted, her temper finding a worthy object at last. "Nicholas? I assure you, wherever he may have gone, 'twas ne'er at my bidding."

"No, my dear lady, not Nicholas," Aristotle said caustically. "Nicholas concerns me but little just now. I meant your Spaniard."

Janette's blue eyes flashed fire. "I have many possessions, monsieur, but a Spaniard is not among them," she shot back.

Aristotle crossed his arms patiently. "Forsooth? Then explain to me how is't that I did see you in his company not half an hour since."

Before she could reply, Dianne opened the door again and ushered in an uncharacteristically troubled LaCroix and his vampire servant, Gaston, lent him by Aristotle. "*Bon Dieu,* what has happened now?" Janette demanded as Dianne went out again.

"Another, er, plague corpse, my lord," Gaston answered, glancing at LaCroix for a nod before addressing himself directly to Aristotle. "I found her in the stables just now—dropped there, by the look of her, with no pretense of discretion."

Aristotle rolled his brown eyes heavenward as if to entreat

wisdom from the gilded cherubim painted on the ceiling. "A woman, I suppose."

"Yea, milord, and more than passing fair to look upon," Gaston replied, glancing at Janette.

"Gaston took certain temporary measures before coming to report this to me," LaCroix said dryly. "These will serve but for the nonce, however. I think it best we make more lasting arrangements as soon as possible."

Janette met her master's inquiring gaze with equal defiance. "You two go, and take your footman," she said. "For myself, I shall retire to our lodging—"

"Nay, lady." Aristotle demurred, his tone pleasant but firm. "I think for this matter, we shall most particularly require your assistance." He gestured gallantly, but inescapably, for her to proceed him through the door.

The girl was sprawled, wide-eyed and unmistakably deceased, half-covered in the straw of one of the empty stalls. "I'faith, milord, I had her covered well," Gaston protested to Aristotle and LaCroix's mutually lifted eyebrows.

"I doubt it not," Aristotle reassured him, clapping him briefly on the shoulder as he bent down to examine the corpse more closely. "What lovely blue eyes these were. And midnight tresses."

LaCroix looked once again at his vampire daughter, but she turned her face away.

Aristotle kicked at a furry object with obvious distaste, and Gaston leaned over and picked it up. "A rat, milord," said the servant.

"Unmistakably so," said LaCroix, crossing his arms. He leaned forward fractionally and peered into the hay. "Several rats, in truth." His tone was a peculiar mixture of disgust and amusement.

Aristotle shot his old friend an annoyed glance. Lucius had a rare gift for staying out of trouble, even when it meant leaving the trouble for other people to deal with—or dodge.

"What of these rats, Gaston?" Aristotle asked. He gestured slightly, and the servant, who had been poking through the straw, straightened up. As he did so, he swung the one rat he held before Janette's delicate nose, seemingly by accident.

Janette stiffened and retreated a half step, with a small cry of disgust.

"Indeed, there are four rats," reported Gaston. "And there were no rats here when I left her before, milord," he insisted.

"So," Aristotle said with a resigned smile as he gestured the servant to let the rat corpse drop. "Two vampires, one a carouche. The rat-sucker follows the seducer."

"Two vampires," LaCroix agreed.

All three men, lord and servant alike, turned to look at Janette.

"Should we not dispose of this person?" she replied coolly. "I understood it to be a matter of some urgency that we do so."

Aristotle turned his questioning eyes on LaCroix, but he would have been better served to take his prayers to a marble god. LaCroix yielded nothing to outsiders whenever a member of his family was concerned, however harshly he might enforce justice upon them himself.

"Gaston and I will take care of the body," Aristotle said coolly. "You two, I pray you, find these wretched vampires."

Elizabeth was no queen, but she had lived her life a virgin princess. Indeed, tonight was the first in all her sixteen years she had ever spent partaking of the world after dark, her first night in the heady crush of adult society. Her first play, and that spoiled by some common wench in breeches. "Still, 'twas passing thrilling," she confessed in careful nursery script to an equally sheltered and so-far-still-cloistered friend. "Lord William Hilliard is very handsome at all events, even more than gossip says, and tonight he was . . ." She paused, at a loss. Nothing in her experience had given her words to describe the sensation she'd felt watching the very handsome Hilliard in a lover's cruelest rage.

She contented herself with a long, ragged sigh, crumpling the page and tossing it into the fire.

"Love letters to the Devil?" a masculine voice queried from the shadowed corner behind her bed.

She whirled around to find an apparition even more delicious than Hilliard, gazing on her with intense dark eyes. *I'm asleep,* she thought with an inward giggle. She'd had dreams like this before . . .

"What is't you say?" she asked boldly, getting up from her

tapestried chair. His hair and beard both looked so soft . . . stroking them would be like stroking a panther's back. She frowned: where had that thought come from?

"Only the Devil can receive tenders posted so," the vampire explained with the barest hint of a smile as he moved into the light. "Do you beg him to come fetch you away?"

Something in his eyes made her pause, shivering—was this a dream or a nightmare? He was so beautiful, but still . . . She wanted to look away, yet his eyes were holding her somehow, making her want even more to keep looking and looking . . . "Nay," she answered, a tremor in her tone. "I do renounce the Devil and all his pomps—I am a Christian."

"His pomps?" The vampire repeated the word with amusement. He smiled at the girl, his lips parting and his eyes narrowing with what looked like friendly appreciation. "So you are a good Christian. Think you not *el Diablo* loves those best of all?" Vachon said, taking another lazy step closer.

He had meant to leave off killing after the last girl, his hunger more than sated. He had meant to lay himself down in some dark, safe den and sleep off the dregs of his black mood. But as he walked back from the stables, the lights of this grand house had called him, glowing eyes that winked and mocked his pride. After so many decades of being his own master, he'd suddenly been forced to remember what it was to be a boy who belonged in the stables, never to be allowed in the big house. Wounded and angry, his vampire heart insisted on reminding him that now he could go wherever he willed, and make himself the master, the absolute possessor, of anyone there. *Anyone mortal,* he'd thought, recalling the image of Janette's dismissal—and that image had made him snarl inside. And at that moment, he'd heard a girl humming in a high window.

It was the easiest thing in the world for a vampire to drift up to a high window ledge, look in, and decide whether he liked what he saw there . . . long black hair, tumbled down for the night, a girl of noble bearing, straightbacked and proud, her eyes large and blue as a holy well.

"Dost thou fear me, Christian?" he whispered, lifting one of her raven curls and pressing it to his lips.

He stood directly behind her chair now. To look at him, Elizabeth had to tip her head back in a way that lengthened her neck, stretched its skin taut, and outlined the treasure of veins beneath it. Vachon's breath quickened to see her pulse. He stroked her cheek lightly, still holding the strand of silken hair twined between his fingers.

"You are one of the players," Elizabeth guessed, every inch of her tingling with chills she could barely define. "Which part did you play? And how did you—"

"Which do you think?" he asked, tracing the curve of her jaw with his fingertips, trailing down the smooth, blameless skin of her throat—and stopping there.

"I know not," she whispered, her voice melting away beneath his touch. "They say Hamlet the prince was deranged . . . But I know not how he ended . . ."

"In his grave, pretty Christian," he answered, his black hair tangling with hers as he bent to the bite. *Where all good Christians end . . .* The delicate touch of his fingertips was suddenly an iron hold beneath her jaw, pulling her head to one side. Her startled motion, her desperate attempt to rise, only brought her skin to his mouth with an even more exciting suddenness.

Aye, an' I might 'ave known, Screed silently despaired, clinging to the ledge outside the window as if he might have been a Bombay monkey. He'd managed to catch a glimpse of Señor Stupid as he'd slipped into the house like a bad dream. Now he crawled through the window as Vachon drained the little ladykins dry as her stableyard sister outside in the hay. "Spanick ships and Spanick soldiers, unhandy and unlovely alike," he grumbled as Vachon let his prey slump back in her seat, and picked up her quill from the desk. "Wot now, mate? Writin' yerself into her will?"

Vachon ignored him. He finished his message and headed for the door, his perverse humor moving him to walk out of the house bold as a lord. "The world'll be runnin' short of lamb-ikins wi' blue eyes and black hair, rate yer cannonadin' 'em," Screed ventured, scrambling to follow. "A few more bastinadoes, an' it's yellow-haired girls for aye." Vachon started down the stairs. "'Tis two now, right?" Screed pressed, running ahead to face him.

Vachon stopped. "Three," he said, meeting his fledgling's eyes for the barest moment before continuing on.

"Three?" Screed goggled. *Must've found a nibble inside the first time . . . Three?* For all the sailor had few morals, he shook his bald head in dismay: *three's evil. Little girls wot barely hurts flies?* And the Conquistador himself, for all he loved his ladies, never hurt 'em but for hunger. *Gone lunatistickal,* Screed concluded, growing fearful. *This'll put us both on the boulders.* He clattered down the last flight, racking his brain for a way to steer his master off this course. "Three's a good string," he persisted, counting off on his skinny fingers. "Ye've got yer *Niña,* yer *Pinta,* an' yer *Santa Maria.*" He got plainer. "Look you, if Duchess Vampiresa said you nay, then you've done. That galleon's sail down on th'orizon, mate—gone a-gone, is what. Give over."

Vachon didn't deign to speak a word. He simply whipped around too fast for a mortal eye to follow, grabbed Screed by the throat, and snarled an inch from Screed's nose, red-eyed and fanged, rumbling deep in his throat like a lion.

Screed cringed as far as his master's grip would permit. "'Ere, 'ere, belay yer murderin'; just pumping the bilge, am I. Just diga-me this: wot's the misery-phiz all for?"

Vachon's first thought was to crush the bones in the persistent little bastard's neck for the interest of watching him mend, but in truth, Screed didn't deserve it. Nor did he deserve any great answer. "I don't belong here," he said, dropping his fledgling and heading back out into the night.

"God's hinders, what of it?" Screed snorted rudely behind him. "Call'em me betters, they do . . . Right-ee-o-aye-aye, better in findin' of troubles where there is none—'e sights a storm on a leeward quarter an' has 'im a tizzical fit." Vachon's hair caught the breeze and waved outward like a pirate flag as he went through the door.

Screed paused a moment longer, considering, then followed on nevertheless. "Be ye warned, little black lambs," he muttered to the winking stars above, in hopes they'd pass the word along. "'Tis a fair night to be fair." He stopped as he saw Vachon pause in the shadow of the stables and heard a woman's musical laugh. "An' a fair night to be foul," he sighed. "But a foul night to be darkly fair." Vachon had altered course and pace, heading back into the stable. Screed shook his head again. "An' Devil take us, little lambs, 'e's not done."

"This entire project is ridiculous," Janette was saying as she and LaCroix stalked through Lord Hunsdon's upper halls.

"How exactly does your so-precious Aristotle imagine we shall find two little vampires in all this great house without arousing suspicion?"

"Sneering at Aristotle is never wise," LaCroix returned. "In your case, *ma chére,* it becomes less wise with each passing hour. As for how—the thought occurs that no such quest would be required had you not made such a foul assignation. Really, Janette—punishing Nicholas is an admirable diversion, but could you not have chosen a more admirable tool?"

"Punish Nicholas?" she demanded, incredulous. "Assignation? *Mille diables!* How many times must I say it? I know naught at all of these rogues—"

"Then why, pray tell, was the Spaniard mooning after you on the street?" LaCroix asked.

"What have I to do with where some Spaniard may choose to look?" she shot back. "Truly, LaCroix, if I were not—" She broke off suddenly. "*Mais silence,*" she ordered in a whisper. "Heard you that?"

"Heard me what?" LaCroix paused.

"I cannot say certainly," she said, moving slowly down the passage. "Someone was speaking . . . one of us." Turning the corner, she found a door standing ajar. "Oh, *mon Dieu,*" she sighed.

"Your *Dieu*?" LaCroix demanded, catching up. "What dark deity might that be?" He would protect what was his, including an errant daughter, to the death, but nothing prevented him from expressing his own irritation. It was most unlike Janette to engage in such willful conduct, and if it had not been for the purpose of provoking Nicholas, what was the point? He paused at the door, surveying the room before him for a long moment. "Ah, how most excellent: another guest at the *fête*," he said mockingly.

The girl was lying in an ungainly heap before her dying fire, the wounds in her throat barely dry. "*C'est magnifique,* think you not?" he added, raising his eyebrows like a connoisseur judging a painting. Despite his tone, LaCroix immediately moved the dead girl onto her bed, covering her so that she looked merely asleep to a casual glance. Then he stood back and became droll again. "Who would guess a single English household held so many beauties?" He looked down at the girl's wide-staring eyes. "All with black hair and blue eyes," he went on, turning back to his child. "*Quelle coincidence.*"

But Janette wasn't listening. She picked up the blotted page lying on the desk near where the body had been:

**Prithee . . . bon Dieu*
**Prithee . . . bon Dieu*
**Prithee . . . bon Dieu*
**Prithee . . . bon Dieu.*

"*Bon Dieu du vrai,*" she breathed, sinking down into the chair.

"What is it?" LaCroix asked, taking the paper. "A religious delirium? Perhaps he drove her mad—"

"*Non.*" Janette waved one hand in a small, tired gesture. "She did not write it. He did."

"Ah," LaCroix said ironically. "Now it makes plain sense—"

"He wrote it for me," she blurted out.

"A poor poem for such a pretty prey," LaCroix remarked. "It lacks a certain . . . *je ne sais quoi.*"

Janette gave him a hard glance. LaCroix usually understood too much, not too little: why was he clinging to his notion that she had consorted with this Spanish pig of a vampire? She mustered an icy civility.

"No, LaCroix—those are the words I taunted him for learning—I called him a parrot, a fool." She waved her hand again, then rested her forehead against it wearily. "I'faith, I scarce remember what I said to him."

"This vampire of whom you have no knowledge?" LaCroix asked dryly.

"Just so," she admitted with an obvious effort. "You must believe I have no part in this madness. Aristotle—"

"Matters but little," LaCroix cut her off. He put a reassuring hand on her shoulder and tried not to smile. As irritating as their present little adventure was becoming, 'twas a rare pleasure to have Janette so contrite. He would not spoil it by being over-stern. And first there was the task at hand: there was not enough time before dawn to trust to Gaston's return. There was a sharp, slender knife for the slicing of seals at hand among the girl's writing things.

"This lovely child must be seen to have died of self-murder,"

LaCroix instructed, placing the sheet of paper before her. "Write, in a delicate hand, something tragic at the bottom of your Spanish suitor's missive." Janette glanced at him. "The words of a maiden about to defile her own sweet throat." He picked up the knife, meeting her eyes. "And then, Janette, I think I must know . . . all."

Vachon's only purpose in heading for the stables had been to walk away from Screed and his harping, though the notion of finding someplace to lie down had begun to infect him again. Drunk from overfeeding, he barely saw the true colors of the woman emerging from the stable door before she blazed up in the glow of vampire hunger: he had a fleeting impression of frank blue eyes and brown hair . . . close enough. And yet he was full beyond full already, and no longer angry, not even with all the dark angels the night world might hold.

He made to simply walk past the woman, thinking of lying on the soft hay for a bit before the hour came to hide from the sun. But he'd forgotten the limitations of mortal sight, and the woman veered almost directly into him, then whooped and jumped as he became visible to her.

"'Sblood, boy, you gave me a start! I didn't see you there at all," the woman laughed, pressing a scullion's red hand to her bosom to emphasize her point. Her usual station was Lord Hunsdon's kitchen, but for the past quarter-hour she had done good service in the stables with a groom from some other lord's house. Vachon nodded with curt courtesy, and swung to one side of her, out of the stable's shadow. The woman took a look at his face in the moonlight and reached out. "Hold, child—mayhap Margery can give you a finish," she added boldly.

Vachon stopped.

Not like the others, who'd been girls or barely past it, Dame Margery was full ripe fruit, and it was in her eyes that she liked a good time with a man. More than that, Vachon's senses, burning at the high pitch of overfeeding, instantly seized on the disarray of her blouse and kirtle, the small, sweet-smelling bits of hay that clung to her skirts and cap, the dark strands of hair that were everywhere escaping their careful moorings under the cap. The woman's hand reached up from his arm to his cheek, cradling it, stroking at his small soft beard and the stubble around it.

“Were his kisses sweet?” Vachon backed her through the stable door with a rogue’s grin. He could smell illicit passion clinging to her skin like Araby perfume—the fragrant wages of sin, *amante*.

“Impudent dog!” she jabbed him. Now this was a beauty, no question. She tugged him back into the dark confines of a hay-filled stall. “Think you to better his game?”

“Most certainly.” Vachon grinned, tumbling her back in the hay. A small, square patch of moonlight came through a stall door to illuminate them: this was no coy dance of seducer with maiden, but a man and a woman both intent on their pleasures. Or so the woman thought, drawing the pretty boy closer.

He kissed her mouth, overwhelming her feigned protest in a moment with a tickle of smaller kisses all over her merry face, tingling pinpricks of blood beneath his lips as she blushed. “Wait, for mercy,” she giggled, pushing him off. “At least tell me how you are called.”

“Javier . . . Javito,” he answered, smiling down on her with something like affection.

“Harvey?” she repeated.

“Close enough,” he growled against her ear.

“Wait,” she protested again, a laughing plea. “Let me have a good look at you before I’m ruined, so please you.” He lifted his head obligingly, and she smiled.

“You are a pretty creature, strange and all,” she mused, caressing his cheek. “God hath gi’en you a maid’s fair mouth for kissing . . .” He kissed her. “Eyes of a gentle hind,” she continued, running her fingers around the edges of his large, slightly slanted eyes. He kissed her again. “A lordling’s pretty nose . . .” He nuzzled her with the praised nose, slid his lips across her cheek, flicker of tongue in her ear, nip of teeth along the lobe, teeth turning to fangs even as her hands came up to tangle in his hair. The vampire breathed a happy sigh in her ear, sliding an arm under her back and lifting her body close against his as his kisses trailed down her jawline, down the side of her neck . . . He held her tighter.

“Nay!” she scolded playfully. “Not yet, hasty boy.” She pulled back to give him a swat, but saw the vampire at last and gasped. “Holy Christ—”

“Gave me not these,” he finished, sinking fangs into her throat.

• • •

"'Anaxeretis bewtifull, when Iphis did behold and see,'" Screed sang, loitering outside the door. He browsed through the tall grass for some object to his purpose. "Now where's a loose spar when ye're wantin o' one, eh?" he muttered, surveying his options. A wheel spoke, too fragile, an old carriage door, likely not thick enough—ah, now, a broken axle-tree from an ox-cart, a good stout yard of seasoned oak—Screed resumed his tune.

"With sighes and sobbings pitifull
That Paragon wooed he.
And when he could not wynne her so
Ladye ladye
He went and honge him selfe for woe
My dear ladye."

He waited until Vachon came out, walking past him again as if he had no shape. "Prithee pardon, matey," he said and sighed, raising the timber high and bringing it down on his master's skull with all the force he could muster. The oak cracked, and the Spaniard paused in mid-step. "Or shall I say, *prithee bon Dieu,* ye codbrained fool? More royal consorts than 'Arry the Eighth, ye're after 'avin'—and bloodier divorces," Screed lectured, watching as Vachon turned . . . blinked once . . . twice . . . and fell to the ground like a stone.

"Thanks be to whiche'er imp gave me the nod," Screed muttered with a puff of long-held breath. "Come along then, me love . . . Ye'll likely feel yerself by the bye. An' 'ere comes the next watch whom we wants nowt o' bein' watched by." The tall, skinny vampire shouldered his ungainly burden, winked at the moon, and took clumsily to flight.

Aristotle and Gaston had just returned from their errand of disposal. Descending from their carriage, they felt more than saw Screed's passage into the sky. "Saw you that, master?" Gaston asked.

"Yea," Aristotle replied, going into the stable to find just what he'd expected.

"That is *not* the same wench," Gaston insisted. He had, after all, just consigned that one to the tender mercies of the Thames.

"Of course not," Aristotle agreed wearily. "Mark you the absence of rats? This prodigality finally o'erstretched even the patience of a carouche." He swept a hand skyward. "Go you and follow them, Gaston—and bring me their direction ere the sun rise."

LaCroix and Janette had arranged the fair Elizabeth, now seemingly dead of despair, into her bed and returned to Janette's chamber when "Secretary Dyer" reappeared. "All's well, my friends," he said cheerfully. "Gaston and I were fortune's favorites—happened upon the wretches in the courtyard." He glanced back and forth between their incredulous faces. "I do hope you two were not hard-pressed," he smirked.

"Of course not," Janette retorted, turning away from him.

"'Twas a rare and enlightening hour," LaCroix finished with a secret smile of his own. "Though methinks you must number your plague victims at two." He inclined his head toward the hall outside. Before Aristotle could speak, LaCroix waved a hand. "I have dealt with it."

"Then there are three," said Aristotle, shaking his head. "There was another in the stables. This Spaniard . . ." Janette shifted restlessly.

"Well-a-day, call it a banquet of several savories, removed with rats." A grin broke across Aristotle's face. "Or shall we say he tasted first of a tender grape, pale and grown wild i' the woods, plucked at earliest bloom; then progressed him to a blushful claret; and for a finish, drank deep of a maturer vintage." LaCroix registered delicate disapproval; Aristotle's absurd mirth was rampant again. Still, the jocularity meant he was not worried. "Even now, Gaston runs the rogues to ground, and all should be settled on the morrow."

A crashing knock on the door was immediately followed by the entrance of an anxious chap in livery. "Milord Dyer, thank heavens you're here!" he cried. "'Tis horrible! Horrible! O, most horrible!"

"And who, pray tell, is this?" Janette asked, trying not to notice the streaks of dawn light appearing in the sky outside the window.

"Osric, milady," the man said, sketching a hasty bow. "Steward to Lord Hunsdon—Master Dyer, you must come with me, sir, and only see—cry mercy, O cry mercy!"

"For my own mercy, what is it, Osric?" Aristotle rubbed his eyes, already guessing what he was about to hear.

"A dead girl, sir . . . dead!" Osric blurted. "Maid to Lady Hilliard—a lovely girl, ta'en in all—now dead, sir, dead as a doornail."

"Where is this girl, monsieur?" LaCroix asked blandly as Janette held up four fingers behind the man's back with an eyebrow quizzically raised.

"In the wine cellar," Osric replied. "I found her abovestairs—only think on't! If someone else had seen, one of the guests? My place—alas, poor Marcia . . ."

"The wine cellar, say you?" Aristotle asked, giving his own glance out the window. That should serve excellent well. He turned to Osric with his most pleasant smile. "Tell me, Osric—who else hath seen this unfortunate corpse?"

"No one, milord, by my faith," the man swore. "I thought best to inform only you."

"And so you did right," LaCroix said, offering his arm to Janette. Janette's hand wafted gently down on his arm; her bearing was that of a great lady, but a wild humor had surfaced in her eyes, and she could barely restrain herself from laughing. She gazed on Osric with an almost affectionate anticipation, then looked back to her elders.

"No one knows but you," Aristotle repeated.

"Milord, none," Osric reaffirmed, sealing his fate.

"So, a young domestic was the first to be decanted," Aristotle sighed. "Iberians . . ."

"Milord?" Osric said uncertainly.

LaCroix coughed slightly. "Come, gentles all—let us to the wine cellar." As if leading a grand procession, LaCroix and Janette started for the door.

12

DIDO. If he forsake me not, I never die;
For in his looks I see eternity,
And he'll make me immortal with a kiss.

—Christopher Marlowe
Dido, Queen of Carthage,
Act IV, sc. iv, 121–123 (c. 1592)

ARISTOTLE WATCHED HIS ANCIENT FRIEND WITH GENUINE CURIOSITY AS the two of them walked west from Whitehall in the frozen night air. Seven nights had come and gone since the Lord Chamberlain's disaster, and no sign had been seen or heard of the errant Nicholas. Yet LaCroix seemed perfectly content—indeed, he had yet to mention his fledgling's name. Could he have given the boy up at last?

The thought made Aristotle smile. *The skies will fall first.*

"I give you thanks for accompanying me, Lucius," he began, watching a pair of mortal drunkards walk by leaning on each other. His hunger flickered, but work before sport, he counseled himself. "Though I wonder at it. My purpose is plain: Gaston says one but follows the trail of rats each night to find this barb'rous pair." Aristotle snorted. "This, he avers, is so far as loyalty takes him, and I must assume their schooling myself. But you—do you come to second me?"

"Dost thou require a second?" LaCroix asked with malicious good humor.

Aristotle smiled as well. "When you sent word of your return from Paris, you purposed but one night. While I do treasure each day of your presence, I cannot but wonder what stays you."

They watched as the mortals stumbled and fell into the gutter as a single two-headed monster. "You know my reason."

"Nicholas . . . " Aristotle sighed. "As ever, since . . . Hastings? Before? Where is he, or do you know?"

"Since a Crusade," LaCroix answered. "'Tis you who dwells so much on this island, not I. As for now . . . ," he smiled benignly, "Nicholas's zeal for missionary work never cooled. I have merely attended until his present project be complete."

"Missionary work," Aristotle repeated, unable to make sense of this.

"Were you not at Hunsdon's play, my friend?"

Aristotle suddenly remembered the madwoman whose real tragedy had ended the false one, and next remembered where he'd seen her before: flirting outrageously with this selfsame Nicholas. "Of course," he mused. "Well, she was most lively before—and is again, think you?"

LaCroix made no answer. He looked around, judging their surroundings dark enough to risk flight, said "I'll take my leave," and was gone before Aristotle could reply.

"Posies, sirs! Pretty posies 'gainst the wind! Penny a bunch!"

It was a thin call, but it drew LaCroix down from the sky to resume his travels on foot in a dark alley nearby. He liked to walk out to see the world at some time each night, usually first thing upon waking, catching it in the blue hour after sunset when mortals finished up their daily toils and found their way home. It was a habit that had stayed with him as a pleasure long after the urgent waking hungers of a young vampire were no more than a dim memory. Tonight, he'd spent that hour with Aristotle, but in return was able to fly even over the thickly inhabited precincts of west London, since the moon was new and cast little light. But here was game . . .

For always, as he walked, he hunted—the hunt, like the walking, not a necessity but a pleasure. He hunted casually, mentally, more as a game than anything, extending his vampire senses into the houses around him to listen for the humans within, using his enhanced vision to look down the unlit streets and alleys. Was someone alone? Was there a musical girl's voice, a beguiling laugh?

Tonight, of course, he was hunting not someone's daughter, but someone's son: his own.

What did Nicholas propose to do with a disease-maddened wench who was within days, if not hours, of death?

The same thought that struck Aristotle had come to LaCroix a week ago and made him laugh aloud. Would Nicholas do that? Would he repeat his experiment, not upon a noble bride all draped in white satin, but upon another man's cast-off mistress? Yes, LaCroix had thought, it would be just like Nicholas to yield to such an impulse. He pictured the room, some little dark corner somewhere, for this would have been all unplanned, and his son sitting there watching as his first fledgling stirred to wakefulness, suddenly aghast at the magnitude of what he'd done. It had been worth leaving Nicholas alone for a time, to live with his experiment.

If, in fact, he had succeeded this time.

"Posies, sirs, sovereign for all ills!" The high, sharp voice broke into his thoughts. Here was a prey calling out to be taken.

Rounding a house to come into the next street, he found the source of the street cry to be a girl. She couldn't have been more than eleven years old, dressed not much better than a beggar, an apron over a worn gray shift, her posies carried in a basket of roughly woven willow wands. Her shawl was no more than a rag, far too thin for the oncoming winter night. How she had gotten flowers in this season was a mystery in itself, but it was a far greater mystery why she was staying out in the hours of darkness, when a hungry vampire was only one of the predators that might happen upon her—

"Posy, good sir?" She had seen him.

LaCroix looked down at her. Poverty, the London winter, a life so hard—never mind what a vampire could do to her: he, as a gentleman, could, if he so desired, slap this child down on the cobblestones, and no one, she least of all, would question his right to do it. She was little more than half his height, dirty, already missing teeth.

"Why should I have one?" he said.

She was flustered, but knew her answer. "'Tis to sweeten the wind 'gainst all agues, and 'tis also the perfectest avoidance of the pest."

LaCroix's eyebrows rose. "For my good health, then?" It amused him, as always, to be offered a sure guardian against the ills that mortal flesh was heir to. He, Lucien LaCroix, already possessed the surest remedy against death the world had ever seen, and he did not peddle it for pennies in the street.

"Oh, and 'tis also very pretty and sweet-smelling for in the house," she said swiftly, for all the world like a child finishing a lesson for a schoolmaster.

The thought made him smile. He had been many, many things in his centuries of life, but schoolmaster to a passel of brats was not one of them. Which brought him another smile: no, LaCroix reflected, he had only one brat to tutor, and a most difficult scholar he was, each lesson no sooner learned than quarreled with.

The urchin girl was hoping for much from that smile. "Penny a posy, sir," she prompted.

It brought LaCroix's thoughts back to the present. "Why are you out this late, little mistress? Have you no mother nor master to get home to?"

The girl blinked, and her eyes turned cunning. LaCroix smiled again. So she was not without wits, young as she was; he watched as her eyes flicked rapidly around her, measuring which would be the best direction to run. *Poor child*, he thought, *you would not be lamb's meat to a wolf, but I am a far greater predator than you can imagine.*

"Never mind," he said, addressing her as he would a lady. "'Twas but an idle question, and an impertinent one."

This took her so off guard she blurted the truth. "He'll whip me an I come home with all these." She held out her basket of flowers.

LaCroix nodded. "No one fears pest come winter, do they?" he said understandingly. Plague deaths, the very best prompter of posy sales, always dropped with cold weather. No one knew why, though the most advanced doctors were speculating that it was because the lower air's plague miasmata were drawn away by the moon in the longer nights.

"No, indeed, your worship!" said the girl, pleased at his comprehension. LaCroix noticed his promotion from gentleman to lord.

"How much?" he said.

"All of 'em?" she cried, her eyes and mouth opening to wide O's. There were tales the gentry took whims like this, but it had never happened to her before.

LaCroix tipped his head back momentarily, chuckling, then looked back down. He drew forth a half crown. "Here's for all," he said. Her eyes flared again, and she stared at it in her palm; it was not a coin she was used to seeing. He held up a sixpence as well, crouching down to look her directly in the eyes. "And here's for you, just you, mistress—don't give it to him."

This struck her dumb—but not so dumb she didn't think to take the coin with a whispered "Ta."

LaCroix took one posy out of her basket, and stood up again, starting to walk away. They struggled so hard, these mortals, and for what? Half a crown and sixpence was nothing to him, a moment's whim, but a revelation to her. What would she say if she knew about that other revelation, immortality? He laughed a little, and then thought of Nicholas, who even now might be attempting to share that revelation with another.

LaCroix turned back.

"Girl!" The little girl turned, wanting to run from the summons in case the gentleman had repented of his generosity, yet wanting to stay in case another coin might be forthcoming. Her eyes were as cautious as a deer's.

He smiled at her. If his son had indeed made himself a sister, Nicholas would be unlikely to have provided for her needs. The girl walked closer, and now LaCroix reached out with his mind, staring down into her eyes. "You've taken a mind to stay here," he told her softly. "To stay and sell posies for another hour."

That should be long enough to find Nicholas, long enough to learn if there was a need. If there was not, the girl could live to enjoy her sixpence.

Aristotle had been a philosophical man as a mortal, and many centuries of living as a vampire had only deepened the natural trend of his character. So it was that he followed the trail of rats to the seedy inn at first with anger, later with resignation, and ultimately with a certain fine amusement.

It was easy to sense them. Vampires. Two. Within, upstairs, and, Aristotle noticed as he listened, still asleep.

He smiled at this last perception. A moment later he stood in the middle of their pitch-black room and said, "Which of you is Hansel, and which Gretel?"

The two vampires were awake in an instant, snarling at the intruder with two pairs of rage-red eyes and bared fangs. One of them attacked, and the elder vampire hurled him aside with as little effort as it would have taken him to swat a mosquito, if one were ever impertinent enough to seek blood from him. After this moment of violence, there was stillness and quiet.

Aristotle saw a flint and used it to light the room's two candles. Bare floors, a single bed, tallow candles, and a pewter basin with little water in it: these vampires were purse-pinched.

"Ship ahoy," said one of them sarcastically. This one was bald, still sitting on the four-man bed, wearing sailor's slops for trousers, as the innkeeper's wife had described, with hairy knees and calves poking out beneath them. Above them, though, he wore successive layers of a fine lawn shirt, a velvet doublet slashed to show silk, and a jerkin of very good wool. All harvested from victims, Aristotle surmised.

The one who'd attacked him looked up from under heavy brows and thick black hair cut short across his forehead and left to grow wild everywhere else, so that he seemed to be looking out from behind a curtain. Hostility and fear were mixed in his expression, but he said nothing and made no effort to rise from the floor where Aristotle had flung him.

The bald one recovered enough composure to make a rude noise with his lips.

Aristotle smiled. "A fair beginning." He sketched a small bow. "I am Aristotle. I have followed your trail of crumbs." The bald one pulled at his fleshy nose, trying to understand. "The rats," Aristotle enlightened him. This produced an impudent grin, revealing a full set of large, yellowy teeth.

"Ordin'ry seaman Screed," said the bald one. "An' not at your service, neither. 'E's Javier Vachon, conquistador." The dark one remained frozen but for a blink.

Aristotle sighed. A Cockney sailor and a Spanish lout—what was the Community coming to? And not an ounce of civility between them. *Never mind making their acquaintance: just bring them into line and go home.*

"You are both very young, methinks." Aristotle's face resumed its usual cheerful demeanor. "I bring you . . . a message. You must learn discretion. Immediately. This is necessary not only for your own sakes, but for the protection of others as well." The one called Vachon threw his hair back, and looked at him with more interest and less threat. Willing to learn. "You may think you are invulnerable, but danger closes in around you."

"Now there's the right readin' o' the mappamundi and a bit o' the gospel fair in church," Screed agreed. "Preachin' that sermon meself, but 'e'll have nowt of it."

Aristotle's eyes swung to Screed. "You are the carouche?"

"The which or what, cap'n?" Screed's brow wrinkled.

"The rat-sucker." Aristotle's tone communicated his contempt for Screed's diet. "Surely your maker told you what you are—it was his duty to instruct you." *Actually,* thought Aristotle, *it was his duty to destroy you, but one thing at a time.*

"Ca-rouche," Screed tasted the word. "Sounds Frenchlike. Smell o' froggy-woggies and mudfish and worse. Snails," he enlarged. "Court-fragrancy, yerself, ye are."

Aristotle took a step forward.

"Touch him not." The dark one had come to life.

"It speaks," chuckled Aristotle, distracted from his reaction to Screed. "I thought that might prove possible."

"What want you here?" Vachon stood up, still wary.

"What want you here?" Aristotle countered. "You bring danger to us all."

The black eyebrows flew up. "All?"

"Do you know *nothing*? Who made you, that you so flout the Code?"

"Code?" said both Vachon and Screed.

"You know nothing of the Code?" Aristotle was taken aback. Such ignorance shouldn't be possible; simple blood knowledge gave a fledgling awareness of the Code at the time of his making. "Truly, who made you?"

"She is dead." This came from the Spaniard.

"Aren't we all?" Aristotle could never resist a joke. Then he frowned. "Dead?"

"She went into the sun the morning I came across."

"There was no one to teach you?" He looked from one to the other in dismay.

"'Ere's me learned tutor," Screed jerked a thumb at Vachon. "Ye mislike me scholarhoodship," he waved his hand around a few times in a mockery of a bow, "ye pick the bare bone wiv 'im."

Vachon shrugged. "No sun. No wood." He smiled a little. "No holy water, I discovered for myself."

Aristotle's patience ran out. As he'd done so many months earlier with Janette, at the beginning of this puzzle, he took the most direct course of action. Flashing over to where Vachon stood, he simply gripped the Spaniard's wrist and bit. Surprised, the young vampire tried to fight, but a hand clenched around his throat stopped him.

Aristotle closed his eyes for a moment, concentrating. When he opened them again, his face bore a look of amazement.

"The New World? That was in the New World?"

Vachon raised his eyebrows and nodded. Why did that matter?

"But this is extraordinary!" Aristotle was positively effusive. "The New World!" He was carried away by the vision in the young one's blood: there were native vampires in the New World—or at least, there had been. This Iberian oaf had been born in blood to a vampire of New Spain.

And had tried to kill his twin. Interesting. Aristotle put that thought away for another time.

"In sooth, you do not know the night. Not here." Aristotle grew serious. "We are a Community here, not wolves hunting singly in the wild." The Spaniard crossed his arms. "We have," his eyes twinkled, "many pleasures to share with each other, but alas, some few burdens as well. Of the providence, we may offer you houses at need, passage from kingdom to kingdom, never minding the mortals' alliances or wars; likewise the petty matters of gilt may be treated easily amongst us. We give each other names, histories, family—"

"Hold! Belay yer babble—did 'ee just say farthin's for nowt?"

Screed's outburst interrupted the quiet tension between Vachon and Aristotle, each of whom shot the carouche a sidelong glance. Aristotle's was neither friendly nor amused.

Screed held up his hands in surrender. "Oh ay, I'm mum, or dumb, or mumchance. But 'e said money for the haver's havin' Har-vee-to, or I'm a wench on a tar's winch."

Vachon reflected, as he often had lately, that learning proper English contributed almost nothing to understanding Screed. Aristotle merely gaped, which made Vachon smile. Screed was a tactical strength all his own in this small war among vampires.

"Of these matters of reliance, good order in the kill is prime." Aristotle let a long subsequent silence drill this point in deeper.

The Spaniard simply watched him, blinking occasionally.

Aristotle's voice became flat. "Do not risk exposing us. That is firstmost. Any one of us will kill to avert such a danger. We move among mortal men, always unmarked, and if you draw attention, if you cause them to look to our existence, we will put an end to it." His eyes opened a little wider. "An end to any troublesome mortal, an end to you. I might have done so here." Vachon simply blinked again, his face completely expressionless. The elder vampire pursed his lips. *Stupid insolence, boy.*

"There cometh to thee no other warning." With that, Aristotle was gone.

At times, Isabella thought she had indeed fallen dead in her lover's hall, murdered by his cruelty. How else to explain this bittersweet purgatory in which she now dwelt, this paradise in squalor? Perhaps the powers of eternity kept her here between Heaven and Hell as they sorted out the chaos of her life to pass fair judgment. Why else leave her in the care of an imperfect angel, a saintly rogue who would neither ruin nor release her?

Nicholas stayed by her side day and night—or day, in any case. He left her alone for a short period every night, a scant hour in which she fretted and burned and thought only of Hilliard and her new love, until the two seemed one and the same. With every moment that passed, she would feel more certain that this phantom, this Hilliard/Nick, had left her at last, until by the time he returned, she could do naught but rush weeping to his arms.

"Kiss me," she demanded when he returned on the seventh night.

"You should be in bed," Nick scolded, taking the cloak he wore from around his own shoulders and putting it around hers instead. "You will be chilled to the bone."

"What of it?" she said, sulking, turning away to go to the window. So many stars, but the moon hid her face in shadow. "Lovers can see to do their amorous rites by their own beauties," she recited, barely remembering from whence the words had come.

"Eat your supper," Nick urged.

"Give me my Romeo," she continued undaunted, wrapping herself more tightly in her cloak and remembering herself an Italian virgin she had never been. "And when he shall die, take him and cut him out in little stars, and he will make the face of Heaven so fine that all the world will be in love with night."

"Very prettily spoke," Nick said. "Come, the floor is cold, Bella; at least put on your shoes."

"Is your true love now made of stars, Nicholas?" she asked. "Is't this makes you so enamored of the night?"

He pressed a kiss to her brow, finding it clammy with fever. She needed a doctor, though there would probably be little enough that he could do. "Stay here," he ordered, picking up his purse and turning for the door.

"No," she protested, clinging to his doublet. "Leave me not—you've only just returned. Let the star maid bide without you till I am as dead as she."

Truth-perceiving madness, Shakespeare called it, Nick thought, meeting the wild black eyes that seemed to see his very soul—his damned soul. "I'll not go far," he promised, pushing her away.

Walking steadily west, LaCroix passed out of the last even remotely respectable neighborhood and into an area where the houses were alternately bawdy houses and brewers, with the golden balls of pawnshop signs relieving the monotony now and then.

In these poorer neighborhoods, he sensed a vampire once or twice, fleetingly; others such as himself, meeting the night's need before turning to other pleasures, feeding among those who would not be missed. None of them was Nicholas, though; his blood did not lift with the special recognition of family.

Nearly an hour went by as he walked backstreets, crowded with pickpockets, sharpers, bawds, beggars, drunkards, slumming noblemen, and a very few honest boys who only wanted to make pennies by holding the quality's horses while they took their pleasure. Several times some rough man set eyes on LaCroix's good clothing and boots, guessing at the purse that lay under that well-lined cloak, and either came forward or fell in behind him, walking softly. In their own way, they were hoping to make a meal of him, LaCroix thought. The smile this fancy brought to his lips was enough to send every one of them off in another direction.

He finally sensed Nicholas in a house of the cheapest sort, somewhere on the upper floors of an alehouse that hung the sign of a yellow dog at its door. He did not feel the presence of another vampire. Pity, really. LaCroix remembered very well the night that he had strolled into Nicholas's wedding chamber and found him with a cold bride. Yet if he'd made the effort and failed, what held him here?

Once inside, LaCroix thought a yellow dog would be a much

better companion than any of the tavern's denizens. The place was a hell of human stinks and human bodies, ruffians drinking at the tables and vomiting under them, wenches trying to deliver full pitchers of ale and wine while having to dodge the unconscious bodies on the floor and the grasping hands on every side of them.

Beyond the voices of the rabble, the raving of the madwoman upstairs could be heard. LaCroix looked upward, seeing Nicholas appear at the top of the stairs.

Thinking his son had sensed him, LaCroix began to pick his way through the crowd to reach him. But Nicholas was not looking for him at all. Instead, he had beckoned to the landlord's lad.

"Know you a physician near here?"

The boy tilted his head. "Dr. Barton, so 'e calls 'isself, in Butcher Lane." The boy nodded wisely. "'Tis where 'e belongs, pardee."

"Fetch him hither. Give him this," said Nicholas, thrusting a golden angel into the boy's hand. The boy gaped: ten shillings would buy a dozen doctors. "Tell him there's more if he comes betimes."

The quality were crazy, the boy was thinking. 'Twas clear as a bell that the man's wench was pox'd; what did he think a doctor could do?

"And there's one for you, stripling, if you run," Nick said.

The boy gaped. For ten shillings, he'd run to Scotland. He was gone in a second.

"So you think to physic her?" LaCroix had reached the top of the stairs, twisting to let the landlord's son speed past him. Amusement colored his voice as he addressed his son. "Or do you only mean to sweeten her for the feast?"

"I will not have her so," Nicholas growled, drawing back into the upstairs hallway. LaCroix followed him. Nicholas met his master's eye. "Nor will you, I think."

It was always a pleasure when Nicholas issued his little threats. LaCroix smiled. "Then you purpose to enlarge our *petite ménage*? If she's to join the family, what matters a physick? Her . . . infirmity?" he said with a mocking lilt, "is nothing to us."

"That neither," said Nicholas.

"What, you've turned nurse?" LaCroix was joking, but he

saw in Nicholas's face that he had at last hit the truth. LaCroix laughed. "What absurd jest is this? One way's as good as another, but end her pain, Nicholas; you would do no less for a suffering dog." Nicholas continued to be silent, and LaCroix's voice turned harsh. "Enough of this. The jettisoned mistresses of thoughtless young men litter the wide world, and not even you, Nicholas, possess time or purse enough to save them all. And this one—do we not agree?—this one's past the saving."

LaCroix's voice dropped to a commanding growl. "Make an end of it, Nicholas, and come with me."

Without a word, Nick turned away and went through one of the doors behind him. LaCroix hesitated a moment, then followed.

Inside, Isabella had apparently abandoned her own new love for the night in favor of false daylight. Every candle in the room was lit, even those Nick had stored away, and every sputtering lamp turned up to full, arranged in a semicircle on the floor with the girl standing behind all, dressed only in her shift. "O serpent heart, hid with a flowering face!" she cried as Nick came in, though her eyes were turned on some phantom on the other side of the room. "Did ever dragon keep so fair a cave?"

"Only a week in your company, and yet she knows you already so well," LaCroix quipped.

"'Tis not to me she speaks," Nick answered softly, fascinated.

"Beautiful tyrant!" she cried, turning toward him. "Fiend angelical!"

"Indeed?" LaCroix asked, raising a brow. "Are you so certain?"

"The words are Will's spoke by his Juliet," Nick explained. "Isabella is oft said t'have been her model."

"Yes, Nicholas, I know," LaCroix responded. "But who is her Romeo?"

Isabella caught her hair tight in her fists as if she meant to tear it out by the roots, keening like a savage. "Dove-feathered raven! Wolvish-ravening lamb!" she wept in helpless fury. "Despised substance of divinest show—a damned saint, an honorable villain!"

LaCroix watched his son's face with a weary heart—Nicholas drank in this drivel as eagerly as innocent blood—

more so, every shriek and whimper from the girl produced another springtime drop of rain on the flower of his new-sprouted shame. "Lady, a mercy, forbear," LaCroix said.

"O nature, what hadst thou to do in hell, when thou didst bower the spirit of a fiend in mortal paradise of such sweet flesh?" Nick finished, pushing past his mentor to reach her. Isabella looked up, stricken and seemingly lost, as if she could scarce remember where she was or who, then fell weeping against his breast.

"Your friend should end all his plays with such tableaux," LaCroix said sardonically as Nick carried her to bed. "'Twould no doubt fill the house."

"Hush now," Nick said soothingly, stroking the girl's brow as she curled herself into a ball of misery beneath the blankets. "Go now, LaCroix, I beseech you."

"As you wish, Nicholas," LaCroix replied. "I shall make your farewells to Janette."

Nick looked up, stunned. "Janette . . . ?"

"Is leaving," LaCroix finished, his tone as neutral as his alabaster face. "Tonight. And she swears she is ne'er to return."

Nick stared at his master. "You lie," he said at last.

"Really, Nicholas," LaCroix scolded, shaking his head. "What need have I to lie when the truth doth suit me so well?"

"Nicholas?" Isabella asked, clutching his wrist.

"All's well," Nick promised, patting her absently, his mind focused far away. He reached out for some perception of his vampire beloved, some clue to her true state of mind. 'Twas true, LaCroix rarely betrayed his ancient dignity with a lie, but surely Janette would never leave London without seeing him herself.

"Where is she?" he demanded, getting up from his nursemaid's chair.

"Whitehall," LaCroix replied. "Aristotle has completed her travel arrangements—a new identity, even, or so I do believe. In truth, she begged me not to ask her, and I have honored her request." He suppressed a smile at the obvious fury this inspired in his rebellious son. "Mayhap you can catch her, though now as I think me, her sending me to you may have been but a device. I doubt not but what she may be gone already."

"She would never abandon me so," Nick insisted.

"Would she not?" LaCroix asked, mock-innocent.

Nick's eyes narrowed in fury—never had he so longed to tear that smug, white mask to ribbons as now, not even with Alyssa lying dead in his arms. But now as then, the bastard had the right of all, leaving him little room to quarrel. "Sleep, Isabella," he said, turning from the vampire who had made him to placate this charge of his own. "I shall return before you wake."

But Isabella was not so easily placated. "Liar," she hissed, making him really look at her in spite of himself. Her lips were drawn back in a snarl that was shockingly like Janette's when the vampire beauty was furious. Or starving. "Waste not thy sins nor breath on me—you will ne'er come back," she said. "Why should you so, when you do fly to your pretty cousin? You forget, *monsieur*—I have lost your favor to her before."

"Isabella," Nick began, pleading, wild with worry that Janette would be lost but unable to ignore the fear behind the fury in Isabella's eyes.

"Soft you, child," LaCroix said soothingly, moving Nick aside. "Look at me . . ." He picked up her hand, focusing his entire attention on her fever-mad eyes, drawing her to his will. "Do you as Nicholas says," he ordered, even her heartbeat pounding in a rhythm of his choosing, so willing was she to sink beneath his spell. She was exhausted—only her will had kept her living so long, and that was weakening fast. "Calm thyself," he commanded, feeling almost sympathetic. "Such tantrums can only do you harm."

"Yes," she answered softly; smooth, even breath rose and fell in her ruined lungs.

LaCroix smiled. "Go, Nicholas," he urged. "Your pretty pet will barely miss you now."

"LaCroix," Nick said as he paused at the door, the beginning of a warning he hadn't a clue how to finish.

"Spare me, *mon fils,*" the older vampire cut him off impatiently, glancing over his shoulder. "Fear me not—I shall treat her as one of my own." Nick waited a moment longer, watching him pass his hand over the girl's face to close her eyes, like a priest attending Death's last whisper. Perhaps it would be better if she were to die out of his sight . . . Turning away, he left the room, racing out into the night.

"There now, *ma pauvre petite,*" LaCroix murmured mockingly as soon as Nick was gone. "What shall become of you now?"

"As if you cared a drab's dirty linen," Isabella retorted, her eyes snapping open again.

LaCroix's own eyes widened, shocked but not altogether displeased to find her still so alert. He chuckled; certes, to have flourished at all among the rough jostling of London's players and nobility, she must have needed the fierce spirit of a weed in a hay field. Perhaps her will was equal to his plan after all. "Waking still, my sweet?" he queried, touching a finger to her face.

"Aye, and little blinded," she answered. Something in the enchantment he had practiced upon her seemed to have done her good, made the air come more willingly to her chest and the fever weaken. Or perhaps she was merely hale in fury. "Thou needst not waste thy comfort on me, my lord," she continued, jerking away from his death-cold touch. "I know thy hatred well—thou'rt more willing to see me die than e'en thy lady cousin."

"And why should either of us wish thee ill, little one?" he asked, intrigued. "I'faith, the lady Janette hath long been thy advocate."

"Yea, so long as I knew her Chevalier not," she retorted. "Think you I am so foolish as to know not how little either of you cares to see him bide here with me? But have no fear, my lord—even if he speaks true and will come to me again, 'twill not be long 'fore I am dead." A sudden fit of coughing racked her slender frame as if to prove her point, a spattering of blood bubbling on her lips.

"*Vraiment, ma belle,* I can see as much," LaCroix replied. He passed his fingertips across her mouth and looked down at the crimson stain, savoring the scent of her blood. "But you mistake me most cruelly when you say I shall be glad," he continued, tasting it with impunity, enjoying her sudden wide-eyed stare. "It shall grieve me sorely to see you die."

"God's truth, I do believe it," she managed, her sarcasm somewhat diluted by shock—what manner of monster was this? "And why, pray, should this be so?"

"Why should it not?" he countered. "You know me but little, lady, yet still you do know me for a lover of beauty, do you not? And you, little queen, are beauty's very glass and fashion."

"Aye," she laughed bitterly, seeing the joke a last. "A sweet jest—never more so than now; is't not so?"

"It is," he promised, his own expression turning serious. "Who could think other who saw your turn upon the stage?" He paused, letting this most rare compliment find its mark. "I'faith, lady, were Nicholas not set so hard against it, I should straightway bring you cure for this illness that plagues you so, this death," he continued, the very soul of sincere regret. "Indeed, had I my will in this, you should ne'er die at all, nay, nor even fade."

"A miracle indeed," she said. Did Will Shakespeare not speak of this man as a fiend? What manner of hellfire meant he to tempt her toward with this? "You lie to keep me quiet. No such physic as this exists, or Nicholas would have given me of it long since."

"Think you so?" LaCroix asked mildly, letting his thorns do their work without further urging.

"Yea, verily," she retorted. But doubt haunted her eyes just as he'd known it must. This girl had known too much betrayal in her short life to have learned trust in one scant week. Even from Saint Nicholas. "Nick cares for me," she insisted. "You will warrant it little, but he doth love me well. If he could save me, he would do and quickly."

"Mayhap you speak aright," LaCroix allowed with his most tender smile. "It could be he is not able to give you this gift." He took her hand and letting his eyes go gold, slowly pressed the palm to the side of his throat where she would find no living pulse. "But I can," he said, showing her his fangs.

"Holy Jesu's blood," Isabella breathed, an incredulous smile on her lips. She dreamed, surely . . . or was this the Devil in truth?

"Wilt thou live, Queen Isabella?" LaCroix asked, raising her from the bed. "Live forever with this Nicholas you think so fond?"

"Yes," she said, not a moment's hesitation. Was she not already well and truly damned?

LaCroix smiled, genuinely pleased—madness could be managed if its creature were so brave as this. "Then come," he said, opening his arms.

She obeyed him eagerly, melting into his embrace, her delicious little heart pounding with surprising power as he kissed her lips, so briefly and so sweet, the delicate traces of blood inflaming his ancient hunger. He lifted her off her feet, barely more than a wisp of blood and breath, and sank his fangs into her throat.

"Please—" she whispered, clutching his velvet-covered shoulders as the vampire fed, a sigh that longed for the strength to scream dying on her lips. Such pain . . . how could she crave such pain? But she wanted it to go on and on, the burning hunger in her soul growing stronger even as her body weakened.

LaCroix held the more savage depths of his hunger in check—the wine was sweet, but its vessel was fragile, and he would keep its beauty intact. As soon as the fevered pounding of her heart began to slow the slightest bit, he pulled away, savoring the mewling protest instead of her heart's blood. "Soft, child," he said soothingly, laying her back on the bed and opening the vein in his wrist. "Now you shall be cured."

Neither Vachon nor Screed said anything for a long, tense moment. Then Screed's face broke out in a goblin's grin. "So now we've seen the fangy magistrate," he said. "Think ye we're to hang?"

"No," Vachon muttered. He was barely able to speak. How to explain the rage he felt, the frustrated fury that he now knew a river of mortal blood would never quench? When he'd awakened in the New World a vampire, he'd known his weakness was at an end at last, that only a single, hated twin stood between himself and the freedom he craved as other men craved riches. The only hobble, this Inca brother—still asleep in the ground—a lesser thing to be dispatched or at least avoided. But now . . .

He'd been the natural son of a Marrano mother, half-Gypsy, half-converso, a girl who had been a beauty with huge, flashing black eyes. As with so many poor girls, her beauty was her misfortune: barely into her teens, she caught the eye of a traveling nobleman who had simply taken her honor for a week's lust, then left her behind when he traveled on. All that was left after that was the gold ring he had given her (or she stole, it didn't matter which), and her swelling belly. That ring, though, had been just enough of a substitute for honor to persuade a stinking tanner to marry her and give little Javier, the Duke de Azuga's bastard boy, a name, while himself siring a long string of half brothers and sisters, all of whom knew that no matter how ugly or stupid they were, as legitimate children of a tanner they were better than the casual get of a lord.

Javier's world had assumed he would live forever on its fringes, a baseborn peasant, destined to be a stable boy, lucky if his stepfather would take him into the tanner's trade. Instead, born on St. Dionysius' day, the pagan god of wild spirits with a thin mantle of Christianizing thrown over him had proved a fitting patron for the boy Javier had been and the man he would become. Still very young, already having fought and beaten every boy and most of the men in Sarriá, he left to brave the New World for its Inca gold. And found instead a treasure much greater than gold, absolute liberty in the night.

A liberty an old, strong vampire cared for so little, he simply presumed he could end it with a few blunt words. Community? Houses, passports, identities, Code? *Que vayan al Diablo . . .* They could all go straight to Hell: he would not be ruled.

" 'No' be the right o' this wrong," Screed cut into his thoughts. The carouche drew himself up to his full height and tucked his chin back into his neck. " 'There cometh to thee no other warning,' " he intoned in perfect imitation of the vampire who'd just left.

Vachon smiled a little despite his rage—who knew Screed could make such a plain and haughty speech, even in jest? "Code . . . in a rat's crammy, parson," Screed finished in his own rare tones.

"Ye're to sea, say ye?" he went on. "I'll show ye the ropes, which is sheets, and the sheets, which is 'ammocks, and the 'ammocks, which is bumps in the ocean sea." Screed's voice warmed as it always did when he talked of the sea. "Blow the Pole-star, we'll steer the Finster-star." Vachon's eyebrows went up. "Finisterre, ye lubber—the Sunset Country, End o' the World, El Grandee Lo Rico Finisterre? 'Tis where the men go about without necks and have their faces in their chests, where unicorns runs awildering. Duke o' Venice gave thirty thousand ducats for one little horn; there's one at Windsor now eight spans an' a half long as the Queen refused ten thousand pounds for. Lyin' on the ground in the Westmost lands, they says . . ."

Still getting no response, he tried sarcasm. "Contemplatin' takin' service with his Vampy Top o' the Toploftness, are ye?"

He returned to his uncanny mimicry: "'. . . likewise the petty matters of gilt may be treated easily amongst us.' Look right benshiply in servants' togs, ye would, yer lady face."

This pulled another unwilling smile from Vachon, but no answer.

"Study to fight him, do ye? Sounds like 'eavy weather and rocks a'leeward," Screed ventured. What ailed the Spaniard, to freeze up so? "Still, fangers 'as their weak spots . . ."

"No."

"'It speaks,'" Screed echoed Aristotle again, but now he got a masterly, and very quelling, glance from Vachon. "All right then, say on, say on: what'll ye have?"

"Liberty," said Vachon softly. "I'm for home, Screed. My home." He blinked, and his eyes focused far away. "'Gainst me, let any man come who dares—or vampire. I've done with servility."

"Aye, aye to that, lubber-man." Screed laughed happily and knuckled his brow. "The New World, mate—saw you how 'e smacked 'is mighty lips at that? He's knowing nowt of it, nowt i' the world. There's our fortune, just as ye said—sure as moonshine it is. Say the word and we're off." A note of worry edged his voice. "'Tis us ye mean . . . both?"

Vachon smiled. He nodded an assent to his accidental fledgling, the Cockney seadog turned carouche, and indulged in a little mimicry of his own. "See me safe to the New World, and I'll ne'er ask ye more."

Nick burst into their shared room as if he were still flying, his hair wild from having taken the risk of traveling by air over the crowded streets of London. Janette could not leave him, she would not leave him again.

But there was a closed trunk near the door, and Janette was dressed in traveling clothes. As he arrived, she was just pulling on dark leather gloves, embroidered delicately with pearls above the wrists.

"'Tis true then," Nick said heavily. "You'll go?"

Janette looked at him. "Have you been this whole week in company with that sick girl? What kind of vampire did she make?" There was an affected carelessness in her voice.

"I have not brought her across," Nick said.

Janette's eyes widened. "You have spent this week closed up with a diseased mortal?"

"Yes," Nick nodded. "She needed care—bathing, food, simple things. She was too weak to go forth." His face lightened. "In sooth, I have learned much from her these seven days that I would share with you."

"Do you study to die?" The words exploded out of Janette. "Nicholas, you fool." The anger was real, but she also was fighting to hide her shock. *He bathes her? He bathes her like the dirtiest servant? Spoon-feeds her like a cooing mother?*

"I have learned much of innocence, Janette," Nick said steadily. "Of what is possible for us, even as we are."

"Innocence?" Janette scoffed. "Very well, Nicholas, instruct me: which is innocent—this girl who depends on men for her clothing and jewels, or the man who made her so? Or shall I say, which is guilty?"

"If I say Hilliard?" Nicholas said. "Would you disagree?"

Janette's voice softened, but her words were stern. "Then I say again that you are a fool. Not because the one is guilty, and the other is not. 'Tis greater presumption to judge between them, or betwixt them and thieves and murderers as you would do, than to take what you must have, as do LaCroix and I."

Nick shook his head. "You do not understand."

Janette snorted. How many days since she'd last heard that phrase from a man? Immortal or no, they could ill bear rebuke from a woman. If a female debated their thinking, it needs must be incomprehension, some intricacy of intellection the feminine brain could not comprehend.

"*Au contraire,* I understand far better than you wish of me. *Mon cher* Nicholas, you protest against your nature, you have ever done so. You cling to the shreds of mortality as if you were a drowning man." Janette laid a hand on Nick's arm, and her voice became low and intense. "*Écoute:* you are not a drowning man, nor any kind of man—you are a vampire, Nicholas."

Nick's blue eyes, usually so lively when they looked on her, were like shuttered windows.

Janette shook her head sadly. "Truly, it is as LaCroix says. You have received the greatest gift there is in all the world, and you set it at naught. It is some madness in you that will not let you be happy."

Nick's manner turned icy. "Do not presume to judge me, Janette."

Nicholas, playing the mortal aristocrat to her commoner? Wounded, Janette retreated into angry magnificence; her voice soared.

"Do you not judge me by embracing this diseased sparrow? I, who have now traveled to this little bog of an island twice for you?" Nick relented, reaching for her, but Janette pushed him away, insulted beyond an easy reconciliation.

"But 'twas you who drew her plight before me," Nick protested. "You pity her condition, Janette, I know you do."

"Pity? *Oui,*" Janette agreed. "*La pauvre petite* is much to be pitied, I think. But to pity her sufferings is a far different thing than to embrace them with one's whole heart."

Now Nick affected to scoff. "You cannot believe I love her better than thee," he said.

"I do not believe that you love her at all," came the reply. "It is her dying you love."

"Not so." It was the reflex denial of a little boy.

"No? Then why did you not bring her across? Is it because of that other, the pretty one who died at Schloss Throbbig, your Alyssa?" Janette spoke more softly. "But this one can still be saved, Nicholas. If 'tis such another failure you fear, LaCroix will do this for you."

"No!" It came out harshly, then more softly. "No." Nick dropped his eyes away from Janette's. "Even dying, innocence is finer than guilt. Mayhap I gave Alyssa the better gift." He smiled. "I will not have to spend eternity knowing that I made her a killer."

"So." Janette bit the little word off. "It is the dying you love, not the girl."

Nick shook his head. "No. You mock because you like it not, but this girl is an innocent, and will remain so. Come, meet her again. Her lodgings are not far."

"I have no stomach to watch you bathe yourself in this girl's death." Janette flung the words at him. Bedazzled with that pitiful girl's sickness, Nicholas reminded her of nothing so much as a religious fanatic who was sure he had only to impart his simple truth to win everyone to his belief. "I have no wish to learn how to sicken, how to die, how to rot."

"Yet stay with me," Nick said softly.

"Nay, I have done with you, until you return to your senses," she snapped. "I will not linger to be infected with your idiot love of perishing mortality." Nick reached for her again, but she backed away, throwing a hand out to stop him following. "I am gone, Nicholas. Stay and see your doxy buried."

She paused as if struck by a thought. Her tone became falsely light. "Ah, but you will not, since that will happen in daylight, *n'est-ce pas? Bon,* stay and lie down upon the dirt of her cold grave—if you can find it," she added contemptuously.

"Janette, please," Nick said, his tone another plea.

She waved a hand in dismissal. "No more: I wish you joy of her," she said cruelly, and turned to leave.

Nick was watching her, she could feel it. He had been like this the night she had beckoned him into the darkness. "How much do you want me?" she had said, tantalizing him, but he might easily have asked it of her: so golden fair, perfect, his eyes so dazzlingly expressive, his face so mobile, the hands that touched her so delicately—at shoulders, at waist, at knees, at the throat—oh, at the throat—

Hands that now were most oft employed in bathing a dying mortal girl.

At the door, she turned to look back at him for a moment. "*Au revoir,* Nicholas. I know not when we shall meet again."

Safely through the door and out of Nicholas's sight, Janette let her head droop. *Joy,* she thought, bitter and weary, enraged and sad all at once, *I wished him joy from spite, when in truth it is what I wish him with all my heart.*

There could be so much joy if Nicholas would accept his nature. Instead, Nicholas would tell himself now that she did not love him enough, when in sooth she loved him more than she loved any other being on Earth. But how should she tarry to be hurt by his adoration of a wench on the brink of death? Had it somehow escaped his notice that this dying girl, with her black hair, blue eyes, and diseased pallor, was like a monstrous mirror of Janette? *It is indeed the mortality he loves,* she thought. *It is the dying.*

"Oh, Nicholas," she said sadly. Alone in the hall, she had spoken aloud, but maybe too softly for even a vampire to hear.

13

I cannot speak and look like a saint
Use wiles for wit, or make deceit a pleasure...
With innocent blood to feed myself fat,
And do most hurt where most help I offer.

—Thomas Wyatt
"Mine Own John Poins,"
ll., 31-32, 34-35 (1557)

LACROIX WATCHED WITH AMUSEMENT AND SOMETHING LIKE GENUINE affection as his newborn child danced the remains of her first meal around the room. "What think you now of leeches, my dear lord doctor?" she laughed, letting the dead man fall to the floor. "I'faith their methods have done me good service at last."

"You are happy, then?" LaCroix asked with a smile.

"Happy?" Isabella laughed. "Yea, and happy and happy and yet more happy still." She twirled around in a pirouette of joy, stepping over the corpse as if it were but a figure in the dance. "And this feeling, this wondrous strength—you say 'twill endure forever?" she asked, still spinning.

"So long as you keep my commandments," he promised.

She stopped, her smile like moonshine. "They are locked inside my heart," she quipped, quoting the doomed virgin she had lately played. "And you shall have the key of it—you and Nicholas." She stopped, her face clouding with concentration. "But what is this?" she mused. "I feel . . . sick?"

"Look you there and see," LaCroix urged as Nick came through the door.

Nick could scarcely believe his eyes. Isabella, the tragic mortal beauty he had left barely more than an hour before bedridden and miserable, on the very brink of death, was now joyfully, vibrantly alive—

"Nay, not alive," he breathed in horror, catching sight of the blood on her mouth, the feral gleam in her eyes. "Immortal."

"Just so," she laughed, rushing to him and throwing her arms around his neck. "My pox is cured, pretty—are you not pleased?"

"A medical miracle," LaCroix agreed. "In one motion, this doctor hath earned his pay twice over, saving two lives at once."

"Two lives?" Nick asked weakly, still too amazed to make sense of his master's words.

"*Oui,* two," LaCroix replied. "That one there and a flower girl in whose coffin he shall lie. Not to mention the bill you shall thus be spared by his passing."

"What care, sweeting?" Isabella demanded, drawing back to look him in the face. "I live . . ." She caressed his cheek with frozen fingertips, her eyes still warm with love. "At last I may live."

She raised herself on tiptoe and kissed his mouth, and he tried to respond as she wished, remembering Janette's words. If 'twere this girl's life he loved and not her death, he needs must love her all the more now this life must last forever . . .

"I cannot," he said, pushing her away.

LaCroix shook his head in disgust. "Oh, Nicholas," he said with a sigh.

"How could you, LaCroix?" Nick demanded, moving past the girl to confront the one who had destroyed her. "How could you so betray my trust—even you should weep for shame at such treachery as this."

"Treachery?" Isabella echoed, looking back and forth between them. "What means he treachery, my lord?" She framed Nick's face with her hands. "Look at me, sweeting," she urged. "I feel naught but joy—my pain is gone. How may such a boon be called treachery?"

"You must forgive Nicholas, my child," LaCroix explained, his eyes locked to Nick's as if the girl did not exist. "In his childish perversity, he has chosen to see our particular manner of living as less a blessing than a curse."

Isabella looked at the dead man sprawled on the floor then back at her loved one's face. "'Tis pity he should die," she admitted slowly.

"Pity for whom?" LaCroix demanded. "Not his patients, I assure you, as you know full well yourself. Your kiss spared more lives this night than it took. But Nicholas perceives of no such reason." He paused, his blue eyes glittering like Arctic ice. "In truth, he did allow his own dear sister to die rather than live so forever."

"Yea, her mortal body did die," Nick retorted angrily. He extricated himself from the girl's grasp, unable to bear her freezing touch a moment longer. "But her immortal soul was saved." He looked at Isabella, so beautiful in unlife, even barefoot in her dirty shift in the midst of meanest squalor. Gazing at her, he could scarcely remember the broken innocent she had been. "And she never lived as a killer. Death is far sweeter than this fate," he finished, turning away.

Isabella looked at LaCroix, but he was silent. "Nicholas, be not so sick at heart," she urged, going to her unhappy protector and touching his shoulder. "In truth, you weep at a wound long healed, a scar now rubbed away. My soul was damned long ere this . . ." She moved around to face him. "Is't not better I should then bide here on th'earth?" she asked with a tender smile. "Think you on it, Nicholas. I do love thee well, as well as aught thy heart can e'er have known, and I would be thine forever." She took his hand and pressed it to her breast. "You need ne'er fear me, dearest," she swore, the heart whose rhythm was gone shining in her eyes as purely as any virgin's. "I shall perish in fires anew ere I desert you as this faithless Janette has done, over and over again."

Nick turned to LaCroix, his eyes reddened with rage. Where else could her words have come but from this new lord and master? No wonder he had given Janette her freedom—she was no longer so easily schooled. "Leave me," he rasped, taking Isabella by the wrists to push her away with all the kindness he still could muster. This horror was not her fault—in this demon's game, she was more innocent than she could ever have dreamed, for all that her soul was now damned. "Let me go—"

"Nay," she insisted, the glow coming back to her eyes as well. "I would be yours—"

"I said go to!" Nick roared, flinging her away in horror at the sight. "I will not love thee so!"

LaCroix stepped back, letting the girl fall to the floor as cruelly as she had once done from Hilliard's slap. "Well done, Nicholas," he said as her tears of blood spilled on the rushes. He reached down and caught a single blood tear on one finger. "That's twice in two months I've seen such tears shed by your violence. Your virtue knows no bounds." He smiled thinly. "Perhaps you intend to knock at Heaven's gate?" He wagged his head from side to side, eyebrows raised, eyes wide and glittering with haughty mockery. "Perhaps you expect St. Peter to embrace you as a brother?"

Nick froze, self-loathing rising like bile in his throat as Isabella wept behind the tangled curtain of her hair. "Forgive me," he said softly, looking up at LaCroix, but his master's face was utterly neutral, a Roman statue of justice. Looking past him, Nick could see the first pink streaks of dawn in the square of sky outside the window. "Damn you, LaCroix," he muttered, fleeing them both.

"A moot point, Nicholas," LaCroix said dryly, though his son was gone. "Particularly at such a moment."

"Why did you not kill me?" Isabella wept. "Better that than to be so despised . . ."

"Don't be foolish, girl," LaCroix cut her off. He held out his hand, waiting with perfect patience until she took it and let him raise her to her feet. "But e'en so, thou art hardly despised," he promised. "You do not yet know Nicholas's nature. He is like quicksilver, and will change his mood utterly in a minute." LaCroix raised her chin with one finger. "He will love you as truly as e'er you may wish, once he and I are returned."

"Let me go with you," she pleaded.

"Isabella, stay here," he ordered, putting a finger to her lips. "You said you had given me your heart's safe key—would you take it again so quickly? I do not like to be disobeyed," he added, very gently.

Her eyes flashed rebellion, but only for a moment. "No," she said, shaking her head.

"'Tis well," he answered, pleased. "Have no fear, *petite*.

Stay here behind the blinds, and I shall bring Nicholas to you ere long."

Only a few seconds had elapsed since Nick had streaked out the window, yet LaCroix could barely feel his son—he must have been flying then, racing for shelter before the coming of the sun.

A thought which he must take for himself, but not quite yet.

LaCroix went first to their rooms in Whitehall, thinking them the logical place for Nick to hide, but Nick had followed the same logic and therefore gone elsewhere.

Where? To the mortal world, of course. And what part of it?

Standing in Janette's empty chamber, LaCroix laughed quietly. Where else? To the theater.

The sky was lightening steadily, which meant flying higher and faster to remain unseen; and the theaters Nicholas would go to were across the river, damnably busy with barges and ferries and small private transports for all of London's morning trade as dawn broke—and all the while, around the edge of the Earth, the line of the sun's fire would be coming lower and lower, reaching like a killing finger, straining to touch a flying vampire.

Let the sun try. The sun must stay itself a minute or two.

Four round buildings standing high in the fetid bog, empty O's housing a stage ringed with rows of benches under a wooden roof—these were the theaters and the animal house. Never mind that last, its stink was enough to repel even a mortal. LaCroix flew past the row of theaters, unwilling to risk a landing in front of a building where mortals could be, unable to simply pause in the air or on the roof with the light growing by the second—unless, as once before, he presented himself as Lucifer in full panoply.

Coming to ground between trees, he went quickly to the first building in the row; it was marked by a sign of Hercules doing what Atlas should do, holding up the world—the Globe then. Shakespeare's theater.

Nicholas was within, he could feel it. LaCroix went to the door and found it bolted. Nicholas had flown in then, trusting the darkness to hide him. But it was growing lighter by the second.

Listen. Don't think of the sun, though its light was now coming to the upper sky. *Listen.* How many mortals? Just the one, stirring, growling, scratching himself, blowing his nose, stamping his feet to start the circulation—an older mortal. Nicholas, not far from him, moving by stealth. Just the one mortal, and a door scraped, and then wood—a privy closet. The mortal would be out of the way for a minute or two.

An instant later, LaCroix was inside the ring, standing onstage, sensing for his son—and realizing that he was literally underfoot, crouched under the stage boards like a dog in its kennel.

LaCroix knocked the trapdoor open with one foot, and hopped down into the pit below, a matter of only five feet. He leaned down until his head was below the stage, and regarded Nicholas. "An excellent vantage for the play, I reck—unless you cared to see it."

Nicholas snarled at him, his eyes baleful. LaCroix smiled. "Methinks thou dost protest too much," he said cheerfully.

Light was begining to show; the vampires both realized the planking was loose enough that the sun would be able to seep in through the cracks between them.

"These will prove warm lodgings. Come away, Nicholas, while there is time." The humor dropped out of LaCroix's face. "Of course, this is Hell, is it not?" he said mockingly. "Is that not exactly what the players call it? How clever of you, Nicholas, to fly straight to Hell for a day."

Nicholas refused to answer. The light from the cracks illuminated a sullen, passionate anger in his face.

"Too warm by half," LaCroix finished flatly. He was disappointed that Nick was not denouncing him furiously. An affectless Nicholas was a very distressed Nicholas indeed. Was his son so sick with this mortality-love as to wish to die?

The light between the cracks increased; the discomfort they brought warned LaCroix that he must look to himself. Fifteen centuries of vampire life were shouting at him to clear out, telling him the sun was mere minutes from showing itself. He loved Nicholas very well indeed, but not enough to burn with him.

And yet he waited one more moment, saying very softly,

"Nicholas, come." The burning in his mind was shrieking that it was all but too late. "Please—"

LaCroix flew straight up through the Globe's trapdoor, relieved to feel his son take flight behind him. LaCroix could see the line of light descending from the upper sky as the burning sun made its way up toward the horizon. Flying, he snarled defiance at it, of anything that dared to strike at him.

A windowless stone building, southerly, stood near a ruined church. Risking human eyes, LaCroix plunged straight for it. And as he went down, he roared, for the first rays of the sun had found him.

Landing below the sunline, LaCroix slapped the hasp off the door's medieval lock with a smoking hand. He slipped inside, Nicholas close behind him. Together, they pushed the thick wooden door back into its frame, and backed away from the tiny cracks of light that came in around it. Both of them sank to the floor, scorched and exhausted. They did not speak to each other for long minutes, unable to do anything but wait out their bodies' healing.

At length, LaCroix stood up and looked around him. They were in a small building lined with shelves, and stored along the shelves, seemingly sorted by size, were row after row of skulls, breastbones, shankbones, forearms, shin bones, and many, many ribs.

A roomful of bones. Monks' bones, LaCroix supposed, relics of nameless faithful men who died in service to a religion whose practice was now unlawful. Yet the hostility against the Pope and his Church had not outrun superstition, and the protesting mortals had left these bones to molder in peace.

An ossuary, this was. The final flower of mortal existence. Charming.

LaCroix brushed the dust off his clothes as best he could. "I'm so pleased you came to pass the day with me, Nicholas." He gestured widely with a now healing hand. "'Tis not oft I make my lodging in a boneyard. What think you the holy brothers—or were they sisters?—would say, knew they who had come to share their shelter?"

He picked up a delicately curved rib, holding it out before his face. "Well, lady, what say you? Will you shelter needy travelers, or do you stand on holy ceremony?" He laughed alone, for Nick was in no mood for LaCroix's arch humor. LaCroix tossed his head, his eyes flashing: "Why, madam, I thank you for your courtesy. I cannot recall that I have shared a nun's bed ere this." He tossed the bone over one shoulder.

"Let me go, LaCroix," Nicholas said.

His master snorted. "Why, certainly." He waved a hand courteously. "There stands the door."

"You know my meaning." Nick's voice was exhausted, melancholic, not at all the exuberant and lusty crusader who'd first drawn LaCroix's notice. "Let me go my own way." His head hung down. "'Twas an act of great cruelty to bring that girl across."

"Do not presume to instruct me in what is cruel and what is not," LaCroix said coldly. "Cruelty was to leave her suffering for a week that she could have spent joying in her new existence." His tone moderated. "You should be thanking me; I thought I did you a favor. Of a certainty, she thought so."

"That is the cruelty. Until today, she was innocent," Nick said, "and now you've made her a killer."

LaCroix lost his patience. "And here," he swept a hand around them, "is her alternative? Let us ask her which she prefers."

"She doesn't understand."

LaCroix laughed. "O Nicholas, I think she well understands. 'Tis you who prefer your ignorance of so many things. If you would have spared her suffering, why did you not simply take her?"

Nick's head dropped.

LaCroix sighed. Yes, Nicholas would be miserable; he always was in his defiant hours. Why did that misery never teach him to yield to himself, his own nature?

"You cannot say that you loved her? Or was her poxy blood too sour for your palate? You might have snapped her neck."

Nick made a gesture of disgust. "You do not understand at all, LaCroix. It was her life: her death."

"It was pain, Nicholas," LaCroix said coldly. "You wallowed in it."

That was too much; Nick turned away and wrapped his arms around himself, shutting his eyes as if for sleep.

"Yes, perhaps you will be less foolish with some rest," LaCroix assented. He looked around him, hoping that by some miracle there was a more pleasant corner in the monastic bonekeep than the one he currently occupied, but that hope was forlorn. Choosing what seemed the least dusty corner to stand in, he too closed his eyes.

Nick was not asleep. While his master relaxed into comfortable rest, he brooded, watching as tiny breaths of wind made their way through the keyhold to raise wisps of dust off the bones.

The image of Isabella danced in his mind: red-mouthed, gleeful with her first kill. Eyes afire not with mortal disease, but her first taste of the endless round of desire, satiation, fresh desire that would be her life—life? what a bitter misuse of the word!—from this day forward.

Dead bones. Nun's bones, LaCroix had said mockingly: the ultimate in innocent mortal girls. Nick closed his eyes, summoning the images of such girls—so many. Tender daughters of peasant woodsmen and farmers, in the early days—had he really kept them alive in his dank little dungeon, the better to sense their knowledge of their own dying as he drank? Common women, easily found in the narrow streets of Paris, easily beckoned into dark places. The sweet daughter of an Italian merchant who crept out to meet him over a series of nights, joying in his vampire's pleasure at possessing her.

Nicholas frowned, torturing himself with this chain of memories. His eyes opened again, and he estimated idly in his mind: were there enough bones here to have belonged to all of them? Three centuries and more of tender young maidens, all of whom he had truly cherished. But what was a vampire's cherishing? Death.

Only death.

His head drooped, thinking of the worst of those deaths. The one time he'd attempted to mix love and the eternal gift. Alyssa in her white shift, proud to be his wife, proud to offer her uttermost trust to her lord. Giving him her throat without an instant's outcry: he had felt her pleasure in being possessed, had felt in his own mind her rapture at being taken by her wedded husband. Joined before God, they were, and nothing could be wrong that her lawful lord wished of her. Yield, and have me drink thy blood? How could there be any answer but a joyful yes?

"Alyssa," he whispered to the bones. "Forgive me."

And now there was Isabella in her place, her face made ugly to him by fangs. Was it suffering that he loved, as LaCroix charged? Or was it only the pleasure of seeing a mortal life have its proper shape, even if it must end all too early? Nick's blue gaze flickered among the neatly ranked bones. Early, yea, but not at the hands of a vampire. Not under the cruelty of a caress at the neck that should have been a kiss but turned into the embrace of the two murdering knives that had been part of him for this eon of nights.

He could not bear to see innocence become a killer. Would Alyssa have retained her nature? It was moot; that preternaturally sweet girl had been a ghost for most of a century now. But Isabella—alive, she had been no Alyssa, for all her tangled desire to be loved. And dead—a vampire—Nick shook his head uncomfortably. He would not go so far as to drive a stake through her heart, but he did not wish to so much as see her, not even glancingly or at a distance—no, never again.

Nick looked around the bones yet again. They did not make for a cheery bedchamber—and yet this was, after all, an excellent place to clarify one's thoughts. Sweet mortal voices these bones must once have had, nuns moving about their mundane tasks of getting milk from cows, churning butter, teasing food out of the boggy turf of Lambeth, praying for all souls . . .

If I have one, pray for mine, Nick thought to them. *There must be a way to live as I am, yet be not a monster. I must find it.* And now he began to sleep.

Both vampires woke shortly before sunset.

LaCroix was in high humor again. "Well, Nicholas, have you repented your sins? Did these excellent ladies assist you?" He swept a bow to the shelves of bones. "And will you not return to the excellent lady who is now your sister? She wishes to give her most sororal love, I trow—and more."

Nicholas did not answer. LaCroix spoke gently. "If you needs must spurn the fair Isabella, will you not hunt with me presently? 'Tis a pleasant hour to stir out, and you have led us to a district with many tender ladies." The stews of Bankside were near—a hundred Isabellas . . .

Nicholas kept his silence.

"Do you bide with the dead, then?" LaCroix's voice whipped harshly. "Will you drink these dry bones?"

"I . . . am . . . *sickened* on innocent blood!" Nick hurled the words at him. "I'll have no more of it. Nevermore, LaCroix! If I must be a plague, a disease, a monster among men, then I shall be the *one* cruelty that truly strikes only the evil."

"O Nicholas, Nicholas—only the evil? Where will you find them?" LaCroix's voice was quiet, almost sad. "There are sermonizing fools abroad who'll blame a mewling child for its fever—or worser still: the poor babe's mother, who all in love doted on her dearling, is instructed that it lies limp in her arms because of some ill word or deed of hers." He snorted. "And she, the sad distracted creature, must not only bury her child, but torture her memory withal, till she finds the fault in herself, like a crack'd glass." He fell silent for a moment.

"Which of them truly does evil, sinner or priest—neither, both?"

LaCroix drew his dagger and played the ossuary's one ray of light, the beam that came through the keyhole, now the low, golden slant of a setting sun, along its blade. He angled the blade to throw the reflected light across Nick's face for an instant.

A burning instant; Nick swatted at the tiny finger of light and moved out of its reach with vampire speed. LaCroix laughed at him, and continued with the lesson.

"Death does not choose; nor shall we. The lion does not interrogate the deer: 'Say you, stag, but hast thou done evil? And thou, pretty doe? Hast thou et of Farmer Brown's grain, hast thou nibbled at his peas?' " LaCroix stretched out his arms and laughed. " 'Tis folly, 'tis madness to imagine. It is a lion. *We* are lions, Nicholas."

"I've made my decision, LaCroix," Nick said.

LaCroix glanced at him, then turned his attention back to the dagger, turning it around and around with the point against one fingertip. Finally he drawled, "Yes, Nicholas, I see that you have."

Despite the battering of the years, some things, LaCroix reflected, seemed never to change. There would always be yet another moment when his child would insist on having his own way. With his jaw set and his bright blue eyes shining with determination, Nicholas looked so much like a stubborn little boy that one could scarcely credit there was a single decade, let alone full four centuries, of experience behind him.

LaCroix sheathed his dagger, snorting with amusement. This whim would play out, as they always had before . . . if it didn't cause some messy disaster first.

Yet even at that, Nicholas's errors usually had no more serious consequence than requiring a hasty departure, sometimes with a few precautionary killings. LaCroix smiled wryly, pondering it: Nick's whims were most often disastrous for the very mortals he'd taken a fancy to help. One might almost think the boy was cursed.

"As you will, Nicholas," he said. "I retain my great curiosity, though: how shall you detect in the general herd of humankind these guilty ones? Will you wait to see murder done ere you feed? Will a treacherous housewife be low enough for you? A lying lawyer? A lazy apprentice? A tapster who o'erwaters his wine? And will a single sin suffice you, or shall you wait to see two, three, or four?" LaCroix looked thoughtful. "'Twill prove a very delicate question, think you not?"

Nicholas was fairly glowering by now, yet holding his tongue. He truly believed he had made a final choice, LaCroix realized. Even more, Nicholas believed himself able to act on his choice with no guidance from his master. Well, he had never been willing to acknowledge how much he needed to learn. LaCroix felt the sun slip below the horizon and lifted his head with the pleasure this moment brought him each day. Time to go.

But first, one last dollop of education for his son: "Nay, I think I shall enjoy this kickshaw of yours, Nicholas," his voice turned harsh in an instant, "watching you sift among the living and the soon to be dead with all-seeing wisdom." LaCroix arched his eyebrows, and his voice became light and mocking again. "Shall I say— Godspeed?" He left, laughing.

Returning to the shabby inn, LaCroix felt no vampire near, and certainly none of his blood: Isabella was no longer here. His anger flaring, he cut a path through the tavern patrons and up the stairs simply by force of the look in his eyes.

The girl was gone indeed, but she had left her meager belongings behind, along with a note written in surprisingly legible script:

My dearest Nicholas, and most kind and gentle LaCroix,

If your promise be kept, know that I did strive to wait as bidden, but hunger hath gotten the upper hand over obedience. I have tenders I have longed long to return . . . In all avers, if you wish not to seek me out, I shall return here once my final debts are paid.

I.

LaCroix crumpled the note with a smile. *Tenders I have longed to return . . .* Vampire perception was hardly required to deduce where his daughter had gone.

"Where is she?" The boy player, Thomas, was standing in the open doorway, looking fit for murder or mourning, whichever his answer required. "Where is Isabella?"

"Dead," LaCroix replied.

Color rose hot in the boy's smooth cheeks, then faded white as flour. "'Sblood," he mumbled, turning slightly away, greensick with grief.

"You can hardly be surprised," the vampire said, watching him stagger, his broken young heart pounding between them. If taken, he would have to be hid—

"No," Thomas admitted, sitting heavily in the bedside chair so lately abandoned by Nicholas. "I knew she would die ere long." He touched the pillow reverently, as if touching his dead lover's face. "But 'tis hard to think on't, my being away, her being . . . I had thought to say good-bye."

The boy wept as shamelessly as a child, the simple drama of his grief giving even this vampire pause. Was it possible to feel pain so purely, even with a mortal heart?

"You were here," LaCroix said, using his hypnosis and cursing himself for a fool. *Nick's madness is apparently contagious,* he thought with a wry inward smile.

The boy was no resistor—even before he looked up, he was utterly captured. "'Sooth—"

"You were by her when she died, just there where now you sit," LaCroix went on. "Held her hand, kissed her cheek—closed her eyes with pennies when she was gone, just as she bid you do." He paused, not entirely certain that even this sudden altruism was sufficient to carry him through such a scene, but strangely game to try. The boy's own love-soaked imagination would certainly fill in the gaps. "I'faith, you did keep her close," he finished as Thomas turned back to the pillow, his tears still falling but his heart at peace. A smile pulled at LaCroix's lips: Nicholas was not the only one who could play at piety. "Go now . . . seek the girl here no more, but hope to meet her again in Heaven."

14

We know diseases of stoppings and suffocations are the most dangerous in the body; and it is not much otherwise in the mind;

you may take sarza to open the liver, steel to open the spleen, flower of sulfur for the lungs, castoreum for the brain;

but no receipt openeth the heart, but a true friend; to whom you may impart griefs, joys, fears, hopes, suspicions, counsels, and whatsoever lieth upon the heart to oppress it, in a kind of civil shrift or confession.

—Sir Francis Bacon,
"Of Friendship," *Essays* (1597)

NICK STAYED IN THE OSSUARY WITH WHAT LACROIX FANCIED TO BE nuns' bones till full dark had settled over the Lambeth marsh around it.

Emerging in the gloom, he was indeed assaulted at once by hunger. He needed to feed. The cooling land around him drew a wind from the Bankside, and again the smell of animal blood taunted the vampire in him. LaCroix had probably already feasted on some unfortunate girl there—if, Nicholas thought belatedly, he hadn't gone back to Isabella's inn to collect her for her first hunt.

Isabella. The mere thought of her heightened Nick's shame. The prancing girl who'd merrily purloined a hat with a big blue feather, the sick, skinny girl who'd turned from fevered rage to whimpering clinging and back again so many times over the past week. But always so human: frail, strong, sly, too wise for her years; laughing, ranting, weeping—always so human.

In the interrupted play, the mad maid—Will had given her Isabella's songs, just as earlier, in the first blush of his own infatuation, he'd given Juliet her willful naïveté, and made her the betraying dark lady in his love poems when the sprite had found herself another lover.

A rage rose in Nick: if he knew, to whom would Shakespeare give her blood-fed dance of this afternoon? What could the playwright, so apt with every form of human madness, make of the hunger that owned Nick's very soul, that gripped him at this very moment?

Blood on the wind—Nick inhaled it, and his eyes paled, the vampire in him responding to that heady promise. He fought it, screaming back inside what was left of his soul that he would not be its pawn anymore, but its ruler. *Never again innocent blood*, Nick said to himself. *This much I can do. This much by sheer will can be possible.* The vampire still showing, he snarled at the sky as if it held his hunger, and flew up into the darkness.

From the street, Lady Hilliard's house seemed as serenely pretentious as ever, a fortress of respectable luxury on the fashionable bank of the Thames. But LaCroix's vampire ears could detect great consternation behind the thickly plastered walls—an old woman's sobbing and a young one's laugh. Glancing about to see who might be watching, he opened the door and went in.

The servants who approached him were turned away with barely a word, even as he moved up the stairs, following his sense of his child and the telltale scent of death. Isabella had chosen to sup in her bedchamber—or Hilliard's anyway, a cozy little nook with a high cabinet bed, thick carpets, and enough tapestries to keep out the most bitter riverside chill, even in this dead of winter. But Hilliard was cold just the same, laid on the bed as if in the most peaceful repose, oblivious at last to his mother's voice.

"Behold!" Isabella cried as LaCroix came in, pointing to the weeping lump crouched before her. "The beauteous majesty of Denmark!"

As annoyed as he was at the girl's disobedience, LaCroix was still tempted to laugh at the picture she presented—pure gleeful malice, with her lover's blood still on her teeth. The fine lady who had ordered her arrested the last time she'd dared appear in her society now huddled weeping at her feet, looking anything but disdainful. Her face was white now with fear rather than paint, her eyes red-rimmed and staring, and the golden wig she wore in remembrance of her youth had apparently been snatched from her head, revealing a soft crop of yellow-white wisps. "My lady, what ails thee, that you appear so disarrayed?" LaCroix asked smoothly, making a deep, mocking bow.

"She is mad, sir; nay, possessed!" Lady Hilliard shrieked, struggling to her feet. "You must help me flee—a fiend!" Isabella lunged forward, and Lady Hilliard screamed again, falling back to the floor, her hands held up to either ward her off or beg her mercy, but which was impossible to tell.

"A fiend she doth know right well," Isabella said, her voice fairly dripping with venom. "Mark you how she makes no show that my face is unfamiliar now."

"Aye, I know thee, harlot, have known thee long, indeed!" the woman hissed. "As I know the Devil lives in Hell."

"Then thy knowledge be but little, lady," LaCroix said silkily. He added a fragment of vampire compulsion to his speech: "Abate thy squalling."

Next he bent his gaze on his new daughter. "Isabella, I am most displeased."

The girl's look of hatred faded into sweet contrition in an instant, though whether the change were feigned or true was beyond even his perceptions. "Prithee, forgive me," she said meekly, leaving off menacing the mortal to come to his side. "I—"

"Such recklessness needs must be punished," LaCroix continued. He held out a hand to Lady Hilliard, raising her to her feet. "Chasing this gentle lady around a bedchamber like a kitten in pursuit of a mouse—'tis badly done, my child." He moved around the woman, holding her motionless and trembling before him by sheer power of his will. "How best shall I chastise my daughter, *madam*?" he asked softly, his lips barely brushing her ear, Isabella's eyes going gold with anticipation as she watched him.

"Send her to Hell, where her friends are," Lady Hilliard managed, grasping desperately at the rags of her hauteur. "That should serve her well."

"As it serves your son, no doubt," LaCroix answered dryly. "Nay, I think her too rare an infant to be so dismissed—so rare that I am tempted to forgive her this silly prank." He laid a hand on the woman's brow and bent her head back against his shoulder, exposing her throat to his fangs and Isabella's eager sight. "What think you, Isabella?" he asked, his own eyes going gold. "Shall you have your prize, or shall I take it now for myself?"

"You," Isabella said, breathless with excitement. "I would see her preyed upon and die."

He sank his fangs into the flesh, righteous fury sweetening the dying woman's noble blood as it coursed hot and rich on his tongue. Isabella watched, fascinated, until the creature's struggles ceased, then her eyes faded back to blue. By the time the heart had stopped, she had turned away completely.

"You needs must take more care," LaCroix said, watching her gaze down on Hilliard. The blood had made him feel uncharacteristically well tempered—sanguine, the physicians called it.

"Forgive me," the girl repeated, tracing the arch of each golden brow, the curve of bluish lips. "E'en now, he is a beauty; think you not so?" she said sadly. "E'en now the worm is hid deep in his heart."

"It will have him soon enough, or its brothers, at any rate," LaCroix replied. "Do you regret his loss?"

"His loss? Yea, very much, and will ever," she answered. "But his death?" She twisted a curl around her fingertip. "Nay, his death I regret not at all." She closed the dead boy's eyes and pressed a tender kiss to each lid. "'Tis passing strange," she mused. "I did truly love him."

"Yet you killed him," LaCroix said, smiling.

"Yes," she agreed, turning to look at her new master. "Without a moment's pause—and for love, mind, not for hunger."

"Not so strange," he answered. "In truth, you will be much

amazed to learn what destruction we creatures may wreak, e'en against ourselves. And how much love may be in such destruction withal."

She smiled sadly as if in agreement, then her face turned serious, realization in her eyes. "What means this?" she demanded. "Where is Nicholas?"

LaCroix moved to her slowly, putting the image of his errant son firmly from his mind. She had begun so well; a lie would let her continue. When she was strong, there would be time enough for the truth. "Nicholas is gone," he said gently.

"What is gone?" she asked, grabbing his arm. "You said yourself we can ne'er die—"

"Unless we choose to do so," he interrupted. "Nicholas exposed himself to the morning sun—"

"Nay, tell me not!" she shrieked, covering her ears with her hands. "I will not know of it, will not think—God's blood, LaCroix, how could you allow him—?"

"I knew not his intention until 'twas far too late," he answered smoothly, his face the picture of fatherly grief.

"I cannot bear it," she wailed, looking frantically around at the tableau of mortal death she'd created, her genuine grief touching his heart even as he knew it for the best. "I will die as well—"

"You will not, by any shift," LaCroix cut her off sternly. "You will live as a princess, far away from this paltry city, in a house to make this one seem but a miserable hovel. You may do as you will, have whatever you choose in any place you wish—Paris, Rome, Constantinople—"

"What care I for Constantinople when my only lover is dead!" she cried. "I want none of those places, none of those things—I want Nick!"

At least she didn't say Hilliard, LaCroix thought. "Nick, as you call him, is gone," he said. "You will find other lovers in immortality, just as you did in life." He held out his hand, and she took it, letting him lead her away. "Believe me," he promised with genuine affection as he led her out into the night. "I will make certain you are so happy, you've forgot Nicholas ever lived. You have a sister in Avignon, Francesca; I will send you to her. She is quite a beauty." LaCroix smiled. "She is also a . . . what shall I say? . . . remarkable hostess. And a woman of infinite ingenuity. She regained control of her ancestral lands and has contrived to hold them for hundreds of years, despite all the inconveniences of human law. She is the right mistress for you."

Isabella pulled away, her eyes flashing defiance. LaCroix reached out and took her chin between thumb and fingers. He spoke in deceptively light tones. "You . . . will . . . obey her as you would me." Contrite again, Isabella nodded. He patted her hand. "I shall come to you soon enough. Come, child, we must arrange a passage for the noble House of Hilliard beyond mortal sight, and a passage for you—"

Aristotle had not been expecting Lucius, far less Lucius with a very young fledge, who had previously been a very young and very sick girl. Nevertheless, they were admitted immediately by Gaston to his innermost chamber at Whitehall, a dark office with a table cluttered with scrolls, and a small, high scrivener's desk at which he now sat.

This was the center of Aristotle's life among the mortals. The presence of any vampire here unbidden was remarkable; the presence of a vampire with a new and potentially uncontrollable fledge . . . Gaston cast his eyes inappropriately heavenward and shut the door behind him, wondering what he would say if the Queen sent for his master now. It was not unheard of: that lady kept late hours, and was wont to send for her counselors at any one of them, to probe their minds over a hand of cards.

Even so, Aristotle regarded the intruders calmly.

"They do say a bad penny turneth ever up," was all he ventured. It was an opening gambit, as both of the old friends knew.

LaCroix granted him the point and the game at once. "Yes, Aristotle, she is, as you perceive, freshly minted, and I have come to confess dire need." He smiled, enjoying his tactic of sudden surrender. "Need of Dyer. Art thou pleased?"

"Nay, no whit," said Aristotle. His brow was so furrowed that his receding hairline almost reached his eyebrows. Lucius bringing that ridiculous chit to his chambers was trouble enough, but Lucius declining a contest? Something must really be wrong.

LaCroix followed Aristotle's train of thought without difficulty. "Yea, old friend, I must draw heavily upon your services.

A noble dynasty is extinguished, and we must extinguish the extinction."

You killed Elizabeth Tudor? was Aristotle's first wild thought. He closed his eyes over it.

"That lady lives yet to die," LaCroix said with gentle amusement. Aristotle could be so transparent. "Guess again."

This was more like Lucius: giving him a headache. "No riddles," said the Undersecretary. "They do hurt my brain."

"No cloud without its silver lining," murmured his friend.

Aristotle made a rolling motion with his hand: *and, and, and?*

"The House of Hilliard hath seen the end of its age," LaCroix reported. "Mistress Isabella and I—"

"Say no more." Aristotle's head dropped into his hands. *Nobility?*

But Lucius did. "There is also the question of a journey for my daughter—"

"Say no more," Aristotle begged, voice muffled by his sleeves. Here he'd been lecturing that unkempt pair from the New World about simply not leaving corpses in the street, and Lucius had wiped out a whole house? And . . . daughter? This mad imp who wrecked mortal lives was now to be a vampire?

Again LaCroix disobeyed. "She must go to Francesca in Avignon."

"Lucius . . ." Aristotle sighed massively. "I beg you, say no more."

"On this tide."

"The night tide?" A bit of desperation tinged his voice, although both vampires knew that Aristotle *always* had a boat available on the night tide: there was no predicting which night he would need it himself. "Say—"

Benevolence shone in LaCroix's smile. "Anything to oblige you, my friend. I shall say no more."

At this, Aristotle's head emerged from between his hands, and he shot his friend a venomous glance. "Will I ever win, Lucius?" he snapped, the laughter in his eyes belying his tone.

LaCroix appeared to give this question careful consideration. "No," he said at length.

Both the ancient vampires laughed, enjoying this latest

round in their friendship, then Aristotle turned to his desk and swept his papers away.

"Passport," he murmured. "Papers. Monies. Francesca du Montaigne is currently on the Costa del Sol. Passage—a woman alone?" he demanded.

LaCroix shrugged. "Servants?"

Aristotle blew air out between his lips. "Servants. Coach. Francesca—you will send to her beforehand?"

"Aye, a courier," LaCroix agreed.

"My courier, you mean." Aristotle sighed. It was fortunate the Queen was willing to spend so much for spies.

Isabella was watching this give-and-take with comprehension, well aware she should not meddle between these two elders, and yet—

"I do not wish to go alone," she said and pouted. "I want Nicholas."

Aristotle's eyes drifted shut slowly, and his lips pressed together to hold back a laugh. Nicholas, the fountain of endless trouble. Two of the strongest vampires in Europe, Lucien LaCroix and Janette DuCharme, had mangled their hearts for golden Nicholas, and now this girl wanted to test her day-old fangs on him?

No wonder LaCroix was packing her off willy-nilly.

His eyes opened again, their brown depths twinkling. "Perhaps I shall live to win just a . . . small . . . victory," he remarked.

LaCroix addressed Isabella. "That is not possible, my child. Have I not told you Nicholas is dead?"

Aristotle's eyes flared, but he was fooled for only that split second. Of all the hearts that wanted to pledge themselves to Nicholas de Brabant, Lucius's was the first, and the most thoroughly ensnared.

"My deepest sympathies," he murmured, jocularity barely suppressed. His sentiments earned him an acid glare. What fun Lucius was, really.

"Now let us prepare," Aristotle said, taking up his quill and seizing a sheet of foolscap. He laughed silently. *"Nicholas is dead"? And the little fool credits it?* So Lucius not only wanted but *needed* her gone on the night's high tide before she discovered his lie. Well, given Lucius's notions of family discipline, the chit was probably better off with Francesca, anyway—now *there* was a lady who understood that being a vampire was *fun*.

LaCroix relaxed a little. There had been a saying in the Rome of his day that it was good to have Gaul but better to have an honest friend. As a mortal, he had preferred Gaul, but now he thought otherwise.

Nicholas was sitting on his bed in the luxurious room at Whitehall, a far cry from the dusty bonehouse where he'd spent the sunny hours. Yet his manner reflected no pleasure in the exquisite luxury of his surroundings; the Flemish tapestry, carpet from the Orient, beeswax tapers, and richly hung bed furnishing seemed not even to reveal themselves to his gaze. Instead, it was dully fixed on the fire that had been kindled in the chamber's hearth; the endless varied turning, shaping, falling and rising of the flame, the occasional crackle when the fire found and popped a bead of sap as it consumed the wood.

"Ah, Nicholas, so good to see your cheer restored." LaCroix strolled in as majestically as the Queen herself might have done. Nick ignored this irony. "Tell me, what oppresses you now? You should be rejoicing to think how much you have accomplished this past day—both my daughters have fled your London." He paused, as if reflecting. "Though by very different routes."

Nick frowned at him. "What trickery is this?"

"Trickery?" LaCroix opened his eyes to their widest. "Nay, simple truth: Janette has gone by water, Isabella by fire." He cocked his head. "'Tis very philosophical, is it not? Elemental passages . . ."

"Fire?" The word choked Nick's throat.

"I was not there in the hours when she needed comfort," LaCroix said evenly. "She begged me fetch you. Doth not your very own poet teach you that spurned maids embrace a lonely end?"

"Do you say that she . . . ?" Nick couldn't bring himself to give voice to LaCroix's terrible implication.

LaCroix met his eyes steadily. "Have you ever known me desert a child upon the day of her making?" His eyebrows quirked upward. "Do you see her here present? She went to the sun." *Costa del Sol, at any rate; not quite an outright lie.*

Nick slumped to the bed, sickened. Though LaCroix had

worked the transformation, he knew himself to be Isabella's killer. *Go to*, he'd spat out with his terrible contempt. "You lie," he ground out, one last effort to avoid this unbearable guilt.

"Ask the boy who hounds her steps if she lives," LaCroix said coolly. "Could he have come nigh her on the day of her first hunger and lived?" He arched one eyebrow. "Go, by all means, and seek for the truth about vampires among the mortals."

He looked into the fire, but his words were a command. "And then return to me."

The players were, as always, gathered in an ordinary, joking and shouting and splashing food or wine about as if the world could never harbor a worse monster than a bad rhyme or a missed cue.

They were joking about the disaster at Lord Hunsdon's house. Nicholas paused just outside a blurry window, seeing them as wavering shadows bobbing in and out of the light of their few candles. Mortal hearing would not have been able to follow the conversation, but Nicholas listened as if to the world's sweetest music.

". . . old basilisk turned my guts to water with a look," said Shakespeare. He meant Lady Hilliard, as his pantomime of her face made perfectly clear.

"Nay, 'tis your guts that turn wine to water," remarked Jonson.

"That is a most excellent practice, sir." This was Dick Burbage, once again adopting the falsely bland tone that irritated Ben the most. "Know ye also the trick o' the bezoar stone that turneth dross to gold?"

"I contain even now the wit that doth change dross to pearl." As always, Will deflected the nascent quarrel between the two.

Dick scoffed. "How say you?"

Jonson laughed, getting the joke. "He means he hath swallowed many oysters."

"Why, it is a most philosophical gut withal," Will agreed, patting the small bulge in his doublet.

Ben was feeling wicked. "Nay, 'tis thy good woman who's the doctor-philosopher." Will's face got a bit tight-lipped, but Jonson ran on. "What way may a husband be turned to a poet? Anne hath a way!"

"Do not practice on our sweet William, gentle Ben, lest your worshipful scholars remark thy gift, who turneth mere empty air to hot quarrel." Dick rubbed his thumb ever so lightly at the place where Ben's thumb wore its fatal brand.

"Now turn I mummer," Ben nodded. Will and Dick had enough trouble on their hands lately, with all of lordly London rumoring about the wild boy/girl who disrupted their great play. "I'll be bound to hold my peace."

Will Sly spoke up. " 'Tis what we thought, Ben, that you held your piece." His smile was even blander than Burbage's.

"Be it still the regulation nine-inch brick o' thy mystery?" said Burbage wickedly.

"I hear no complaints from ladies." Now Ben was bland. "Certainly none from your good lady, Dick."

Before a brawl could start, Nick made his entrance.

"Nicholas! Where have you hidden yourself these seven days?" Burbage was cheery. "God's blood, you look a Danish prince!"

Nick froze, startled into awareness of himself. He'd changed at Whitehall into whatever clothes were in reach, but it was true: he was dressed in sober black, over a simple shirt with ruffled cuffs that greatly resembled Dick's Hamlet costume.

"Your pardon, Nick." Suddenly Burbage had his observer's look, the scrutiny that would peek out of his face in even his most pot-valiant moments and lock someone's bearing, expression, or quality of voice into his actor's box of tricks forever.

Nick forced a small laugh. "Oh, I have been private with . . ." His throat closed. He couldn't make a joke of it.

They were all staring. "Come, sit you," said the usually caustic Will Sly, sliding down the bench to make him a space by Shakespeare. Jonson poured a cup of wine and pushed it at him.

Nick looked at the cup and laughed again with no mirth in his face. He might as well drink it: the pain of mortal food would suit his humor.

"You have been closeted with her, then," said the playwright beside him, very quietly. Everyone knew he'd last been seen carrying Isabella away from her would-be jailors. "Young Tom has told us how he did see her die."

Tom Saddler was sitting, miserable and silent, at the end of the table, his young head bowed over a huge, untasted, mug of ale.

So that was how LaCroix had spread the tale. Well, it was probably easier for the poor boy than the actual truth would have been, even before the girl had immolated herself.

Bitterness rocked Nick. "Ay, she's dead," he answered. "Very dead. Dead dead." His fingers closed around the pewter cup in his hand until it dented, a mistake he rarely made.

He stood up abruptly. "Your pardons, all." His eyes swept the table, a group of decent men who'd been laughing until he came in. His voice was a rasp. "I am not fit." He climbed over the bench to leave, but Shakespeare caught his arm, and his eye.

"Will you go with me, Will?" he asked, almost too softly for a mortal to hear.

The player poet, his big owl eyes deep and thoughtful under his high forehead, looked up at Nick, nodded, and rose.

The door let them out into Southwark High Street, and Will swung north for Maid Lane as by habit.

"We played our prince," he said. Nicholas was just a figure in black walking beside him, his head sunk nearly to his chest. "At Hunsdon's, you saw only . . ." Will broke off.

"Ay, the spurning of the girl who dies. And then the dying girl," Nick said. "A tragedy, a tragedy, and then another tragedy." The roughness was still in his voice.

"Loved you her?" Will asked. Such bitterness, what could it come from? "I did love her well once," he added very quietly.

"I am told I loved only her dying." Nick pursed his lips. "That I am a great lover of death."

Shakespeare chafed his arms under his cloak. "The night is cold," he said. In truth, his friend's manner would chill midsummer. He rubbed harder, wanting to shake off this mood, and led Nick onto the way to the Globe.

"Doth your prince kill?" Nick rasped out suddenly. "Doth he so master himself?"

This was frightening. "Claudius dies," Will said carefully. "He kills the usurper in the end by hap more than present purpose, for he is dueling with Laertes. There is a poison blade, a pearl'd and poisoned cup." *Why do you ask?* he left unsaid.

"Many die unpurpos'd in this tale," he added, still offering words as cautiously as a cat would place its feet.

Nick made a noise like a growl.

Will brought a gloved hand out from under his cloak to scratch his mustache. *Turn the topic.* "We played the story entire at the Globe three times this se'nnight." He rubbed at his cold ears. "A fortunate string of warm days let us run up the flag." Nick was unresponsive. Shakespeare bent his head a little to peer at Nick's face, but Nick turned away. "'Tis how we signal we show a play; the banner may be seen e'en from St. Paul's."

"I think any man may come to kill," Nick said. "And drink hot blood. Or any maid."

Shakespeare choked, his wind puffing out in a coughing fit.

Nick whirled to face him, blocking his path.

"We spoke of it on this very road," he said. Will nodded, bent over with his coughing. "Well, I have seen a maid drink blood this day. She then destroyed herself in flame, but not for that."

Will's breath came out in one long exhalation that made a cloud on the night air. "What are you?" he whispered.

For he had straightened up to find his French friend looking at him with yellow eyes that burned like the fires of Hell.

"A vampire," said Nick, feeling the weight of the world come off his shoulders. He said it like a lord: "I am Nicholas de Brabant, vampire."

"You have led me aside to kill me?"

Hearing his own words gasped out, Will was astonished he still had the power of speech, but Nick had heard the question before. Mortals screamed, fled, or fainted; some of them fought; a few gave themselves to the demon passionately; and a few retained their reason. Of those who could speak, most asked this very question.

Most were told yes.

Nick shook his head very, very slowly. "I have not."

The Globe's stage was still strewn with fragrant rushes from the day's work. Nutshells and orange peels littered the yard.

The door to the player's Hell hung open and a skull sat next to it.

"This should not be here," Shakespeare said, irritation

briefly distracting him from terror. They had walked the rest of the way to the Globe in complete silence, Nick constantly aware that Will was trying to look at him without being seen. "The gravedigger's to carry this off."

Nick had let his eyes go blue again, and his face had softened to its normal humanlike friendliness. He stooped to pick it up, then sat down on the stage, holding it, opening his doublet and unlacing his shirt at the neck as if he were hot on this chilly night.

It was eerie. Shakespeare tried a joke. "Your speech is: 'Alas, poor Yorick. I knew him, Horatio; a fellow of infinite jest . . . He hath carried me upon his back a thousand times—'" but the terror closed his throat again.

Nick's mouth twisted bitterly. "I passed the day with bones," he said. "I'll ha' no more of 'em." He tossed the skull to Will, whose numb hands nearly dropped it.

Now he met the playwright's eyes again. "I cannot stand the sun. One minute of it would be my death—my final death." A humorless smile pulled at his lips. "You want to know the monster's nature, do you not, my friend?"

Will nodded, lowering himself to sit on the other side of the trapdoor, still cradling the skull.

Nick stared at the stage. "I was brought across in 1228. LaCroix, my 'father,'" he gave the word a harsh inflection, "is my master, the one who made me into this thing that I am." His eyes darted up to Shakespeare's for an instant. "'A father who comes from Hell to rule his son,' you said." He fell silent, staring into the stage "grave."

"Forsooth," Nick said. "I am so ruled." Another unhappy smile. "And I am cared for so." Now he looked up at the stars, his voice climbing until it easily reached the upper tiers. "Have I not father, lover, house, and history? May I not taste any pleasure the world can devise?" Another silence. "For a while." This was almost a whisper. "For a very little while."

He looked over at Will. "Then it is time to take leave. Then it is all ash and shadow and bone." He gestured at the skull in Will's lap. "Then they are gone, cold, stilled, silent, dead." A silence. "And I have . . . drunk." His face was twisted with contempt and a strangely passive rage.

Will shifted his seat slightly, pulling in his legs and wrapping his cloak around him against the cold. It was worth a chill to hear such a tale—and besides, would his "friend" let him leave?

"Blood," said Nicholas. Will shivered. "'Tis the only food I may have." He tipped his head back to stare at the stars again and his voice lightened. "I must not lie to you; it is a most excellent sustenance." Nick gave a slow exhalation, thinking of the satisfaction; his fangs appeared, and Shakespeare had another coughing fit.

Nick understood. He turned a warm human gaze on his friend. "You must not fear me, Will."

"How not?" the player choked out.

"Thou art my friend." This was Nicholas Chevalier, exactly as he always had been, a little lighthearted, a little secretive, a puzzle. Speaking now in the high diction to emphasize his meaning.

Will shook his head. "How can it be?"

Nick smiled a little. "Have I not just put my life into your hands?"

It made Will stare at the skull that he truly held. "Immortality," he said wonderingly. "At the price of bloody murders of men." He looked up.

The bitterness was back. Nick stared hard into his friend's eyes. "Men . . . women . . . children. Horses, cows, pigs, dogs at need, what have you, at need, anything for the blood, every night, every night for the rest of time." The words raced out of Nick. "You will do *anything* to feed the hunger. Once fed, you will do it again, for it is a fire with no embering. It is damnation and paradise together."

Will nodded, realizing why he was being trusted. "The hunger you speak of exceedeth any I have ever known," he said gently. "So any man may come to kill, in sooth."

Nick's humor turned. "Or woman, child . . . ," he said. What a luxury to say it, just once.

"Isabella?" Will spoke in alarm as the idea struck him.

"No!" The lie was reflexive; it was one thing to trust a friend with his own life, but Isabella's fate was a matter belonging to LaCroix, even if her damnation had lasted but a single day.

"No." This was the answer Will preferred, it was clear. *The cousin Janette,* the playwright was thinking. *She was his blood-drinking maiden.* An image formed in his mind of the woman, her long black hair tumbled loose, blood at her mouth. He furrowed his brow, looking at Nick. "What do you now?" He pointed a finger at the sky. "To outlive these stars; how can that be borne? And to support that life . . ." His shoulders sagged. "I can hardly bear to have outlived one little boy."

Nick smiled. "'Tis the answer. To hardly bear it, but bear it. And then there is laughter, sometimes. Love, sometimes. Hold where you belong, find a friend . . ." He met Will's eyes and said the hardest thing. "Take no sweet life."

Hearing himself say the words, Nick knew them for a vow.

His smile became wistful. "Perhaps watch for a better existence. 'Tis what I wish—what I may wish."

The two men looked at each other across the Globe's stage grave. Will shook his head slowly. "You came to say you are going again," he said, realization dawning.

"And have said rather more," Nick said steadily.

"And you'll not come here again, methinks."

Nick nodded confirmation. "Not while you live," he said gently. Any vampire who guessed the playwright knew of their existence would simply kill him; it was bad enough that LaCroix and Aristotle knew they were friends. If Will were visibly easy with Nick . . . if a joke with too much knowledge in it slipped out in a careless instant . . . It was a chance that could not be taken. "And you must never speak of it."

"No play of . . . what was your word? vampires?" Will shivered. "Eternal, unnatural hunger . . ."

"One more thing between Heaven and Earth," Nick said, attempting lightness. "'Tis both our deaths if you fail."

"Then I'll not." Will nodded slightly.

Nick rose. "I must go."

The playwright stood up too, his limbs stiff with both chill and a bit of renewed fear. The strangeness had come back in his friend, the distant, lordly quality. Yet, withal, this was, or had been, Nicholas Chevalier.

"Stay for me a moment," Will said. He disappeared into the tiring house with Yorick's skull tucked in the crook of one elbow.

He returned a minute or two later with a thick scroll bearing the seal of the Queen's Master of Revels, and gave it to Nick.

The vampire held it in both hands, looking down at it. He knew what it was. He took a quick breath, and looked up to Will's face.

"'Tis the whole of Prince Hamlet's tragedy," Shakespeare said softly, running a finger over the lapped pages. "Take it for token of me." He leaned forward, put a hand on Nick's shoulder, and kissed him ceremonially on each cheek, in the courtly fashion. "Myself must go into a warm place before an ague seizes all that's left of me." His eyes dropped involuntarily to the hole in the floor called "Hell." "But I did leave the box unlocked and thou may'st read as thou likest this night."

Nick nodded.

"I wish thee well, Nicholas," said the player. The owl eyes were touched by a smile. "'Tis a wish must last you until you find your own wish." He clapped Nicholas on the shoulder, an actor trying business to find his way out of the scene. He waved a hand at the inner door. "Go in, boy, and read."

Nick watched him go down the stage stairs and across the groundlings' yard, then called after him in joking protest.

"I am full four hundred year, sirrah."

Will looked over his shoulder, puffing out a small laugh, shook his head, and disappeared into the tunnel that led out to Globe Alley.

Nick turned toward the door to the theater's closed chambers—green room, tireroom, property room, account room—the warren of inner places that were Globe's private heart. Or perhaps those rooms should be called the theater's inner mind, from which the dreams issued forth, an ever-changing panoply of costumes and characters, acting out a world's worth of story on a few square yards of oak planking. Later this very day, more of them would spill out, laughing and dancing and making man's life a merry fiction or a grievous tragedy, all in the span of a few hours. By tomorrow, the clothes and names would all change again. At the moment, all was silence—or almost all; Nick's enhanced senses told him the night watchman was stretched out on a cot and watching only his own dreams, snoring to give them a chorus.

Tomorrow he must belong to LaCroix again, probably returning with him to Paris, maybe traveling to Italy; he knew he would go as he was bid. But he also knew he would go with this new vow clenched tightly in his own private heart, and tonight he could have a last dream of his own as a man among men, poring over the playscripts of a generous friend. He held the one manuscript that was his to keep a little closer and walked toward the small door.

Tonight, these things were enough.

EPILOGUE

Be a physician . . . and be eternis'd for some wondrous cure!

—Christopher Marlowe,
The Tragicall Historie of Doctor Faustus,
Act I, sc. i, 14–15 (1588)

"NICK, WHAT?"

He shook his head, snapping out of it. "Nothing."

Nat folded her arms. "Aw, c'mon. It was *something*—you got that out of focus, fade to black, cue the ghosts look."

"Guilty." Nick looked up and met her eyes with a frank smile. "Cue the ghosts?" he teased. Had anyone else in history ever made fun of him like this?

Nat tilted her chin. She was still a little winded, and her hair was fanned around her head from whirling around in her dance.

"Okay, let's say you sing it a little differently than the first girl I ever heard sing that song."

"Who was . . . ?"

"Ophelia," Nick said. He smiled. "Part of her was, anyway. She wasn't a highborn virgin of Denmark, though. Just another unlucky young woman who got mixed up with the wrong guy, and . . . well, you know the story." Nick's eyes blurred thoughtfully. "Who knows what she could have been today."

"Wait a minute, you're saying you knew the actual girl

Ophelia was based on?" Nat caught herself. "*Why* do I always wind up sounding like the straight man in a comedy act?"

Nick grinned. "Okay, I give up: why?"

Nat sat down on the piano bench, leaning toward him. "Ophelia, really? Who was she? Where was she? Where were *you*?" Her breath stopped for a moment. "So tell me, Mr. Bones, does this mean you met Shakespeare?"

Nick looked out the window.

"Ni-ick, don't make me work for this," Nat griped.

Nick yielded, nodding as he turned around to face her. "Yeah, I knew Shakespeare."

"*So what was he like?* . . . You *are* going to make me work for this, aren't you?"

"He was nice," Nick said, with a grin and a shrug. "You think that's a nothing answer, but it's not. He was funny, and he worked all the time, and he tried to be a nice guy."

Nat deflated. "This I do not believe." She stood up and glared at him. "Shakespeare was *nice.* Boy, immortality is really wasted on some people."

Nick spread his hands, still teasing. "What can I tell ya?"

Nat moved over to the black leather sofa and let herself fall deeply into it. Nick nodded: she was settling in for a long story.

"So does this also mean you sat around the Mermaid Tavern with the other playwrights quaffing ale and quothing 'O rare Ben Jonson'?"

Nick came around to the other end of the sofa and also settled in. "Actually," he grinned, "it was fish stew the Mermaid was famous for, and it wasn't me who said it, and I was never a playwright, but otherwise—yeah."

Nat's eyes were big and shining. There were some parts of Nick's long life that she really enjoyed learning about; her ability to take pleasure in these things sometimes helped Nick remember it hadn't all been gloom and doom and murder for eight hundred years.

"So, Ophelia . . . ," she prompted.

"Her name was Isabella," Nick said. "She was sick, Nat. I think it was syphilis, but in those days they called it French pox. She wasn't insane—mad—or at least, not just mad."

Nat nodded, the doctor gears grinding in her brain. "It must have been tertiary. Poor thing, there wasn't a treatment," Nat's eyebrows quirked up, "pretty much until now, really."

"Oh, sure there was," said Nick, a trace of bitterness entering his voice. He looked at the wall. "Bloodletting. Immersion in scalding water. A visit to a holy well, purgative of lead, purgative of garlic, posset of arsenic. Tincture of weasel's brain."

"Oh my God," Nat said softly. She scooched forward on the sofa so she could put a hand on Nick's knee. "I'm sorry. You really cared."

"No." Nick covered her hand with his own. "No, I'm sorry, Nat."

"Weasel's brain." Nat took a breath. "I never heard that one before." It was all too clear on Nick's face that he'd seen that one, and worse, in actual use. She tried to lighten the mood.

"Hey, does this mean you wore those Mr. Sta-Puft pants?" Nat's hands shaped their curves in the air, and they both laughed. "How did you get them to be so . . . round?"

"Whalebone, wire, paper, whatever it took. Some guys stuffed 'em with buckram or paper."

"And tights?" Nat pursued. "You wore *tights*?"

Nick cocked his head. "I was told I had a very pretty calf."

"By Ophelia," Nat said sarcastically.

Nick smirked. "Among others."

"Uh-huh," said Nat. "Sure. Now I bet you're going to tell me Shakespeare thought you had nice legs."

Nick laughed and let a moment pass. "Well, he hired me twice," he said.

"*You* . . . ," Nat sputtered. "You're going to make me crazy." She raised a hand. "No, wait a minute: I believe in vampires, I've been turning down a transfer to the day shift for three years, and I almost, almost believe you met Shakespeare—yes, folks, the ballots are in: I *am* crazy."

Nick got up and hugged her shoulders from behind. "Good," he said into her hair. "Then you can be Ophelia in Neeson's play."

Nat twisted to look at him. "You're really going to do that? Fund his play?"

Nick nodded.

"Lemme guess, you're going to give him pointers from when you played Hamlet."

Nick gave her a funny look and veered off toward the bookshelves in the back of his loft. A moment later he came back with a cedar box. "Have a look," he said, putting it in her lap.

Nat gave him a suspicious look, but it was just for show. There were all kinds of odd treasures lurking in boxes in Nick's place: Joan of Arc's cross was here somewhere, and a jeweled treasure that was supposed to have gone down with the *Titanic* . . . Nat pushed the hinged lid up and found a yellowed sheaf of paper rolled and tied with a ribbon. Very gently, she took it out and pulled the ribbon to loose the paper.

"*The Historie of Hamlet, Prince of* . . . ," she read. "Oh my God, Nick." She touched a wax seal. "What's this?"

"Their permission to put on the play. It had to be approved by the Queen's office."

"This is the *original*?"

Nick didn't answer. He was looking at the fragile paper, and he reached out and ran a fingertip across the lapped edges of the curled pages. *Take no sweet life.* Nat was watching him closely. Somehow he couldn't quite bring himself to tell her that he'd visited the church at Stratford-upon-Avon just after the Second World War and whispered to his friend's grave that he'd not only kept his vow, but bettered it.

Nat retied the ribbon very gently and closed the box. She took a deep breath. "Time for work."

They got their coats, and Nick took them down in the elevator. As they were about to leave the elevator car, Natalie blocked his path, pressed him against the wall, and threw her head back at a dramatic angle until she was looking almost straight up at him.

"If you're really going big-time into the thee-ay-ter, I'd be a terrific Scarlett O'Hara," she said huskily, batting her eyelashes a few times for emphasis.

Nick looked straight down into her eyes, a movie-poster Rhett Butler with bright blond hair and a boyish smile, and their eyes locked. The humor fell away from their faces; they simply stood frozen for long seconds, neither saying anything. Neither even breathing.

It was Nick who broke the moment, sliding away to unlock his vintage Cadillac. Getting in, he looked at her across the car's roof and said, "I'll think about it." He disappeared from view into the car, then popped up again with a mischievous grin. "Tomorrow."